# Dangerous Alliance

# Randall Krzak

## ALL RIGHTS RESERVED

No part of this book may be reproduced or transmitted in any form or by any means, electronic or mechanical, including photocopying, recording, or by any information storage and retrieval system, without permission in writing from the author, except in the case of brief quotations embodied in reviews.

Publisher's Note:

This is a work of fiction. All names, characters, places, and events are the work of the author's imagination.

Any resemblance to real persons, places, or events is coincidental.

Solstice Publishing - www.solsticepublishing.com

Copyright 2018 – Randall Krzak

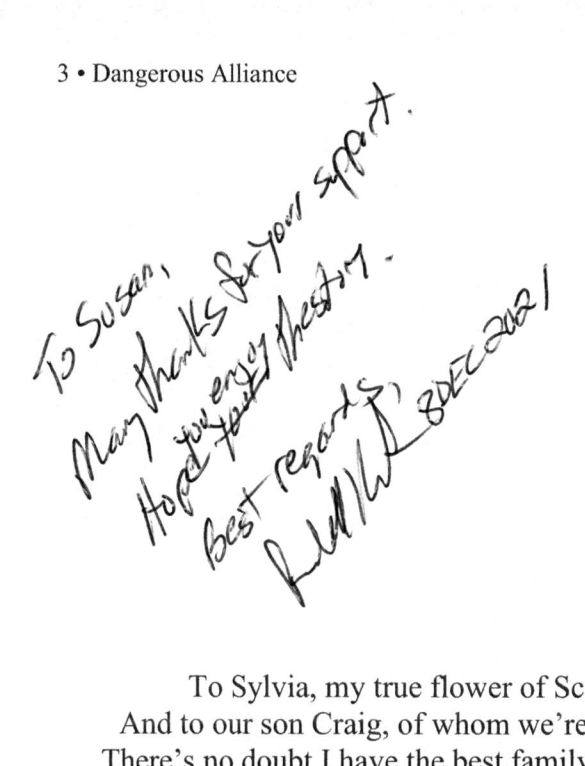

To Sylvia, my true flower of Scotland,
And to our son Craig, of whom we're very proud.
There's no doubt I have the best family in the world.
Thank you for loving me.
I love you.

# Chapter One

Port Rashid, Dubai
United Arab Emirates

In the moonless night, the target floated in the harbor's dark water, anchored fore and aft. A faint hiss broke the silence as climbing ropes and grappling hooks sailed into the air from Plumett NS50 Silent Launchers. Within moments, a sharp tug secured each hook to a quarterdeck railing on the cruise ship, two each on the port side, the starboard, and from the stern.

The men, dressed in the colors of the night, facial features distorted by brown, black, and green camouflage paint, raced up the lines using ascenders. The whisper of their rubber-soled shoes on the ship's sides the only hint of their invasion.

With a single click of their radio, each man signaled when he was in position. They readied their TGR2 rifles and waited for the command.

Colonel Trevor Franklin (Ret.) anticipated the go-ahead from Craig Cameron, Bedlam Alpha Team Leader, and senior commander of the mission. He performed a mental review of their intel. *Ship in port for routine maintenance. Crew spending time with family and friends. Seven friends, attending a private onboard dinner arranged by the ship's owner, taken hostage by at least ten terrorists. Threatening to kill them if their demands aren't met. Maintain silence and minimize casualties.*

Craig watched the seconds tick away and nodded to Trevor.

"Go."

Trevor, leader of the new Bedlam Bravo team, issued the order as he positioned his ATN night vision goggles and slithered through the stern rail. Craig slipped through the stanchions ten feet away.

Calm. Dark. Perfect time for a raid.

Trevor's eyes swept the decks above. By now the other men should be at their designated search areas on decks one through seven. He located the stairwell leading to the signal deck. From behind, he felt Craig's hot breath on his neck.

They mounted the steps, listening for the creak of movement, the strike of a match, anything indicating a terrorist. Silence greeted them. As they reached the bridge, Trevor lifted his head to peer inside. A tall man with shaggy brown hair stood in front of a control panel.

Trevor turned to Craig and raised a finger. One occupant. *Need more intel.*

He reached into his pack, grabbed his Double Trouble stun gun, and worked his way to the door. It gave a light squeak as he pulled it open. The man turned at the sound. Trevor lunged at the hijacker, pressed his weapon against the man's chest and zapped him.

The target collapsed. The wriggling stopped, Trevor flipped him over and secured his wrists with plastic zip ties.

"Where are the hostages?"

"Go to hell." The thug turned his head and tried to spit.

Trevor shoved a gag into the man's mouth and secured his ankles. "Don't go away, mate."

He rejoined Craig. "One tango captured. He won't be giving any trouble."

"Aye. Good job. Don't forget to swap your stun gun's batteries."

"Thanks." Charge restored, he returned the gun to his pack and grabbed his radio. He whispered to his team: "One tango down. Continuing search."

\*\*\*

Built like a heavyweight wrestler, Gerhard Badenhorst's bulk belied his ability to move with silent speed. Wall-to-wall carpet muffled his movements. Former Gurkha Sergeant Agam Bahadir Pun, a stealthy shadow, stood behind the huge man, his TGR2 at the ready.

Tasked with investigating decks four through seven, they hurried down the stairs, checking each passageway before continuing.

Once on deck seven, the men peered into the lounge and the well-equipped gymnasium before working their way through areas off-limits to passengers. They cleared possible hiding areas in rapid succession before returning to the staircase.

The acrid smell of antiseptic on deck six greeted Gerhard and Pun as they entered the ship's medical facility. Gerhard stood guard while Pun slid a fiber optic cable under each door for a peek before moving on.

A sliver of light appeared underneath a door labeled 'Doctor.' Gerhard listened as he grasped the knob. Silence. He twisted the handle to the open position and pushed, keeping his body to the side of the doorframe. Pun wormed inside to the right while Gerhard veered left.

A shadow flew past Gerhard's face. He dropped to the floor, kicked out, and connected with something solid. Someone grunted. As Gerhard scrambled to his feet, a strong punch to his stomach knocked the wind out of him, forcing him back to the floor.

The assailant kicked at Gerhard's head. Missed.

Gerhard landed a side thrust kick to the nerve point above the man's right knee, causing it to buckle. He grabbed his attacker in a chokehold, pressing on the carotid arteries until the man became limp.

After binding his hands and feet, Gerhard slapped the man until he regained consciousness.

"No *dossing*. Where are the hostages?"

"Huh?" The man shook his head.

"*Ag, man*. Are you *dof* (stupid)? Where are they?"

The dazed thug raised a shaking arm and pointed to an inner door. Gerhard grabbed the man and propelled him into the wall, knocking him out.

"*Lekker droom.*" Gerhard turned to Pun. "Why didn't you help me?"

"You didn't need any to give stupid man sweet dreams."

After securing the intruder, they approached a wood-paneled door. Gerhard heard a muffled moan from inside and eased the door open.

A woman, long blonde hair falling over her face, sat bound to a chair with strips of elastic bandages. Gauze held her hands together while a piece of tape covered her mouth. Her eyes widened in fear when the men entered.

Pun scanned the room. "Clear."

Gerhard raised his eyebrows in concern, pulled out his knife, and sliced the gauze, freeing the woman. "You okay?" He yanked the tape from her mouth.

"Ow! I will be." She coughed and flexed her arms, rubbing at her chaffed wrists. "Who are you?" She inhaled several sharp breaths and appeared to calm down.

"*Ag*, no one. Stay here until I return."

"What about the guy who snatched me?"

"Asleep—fought with a wall. He lost." Gerhard smirked. "He won't be bothering anyone for a few hours."

\*\*\*

Gerhard and Pun climbed the stairs to deck five. They moved from cabin to cabin, using master key cards to gain access through locked doors. Each room appeared the same: bed, built-in side tables and lamps, dressers, and two easy chairs, a coffee table snuggled between them. A small bathroom completed the amenities.

Each room shared a common similarity—empty.

After inspecting the last cabin, Pun returned to the staircase. As he placed a foot on the first step, an arm snaked over his shoulder.

His instincts kicked in. Pun jumped on the next step, yanked his *kukri* from its wooden scabbard on the back of his belt, and swung to face his opponent.

"Shh." Gerhard pulled his hand back. "Ag, man, put your toy away before you *steek* someone."

"Why you grab me?"

"To check your reflexes."

Pun grinned and replaced his blade. "This deck is clear."

Gerhard nodded and keyed his radio. "This is Green. Moving to next deck." He turned to his partner. "Let's go."

A man of few words, Pun tilted his head toward the stairs. Together they crept up to deck four, each taking a side of the hallway to check the cabins.

There was no activity until they reached a small corridor on the right between two inner cabins.

They scooted along the short hallway. Straight ahead were three cabins. Pun went left, Gerhard to the right. Moments later, they returned to the corridor, shaking their heads. Gerhard stepped to the middle door and tried the handle. Locked.

He pointed to himself, giving a high sign and indicated Pun should go low. Gerhard reared back and kicked the door with his foot.

When the door flew open, they powered into the room. Four men sitting around a card table jumped to their feet. With no weapons in sight, Gerhard hauled out his stun gun and pressed it against the chest of a man with a purple snake tattoo running down his arm. Gerhard pulled the trigger and the man dropped to the floor in apparent agony.

He prepared to meet the challenge of two others rushing at him.

He flipped one thug over his shoulder. The man crashed through the card table to the floor, stunned. The other terrorist grabbed Gerhard's arm and tried to force it behind his back.

"You fight like girl." Gerhard chuckled, twisted his body, and dropped to the floor. He stomped his right foot on the man's ankle, placing the other in the back of his calf. The assailant fell face-first to the floor, dazed.

Pun launched himself through the air at the fourth terrorist as the man grabbed his pistol.

They struggled for control and the gun discharged, smashing a nearby lamp. Pun leveraged himself and thrust his opponent against the wall, where the terrorist collapsed, the pistol spinning out of his hand.

The men trussed and gagged, Pun and Gerhard searched the remainder of the cabin. They stood on either side of the closet doors, grabbed a knob and tugged.

A man and woman sat on the floor, tied back-to-back, their eyes covered with blackout masks. Gerhard and Pun released the couple from their makeshift prison. Both captives were shaking, massaging their wrists where ropes had cut.

"You're safe now." Gerhard glanced at Pun, who helped the couple back to chairs.

"We were playing chess when the door burst open." A young man with bright orange hair and blue eyes pointed at the table. "They knocked us down and tied us up before dragging us into the closet."

"What did they want?" Gerhard asked the questions, leaving Pun to stand guard.

"They never spoke." The woman, about five feet tall, with black hair, shook her head. Her hazel eyes remained wide with fright.

"We'll move you to another cabin before we continue our recce of the ship. Pun, take them to a room by the stern stairs. I'll retrieve the hostage from deck six. Meet you there."

The three passengers now safe in one location, Gerhard turned to Pun. "Let's help Nate and Fergus."

\*\*\*

Nathaniel 'Nate' Webster scampered along the passageway on deck three toward the stern. He threw an occasional glance over his shoulder.

As Nate approached the stairwell, a faint shoe scuff on the rich pile carpet gave warning. He ducked around a corner and dropped into a crouch, his TGR2 ready.

Two shadows appeared—Pun and Gerhard. Nate waved for them to follow and the three men entered the launderette.

Gerhard glanced around. "Where's Fergus?"

"We decided to split up. He should be on deck two."

Gerhard shook his head but kept silent.

"You guys find anyone?" Nate gazed at Gerhard, knowing Pun's aversion to speaking.

"*Ja*. We found five baddies and three hostages. We moved them to a cabin on the deck below. What about you?"

"I found a hostage in the chapel. He's wrapped up, lying on the floor."

"Why didn't you bring him?"

"Forgot to mention. Four terrorists with him. Two, perhaps three, I'd have gone in. Four is too many."

"We help." Pun raised his kukri in the air.

"This way." Nate headed for the port hallway, while the others zipped down the starboard passageway.

Once in position, Nate crawled along the wall of the synagogue to the glass-partitioned doors. He snaked a miniaturized camera through a gap to verify the terrorists' positions.

The device removed from under the door, Nate pointed to the left and raised one finger. He motioned to the right, with three upright fingers. He pulled his stun gun from its holster and waved at the others, who nodded and retrieved theirs. Gerhard swapped out the batteries before signaling he was ready.

Nate tried the doorknob. It turned, and he raised three fingers again, counting down. His hand now a fist, he thrust the door open and dove for the deck, reached out to make contact, and sent an electrical charge into the single terrorist on the left.

From the right, bullets chewed into the doorframe above the heads of Pun and Gerhard, who hugged the floor. When the firing stopped, they charged forward, two terrorists receiving a single charge from their stun guns. Pun reached the shooter. He pressed his weapon against the man's shoulder and fired. The man's body seized in violent spasms.

While Nate undid the ropes around the hostage, Gerhard and Pun bound the four terrorists with zip ties from their backpacks.

"I think we should consolidate the people we've freed in one spot, perhaps the launderette." Nate pointed toward the stern as he spoke. "Since we're using the staircases for movement between decks, it'll be easier to collect them when we finish."

Gerhard stuck his head out of the doorway. "Okay, all clear. I'll bring the three up."

"I guard."

Nate nodded at Pun's offer. "Good. I'll head to deck two. Tell Gerhard to follow once he brings you the others."

*\*\**

Fergus Mulligan, the newest member of Bedlam Bravo, pushed long reddish hair from his forehead, and finished clearing the starboard side of deck one. As he turned the corner to work through the port side cabins, a scream echoed along the passageway.

A woman with long brown hair in a ponytail ran out of a cabin midway along the hallway and headed away from Fergus. A turbaned man brandishing a knife followed in close pursuit. Fergus let loose a shot from his TGR2. Missed. They turned into another passageway and disappeared before he could fire again.

He ran to the cabin's door and peeked inside. A man lay on the floor, the remnants of a red ceramic flowerpot scattered around him, clumps of earth and roses spread along his back. Fergus rushed back into the corridor and continued pursuit.

He reached the stern and turned toward the staircase, skidding to a stop. The turbaned man lay motionless on the floor. The tall woman leaped across the body and flung her arms around Nate, holding on to her savior.

"You're a chancer. Why do you always get the girls?" Fergus laughed. "One day you must clue me in."

"All about being in the right place. Being handsome helps, too."

"Don't forget modesty. I'll take a gander for the others, give you time to introduce yourself to the young lady."

"That's okay, boys." She gave Nate and Fergus a peck on the cheek. "You rescued me, and I'm thankful. Now, how do I get off this tub?" A wary smile surfaced on her lips before she screwed up her face. "I've had enough excitement for one evening."

A few minutes later, the rest of the team and the freed hostages arrived. Stashed in a cabin, Pun stayed with them. The others headed up the stairs to deck one.

\*\*\*

Trevor and Craig moved from the signal deck to the sun deck. They cleared the few suites in rapid fashion and headed to the cinema. Craig eased the door open far enough to squeeze in. Trevor followed.

In a crouch, they waited for their eyes to adjust to the dim light. Craig remained by the door while Trevor glanced around the room seeking anything out of place.

A shadow moved up front. Trevor ducked and crabbed along a row of seats. He peered through the gap between two backrests toward the figure.

More movement—someone's head lolled on the back of a seat. Trevor crept forward for a better view. A TCR rifle across the man's lap, he appeared to be asleep.

Trevor snuck behind the terrorist, grabbed him in a chokehold, and subdued him. After securing the man to the seat, he motioned to Craig and they continued. Not finding anyone else, they moved to the stern and proceeded to the boat deck.

Picking up their pace, they circled via the promenade, ducking as they came along a row of windows. Craig raised his head above the ledge. A gold placard on a window read: 'Queens Grill Lounge.' Sprawled across the bar, a gagged man lay bound by several strands of rope.

"One man tied on top of the bar," Craig whispered. "You go and I'll cover."

Trevor nodded, glanced around for any further movement, and crept forward. After he had untied the cord around the man's hands and ankles, the freed captive slid off the bar and stumbled into a chair.

"Thank you. My friends—a couple—the terrorists took them away after they trussed me up like a chicken. Find them, okay?"

"Don't worry. My team's clearing the other decks. Stay here with my partner until I return."

The man nodded. Craig reached over the bar, grabbed a glass, and pulled a pint. He handed it to the still shaking man, who sucked air in with great gulps.

"Here, this will help. Try to relax. You're safe now."

The man downed the pint in three swallows and held the glass out, smacking his lips. "Couldn't have another one by any chance?" He stood, twisted his body to work out the kinks and rolled his shoulders before sitting.

"Aye." Craig grinned at the man's audacity and got him another pint.

Trevor cleared the remainder of the deck and grabbed his radio. "Team, this is Black, report."

"Black this is Red. I guard five hostages. Rest of team on quarter deck."

"Confirmed. Haggis tending to one hostage. Proceeding to stern end of the upper deck. Rendezvous with hostages."

"Black this is Green. Ag, man, as soon as we clear the upper deck, we'll join you."

"Roger. Black out."

\*\*\*

Trevor and Nate took the port side, Fergus and Gerhard proceeded along the starboard. As they searched, a clinking sound came from the direction of the bow.

"What's that?" Nate stopped to listen.

Fergus laughed. "A fruit machine."

"What?"

"I tink you Yanks would call it a slot machine."

They hurried forward, the sound growing louder with each step. An alarm triggered and bells rang, the clinking became a rush.

"Casino," Trevor mouthed to Nate.

Nate grabbed Trevor's arm and pointed to starboard. The other pair gave a thumbs-up. The four men rushed the casino, weapons leading the way.

"Down, down, down," Trevor shouted. Three thugs crowded around a slot machine, one with his hand poised to pull the lever, froze in position. One glanced at his TCR on a nearby table. Gerhard moved forward, his TGR2 aimed at the terrorist's stomach.

Hands in the air, they sank to their knees as the team swarmed over them. A terrorist, his arm hidden behind one of the others, raised his pistol and fired.

"Ow! Bastard winged me." Fergus grabbed his ear, blood seeping through his hand.

Nate spun, his TGR2 sighted on the shooter and nailed him in the chest. The man collapsed. The team secured the remaining terrorists and continued their search for the final hostage.

They located their goal in the cruise director's office on the upper deck ten minutes later. Once the team removed his gag and bindings, the distinguished-looking gentleman in a Savile Row suit, trimmed black beard, and manicured hands stood. He gazed at the team.

"I say, about time you arrived." Sir Alexander Jackson, the British National Security Advisor, glanced at his watch. "Only an hour and forty-seven minutes to find me. Not bad on a ship the size of the QE2.

"CC, what's your assessment? It was entertaining to watch on the monitors."

"Aye, Sir Alex. The team did a good job for their first training scenario. Some of the terrorists overplayed their parts when they were hit with non-working stun guns, but their actions helped add realism. Same with the hostages, too—great acting.

"When Bedlam Alpha held their first training mission, we used Tipmman Tactical Compact Rifles and TiPX pistols. More realistic using the TGR2s for the team giving the terrorists TCR rifles and TiPX pistols for returning fire."

After each man stripped off his Kevlar vest, extra protective padding, and helmet, Sir Alex shook their hands. "The exercise is concluded. Release the Navy volunteers who played our terrorists and hostages. I hope you didn't pound them too hard. I'll meet you at Whitehall in a week."

## Chapter Two

Zhongnanhai, Imperial City
Beijing

Soo Khan Chin paced back and forth in the Zhongnanhai imperial palace waiting room. He glanced at his watch a second time.

*Outrageous. I arrived an hour ago, and I'm still waiting. This is no way to treat the Democratic People's Republic of Korea's ambassador to China.* Soo raked his hands through his gray hair and tugged on his jacket to straighten out any wrinkles. He glanced at the massive tapestries covering the walls, depicting happy Chinese workers and frowned.

"His Excellency offers you some refreshment while you wait." A Chinese servant appeared, holding a tray with tea and several plates of dim sum. He bowed to the ambassador.

Soo sat on an orange, overstuffed chair next to a hand-carved rosewood table. The attendant placed the items in front of him and poured the tea.

"*Xiè xie* nĭ (thank you)."

The man backed away from Soo, gave a final bow before he turned and left the hall.

He added sugar and stirred. *Did they add something to the tea or food?*

Soo dropped the spoon and pushed the tea and dim sum across the table. Despite the delectable aromas wafting from the dishes, causing his empty stomach to rumble, he resisted the urge to partake.

The ambassador stood and resumed pacing. His thoughts swirled as he searched for a way out of his current dilemma, which began two days ago.

\*\*\*

Summoned from Beijing, he stood in front of the DPRK's Supreme Leader, Wook Sung. Dressed in black, Wook presented a foreboding figure to all who met with him.

"Soo, we are facing the most serious problem since my family assumed leadership of our glorious country. My people now possess more freedom and rights than any nation in the world. I give them the right to work, play, learn, and provide free medical care. In return, they may petition me whenever an issue arises."

"Yes, Supreme Leader."

"Today's demonstration went too far. The Army arrested those responsible for organizing the uprising, and they will receive a fair trial." Wook slammed a plump hand on his desk, causing Soo to jump. "Afterward, they will visit Camp Fourteen.

"I realize there is a food shortage. Our factories no longer produce because there is no oil to keep them running. Our military strength teeters toward disaster. This is not my fault. The problem lies with our sworn enemy—America and their puppets in Seoul. We are peaceful, but America wishes for our death."

He paced, his hands clasped behind his back. "Their sanctions have caused our people to go hungry." He whirled about and stabbed the air with his finger. "They are the reason our factories are idle because the lack of oil stops them from producing goods."

Wook sat, grasping the arms of his chair until his knuckles turned white. "America wishes for our death, and the ruin of a peaceful people. They believe us isolated, but they are wrong. We still have friends."

"Yes, Supreme Leader."

"Return to Beijing. Request an immediate audience with that fat goat, Huang Fen." Wook stared at Soo through beady eyes. "Get us oil."

"Yes, Supreme Leader."

"And Soo, just because we grew up together, doesn't mean I will accept failure." Wook sank back into his chair, steepling his fingers. "What will become of your family if something happens to you?"

\*\*\*

Soo shook his head to erase the memory of the meeting. He required clear thinking when he met with Premier Huang. He must not falter—his life and those of his family were at stake.

Glancing at his gold watch, a gift from the supreme leader many years ago, Soo noted another thirty minutes had passed with no indication when his audience with the premier would occur. Tired of pacing, he resumed his seat.

Two tall, white doors with engraved red dragons opened without a sound. The same servant who brought him the refreshments tilted his head and swept the air in front of him with his right hand, indicating Soo should follow.

Seated on an oversized, but unadorned chair, the Premier of the People's Republic of China, Huang Fen, bid the ambassador forward.

Soo stepped to a faint line painted on the marble floor and bowed. He held the pose long enough not to appear disrespectful and stood taller than his five-foot-six-inch frame might suggest.

"What does your glorious leader want this time, Soo? Last month he wanted rice. The month before he pleaded for wheat." Huang rubbed his hairless double chin with fingers so thick, the rings he wore were dwarfed by the size of them.

On previous occasions, after the initial greeting, Soo had been offered a chair. None were in view for this session. Even an official painting of Chairman Mao Tse-tung seemed to scowl at him.

"Your Excellency, it is my great hon—"

"Enough." Huang waved a hand to cut off Soo's diplomatic speak. "What. Does. He. Want?"

Horrified at the breach of etiquette, Soo took a step back. "Y-your Excellency, Supreme Leader Wook requests assistance from the People's Republic of China—"

"Stop the formal chatter, Soo. What do you require?"

"Oil, Excellency. My country is suffering because of the United Nations' sanctions. Our industries are crippled. There isn't enough food. The military cannot function." Soo took a deep breath and relaxed before releasing his frustration. "Excellency, without your help I fear the imperialist Americans and their lackeys in Seoul will attack at any moment."

"My sources tell me the Americans will not attack Pyongyang or anywhere else in the North." A grim, half-smile quivered upon Huang's lips. "Wook should nurture his allies, not distress them, as he did to me. He embarrassed me in front of the Security Council again." He shook his head, his face void of expression. "I won't let anyone treat me in this manner."

"Your Excellency, I implore you to support us in our time of need." Soo wrung his hands.

Huang stared out a window. He seemed more interested in the cumulonimbus clouds sweeping the deep blue sky. After a few moments, he turned back to Soo.

"I cannot help you. China requires every last drop of oil we purchase on the foreign market. Our expansionist plans require the mobilization of the People's Liberation Army at a moment's notice."

"But …." Soo hung his head in desperation.

"I'm sorry. You are a good man, Soo, but that knowledge alters nothing." Huang heaved a deep sigh. "Did your despot threaten you or your family? Bring them here. In recognition of your many years of honorable service between our countries, I offer you and your family sanctuary."

"Thank you, Excellency. But your generous offer might be too late. I believe he is holding my wife and sons at Camp Fourteen, our most feared political prison." Tears dripped from Soo's eyes as despair set in.

"My offer stands. If you find your family, bring them here."

\*\*\*

The DPRK-chartered flight departed from Beijing amid a subdued atmosphere. The sole passenger, Soo sat in a first-class seat, staring at the photograph of the supreme leader on the bulkhead. His shoulders trembled and he dropped his face in his hands but couldn't hold back his tears.

Ninety minutes later, tires squealed as the plane touched down at Pyongyang's Sunan International Airport. The solitary attendant bid him good day as he trudged down the stairs to a waiting vehicle.

Unlike standard protocol, when Soo approached the limousine, he found the driver had not gotten out to open the door and see him settled. Frowning, Soo jerked the door open himself, and collapsed onto the leather seat. The driver started the limo into motion before Soo had closed the door.

"Where are you taking me?"

Silence.

"I asked, where are you taking me?"

"To our Supreme Leader."

"But where?"

"Ryongsong Residence."

Soo swallowed hard. He knew what happened when someone was sent to Ryongsong. He'd seen it many times.

They disappeared.

The driver continued through the empty streets. Both men remained silent. Soo wrestled with his emotions, despair overriding any glimmer of hope he might come out of this meeting alive. He paid little attention to the journey, his stomach churning at what might happen at the residence. *Will I be taken prisoner? Accused of treason?* He wiped his sweaty hands on his trousers. He shivered.

When the vehicle stopped at a side entrance to the residence, two guards met Soo and ushered him inside. Without a word, they escorted him to an opulent antechamber filled with priceless statues, paintings, and tapestries. Silk carpets adorned the marble floor.

As Soo sat on a straight-back chair awaiting his audience, his escorts stood on either side. A simple clock resting on a glass table ticked the seconds away. The fragrant scent of orchids teased the air from the arrangements dotted around the room.

A door opened. The sentinels led Soo into the passage toward his uncertain destiny.

Wook Sung, dressed again in black, sat on a red leather sofa, a low coffee table in front, holding a single glass. Ranged on either side of him, six generals stood stone-faced, with their trademark notepads and pens, ready to capture the Supreme Leader's words.

Soo and his escort stopped several paces from Wook. The guards saluted, while Soo bowed.

"What news do you bring me, Soo?"

"Supreme Leader, the Chinese premier sends his regards to you. He ... he said no ... oil." Soo spat out the last word, certain this would lead to his demise.

Wook slammed his fist on the table. The glass toppled, spilling its contents over the polished surface. A servant standing near the door rushed forward to clean the table. Wook waved him away.

"I gave you fair warning before you traveled to Beijing. One simple task. Traitors fail. You failed."

"B-but, Supreme Leader, I did my b-best."

"Heroes do their best, Soo. What did you achieve? Nothing." Wook wiped a hand along the side of his head, pushing an errant hair back into place. "I'm a kind-hearted man." He placed his hands in front of him, appearing to gaze at his nails. "I love your family. You have a beautiful wife and she's given you wonderful children. You'll be given one more chance because of our long friendship. I'll provide the details in a day or so."

"Thank you, Supreme Leader. I won't—"

"I know you won't let me down. To ensure your success, your wife, Jung Gi, will be transported to the Chongori correctional facility. Tonight. She will service the guards until you return victorious or they tire of her."

"No, Supreme Leader. I beg you. Please, don't send her to the camp."

"I didn't send her to a re-education facility. Your ineptitude is responsible. Succeed, and she might be returned to you. Fail, and she will die."

Crestfallen, Soo stared at the floor. "What about my boys? What will become of them?" *Evil bastard.*

"They will stay with me. Fail me again, and I'll erase your entire family from history."

## **Chapter Three**

Ministry of Foreign Affairs
Pyongyang, North Korea

Soo Khan Chin stormed past his secretary into his office at the Ministry of Foreign Affairs, slamming the door behind him. He marched to his desk and swept his arm across the surface, knocking everything to the floor.

He flung himself into the chair and cradled his head in his hands. His body wracked with sobs, he contemplated the future.

*Bleak.*

Soo unlocked the bottom right drawer, removed a wooden box, and opened the lid. He stared at the hardware as he leaned back in his chair. Placing the cold, black barrel against his temple, Soo thought of taking the easy way out. Then the faces of his wife and children swam into his thoughts. He jerked the Chinese Norinco away.

*No! This is the coward's way. I'll show Wook.*

Soo placed the pistol back in the drawer and pushed the intercom button.

"Yes, Ambassador?"

"Nari, please come in."

"At once." A moment later, Nari, gray-haired and stooped, entered Soo's office.

"Oh! What happened?" Bug-eyed, she bent down to pick up the papers and photo frames strewn across the floor.

"I slipped when I entered and fell against the desk. Once you finish, I have instructions."

\*\*\*

Ambassador Soo requested an immediate audience with Supreme Leader Wook.

Two days later, Soo entered Wook's chambers, surrounded by armed guards. Two generals stood in the background, notebooks and pens in hand.

"Well, Soo, did you bring me results?"

"Not yet, Supreme Leader. I-I brought a plan—one which should gain us the oil you require."

"I'm listening. But don't try my patience."

"No, Supreme Leader." Soo trembled and dipped his head. "Since China won't help us during this crisis, I propose seeking help from other allies who possess oil or influence."

"Hmm." Wook rubbed his right index finger across his lips. "Which countries?"

"I did some investigation: Russia and Iran first. Angola and Equatorial Guinea next. Venezuela last, because of the distance to travel. They all produce oil. Russia, Iran, and Venezuela also maintain international influence." *No need to let him know Nari did the research.*

Wook paced the room, hands clasped behind his back. Soo waited for his leader to decide, the only sound the click-clack of Wook's shoes on the marble floor.

The pacing stopped. Wook turned to the ambassador, a glint in his eye. "Make it happen."

"Yes, Supreme Leader." Soo bowed his head, assuming he had been dismissed.

"And, Soo … don't fail. Remember the penalty—your family's lives are at stake."

"Yes, Supreme Leader." He rushed out of the room, fighting back his anger. *Bastard.*

\*\*\*

Back in his office, Soo summoned Nari. "Our Supreme Leader gave me permission to travel. Set up appointments beginning in two weeks with the foreign ministers of Angola, Equatorial Guinea, and Venezuela. I'll take care of Russia and Iran myself—they're more important, so I'll meet with them first. Contact our embassies and advise them of my impending arrival."

"Yes, Ambassador. Anything else?"

"No—wait. Yes, thank you, Nari. Without your help, my family would be doomed. Now, there might still be a chance to rescue them."

Nari glanced at Soo, bewilderment etched on her face with the unusual offer of thanks. She contained her emotions before speaking. "Thank you, Ambassador."

Soo dismissed Nari and placed a call to the Russian Ministry. "Hello, this is Ambassador Soo Khan Chin, from the Democratic People's Republic of Korea."

"Yes, sir. How might I help you today, Ambassador?"

"Please connect me with Foreign Minister Andropov."

The Russian aide whispered to someone in the background, but Soo couldn't understand a word. "I'm sorry, Ambassador, but Minister Andropov isn't available. Is there a message?"

"Yes, I have an urgent matter to discuss with him. Please arrange for me to meet with him within the next forty-eight hours."

"I'll do my best for you, Ambassador. Good day." The aide broke the connection.

Soo stared at the receiver. The pitch of the dial tone sent an ominous warning. "The insolent creature better make the appointment." He slammed the receiver back in the cradle before flipping through a Rolodex file for the Iranian Foreign Ministry's number.

Before he dialed, his phone rang.

"Ambassador Soo, this is Minister Andropov's aide. You're scheduled for thirty minutes at ten a.m. on

Thursday. This is the only time he is available before his two-week international trip." The man didn't wait for a response.

*Yes!* Soo's spirits lifted and he hoped the Russians would help him. He dialed Tehran and was connected to Foreign Minister Rahmani's office.

"I require an immediate meeting with Minister Rahmani." Soo waited, but the person who answered didn't speak. "There is an important issue to discuss with him."

"It will be a month before the minister can meet with you. Give me your name and number and someone will get back to you."

"I told you the matter is urgent!" Soo's hands shook with rage at the insolent attitude of this mere aide.

"And I said he isn't available. You have an option—meet with the third secretary or wait like everyone else." The man hung up without waiting for a response.

Soo muttered a string of curses before setting the receiver down. He cradled his head in his hands, with his elbows propped on the edge of the desk. Ten minutes later, a knock on his door disrupted Soo's preoccupation with his predicament. He raised his head and stared as Nari entered.

"Ambassador, excellent news. I arranged appointments with the Angolan, Venezuelan, and Equatorial Guinean foreign ministers, which will begin this weekend. Did you make arrangements with Russia and Iran or should I contact them?"

Soo's abysmal mood shifted. "Excellent work, Nari. I have thirty minutes with the Russians this Thursday. The Iranian Foreign Minister isn't available. They hung up before I scheduled an appointment with someone else."

"Yes, sir. You meet with the Angolans on Sunday, Equatorial Guinea on Monday, and Venezuela on Tuesday. Should I try to schedule an appointment for late next week with the Iranians?"

"I'd prefer to ignore them, but they might hold the key to my family's freedom. Please set up a meeting—if possible."

\*\*\*

An old Russian TU-114 carrying Soo touched down at Moscow's Sheremetyevo International Airport. Smoke streamed from the tires before it slowed to a disembarkment area. After the Russians retired the Tupolev turbojets in 1991, they presented three of the aged aircraft to the DPRK government. They were used for high-level delegations.

An immigration official handled formalities onboard the aircraft. Once completed, the officer led Soo to a waiting embassy vehicle, which whisked him away to the Russian Foreign Ministry.

Soo ignored the city sights, his eyes half-closed as he rehearsed his plea. He rubbed the pulsating vein near his temple. *They must help us—help me.*

Security guards escorted him to the foreign minister's office. He glanced at the ornate wall clock above an aide's desk. Five minutes past ten. After he was seated, the assistant beckoned to him and stepped to a closed door. A quick knock before he opened the door and ushered Soo inside.

"Minister Andropov, I am honored to meet you at last." Soo walked forward, hand out.

Andropov grasped Soo's hand in his huge paw and gave a slight squeeze, causing Soo to wince.

"Your urgent insistence led to this meeting." Andropov gestured to chairs positioned on either side of a carved rosewood table. An elaborate silver tea set adorned its center. After they sat, the aide poured tea for both men and left the room.

"Now, what does your country possess which would interest Russia? I can't think of anything."

"Foreign Minister, our ambassador to the United Nations will support any proposal put forward by the Russian government. In return, we require oil."

"Why are you approaching us and not your foreign minister?"

Soo waved a hand in the air. "Supreme Leader Wook gave me this task as a reward for our long-time friendship."

"Didn't the Chinese turn you down?"

A shocked expression etched across Soo's face and disappeared in a moment. He fought to control his emotions while he felt his face flush with heat and his muscles tightened. "Yes … yes, they did." Soo grimaced and clenched his hands. "Minister Andropov, I must be honest with you. Wook took my family as hostages. If I fail, they're—they will die."

Andropov finished his tea and set the cup on the saucer. "I see." He dragged his hand over his chin and leaned back in his chair. "Russia will always assist other nations. But what you offer isn't of interest. Your country has little influence with the rest of the world. Supporting us in the U.N. doesn't provide sufficient gain relative to the backlash from the West."

"What might be of assistance to Russia?" *I hope he comes up with something to help.*

"Hmm." Andropov remained silent, his forehead puckered. "Well, I suppose there is one thing we are interested in—your country's cessation of its nuclear weapons program."

"What?" Soo blinked and squeezed his eyelids together. "Impossible." *Can't suggest their terms for assistance to Wook. I'll be shot for treason!*

"I'm sorry, Ambassador." Andropov glanced up as a door opened and his aide pointed at his watch. "My day is filled with other meetings. I can give you no more time. I must depart. Convince Wook to give up his weapons and we'll meet your country's oil requirements."

The aide escorted Soo out of the minister's office and into the outer area where two security guards waited. They escorted him back to his car, which returned to the airport.

*Damn him! The Russians always press for their own advantage and beyond, as does every other country. The hell with Wook. I'll find another way to help my family—somehow.*

Once back at the aircraft, Soo slammed the car door, stormed up the stairs, and collapsed into a seat. The plane lumbered down the runway and clawed its way into the air.

Kim, Soo's aide, shook his shoulder. "Excuse me, Ambassador. A message for you."

Soo took the proffered sheet of paper and Kim returned to his seat near the rear of the aircraft. From Nari. *Perhaps the Iranians will help.* He opened the single sheet of paper, scanned its contents, and screamed in anger and frustration. *No!*

He crumbled the note and tossed it on the floor. *The Chinese won't help and the same with the Russians. Now the Iranians are too busy to meet. It's a conspiracy.*

Soo buzzed for Kim. When he arrived pushing a cart filled with drinks and snacks, Soo uttered, "Whiskey." He downed his choice in a single gulp. "More."

Several drinks later, Soo slouched in his seat and passed out. Kim covered him with a blanket.

\*\*\*

The next few days passed in a blur. Soo met with the foreign ministers from Angola, Equatorial Guinea, and Venezuela. Different stories, same result. "We're sorry, Ambassador. We want the weapons you offer, but our oil is committed elsewhere. Try the Russians or the Iranians. They might help you."

After each rejection, Soo's mood blackened. He skipped dinners planned at the embassies in his honor, feigning a headache and shortness of breath, and returned to the aircraft.

Soo ate little, seeking solace in whiskey. His demeanor worsened. Dark patches appeared under his eyes, and his once-fastidious appearance became ragged. He slipped into a funk, knowing he had failed his family—and himself.

On his return flight to Pyongyang, Soo grieved for his family and cursed Wook. Tears of desperation dripped down his face. Where could he turn for help? *Is my family being tortured? Are they still alive?*

He tossed and turned as he tried to get comfortable, hoping sleep might put his misery aside. Unable to rest, he requested tea and any available newspapers.

Sipping his lukewarm refreshment, Soo skimmed through the headlines. Most were in English, and he struggled with many words. A caption he understood made him bolt upright: "Al-Shabaab Seizes Another Freighter, Eighth This Month."

*Perfect. We have weapons to spare—they'll want more. They can capture oil tankers in exchange. How to contact them?*

A smile creased Soo's face as a glimmer of hope surfaced after a bitter week. He wrote a note to Nari and asked Kim to send it. For the first time since his departure on this ill-fated trip, Soo slept.

***

Kim read the message and smiled. *Should I fulfill my mission or wait in case he's lucky?* He glanced at the ambassador. *He's been decent, unlike some of the others. I'll give him more time.* Once he completed the transmission, he placed his weapon in its case. Unbeknownst to Soo, Kim was a major in the Ministry of State Security. He sent a high priority message to Supreme Leader Wook: *Termination delayed pending review of possible solution.*

## Chapter Four

Indian Ocean
Off the Somali Coast

A tall, black man, almost too thin to keep his baggy pants from falling to the deck of the freighter as it rocked on the gentle waves, stood at the railing, gazing at the rough sea. No one would describe him as handsome because of his pockmarked skin, caused by popping and scratching chickenpox blisters during childhood.

A gunshot sounded from the bow of the ship. *Another crewman refused to surrender.* Dacar Khadaafi, once an Oxford University student and now leader of a group of marauders, turned away from the dying echo and returned to the bridge. Inside, the ship's captain sat in his chair, a bloody bandage wrapped around his head. He glared as Dacar approached. Two armed men stood guard.

"Once again, Captain. How many are in your crew? Where are their stations? How do you contact them?"

"I told you before. The *Napoli* carries a crew of fifteen. We keep in contact via radio. Other than the engine room and the bridge, the rest of the men work wherever they're needed at the time."

Dacar nodded at one of his men. The man placed his weapon near the captain's head and pulled the trigger.

Captain Rossi shuddered at the blast. Deadened by the sound, urine trickled to the floor. He closed his eyes as he cursed the pirates. "Animals. I hope you rot in hell!"

"Last chance, Captain. We captured fifteen men. At least one more is on the ship. He shot one of my men a few minutes—"

"Dacar! Dacar!" The newest and youngest member of the pirate group burst into the cabin. He panted, eyes glowing with excitement. "Two small boats are approaching."

Dacar glanced at his watch. "Right on time. The boats will take the crew to our base. Did you send the message to the ship's owners? We want two million dollars for the freighter and its cargo."

"Yes. I sent it not five minutes ago."

"Go back to the radio room and wait for an answer."

Dacar grabbed the intercom handset from a counter and thrust it in the captain's face. "Tell whoever is still hiding to surrender now. Otherwise, we'll begin shooting a captive every minute."

"You wouldn't dare." Rossi's face contorted with anger. "The company will never pay a ransom if anyone is killed."

"That's guesswork, Captain. Do you want to take a chance with their lives? Or yours?"

The captain snatched the handset from Dacar's hand and pressed the transmit button. "This is Captain Rossi. Toss out your weapons and come out so the pirates can see you. Do this now or they'll kill the crew."

Moments later, two shots rang out, followed by cheers from the pirates.

Captain Rossi turned to Dacar. "You bastard. They killed him."

Dacar waved a hand in the air and shrugged. "He shot one of my men. He paid for his crime."

Rossi glared at the pirate but kept silent. Two of Dacar's gang entered the bridge and shoved the captain to the door.

"Farewell, Captain. Perhaps we'll meet again." Dacar turned his attention to a chart to plot the freighter's new course.

\*\*\*

In the crew's galley, Dacar's team bound the hands of the crewmen, linking two together. Whenever one of the crew struggled, they received a blow from a rifle butt.

"Hurry." Sahid Barre, Dacar's number two, prodded the first pair. "We go now."

The pirates led their captives from the mess up to the main deck, and to the side. They were lowered by a winch into the waiting boats. Any delay meant a quick trip over the railing for the offending pair, falling in a heap into a rocking boat.

Sahid joined Dacar on the bridge, rendering a haphazard salute. "All loaded." Sahid raised the patch over his left eye and scratched around the empty socket. After replacing the filthy, tattered cloth, he grinned. "We'll take them to the camp. Hope you receive a good price."

"Don't worry, Sahid. We'll do our best. If not, the order will be given to make an example. We can't let reluctant ship owners defy us."

Sahid nodded and headed outside. Moments later, the two boats separated from the freighter and journeyed to a small village along the northern part of the Somali coast.

Unlike many of the pirates working for al-Shabaab, Sahid didn't join the organization for religious beliefs. Profit and love of killing drove him. Successful negotiations with ship owners gave each man ten thousand dollars, more than he would ever make in a lifetime as a simple fisherman.

As the boat bounced over the waves, Sahid carved the fifth notch in the wooden stock of his weapon. *Five kills, fifty thousand dollars. When I have five more, I'll disappear. Perhaps to London or America.*

\*\*\*

Once the boats had separated from the ship, it changed course for the Seychelles. Although possible to make the trip in a shorter time, caution meant a zigzag course as they eluded international navies searching for them. Dacar paced the bridge, waiting for word from the freighter's owners. He relished a break after this latest adventure, their ninth hijacking in two months. He'd had enough of saltwater and the smell of diesel.

Pounding feet broke Dacar from his reverie. He glanced up as the youngest of the crew assigned to radio duty, rushed forward.

"Dacar, the ship's owners refuse to pay. What should I tell them?"

"They have twenty-four hours to change their minds and transfer the money. Otherwise, they can find Rossie and their ship at the bottom of the ocean."

\*\*\*

The two boats, loaded with Captain Rossi and his crew, approached a narrow bay near Ras Hafun. Once on the beach, the pirates poked and prodded their stumbling captives along a dusty street to a whitewashed stone wall surrounding a two-story house as residents grabbed their children and hurried inside their homes.

A hand appeared from inside the compound and edged the wooden gate open, allowing the prisoners access to the sandy courtyard. Two goats chewed on stunted bushes struggling for survival. A one-armed man led the crew to an outbuilding near the rear of the compound. Once the captives entered, the man slammed the doors. He wrapped a chain through the handles and used a padlock to secure the ends before sauntering away.

"Hey, Captain, what now?" Smith, an English engineer on his first voyage with Captain Rossi, glared at him as he tried to find a comfortable spot on the rough concrete floor.

"I don't know. They'll want a ransom. When other owners paid the money demanded, their ships and crew were released."

"Cap'n Rossi, what if the company won't pay?" A young man, a bloody rag wrapped around his upper right arm, asked in a trembling voice, "What happens to us?"

Rossi eyed each of his men.

\*\*\*

After the owners and shareholders of the *Napoli* received Dacar's ultimatum, they discussed the possible destruction of the ship, the death of the men manning it, and the damage this would do to the company's reputation. For twenty-three hours they argued back and forth and finally acquiesced.

Dacar held the handwritten note the radioman gave him, his eyes gleaming.

*Two million dollars paid into Freedom Bank, Malta, account DK90123. Please advise disbursement instructions.*

He grabbed the intercom. "They paid the money. We head to Victoria. We'll relax in the Seychelles."

The pirates moored the *Napoli* outside the entrance to the harbor and boarded a fishing boat sent to meet them. The trawler took them to the dock in the inner harbor, east of the town. Dacar strolled through the streets to a small apartment overlooking the Victoria Botanical Gardens.

After unlocking the door, he cleared the small apartment. Satisfied there hadn't been any intruders during his absence, Dacar went into the bedroom closet. He reached down, stuck his index finger in a knothole, and yanked the board out. Underneath, a cash box, a spare pistol, ammunition, and a black laptop filled the space. He grabbed the box and computer, booting it as he strolled into the living room, and collapsed on a faded blue sofa.

One email waited for his attention—from Tahliil Wardi, the latest al-Shabaab leader.

*Congratulations—money is in the bank. Release ship and crew. New assignment. Tomorrow at two p.m. meet a Korean named Major Kim near the Lai Lam Food Shop. He offers a way for our organization to maintain a steady supply of hardware to assist us in our efforts. Acknowledge.*

Dacar confirmed receipt of the message before rifling through the moneybox. He grabbed a handful of different currencies and replaced the box and laptop in the closet. A smile wreathing his mouth, he secured the apartment and headed outdoors for an evening of pleasure. *The owners can wait until I'm ready to release their ship.*

\*\*\*

Dacar arrived at the Lai Lam Food Shop a few minutes before the scheduled meeting to scout the area. *Should be easy to spot Kim—not many Koreans visit here.* He stopped at a store to buy grain to toss to the birds and sat on a nearby bench. Keeping an eye out for Kim, Dacar fed the seeds to black and white magpie-robins, zebra pigeons, and a lone blue pigeon.

A man wearing dark sunglasses, dressed in drab clothing and a black hat, sat next to him. He glanced around before he turned toward Dacar and pulled off his shades. A ragged scar stretched along the left side of his chin.

"I am Kim."

Dacar stared at the man. To be sure this wasn't a trap, he uttered the phrase he was instructed to use, "Hail to the Supreme Leader."

Kim responded, "*Salan. Iska waran* (Peace. Talk about yourself)." He nodded toward the food shop and put his glasses back on. They ordered smoked fish with rice from the take-out window, and returned to the bench, appearing to be another pair of workers eating a late lunch.

"I am here for Ambassador Soo. He wants to trade."

"What kind of trade?"

Kim scanned the area and leaned toward Dacar. "Weapons for oil."

*Hmm. A ready-made market for our hijackings?* "How much oil? What kind of weapons?"

"Ambassador Soo says any weapons you want, including missiles, launchers, and military vehicles. We will take every oil tanker you capture. Two tankers—one freighter full of weapons."

Dacar tried not to appear too eager at the offer. *Is Allah behind this? Our next prize requires more weapons.* "Agreed."

Kim stood. "We have more details to discuss. We should go where no one can overhear us."

"We'll go to the botanical gardens. There are secluded areas we can use for our conversation."

\*\*\*

Logistics and communications arranged, the men shook hands ninety minutes later, and agreed to meet in five days near the inner port entrance. Kim headed toward one of the park's exits while Dacar meandered through the luscious gardens toward his building.

Once out of sight, Kim turned back. The palm, fruit, and spice trees, along with sculpted orchid displays, provided a natural cover for Kim to follow Dacar undetected. The man seemed unaware Kim watched him. *Simpleton. But useful, at least for now.*

Dacar entered a three-story brick apartment building without a backward glance. Kim waited, keeping an eye on the buildings' windows to determine which apartment Dacar used. His patience was rewarded as the pirate came into view on the middle floor and opened a window overlooking the botanical gardens. Horns blared and myriad bird calls filled the air.

Kim strolled through the paved streets, mixing in with pedestrians when they crossed between vehicles and bicycles, doubling back on himself as if he was lost and used store windows to check for surveillance. No one appeared to be following him as he approached a small hotel near the port used by fishermen.

He placed a call on his secure cell phone to the North Korean Embassy in Pretoria. Responsible for interests in the Seychelles, they would relay the agreement to Ambassador Soo and provide any ground support required in the area.

Task completed, Kim thought about the Somali. *Another who will meet with an unexpected accident once we are finished. Perhaps a gas explosion? Or a fall in front of a bus?*

# Chapter Five

Bedlam Headquarters
Whitehall, London, England

Craig Cameron plodded through the slanted rain. He pushed through throngs of tourists gazing at 10 Downing Street and turned right on Whitehall. He stopped near the intersection of Horse Guards Avenue, checking for surveillance. Unlike the visitors struggling with their umbrellas, Craig tugged on his green Scottish Tweed cap and pulled the collar of his Mac tighter around his neck.

No covert observers spotted, he ducked into an unobtrusive side door of the Old War Office Building. Although the structure was for sale, an ultra-secret intelligence group maintained its headquarters in a sub-basement once used by Winston Churchill.

An armed Ministry of Defence police officer requested his identification. After confirming Craig's identity and access to the building, another official flicked a switch, opening a door leading down to the inner sanctum. Energy-efficient downlighters snapped on and off, marking his passage through the corridors.

Every door appeared the same, except for their numbers. Craig stopped in front of number twelve. He knocked. The door buzzed, and he stepped inside.

"You're late again, Mr. Cameron." A mature woman, gray-hair pulled into a severe bun, pointed at the clock. A sign on her desk identified her as Miss Evelyn Evinrude.

"Aye, Miss E, the weather's a bit temperamental, causing a ruckus on the roads." Craig removed his cap and raincoat, hanging them on a wooden rack.

"You know Sir Alex doesn't like to be kept waiting." A hint of a smile graced Evelyn's face. "You better go right in."

"Aye."

Craig, better known as CC to his friends, stepped into an austere room. Four straight-backed chairs formed a semicircle facing a wooden desk. A four-drawer, gray safe sat near a closed door in the back wall. The remainder of the room was bare without even the requisite portrait of the queen found in most government offices.

"It's a long way from the Highlands, CC, but I expected you to arrive sooner." Sir Alex's lips twitched until he could no longer keep a straight face and broke into a broad smile. "Good to see you again."

"Hello, Sir Alex. Thank you for the invitation." The two men shook hands and dropped into adjacent chairs.

"Before we join Bedlam Bravo, what's your assessment of their recent training scenario on the QE2?"

"Trevor's team did an excellent job of searching the ship for captives. They demonstrated efficient teamwork and settled in with one another." CC took a deep breath. "Sir Alex, the scenario was unrealistic for a ship the size of the QE2. At least twice as many men should have been involved."

"I agree, but Admiral Blakely wouldn't loan me the entire Bedlam Alpha team."

"We might require more flexibility, depending on a given situation."

"Agreed. The admiral also concurs with our assessment. Shall we join the others?"

Sir Alex led the way through the door in the back of his office. They stepped into a conference room, where a polished oak table, capable of handling a dozen people, dominated the area. Five men stood as they entered.

"Relax, men. No need for the formalities." Sir Alex smiled at his Bedlam team and took a chair at the head of the table. "I'm pleased with how everyone handled last week's drill on the QE2. What's your opinion, CC?"

"Everyone performed well. Using the paintball weapons and inoperable stun guns gave the team a proper workout. Of course, in a real situation, more men would be required to clear a ship of this size in an efficient manner."

Sir Alex nodded. "I concur. We used the QE2 because we had ready access. The team is new, and we needed a stable platform for their training. We'll also use several British bases within the UK for further scenarios."

"So what background do the team members possess? If we need to use both teams in a joint mission, it'll be useful to know what's what."

"Excellent suggestion." Sir Alex glanced at Trevor. "Colonel, would you do the honors?"

"Of course, Sir Alex. As you are aware, CC, I'm Bravo's team leader. Graduated from Sandhurst ... well, a long time ago. Retired from the Paras. Saw action in Iraq, Afghanistan, and a few other locations." He fingered a one-inch scar on his left temple. "This is my barometer—turns white when I'm under severe stress."

"I've visited some of those vacation spots, too." CC rubbed both of his temples. "Didn't bring any souvenirs back with me."

Everyone laughed.

A massive, bald-headed figure lumbered to his feet. "Ag, I'm Gerhard. I did a spell in the Recces. For the uninformed, this is the South African Special Forces Brigade. My specialty—extracting intelligence."

The next to introduce himself appeared to be a carbon copy of a young Clint Eastwood. "I'm Nate. I met one of CC's men when I visited Turkey as a freelance writer. Not my most impressive performance I have to admit, as I was captured. I used to work for the Drug Enforcement Agency and spent most of my time moving from continent to continent."

"Aye. I didn't recognize you on the ship. Glad the shiner and other bruises have healed."

A discreet knock on the door interrupted the team's introductions. Miss E pushed the door open and wheeled in a cart loaded with an ornate tea service and several plates of finger sandwiches and biscuits. She arranged the cups, saucers, and side plates at each occupied seat before serving Sir Alex and leaving the room.

After everyone helped themselves to tea and a snack, a lanky man with red hair, his face covered in freckles, stood. "No point farting around—I'm Fergus. I used to be in the Garda Siochana, the Irish Special Branch. Once this opportunity came up, I jumped ship."

After Fergus sat, the final member of the team jumped to his feet. The shortest of the team at five feet, his swarthy complexion and piercing dark eyes appeared to be in a constant scowl. Once he smiled, his face beamed. "I am Pun. Before in the Second Battalion, the Royal Gurkha Rifles. I served many places for the British Army. I live by our motto: 'Better to die than live a coward.'"

Sir Alex resumed control of the meeting. "With introductions completed, we must turn to the latest intel concerning our area of responsibility. You might recall BBC and ITV reporting on the continued instability in Somalia caused by a terrorist group called al-Shabaab. They became a thorn in the side of several of our closest allies when they started hijacking ships for ransom. So far, they've earned millions of pounds. They must be stopped."

"Excuse me, Sir Alex, is this why the team trained on the QE2? I don't tink the group ever seized a cruise ship."

"You're correct, Fergus. However, we must be prepared for any eventuality. They're becoming bolder and no one appears capable of halting their activities, at least so far. But—"

Another discrete knock silenced the room. Miss E limped inside, her arms full of binders. After handing one to each man, she departed.

On the front of each binder, a white sheet of paper was outlined in red with TOP SECRET stamped at the top and bottom. In the middle of the page, three words gave a hint to the contents: Operation Just Pursuit.

"Each folder contains background information on al-Shabaab gleaned from various intelligence sources. It also provides details regarding the hijacked ships, their cargos, and the ransoms paid. The information's too sensitive to upload, hence the binders.

"Are there any questions?" Everyone shook their heads. "Very good. This meeting will reconvene in one hour. CC, would you please join me?" Sir Alex and CC left for Sir Alex's office.

"So, CC, do you think they're ready to go undercover as part of a ship's crew?"

"Aye, Sir Alex. Ah dinnae ken any major problems. They all are experienced in various operations. Together, they should be a formidable team." *Wonder if Trevor is up to the physical demands? He's much older than everyone else.*

"Excellent. I appreciate you helping us out. Please give my regards to Admiral Blakely when you return to Washington."

"Aye, I shall. Should you ever need us, give the admiral a bell and we'll be on the way."

The two men rose and shook hands. CC departed to catch his late afternoon commercial flight to Dulles International Airport.

After CC left, Miss E handed Sir Alex a new folder. She followed him into his office and waited for a response to the information. The file bore the same classification as the binders in the team's possession; no label attested to its contents.

When he finished, he leaned back in his chair. "Excellent. Miss E, thank them for the offer. Our team will join them in forty-eight hours."

\*\*\*

After giving the team sufficient time to read and digest the intel, Sir Alex returned to the conference room. "Questions, gentlemen?"

"One, Sir Alex." Trevor gazed around the table before turning his attention back to their mentor. "I'm certain the best way for us to take on the terrorists is to be on a ship they hijack. With various ships transiting through the waters near Somali, how will we be able to go after the right one? From the intel, it appears the owners paid the ransom demands before any navy responded."

"The Italians have provided the perfect bait. Fiat is sending a shipload of parts to their Brosslyn plant in South Africa. The Italian Navy is unable to escort the ship for the entire journey due to other commitments. Without telling them who you are, I volunteered Bedlam Bravo." Sir Alex coughed and stroked his chin. "We also have some intel indicating the pirates have been interested in the Fiat ships."

Trevor tipped his head in understanding as hands shot in the air.

Gerhard stood. "Sir Alex, it's one thing to train on the QE2. But what do we know about their ship? Will we receive deck plans?"

The others nodded at the questions, turning to Sir Alex with anticipation.

"It's quite simple. The team leaves for Naples in forty-eight hours. You'll have a week to learn your cover duties and everything about the ship before you sail for the Suez Canal."

"What about the crew?" Nate stroked a forefinger along his jawline. "Are they Italian or a mixed group?"

"They're from several countries, so your addition won't pose any problems. Pun, you'll need to keep your kukri hidden. Trevor, work with Miss E regarding logistics."

Pun flashed an evil grin while Trevor nodded and remained stoic.

Sir Alex stared into the eyes of each team member, taking into account their excitement and apprehension regarding their first mission. Satisfied they were up to the task, he stood and shook each man's hand.

"With any luck, your ship will be al-Shabaab's next target. If attacked, repel boarders. Capture a hijacker—alive, if possible."

# Chapter Six

Bedlam Headquarters
Whitehall, London, England

The team remained in the conference room when Sir Alex returned to his office. Miss E limped in with two cups of tea. After handing one to Sir Alex, she settled into a seat across from him.

"Well, Lady Evelyn, what do you think of my new group?"

Evelyn laughed while she rubbed her right hip.

Sir Alex noticed her discomfort. "Hip bothering you again?"

She stopped rubbing and adjusted her position. "I deal with it." She sipped her tea. "My meds make sure it doesn't become a problem." She winced and stroked the area again.

"Alex, you've outdone yourself putting this team together. I believe they'll do fine." Eyes twinkling, she added, "Any chance CC might return?"

"Perhaps—if a situation would warrant the inclusion of Bedlam Alpha. Otherwise, you'll need to pursue him on your own time."

"Once my hip recovers, I want to deploy again." Evelyn ran a hand through her hair. "I don't mind the charade of pretending to be your doting personal assistant. Don't become too comfortable. I shan't be here long."

"What do the doctors say?"

"What they always do, dear cousin. Time will tell if the limp is permanent. I wish they'd hurry with the physical therapy. I've sat on my backside long enough."

Alex nodded. "Patience, dearest Evelyn. My PA returns to work a week on Monday. Until she does, try to control yourself."

"I'll do so, Alex, but I can't wait to resume my duty and join Bedlam Charlie when the team is formalized."

"Once the doctors give you a clean bill of health, your position on the third Bedlam team is locked in. Now, would you be so kind to assist Bravo with their first deployment?"

"Of course."

\*\*\*

The following morning, Bedlam Bravo assembled in the conference room. Tea and biscuits were laid out on a polished credenza near the door. The team helped themselves and took seats. They thumbed through the folders left on the table while they waited for Miss E's arrival.

The door opened and she struggled to enter, her arms filled with tablets. Nate jumped to his feet and helped her to the chair at the head of the table.

Miss E gave Nate a warm smile. "Good morning, gentlemen. Shall we begin? We must cover several items today. No need for notes as briefing files are included on these tablets. First things first." Evelyn pulled the gray wig from her head, revealing spiky, blonde hair. She tugged at one of her hands, removing a thin synthetic glove. She pulled the other one off, revealing flawless hands rather than the aged appearance caused by the gloves.

Without exception, the team stared, speechless.

Pun, a man of few words, spoke first. "Wow."

Everyone laughed, lightening the mood.

"Don't worry, boys." Evelyn smiled. "I don't bite. Sir Alex and I owe you an explanation. You see, I'm rather like you." She sipped her tea, gazing at each man.

"I'm Lady Evelyn Jackson. Sir Alex is my first cousin. For the past five years, I've been a field agent for MI6. My deployment name is Evelyn Evinrude. Please keep my real name to yourselves. The wig and gloves are one of the changes I make when meeting certain foreign operatives."

Trevor and Jake spoke at the same time. "What should we call you?"

"I think Miss E works fine, don't you? About three months ago, a Middle East operation soured. A complete balls up. Ended in a fire fight and I was unfortunate enough to stop a bullet. Hit me near the hip. No major damage, but the area is tender, causing me to limp. After I'm cleared for duty, I'll return to MI6. I'm helping Sir Alex while his PA is on her annual holiday to Ibiza."

"I never would have—what—I agree with Pun. Wow. Will you be joining us?"

Evelyn shook her head. "I have other commitments, but I'll help you with your deployment." She picked up a remote-control unit and pointed it at the far end of the table. A flat screen monitor descended from the ceiling. The background showed a world map with the locations of the hijacked ships blinking red.

"Hmm. No definite pattern." Gerhard stretched and locked his hands behind his head. "Some in Somali waters, others farther away from land."

Evelyn clicked the remote. Small flags representing the countries under which the ships had operated appeared next to the blips.

"Eight ships, each registered in a different country. No obvious flags of convenience." Nate frowned, his fingers doing a tap dance on the table. "Unless there's something significant about their cargos, the pirates are opportunistic, going after whatever ship comes within their clutches."

"The ships' manifests are in a folder on your tablets." The screen changed. "No real similarities between the crews' nationalities—they represent thirty-four countries. This makes it easier to place a mixed group like Bravo on the Italian ship."

Trevor stood and waved at the screen. "So, what do we know? Everything seems to be random. This doesn't make our assignment any easier—nothing to focus our efforts on. Will we get lucky and the pirates come after the ship we're on? Maybe they'll take another."

Everyone nodded at Trevor's words. Grim-faced, the team glanced at one another.

A hand slapped the table, breaking the silence. "We go. We try." Pun jumped to his feet. "No success, try again. We will be victor—they lose."

"I agree with our man of few—"

A soft gong sounded as the lights flickered. Evelyn stood. "Nothing to worry about, it's Sir Alex requesting my presence in his office. Be back soon."

After she left, the team members activated their tablets and began reading. Quiet permeated the room as they concentrated on the information, broken by the occasional whoosh of the air conditioning and Nate's light tapping on the table.

Fifteen minutes later, Evelyn returned. "Sorry for the interruption. Sir Alex received new intel pertinent to your mission." She clicked the remote, and a photograph appeared. "Meet Captain Rossi, the skipper of the hijacked *Napoli*."

"He doesn't look too good." Gerhard sat upright as he studied the photo. "Did the pirates give him the black eyes? What happened to the side of his head?"

"Yes, they beat him when he refused to cooperate. One also fired a weapon near his head, causing cordite burns and damaging his eardrum. Prior to the release of Captain Rossi and most of his crew, each captive received a blow to the head from a rifle butt. In his case, he required several stitches."

"Bastards." Trevor shook his head, inward-facing eyebrows and a scowl etched across his features.

"Agreed. The worst part is, they kept two crewmen as hostages—Smith, the senior engineer, and Patterson, a young lad on his first voyage."

A low grumble of disapproval spread through the room.

"From Captain Rossi's debriefing, we've learned the possible identity of the pirate leader—Dachau, Dacar, or Dacker. Another pirate spoke the leader's name, but his accent was heavy. Captain Rossi couldn't be sure of the name."

"An alias or his real name?" Nate continued staring at Captain Rossi's photo before making notes.

"Anything is possible." Evelyn flipped to a new photograph. A grainy black-and-white image appeared on the screen, but several features were distinguishable.

"This came to us courtesy of another agency who debriefed crewmen from the fourth hijacking. The engineer snapped this photo with a disposable camera when the pirates dragged him to the bridge. Not the greatest, but it's all we have."

"Hmm. The cheekbones and aquiline nose suggest he might be Somali." Trevor stroked his chin as he studied the photo. "Tall and slender build, might be handsome to some, although his face is strange."

"A doctor examined the photograph and believed this is scarring from an untreated childhood illness, perhaps chickenpox. Nothing confirmed, of course." Evelyn glanced at the clock. "Let's take a short break. On the floor above us is a decent canteen if you fancy something to eat. It's filling and inexpensive. We'll meet back here in an hour."

\*\*\*

When the team returned, they found Evelyn seated in front of an array of equipment. At the end of the table were several backpacks.

"When the organizers established Bedlam, they insisted each team use the same communications equipment to ensure compatibility. Daily SITREPs are required from the team during deployment. Trevor, you can decide who'll do this."

"What if we need to separate?" Trevor scratched his chin. "On board the ship, I agree a single SITREP would suffice, but not if we're in different locales."

"Agree. Separate reports would be required. Contact will be via encrypted satellite phone or a government-built device similar to an iPad. The iPad uses burst transmission, lasting milliseconds and connects to the phone to reach the satellites. Email or text is the preferred method to minimize mistakes."

"What about designated call signs?" Fergus glanced around the room. "I don't want to be called Irish."

Everyone laughed and Gerhard gave Fergus an elbow to his ribs.

"Bedlam Bravo Headquarters will be Topaz. The color call signs used in your QE2 training will suffice for now."

Evelyn pointed to the bags. "I brought a backpack labeled for each of you. Inside, you'll find your comms gear, passports and tickets. A study packet about the ship you'll be joining in Naples will be uploaded to your iPads."

"Evelyn, you've thought of everything we'll need to begin our mission—except weapons." Trevor gazed at the others. "While we all possess hand-to-hand combat skills, I'd like something else."

"A courier from the British Consulate will meet you when you arrive in Naples. He'll identify himself as Topaz and will provide pistols and stun guns for you."

Trevor nodded "Excellent. More firepower would be better, but since we're supposed to be noncombatants, it makes sense to maintain a low profile. Is there anything—"

The conference room door opened. Sir Alex entered, waved everyone to remain seated, and made his way to an empty chair.

"There's additional intel to share with you. While it doesn't impact your current mission, you should be aware. We've learned North Korea is trying to expand their ties with Angola and Equatorial Guinea." Sir Alex referred to a printout he brought with him.

"What's strange is their foreign minister doesn't appear to be involved in this, nor are any of their ambassadors in Africa. Instead, Soo Khan Chin, the DPRK ambassador to China, is the one trying to cozy up. We don't know what this means yet."

"Thank you, Sir Alex. We'll keep this information in mind. Anything else?"

"Trevor, your primary task is to capture the Somali pirate leader known as Dacar." He shook his finger. "I want this son-of-a-bitch. Alive, if possible."

# Chapter Seven

Ministry of Foreign Affairs
Pyongyang, North Korea

After Ambassador Soo received the details of Kim's meeting with Dacar, he prepared a presentation for Supreme Leader Wook. *I hope this will win my family's release. If only I could kill him—and get away.*

Unable to focus, he shook his head and stared at his handwritten notes. *Knowing Wook's mentality, what will satisfy him?* Soo hit a button on the intercom. Moments later, his secretary entered his office.

"Yes, Ambassador?" Nari sat in a chair next to Soo's desk, pen poised over a notepad.

He handed over his notes. "Type these up and make an appointment for me with the Supreme Leader." He stared at a blank piece of the wall.

"Yes, sir. When do you want the meeting?"

"How soon will my report be ready?"

"About an hour, Ambassador."

"This afternoon, if possible. I'll need time to review."

She took the notes and headed to the door.

"Nari, a moment, please."

She turned back. "Yes, Ambassador?"

"Thank you."

Surprised at his words, she remained speechless. Nari nodded and closed the door.

Three days later, Wook granted Soo a brief audience. Unlike the previous meeting, held under tense circumstances, Soo was escorted into a private room. A small table held place settings for two. Guards stood in each corner, alert eyes capturing every movement.

A servant acknowledged Soo with a deep bow, led him to the table, and whisked out a chair. Moments after Soo was seated and the waiter poured him a goblet of water, the guards stiffened, and a door slammed open against the wall.

Wook, dressed in a gray, pinstriped suit, matching tie, and cream-colored shirt instead of his normal black cover-all suit, strolled into the room. The guards came to attention and the servant bowed.

Soo jumped to his feet and gave a deep bow. "S-Supreme L-Leader. Good to see you again."

Wook nodded and sat at the table, his right arm draped over the back of the chair. Soo remained standing while two servants maneuvered a cart containing several covered dishes. One placed a linen napkin on Wook's lap while the other uncovered platters and placed an array of tempting delicacies in front of him.

"Soo, what news do you bring me?" Wook pointed at several dishes, including brined fish, grilled beef, roasted duck, noodles, and an assortment of vegetables. A servant filled a plate with Wook's choices.

Soo's nervous stomach rumbled from the aromas of ginger and coriander. He swallowed. *I hope I don't vomit in front of Wook.*

"S-Supreme Leader. Through Kim, I have established a workable plan with Dacar." He offered a folder containing his report to Wook, who waved his hand. "They will hijack oil tankers and exchange them with us for weapons."

"How will this serve us?" Wook alternated with a spoon and metal chopsticks to scoop food into his mouth. "The West will seize the ships."

"Once the pirates hijack a ship, they'll repaint the port of registry and change the flag. They'll also change the ship's name. If there's time, the crew will repaint the stack and remove any company emblems."

"I see." Wook slurped the last of his meal. He raised a hand and the servant hurried to replenish the plate. "What country have you chosen for this—?"

"A flag of convenience, Supreme Leader. I've selected Cambodia."

Soo shifted back and forth to relax the pressure building in his legs from his stationary position. "They provide this service to our friends in China and Russia. More than half of the ships flying the Cambodian flag belong to other nations."

A bowl of soup placed in front of him, Wook dropped the chopsticks and tackled the bowl with his spoon. "Won't the West be able to track the ships to one of our ports?"

"Only if the ships come straight here. They'll sail to the tanker terminal in Sihanoukville first. After an appropriate length of time, they'll leave Cambodia and proceed to our port in Wonsan by way of Macau."

"Hmmm." Wook finished the soup and pushed the bowl away. The servant removed the used dishes and handed him a glass of Taedonggang, a beer produced in Pyongyang and one of Wook's favorites. Wook drained the glass and handed it back for a refill.

Soo licked his lips as his mouth watered. *What a bastard—tempting me with the food and beer but not offering any.*

"What is the oil to weapons ratio? I would demand the most favorable terms."

"Two tankers for each shipload of eh, arms, Supreme Leader." Soo continued to rock on his heels. *I wish he'd let me sit. Dare I hope he'll offer me something to eat?* "They gave me a list of weapons and vehicles they want in exchange."

"Generous terms—too generous. Three tankers for two twenty-foot containers of weapons. No missiles requiring a mobile launcher, hand-held only. Assault rifles, pistols, ammunition, and grenades. Toss in a few military vehicles."

"B-But we agreed to—"

Wook waved a hand. "Make the change. I decide what agreements are approved—no one else." He stood and emptied his glass. Using it as a pointer, he directed attention to the half-empty plate on the other side of the table. "Weren't you hungry, Soo? You missed an excellent meal."

*As if I would sit without permission. The guards would have hauled me away.* "No, Supreme Leader."

Wook turned to leave and stopped. "I almost forgot. Jung Gi—she's doing fine in—what's it called?" He snapped his fingers. "Oh, yes. Protective custody. Not at Camp Fourteen. She hasn't been transferred yet."

Soo glanced toward the ceiling. *If there's a God, thank you.* "May I speak with her? What about my sons?"

"Should you complete the oil arrangement to my satisfaction, I might grant five minutes with them upon your return. Fail to correct your mistaken agreement, and their fate is sealed."

***

Soo yanked his outer office door open. Nari jumped to her feet. Without a word, he stormed into his private room and slammed the door. He fell into his swivel chair and pounded a fist into the palm of his other hand.

*Bastard! What I'd do if I .... I'd strangle him and feed him to the dogs.*

A discreet knock shook him from his reverie. Nari entered, carrying a cup of Daechucha tea. She handed the tea to him and took her normal station, waiting for his instructions.

"Thank you, Nari." Soo sipped the tea made from jujube fruit and leaned back in his chair. "Make arrangements for Kim and me to travel to the Seychelles. Tell Kim to set up a meeting with the man named Dacar."

"At once, Ambassador. When do you want to travel?"

"As soon as I can. Lives are at stake."

\*\*\*

Four days later, the Air Seychelles flight from Dubai screeched to a halt midway along the runway. The pilot made a sharp turn at the first available taxiway and lumbered toward the terminal. After the plane stopped, Soo and Kim leaped from their seats and headed for the door.

"Gentlemen, please sit down until the pilot turns off the fasten seatbelt sign." The flight attendant pointed to an illuminated logo. "Your safety is important, and you'll soon disembark."

*Ping.* The illumination disappeared.

Kim turned to the flight attendant. "Seems we may go now. Please step aside."

She glared at the two men before moving out of their way. Soo and Kim hurried to baggage claim. Soo's oversized luggage pulled from the conveyor belt, they pushed through other passengers waiting to collect their bags and strode to the exit.

The terminal teemed with visitors, each trying to find their way around the building. Excited voices and laughter created a welcoming presence. A hint of cooking meat wafted from one of the small booths near the entrance to the terminal.

Soo exited first, wearing his normal black clothes, but donned a Panama hat and blue Ray-Ban Aviator sunglasses. He tipped his Ray-Bans as he glanced around.

"Ambassador, perhaps it would be better to get rid of the glasses." Kim shook his head. "We don't want to stand out, and your hat does enough."

Soo pursed his lips. "The hat is to keep the sun off me and the glasses are to protect my eyes." He tutted. "I don't understand how people can live in this heat and intense sunlight."

"Millions do, Ambassador." Kim hailed a taxi and gave the name of their hotel.

Soo moved to the door and waited for Kim to open it.

Kim lowered his voice. "We must maintain character, sir. For the duration of this mission, you will be a nobody named Soo, and can open your own doors."

"Hmph. If I must."

Once at the hotel, they checked into adjoining rooms and retired for the evening.

***

The next morning, Kim knocked on the connecting door. No answer. He knocked again. Nothing. Kim tried the handle—unlocked. He entered. A noise startled him as he checked in the bathroom. He stepped back into the bedroom and spotted the doorknob turning. He hurried behind the door—and waited. The door swung open, a shadow crept across the carpet. Kim slammed the door shut and jumped on the intruder's back. He shoved him to the floor and rolled him over.

Soo stared up at him. "What are you doing? Help me up."

"Ambassador, what were you thinking? Where did you go?" Kim jumped to his feet and pulled Soo up. "You know nothing about this place."

"I-I woke early and went for a walk. No one saw me—at least I don't think so."

Kim sat on the edge of the bed and motioned for Soo to do the same. He sighed, easing the adrenaline, which had built up in his system as he went into fight mode.

"Ambassador—Soo, you must understand. This is not Pyongyang or Beijing, where you travel with at least six bodyguards. I am your only protection, and if you disappear without my knowledge, what might happen?"

"You speak to me like I'm a child. I am the ambassador to China, and you're a lowly aide."

Kim nostrils flared. "Must I treat you like an infant who needs monitoring at all times? You're in my world now, Soo. Someone might be waiting for an unsuspecting tourist to wander by. What would you do? Can you protect yourself?"

*I guess he's right, but I don't like his attitude.* "I will try to remember my place while we are here." Soo's eyes focused on his minder. "Kim, don't lose sight of who is responsible for the success of this mission—me."

Kim gave Soo a narrowed-eye stare but remained silent.

\*\*\*

They ate a light breakfast and left the hotel, setting off toward the city center. Kim led the way, Soo trailing several steps behind. They traversed street after street, doubling back on their tracks. Kim used shop windows to check for possible surveillance.

Satisfied no one followed, Kim and Soo entered the Lai Lam Food Shop and stepped to the counter.

"What are we doing here, Kim? It's too early to eat." Soo glanced at the menu board.

"Order something, anything. We'll take the food with us."

They found an empty bench not far away after their food was ready. Kim sampled his chicken and noodles, maintaining a close eye on their surroundings.

Soo decided he was hungry after all and wolfed down his fish and noodles.

A shadow drifted over his face. It blocked the sun. For a moment Soo was relieved with the respite from the searing heat.

He glanced up. A man with a scar running along the left side of his chin stood with an older man beside him, also dressed in dark clothing, with a red bandanna covering his head. Both men wore Adidas tennis shoes.

"You must be Ambassador Soo. I am Dacar." He gestured toward his associate with an open right hand. "This is Tahliil Wardi. He is my leader. He doesn't speak much English. I will translate."

Kim stood, Soo following. "I suggest we proceed to the botanical gardens where we might have more privacy."

Dacar nodded, translated for Tahliil. The Somalis departed, with the Koreans crossing the street and walking a few paces behind through the crowded streets.

Once they reached the gardens and found a secluded area, Soo began the negotiations. "On behalf of the Supreme Leader, we look forward to our joint venture ...." He turned his head, first to the right, then left before lowering his voice. "Our sharing of weapons and oil."

After Dacar had translated, Tahliil nodded.

"I must amend the agreement you and Kim reached earlier. He didn't follow my instructions."

Kim glanced at Soo, his brow knitted in confusion.

"The Supreme Leader wants three oil tankers for each agreed upon load of weapons." Soo raised his hands as if anticipating a negative reaction to this change. "To show our good faith, we will arrange a delivery wherever you want before you provide a single ship."

As he listened to the translation, Tahliil stood motionless. By the time Dacar finished speaking, he had dipped his head, smiled, and spoken a few words.

"Tahliil agrees to the change in our agreement, providing the weapons are received within two weeks."

Soo stuck out his hand. "It will be arranged."

Dacar shook the offered hand, followed by Tahliil. Kim continued to scan the area, paying little attention to the negotiations.

Further arrangements made, the men departed and appeared to go their separate ways.

Soo beamed as he jabbed Kim with a finger. "I showed them how to negotiate. We obtained what the Supreme Leader wants."

"Did he suggest a shipload of weapons upfront?"

"Well, no, but it's my decision. It's not a shipload—two twenty-foot containers and a dozen military vehicles. I'll discuss this goodwill payment with the Supreme Leader when we return to Pyongyang." Soo glanced around. "All this work has made me hungry again."

They returned to the Lai Lam Food Shop. Kim went inside to place their order, while Soo sat on the same bench as earlier.

Soo closed his eyes and hummed a Korean ballad.

"Psst."

Soo opened his eyes and stared at a short, stocky man. Darkness descended over Soo as an individual behind the bench shoved a black bag over his head. Despite his struggles, he couldn't break free. Two quick punches to his head knocked him out.

\*\*\*

When Kim returned with the food, he scanned the area for Soo. Not finding him, he dropped the food and dashed back and forth, looking in shop fronts and along the shaded paths.

No sign. The ambassador had disappeared.

Kim returned to the bench where he'd left Soo. He sat and pulled his feet back under the seat. Something clattered. He tipped his head to check under the bench—he had kicked a pair of crushed Ray-Ban Aviators, which lay in the shadows. He bent down and picked up the sunglasses—one lens was missing.

Glancing around, something glittered a few feet away in the sunshine. The item causing the sparkle was the missing lens—drops of dried blood streaked the surface.

Kim shoved the pieces in a pocket. Chest heaving with panic, he scurried away. *What's happened to Soo?*

## Chapter Eight

Naples, Italy
Port Area

Trevor and his team paced the sidewalk outside a metro station in Naples, large backpacks on their shoulders. Commuters shoved past as they streamed in and out of the station. They had rooms booked at the nearby Ponapace Porta Nolana Bed & Breakfast. Merchant seamen stayed there while working in the port or waiting for their next ship to sail.

"Ag, man. These Italians are pushy." Gerhard lifted his bag out of the way as another pedestrian, running for the metro, shoved the backpack out of his way.

Nate coughed. "Time to move out of here before we suffocate on the diesel fumes from the buses."

"Let's find our rooms and check out the harbor." Trevor set off at a rapid pace. The others followed. They nudged their way through the area, crowded with shoppers and tourists.

A horn blew, warning the team of a tram approaching. They scrambled out of the way and continued to their hotel.

Minutes later, the group hovered around the lobby.

Trevor glanced at his team. "There's one room with a view. Shall we flip a coin for it?"

"Fine by me." Nate's nose twitched in the air. "I'm hungry. I'm going to find out where the aroma is coming from."

Fergus frowned. "You're always hungry."

"I have to feed my metabolism."

While Nate disappeared around the corner, Trevor won the coin toss.

Nate returned moments later. "No food. It was leftovers from someone sitting in the common room."

Trevor nodded. "Rooms are sorted. I won the coin toss. You and Fergus have single rooms, while Gerhard will share the remaining room with Pun. Drop your stuff and meet back here as soon as possible."

Each man reappeared a few minutes later, dressed in jeans, boots, and work shirts, with smaller backpacks, each in a different color, tossed over their shoulders.

The first to arrive, Nate asked the others about their rooms. "Mine has a threadbare carpet on the floor, a lump which is to pass as a pillow and stains everywhere."

"Ag, what did you expect, the Hilton?"

Everyone laughed as Gerhard took point and led them toward the harbor.

They stopped at a busy sidewalk café across from the port. After ordering coffees and beef sandwiches, Trevor scanned the area before returning his attention to the team.

"I sent a note informing Topaz we've arrived. A message waited—slight change of plans. The vessel we planned to sail on is delayed by a week before returning to South Africa."

Fergus looked at the other tables. No one appeared to be paying any attention to them. "What does this mean for us? Did they find another ship?"

Trevor lowered his voice. "Yes, they did. We'll be working in the port for about a week aboard the *Ventrusco*. This one's also owned by Fiat and is a sister ship to the original. This will work out better for us."

"Ag. We'll learn how to act like proper seamen and become familiar with the ship before we cast off."

At five in the afternoon, a long, shrill whistle blew near the docks where several freighters were berthed.

Workers assembled, going through a turnstile to leave the port. The guards stopped some and asked questions, while others strolled past.

Trevor nodded toward the turnstile. "Checks seem random. No consistency in examining what workers are carrying."

"Ag, man." Gerhard downed his beer. "The guards appeared bored. Wouldn't you be?"

"Good point."

The team ordered another round of drinks as they continued to monitor the workers' egress. The flow trickled to a few. At last, the guards locked the gate and disappeared into their hut.

"I'm heading back to the B&B for the evening." Trevor stood. "We have an early start tomorrow."

"Hey, Trevor. Fergus and I will check out the other side of the port. Catch everyone in the morning."

***

Dawn broke with the promise of a pleasant day. No clouds lingered. Oranges and reds gave way to a deep azure.

The B&B's door swung open. Out stepped Bedlam Bravo, dressed in jeans, short-sleeved work shirts, and steel-toed work boots.

"Fergus, did you learn anything last night on your stroll with Nate?" Gerhard laughed and elbowed him.

"I learned it's better to go without you." A smirk appeared on Fergus's face. "We went somewhere with class. You wouldn't have been allowed in."

The laughter subsided as the men joined the queue of workers waiting to enter the shipyard. Ahead of them, the guard stopped four men dressed in the same attire.

Fergus nudged Nate. "One of the guys could have been your twin. Must lack your class."

Nate rolled his eyes and stepped up to the guard.

After he gave a brief glance at their passports and entry authorizations, he waved them through.

The *Ventrusco*, painted bright orange with a white bridge castle and a green and white funnel, was moored two berths to their left.

The men headed toward the gangway, where the foreman, a burly Italian holding a clipboard, stopped them. He glanced at each one and scratched his right ear.

Nate whispered, "When did Grizzly Adams begin working on freighters?"

"Who's he?" Fergus asked.

"Grizzly Adams came from California—about the same size as this guy. Adams trained grizzly bears and other wild animals."

"I thought that was Arnold."

"You're thinking of the former governor." Nate threw out his chest and flexed his biceps.

"What's the difference?"

Nate rolled his eyes.

Trevor stepped up to the foreman. "We were supposed to ship out on another freighter, but it's been delayed. Our foreman told us to report here."

"*Kohmeh see. Excusi.* What are your names?"

They each stepped forward and identified themselves. The foreman found their names and scrawled check marks on his list. "I show you the ship. After, you begin work. Come." He turned and dashed up the gangway. The team struggled to match his pace.

Two hours later, the foreman, who gave his name as Lorenzo, completed the team's tour. He fast-marched them through the bridge castle, between stacks of different colored containers on the main deck, into the holds where insulated containers would be placed, and ended at the forecastle.

"You now know way around. If lost, ask. Some help. Luigi will teach how to secure containers."

Lorenzo walked away as a man resembling a fireplug stepped forward. "*Salve*. I'm Luigi. You will be on Fabio's team. First, I'll teach you about containers and cranes, *capisce*?"

The men nodded. Pun gazed at the tall crane before turning to Luigi. "I no like heights. Me stay on deck."

Everyone laughed as Gerhard jostled Pun, almost knocking him over the railing.

"None of you will work the crane. Must be experienced and licensed to do so. But you need to learn how the crane moves in case a container comes loose."

"Does this occur often?" Nate glanced around the busy ship. Noise levels rose as the workday commenced in earnest.

"No, not often, but it happens." Luigi slapped Nate on the back. "I'll show you where to run if it does."

Throughout the day, the team learned about fittings for the deck and bottom, stacking, and locking. The shift-end whistle signaled welcome relief for their tired muscles.

They removed their hard hats and gloves, tucked them under an arm, and headed to the gangway.

"Salve." Luigi ran up to them, lanyards swinging from his hand. "Here are your passes. Tomorrow, boarding will be easier for you. *A domani*."

"Grazie." Nate shook Luigi's hand. "A donimi."

"No, no, Nate. A domani. It means see you tomorrow."

"My mistake. Thank you." Nate joined the others who had made their way ashore. "Luigi appears to be a standup guy."

"Ag, man. As long as we do as they want, they'll all be okay. But what will happen when we screw up?"

"Never mind, guys." Trevor pointed at the café they'd visited the previous day. "Let's grab a *birra* and a bite."

\*\*\*

The team gathered at an outside table.

Not far away, two men, hidden by a bush-covered trellis at another outdoor restaurant, monitored their activities. One used a pair of binoculars, while the other gazed at them through a camera with a telephoto lens, taking the occasional picture.

"Make sure you have photos of their faces. The boss wants pictures of any possible military men."

Rooble lowered his camera and turned to Cumar. "I will. They show the mannerisms of the military—short hair and straight-backed. The one with the gray hair and a scar on the side of his head struts as if he commanded a parade ground."

"I agree. Let's finish and go."

Rooble took several more snaps. "I captured all of their faces."

"Wait—they're leaving. Should we follow to find out where they're staying?"

"Yes, I think so."

Cumar and Rooble strolled a distance behind the five men until they disappeared inside a small building near the Nolana Metro Station.

"Take a picture of the front of the hotel, Rooble."

*** 

Nate ruffled the curtains to peer outside. The two men had disappeared. He turned back to the others and gave a thumbs-up. "Coast is clear."

Trevor gazed at Pun. "Excellent job spotting the tail. We'll wait a few minutes before returning to the B&B in case they come back."

Pun nodded at the compliment but he remained silent as usual. He walked to the entrance, tilted his head, and gazed outside.

Certain they weren't followed, they returned to their accommodations. Trevor bid the others a good evening. "I'll send an update to Bedlam and catch up on the news. See you in the morning."

*To: Topaz*
*From: Black*
*First day on new ship passed without incident. The foreman expected us, so process worked. Picked up tail while at a café near the port—two men, either Somali or Ethiopian. Tall, with slender builds, aquiline noses, and oval faces. Dropped them before reaching B&B. Will continue mission as planned.*

Trevor closed his iPad and flicked through the television channels until he found BBC World. He half-listened as he considered the beginning of the mission. *No new hijackings noted. Need to keep alert for more surveillance. Are they part of al-Shabaab?*

\*\*\*

No tail in sight, the team boarded the *Ventrusco*. The foreman, Lorenzo, greeted them like long-time friends. "*Buongiorno*! Hard work today, capisce?"

They continued up to the deck and weaved their way to the forecastle. Luigi waited for them. With black hair and a short, stocky build, his face appeared to be in a habitual scowl. After sharing greetings, Pun and Gerhard, and Nate and Fergus were paired together, while Trevor joined an Italian worker named Marco. The three teams climbed onto the first layer of containers, waiting for a crane to shift a new one into place so it could be secured.

One after another, new units were lowered, stacked and tied to the ones below and adjacent. The three teams worked in a well-orchestrated manner, each member responsible for specific tasks.

After a fifteen-minute breather, Gerhard and Pun climbed atop the highest container. Grabbing a rope,

Gerhard dashed to the edge of their perch, preparing to leap to the next platform to wait for the crane to lower another box. His foot caught in a coiled rope dangling over the side. He slipped over the edge trying to free his foot.

A shadow descended—the crane lowered a new container straight for Gerhard. "Pun! Help! My foot's trapped!"

Pun grabbed a rope, tied it around a stanchion, and jumped. The unit shuddered to a halt in its resting place.

A thick smear of red trickled from beneath the container, oozing down the side. Luigi and several others rushed to the scene. Suspended between containers, two men clung to the rope—Pun and Gerhard.

Several workers maneuvered into position to grab the rope. Brute force lifted the trapped men upward until they scrambled onto the container.

Pun and Gerhard heaved sighs of relief and patted each other on the shoulder. They gained their feet. "Ag, man. I thought this was the end."

"What happened?" Luigi checked the men over for any unseen injuries.

"I jumped to the next container. While I was in the air, someone yanked on a rope. My foot caught on something and I fell. I couldn't free my foot and yelled for Pun ...." Gerhard sucked in a deep breath of air. "He raced to me and shoved me over the side moments before the crane dropped its load. Someone screamed ...."

Nate slapped Gerhard on the back. "Good thing Pun was there to save your sorry hide."

He nodded and gazed upward. *I might have met my Maker—sooner than planned.*

"Is everyone accounted for?" Luigi glanced around. "Where's the new guy, Cumar?"

Pun pointed at the smear. "Bad man no more."

\*\*\*

Once the whistle had blown, the team headed back to the café. After the waiter delivered their drinks and food, Trevor raised his glass. "Here's to a happy ending instead of a disaster for Gerhard." Everyone drank before Trevor continued. "Luigi said there would be an accident investigation. Shouldn't take more than a day or so." He glanced at Nate. "Let's eat, I'm hungry."

Glasses were clinked, tipped back, and drained. Another round appeared. They dug into their food. Conversation ceased until the last plate was cleared.

"Guys, today was a narrow escape. We must remain alert at all times. Tomorrow we'll find a different café or restaurant to use, away from the docks."

Everyone nodded, somber expressions etched upon their faces.

"Enjoy the rest of the evening. I've a report to send."

*To: Topaz*
*From: Black*

*Contact with possible terrorist-related individual, one who might have surveilled the team yesterday. Red and Green escaped serious injury/death while on ship. Suspected culprit died—crushed by a container. Accident investigation will delay ship's departure. Will advise.*

Trevor clicked send, leaned back in the chair, and rubbed the scar by his temple. *Where's the other guy? Will he reappear or will another accident happen?*

While he watched BBC World, his iPad signaled an incoming message.

*To: Black*
*From: Topaz*

*Last report acknowledged. Courier from British Consulate will rendezvous with team tomorrow evening. Details to follow. Expect increased weaponry. Remain vigilant.*

# Chapter Nine

Jujubba Refugee Camp
Malindi, Kenya

A tall, broad-shouldered man twisted his body to work out the kinks, grabbed a red and white-checkered bandana from his pocket and wiped the perspiration from his face. His nose, plastered with layers of white sunscreen, vied for attention, and reddish hair was his most prominent feature.

George had arrived from England the previous day to spend six months assisting a charity called 'Save the World'. The group's coordinator assigned him to work with several new arrivals to mend the fence around the refugee camp.

He turned to Alf, who'd joined 'Save the World' for his gap year before returning to university to study history. "Want a drink of water? I'm getting one."

Alf stopped digging a hole for a new post and leaned on his shovel. "I could kill for a beer about now."

George laughed. "There's rumor going around Tusker Beer is drinkable. Perhaps we'll try one tonight. Until then, it's water."

After they had grabbed bottles of warm water, they returned to work. Both drank half of a bottle, pouring the remainder over their hot, sweaty heads. Afterward, George and Alf dropped a round wooden pillar in their latest hole, filled in around the post, and tamped the earth down. They trudged back to the pile to fetch another. Before long, they completed their ninth posthole.

"Who or what damaged the previous posts?" Alf gazed at the broken remains. "Wild animals?"

"When I arrived, they told me refugees trying to flee caused the damage." George shook his head. "Something or someone spooked them. They ran for their lives."

"Let's finish up. Be dark soon. This close to the equator there's a short period of dusk between daylight and nighttime. Forgot to bring my torch."

"Lift the other end of the pole, and we'll spread out the barbed wire."

They donned thick gloves and rolled the wire along the damaged area. George used a pair of cutters to snip the metal strands and they returned to the beginning, feeding out another length. Once four pieces were ready, they set aside the roll. Employing a stretcher to make the wire taut, they used a heavy-duty staple gun to secure the strands, and returned to the group's encampment, where they shared a two-person tent.

"Did you check out the shower? Two small cubicles, each has a bucket with holes. Pull a lever and the water splashes over you." Alf clasped his arms around himself. "Brrr. No hot water unless you heat it yourself. Might be okay after a hard day's work, but don't leave it to the evening when the temperature drops."

"No problem, Alf. Pretend you're camping."

"Right. There's camping and then there's—whatever this is."

Both men laughed as the dinner gong sounded not far away. They joined the others at the outdoor canteen, dipping a ladle into a pot of baked beans and sausage augmented by chapatis. After filling their plates, they found empty camp chairs.

Once everyone finished, dishes and utensils cleaned, Ian, the group coordinator, stood and addressed the fifteen men and women. "In honor of George and Alf, our newest members, Tusker beer is available. Warm, but there it is. Alf, George, welcome to Save the World."

A polite round of applause ensued, followed by the clicks and clinks of bottle caps popping and hitting various rocks. Someone said, "Cheers," and sixteen bottles were raised and the contents consumed.

"Yech." Ian screwed up his face. "I'll never become used to warm beer. Wish we had ice to chill this. Never mind—at least there's beer."

The temperature dropped as the night wore on. Someone lit a fire, and everyone huddled to absorb some of the radiating warmth. Snarling and growling echoed over the camp. A bleating sound ensued, followed by a scream as an animal's life ended.

"What made the noise?" Alf's eyes widened as he glanced around the encampment.

"Nothing to worry about—probably a lion or cheetah caught an impala or some other animal. You'll get used to the sounds."

By midnight, everyone left the fading embers and traipsed to their tents for a few hours of sleep.

\*\*\*

The following morning, after a simple breakfast of leftover chapatis, beans, and runny eggs, chased down with lukewarm tea, Ian escorted George and Alf on a tour of the refugee camp.

Ian pointed at the fence. "We use barbed wire to keep the animal and undesirables out of the camp."

"Who are the undesirables?" George shielded his eyes with a hand and gazed at the fence they had been working on.

"Thieves trying to find something to sell are our main concern."

Row upon row of sun-bleached tents filled the space. Kids chased each other in a game of tag, while women tried to wash clothes in small barrels. Older children kicked around several soccer balls. The smell of human waste, garbage, and the buzz of countless flies were constant companions.

"The camp was built to handle fifty thousand people." Ian's hands swept through the air, encompassing the overpopulated facility. "We're overwhelmed with almost seventy-five thousand and more arriving each day."

"How does everyone cope?" George glanced at the squalid conditions, caused by too many people, erratic rainfall, and intense sunlight. "Isn't everyone on your team a volunteer?"

"I'm one of two full-time employees at this camp." Ian fielded a soccer ball headed his way and chased it back to a group of youths playing on one of the drier areas. "We have sixteen foreign volunteers and several Kenya and Somali assistants. Thank God people such as you and Alf donate their time to help us. The refugees appreciate what we're doing for them, but it's never enough."

They continued their tour of the camp, walking between the rows of roomy wall tents donated by several charities. These structures held up to twenty people. In several locations, refugees squatted under black, plastic sheeting to block the sun. Each person received a single small blanket to ward off the evening chill.

"How come some people are under plastic and not in a tent?" Alf pointed to a group of small children, stomachs distended by lack of nourishment, who remained motionless under a plastic sheet, ignoring the flies on their bare skin.

"They're the latest arrivals. Until we process them, they remain here. It's the best we can do with the current supplies."

"We've repaired the fence. What do you want us to do next?" George kicked another loose soccer ball back to the kids.

"This is why we're taking a tour. Our most pressing need is helping the latest arrivals. Some require immediate medical treatment, while others need high-energy food. Would you be willing to work with them? Not everyone wants to as they find it too stressful to witness human misery first-hand."

"Of course," George said, Alf echoing him.

"Fantastic. We're almost finished. I'll drop you off at the processing tables."

\*\*\*

Ian introduced the men to David, who was responsible for processing arriving refugees. David, a gaunt man with blond hair tucked under a bush hat, welcomed them.

"Thank you for volunteering to help. In some ways, this is the toughest job as we meet them after their arduous journeys. Many times, others died along the way. Gut-wrenching stories."

"Thank you, David." George shook his hand, followed by Alf. "What should we do first?"

"It's quiet now. New refugees arrive at any time, day or night. Many don't possess documentation.

"We take their names, where they're from, age, and other details, and complete a registration form. If they can write their names, they sign at the bottom. If they can't, we do it for them. The next step is giving them a bit of high-calorie food. A little at first—they'll vomit if they eat too much at once when they're near starvation. When a doctor is available, they'll also receive a medical check. Afterward, we assign them a space to sleep."

Alf gazed through the gates, edged with remnants of thorny bushes and tufts of elephant grass battling for any available moisture. Beyond, dusty, parched land stretched for miles. "Does it ever rain?"

"Oh, yes. Almost every month. Most of the time it's insufficient in this part of Kenya to restore the land to its once-fertile state. When there's enough, everything greens up."

David continued to explain the processing procedures as a frail Somali woman with two children approached. She straightened her stained *guntiino* so her ankles were less exposed, pulled her *garbasaar* tight around her head, and tied a knot in her *shash*, centering it on her neck. She leaned on a post, struggling to remain upright. The children, covered in tattered Western clothing, slumped to the ground.

The three men hurried to tie their face masks and don gloves before they dashed forward, David carrying water bottles. "Give them small sips. They'll be dehydrated and thirsty. Too dangerous to let them drink fast—it might kill them."

They gave the refugees several sips, stopping them from taking huge gulps. Even warm, the life-sustaining liquid appeared to energize the Somalis. George helped the woman to her feet, while David and Alf each lifted a child and carried them to the relative shelter of the processing table underneath a stretched tarp.

Paperwork completed, a couple took the woman and her children to an area for a medical check and food.

"How do you cope with this?" George's face remained expressionless, his hands on his hips. "You helped open the facility."

"It can be difficult." David nodded and wiped his eyes. "The children are the worst. Innocent—yet most don't survive."

"I-I don't think I can help with any further processing." Alf hung his head. "This is tragic. I'll do anything to help while I'm here, but I can't handle their desperate state."

"These are the lucky ones, Alf. They've made it here so they'll be taken care of. There are untold number of people who suffer the same plights—no food or medicine, physical attacks, and even village massacre."

"When you put it in that way, I'll maintain control of my emotions and help." Alf's hands trembled, his eyes welled up with tears. "It's the least any of us can do. I've seen plenty of human suffering in war zones and dealt with it because we were concerned with self-preservation, but this is the first time I've experienced anything like this."

"Not to worry, Alf. There's plenty of other tasks you can help with if this becomes too much for you. What about you, George?"

"If you don't mind, I want to work on the processing desk." *My mother would approve if she were still with us.*

"Fantastic! I think we've covered enough for today. Go clean up. We have a treat for dinner—American style hot dogs, provided by the American Embassy in Nairobi. Marshmallows, too."

\*\*\*

After dusk, George and Alf took their turn building the evening fire. They stacked the kindling, placed a bit of paper under some of the smallest pieces, and added larger pieces of wood in a small pyramid shape.

Alf struck a match—a slight breeze snuffed it out before he applied the flame to the paper. Whistles and catcalls came from the other volunteers as they waited. He tried again. This time the match touched the paper. Curling, brown smoke swirled before it ceased.

"Here, you try." Alf handed the box of matches to George.

He took the box and examined the sides and ends before pulling out a match. George showed the others what was in his hand. "I say, Alf. I believe you strike the match against the rough bit."

Laughter erupted as George pantomimed the action. Satisfied he had everyone's attention, he struck the match and brushed the paper. It burst into flames and the kindling smoked and burned.

Once the fire was established, George tossed the match into the flames and bowed to the others amid claps and cheers.

All Alf could do was shake his head.

Hot dogs roasted, marshmallows burned to a crisp, appetites were satiated. As the embers died, the group headed to their tents.

"I wonder how the refugees are doing?" George stifled a yawn as he stretched out on his bed. "We shouldn't forget about them."

"You're right, but remember, we're doing what we can do to help them. More people need to do their share."

"Night, Alf." George turned the lantern off.

"Night."

\*\*\*

The nighttime chorus began—snarls, growls, whimpers, and the occasional howl. George covered his head with his pillow and tried to sleep. *Some animal hunting for its food, perhaps to feed its young. If I don't get used to these sounds, six months will last forever.*

The nocturnal sounds stopped. George smiled and rolled over. *At last—time for some sleep.*

Before long, the tent filled with snorts and heavy breathing. *Alf.* George threw a pillow—silence returned and he drifted off.

Two hours later, George woke with a start. Total quiet engulfed the camp. Not a sound ventured forward to break the calm.

*What woke me?*

Sounds like several cars backfiring disturbed the night.

Gunfire!

Adults screamed. Children cried. George and Alf dove off their cots and hugged the ground. The gunfire and shrieks intensified.

"Alf. Stay down. I'll find out what's happening."

"George, are you crazy? Keep on the floor until Ian or David contact us."

"But what if the camp is under attack? Perhaps I can do something."

"Are you insane?" Alf grabbed George's arm. "Stay put. We'll find out soon enough."

Quiet returned. Hushed voices wafted over the camp, encouraging children to go back to sleep.

Footsteps. Closer—stopped outside the tent.

George grabbed a small shovel used for the latrine and readied himself.

"Psst. It's Ian. Are you okay?"

Alf opened the tent flap. He and George scooted outside.

Ian scanned the area with a flashlight. The beam caught nothing useful—footprints in the sand, a broken section of the perimeter fence. Nothing to indicate who entered the camp. He turned to the men. "Raiders." He spat on the ground.

"What would they be after?" George pursed his lips, his forehead wrinkled. "Are any valuables stored here?"

"One thing they're interested in—women. Wouldn't be the first time raiders came and carried away several female refugees, sometimes in their early teens. We'll find out more in the morning."

\*\*\*

George and Alf remained awake the rest of the night, listening to the night sounds. Alf yawned. "Get some sleep, George. I'll keep watch for now. I'm too wound up to sleep. If I become drowsy later on, I'll wake you."

"I'm too much on edge to sleep so I'll keep you company."

When dawn broke, they dressed and headed to the communal area. The other volunteers milled about, waiting for instructions.

Ian arrived and conducted a headcount. "Good. Our team is accounted for. David's checking with the refugee leaders to … here he comes."

David joined the group and shared the news. "Ten women are missing. We found another outside the perimeter—dead." He glanced at George and Alf, anger etched across his face. "The woman you processed yesterday is one of those missing."

## Chapter Ten

Indian Ocean
Near Mogadishu, Somalia

The small blue and white motorboat skipped over the breaking waves as it pushed between sandbars and entered a small bay. A dozen houses overlooked the beach along the crescent-shaped shoreline. Built as vacation homes for foreigners and wealthy Somalis, they stood dilapidated and silent, testament to the country's turmoil.

A cloudless day, the sun baked everything.

Two guards hopped from the boat into the bath-like water as they approached the shore. Engine stopped, they helped guide the craft. A third leaped from the bow, pulling a rope with him while a fourth remained aboard, an AK-47 cradled in his arms.

The boat secured, Tahliil and Dacar jumped ashore. Sahid Barre trudged through the soft sand to greet them. He relieved Tahliil of his backpack and led the terrorist leader toward a white house with blue shutters and trim, and a pink tiled roof. The property hadn't been used by foreigners since the Americans fled the country.

They climbed the six steps to the covered porch. In a corner, a brazier sizzled, heating water. Sahid poured it over the tea, passing a cup to each man. They thanked him and took a tentative sip.

"How was the meeting with the Koreans?" Sahid's eyes shone and his face beamed. "Will they give us more weapons? How soon?"

"Patience, Sahid." Dacar raised his cup. "Let's finish our tea and all will be revealed."

"You're right, my friend. I'll grill some fish and vegetables while you both relax."

By the time the men finished eating, dusk had fallen. So had the temperature. They huddled around the brazier for warmth. With no electricity this far from the city, one of the men lit candles and spaced them around the porch. The two-room house still held the day's heat, well over ninety degrees, and no one wanted to sit inside.

"The Koreans changed our agreement." Dacar shrugged and motioned for Sahid to remain seated. "They want three tankers for two containers of weapons. A shipment will be on the way soon, before we provide any tankers."

"Where will the ship dock—Mogadishu?"

Tahliil joined the men after a trip to the latrine. "No, I want weapons in Kismaayo. Easier to move where needed. More training in camps west of city."

"Should we include an empty tanker as part of the three?" Dacar glanced at Tahliil. "Once taken to Cambodia, we will say the ship carried a full load—must have been stolen in Sihanoukville, by the Cambodians."

"Hmm." Tahliil rubbed his chin as he considered Dacar's suggestion. "Not now, perhaps later. If weapons inferior or double-crossed, we do this."

"Should we continue to seize freighters?" Sahid asked. "Or concentrate on the oil carriers?"

"Both. If one kind of ship, easy spot pattern. Make more difficult do both."

Dacar nodded and changed the subject. "Okay, we'll do this. What about the money wired to the Freedom Bank in Malta? How should we disburse the funds?"

"Leave alone. Mistake to accept wired money. Why you think I want cash? Money sent to bank is traceable—cash much harder. Don't plan more without approval. You learned English and received schooling in America and England, but wits more important."

"Yes, Tahliil. Forgive my rash behavior." Dacar gazed at the floor. Silent for a moment, he looked up and stared at Tahliil. "I wanted to show my expertise. I was wrong." *He always treats me like a child. Will he ever trust my judgment?*

"Yes. Very wrong but done now." Tahliil stretched his legs toward the fire and sighed. "I tell you story about rashness." He glanced out at the water before continuing. "I was fourteen. Ran around the streets of Mogadishu. I took things from stores, not pay. I shared with family and tribe. Right? No. *Boolis* no catch me. I steal more.

"My father said carry identification. Did I? No. My name my own. At fourteen, I knew everything." Tahliil chuckled. "Thought I did. One day, I ran from store. Huge man stop me—Somali Army sergeant. He demanded identification. I try get away."

"What happened?" Dacar's eyes grew wide as he listened. "Did you escape?"

"No. My father right. Should have listened. Too late. No identification. Sergeant dragged me to army truck, cage on back. Soldier opened door. Two more throw me in cage."

"Where did they take you? Did they let you go?"

Tahliil shook his head. "When let out, we at camp. Others in cage, too. They say belong Somali Army." His eyes misted as he swayed in his chair. "I watched many boys, young men die fighting Ethiopians. Two years, they let me go—my time finished.

"Must have discipline and training. I learned from army. My rules be burden, but everyone better off."

Tahliil stared at Dacar and Sahid in turn. "This why obey. I listen suggestions. I make decision. Always."

"Yes, Tahliil," both men responded.

"Sleep now. Tomorrow go Kismaayo."

Tahliil went into a room and shut the door. Sahid banked the fire. Dacar handed him a woolen blanket. Both men draped the covers over their shoulders and curled up near the brazier.

One of the remaining men pulled several strands from a straw broom, breaking them into different lengths. They each drew a piece from the man's hand. The one with the shortest piece began sentry duty while the others tried to sleep.

\*\*\*

Before dawn, the men rose and cleansed themselves with water and sand at the shoreline. Mats aligned with Mecca, they completed the *Salat al-fajr*. Afterward, Sahid, the designated cook, made chickpea pancakes and sweet tea. They ate and prepared to travel to Kismaayo. Some had small packs with a change of clothes while others used plastic bags. All ensured their weapons were slung over their backs by straps and extra ammunition was packed in magazines and clipped to belts at the waist.

Tahliil gave orders to two men before they boarded the boat. "Take technical. Inform others in Mogadishu I return soon."

The men nodded and jumped into a brown Jeep Cherokee. The windshield was missing, bullet holes riddled the body, and the side mirrors no longer existed. A Browning .50 caliber machine gun was attached to the roof.

The property of a former American diplomat, during the fighting with Siad Barre's government, vehicles such as this became known as technicals. Now, they belonged to the strongest, the ones who could keep them from thieves.

The driver gunned the engine, spewing sand everywhere as he rocked the vehicle to lengthen the small depression in the sand caused by the weight of the Jeep. Clear of the obstruction, he headed for the main road, both men swaying to the movement of the vehicle. Within moments, the vehicle was out of sight, the dust churned up by the tires marking their departure.

***

After Tahliil, Dacar, and Sahid were seated on the boat, the remaining two men pushed the craft farther into the water and jumped aboard.

Dacar took over the controls, steered through the small gap in the sand bars, and drove south along the Somali coast. Small, thorny bushes and low scrub trees dotted the coastline between the sand dunes. They passed the occasional shepherd tending to his flock of sheep and goats.

Tahliil dozed under a small awning. Sahid sat next to Dacar, while the other two, armed with AK-47s, maintained their station in the stern and bow. Whenever they approached a small village, Dacar turned east and headed farther out in the water. No one could identify the boat's passengers.

As dusk approached, Dacar guided the craft into a small inlet north of Kismaayo. He stopped against a rickety dock where two armed men waited. Recognizing the boat, they waved and caught the ropes tossed to them.

Tahliil, first to disembark, stumbled as he stepped on the shifting pier. One of the men grabbed his arm to steady him.

"Thank you." He straightened and patted the man on the shoulder. "Help others, and we go camp."

"Yes, Tahliil. Our transport is ready." The man pointed through the dense brush. "Two vehicles are prepared. It will take two, perhaps three hours in the dark to reach the compound."

"Proceed."

The SUVs bounced along the road. More a track than a proper highway, they sped over areas with firm sand, slowing down as it became softer and the vehicles threatened to become bogged down. Occasional trees and bushes marked the edge of their route. A slight glow in front of them indicated their destination.

As they approached, men fired their weapons in the air. The Toyotas stopped in the middle of the camp near a smoldering fire. When Tahliil stepped out of a vehicle, his followers shouted and stomped their feet.

Tahliil waved his hands in a downward motion. Once the noise level dropped, he spoke. "Thank you. More weapons coming to us. We make sacrifice for Allah. Lieutenants, join me."

The men reveled as Tahliil strode into a military-style tent, followed by Dacar, Sahid, and three others. He eased himself into a camp chair, while everyone else sat on the floor.

"Report."

Gari Shire, a lanky man with a patch over one eye, stood. "Tahliil, things progress. My men raided a Kenyan police barracks. Confiscated whatever they could carry. Our new supplies will arrive in three or four days."

"Excellent. Any casualties?"

"Not on our side."

"Well done. Busuri?"

A short, rotund man, unusual for a Somali, lurched to his feet. Busuri Kablan gazed at the others before turning to Tahliil. "Much success with our raid in the Kenya border region near Malindi. No supplies—but entertainment."

Those assembled laughed, knowing Busuri's men had seized female refugees for their pleasure. Several men nudged one another as Busuri clasped his hands together and raised them above his head, crowning himself their new champion.

"When will the entertainment arrive?" a man asked.

"Quicker than last time, I hope. Took forever."

"Their travel will be slow. Perhaps a week, they need to gain their strength." Busuri laughed, waving his hand in an arc. "Still makes me the champion."

"Wait a moment, Busuri." A gray-haired man addressed the group. Most of the time he dressed in Western clothes, but today Harbi Kuusow chose a *macawiis*, a brown and gray-checkered sarong-like garment. A yellow and red cloth covered his upper body, his head crowned with a *koofiyad*, a colorful turban. One of the oldest in the group, he had also served in the Somali Army, where he met Tahliil.

"I believe my men take the prize for the best raid. They intercepted a Kenyan army team, which ventured into our lands near Buur Gaabo. The patrol comprised a dozen men." Harbi stretched upward, thrusting his head out in rapid movements like a chicken, hence his nickname, Chicken Man. "My men brought four survivors."

Whistles and foot stomping erupted as the others praised Harbi. Tahliil stood and clasped Harbi's shoulder. "This week's winner. Now, where trophies?"

"In the back tent. They're not going anywhere."

Dacar held the flaps open. Tahliil stepped into the night air. A clear evening, a myriad of stars covered the heavens, providing sufficient light to traverse the small camp without a flashlight or lantern.

Together Tahliil and Dacar led the others between two rows of smaller tents, erected between piles of rocks and thorny bushes. At the end of the alley, another military-style tent ended the encampment.

Inside, four Kenyan soldiers cowered on the floor. A dim lantern revealed they were gagged, blindfolded, with hands and ankles bound. Cuts and bruises showed through torn clothing. One man whimpered. A stench permeated the air, as if each man had soiled himself.

Harbi approached the nearest soldier and kicked him in the ribs. The man groaned and tried to roll away from further jabs. Harbi kicked him again, a pitiful whine escaping from his lips.

"Enough, Harbi." Tahliil bent down to examine each soldier. "Treat their wounds. Feed and water. Allow them regain strength." He stood and glared at Harbi. "No further mistreatment. If abused, someone will answer."

"What's the point, Tahliil?"

"The point is—" He jabbed a finger into Harbi's ribs. "I spoke. Do as told. Must be healthy." He left the tent, followed by the others.

*Perhaps time for me to take over.* "They are my trophy. I claim my rights." Harbi thumped his chest.

"No. My right as chief. I decide. No one else."

"Tahliil, what do you plan to do with them?" Dacar stepped between the two men before tempers flared beyond breaking point. *Is Tahliil becoming too old to be our leader?*

"Easy. This training camp. Men must train. Healthy soldiers make better targets."

# Chapter Eleven

Port Area
Naples, Italy

After the close encounter with an errant container three days ago, Pun and Gerhard moved to a bunkhouse operated by the port authorities. Trevor, Nate, and Fergus also switched accommodations, electing to room in a small pensione away from the area.

No longer traveling as a group, the team relied on their training to enter a mission mindset, maintaining vigilance. Surveillance detection routes led the men throughout the city before converging at pre-arranged locations.

On the other side of Naples, Bedlam Bravo, now dressed like mid-level businessmen, entered Palazzo Perucci Ristorante, an upscale establishment overlooking the harbor. Trevor entered alone, the others arriving before him in pairs. Since it was still early, the restaurant was almost empty. He asked for the Topaz party and was escorted toward the back of the room, where several areas were concealed behind red velvet curtains.

The maître d' pulled the curtains apart, revealing a partitioned door. A brief knock and he pushed it open, stepping aside for Trevor to enter.

Laughter and the clinking of glassware dominated the room. Besides the other members of Bedlam Bravo, a fifth person stood with them. Trevor's mouth dropped.

"Hello, Trevor. Shocked? Me, too." Evelyn Evinrude, offered her hand. "The doctors declared me fit for duty even with my slight limp. Sir Alex figured I could handle the exchange as I returned to the Middle East."

"Welcome to Naples, Evelyn." He released her hand. "I suspected we'd meet again."

She laughed, pulled out a chair, and sat at the table prepared for six. "I have packages for you. The equipment mentioned in London, plus two extra items."

While they conversed, the others grabbed seats and scanned the menu. Written in Italian and English they identified preferred dishes.

Nate frowned as he scanned the menu.

"What's the matter? Nothing to your liking?" Gerhard laughed. "I thought as long as it was food, you'd eat it."

Everyone laughed.

"I wanted a hamburger."

"What?" Fergus raised his head and glanced at the ceiling. "You're in Italy and you want a burger?"

"The pasta didn't fill me up and I'm not big on Italian. A burger and fries would be perfect."

"Shall we eat and do the handover?" Trevor nodded at the others. "They seem ready to order."

"Yes. I'll have today's special with a glass of the house white."

Instructed by the maître d' to push a concealed button when they were ready to order, their selections were announced when a waiter returned with their starters. All began with pasta, except Nate, who went for an antipasto salad. After the waiter departed, Evelyn addressed the group.

"Sir Alex instructed me to wish you good luck on your voyage. No change of plans, but instructions will be relayed when necessary. Recommend checking for messages at least three times a day."

Trevor nodded. "Not a problem. Once we're underway, it should be easy to find the horizon with the satellite phone. Only need a few seconds to set up, transmit, and finish."

The conversation switched to their recent visits to local sites of interest as two waiters delivered their main entrees, which varied from traditional Italian to seafood. Finished handing out the dishes, the waiters departed.

"I checked out the Pompeii exhibit." Fergus waved his forkful of spaghetti in the air. "Hard to imagine fleeing from the lava, yet still being caught. A horrible way to go."

"Agreed." Nate sipped his red wine before popping a green olive in his mouth. "I'd rather die in bed, with a beautiful woman at my side."

"Ag, man. The catacombs are the best attraction in Naples. Imagine how many people visit the site."

"You have a strange sense of entertainment, Gerhard." Nate finished his antipasto salad and drained his glass. "Hope you haven't warped Pun's mind."

Pun speared a piece of meat from his plate and smiled as he shook his head.

"Let's eat and run." Trevor took charge of his team. "Sorry to be a spoilsport. Evelyn will want to be rid of the packages, and we must head back to our rooms."

After they'd finished, Trevor paid the bill. They departed in ones and twos and reconvened in a black and white van with Pasticceria Alessandro Romano displayed above a picture of a loaf of bread.

Inside, Evelyn introduced them to the driver.

"Meet Mark. He kept an eye on things while I joined you for dinner." Evelyn passed a bag to Trevor. "What you asked for."

"We'll take you close to the pensione and the bunkhouse after we finish."

"Where are the weapons?" Nate glanced around the back of the empty van. "Do we go somewhere to pick them up?"

"You're sitting on them." Mark pointed to the floor. "It's false. Grab an edge near the door and pull."

Nate, Fergus, and Gerhard tugged on the carpet while the others moved out of the way. A grated surface appeared below a lifted section.

"Underneath," Evelyn said. "Five black backpacks and two Pelican cases. Should be two black tennis bags, too."

Gerhard hauled each item from the concealed compartment as Nate passed them around.

"Each backpack contains a Glock-17, ammunition, and a stun gun. The cases hold MP5s. I didn't know if you wanted to keep them in their carriers or switch to the tennis bags."

"I think the tennis bags will work better." Trevor pointed at Gerhard and Nate. "Take the MP5s."

Evelyn turned to Mark. "Head out—the pensione first."

Dropping each group off, Evelyn wished them success. Once Gerhard and Pun entered the bunkhouse, Mark and Evelyn disappeared into the darkness.

*\*\**

Thick, greasy ropes were cast off bollards, engines churned the water into a white froth, and a tug assisted the *Ventrusco* away from the dock. Light rain didn't stop people from lining the street to catch a glimpse of their loved ones as they departed. Off duty crew members waved from vantage points. Several ship horns sounded as they moved about the harbor. The tug released the ship, which headed out to sea.

"Ag, man. We're off." Gerhard waved at his non-existent family.

Pun nodded. Assigned to one of the cargo maintenance teams, Gerhard and Pun squeezed between containers, checking cables and connectors on the port side as Luigi had taught them.

As the *Ventrusco* left the confines of the harbor, Nate and Fergus worked their way through the containers on the starboard side, ensuring every harness was in place and secured.

Trevor teamed with Marco in the central hold, used to store refrigerated containers. They scooted between each one and checked cooling settings and refrigeration hoses. The ship began a gentle rocking.

"We're in open water." Marco shifted his hands back and forth to emphasize the movement. "Now in the Tyrrhenian Sea. A few hours from now, we'll be in the Mediterranean and sail through the Strait of Sicily."

"Why not through the Strait of Messina? Wouldn't that save time?"

"Yes, but more dangerous. In two areas the gap is less than two miles, with heavy commercial traffic. Safer going around and we can move faster, too."

"Makes sense." Trevor checked the final meter before they climbed out of the hold, their shift finished.

Three hours later, Bedlam Bravo joined the other off-duty crew for a spaghetti and meatball dinner. Finished, they headed to the deck for a stroll before retiring to their quarters.

"Should be quiet until we're in the Indian Ocean." Trevor nodded toward the bow, where bolts of lightning crisscrossed the heavens. Deep rumbling followed. "The pirates haven't attacked in the Mediterranean before, but we should remain alert."

"I don't like the sky. I was once onboard a ship in the North Sea." Fergus wiped his face with a handkerchief as water sprayed over the side of the ship. "Shaking, rocking, and rolling like a massive rollercoaster. People sick everywhere. Never want to go through dat again."

"Appears the squall will pass to the south before we reach the area." Trevor shook his head. "Hope so—never did like rollercoasters." He glanced at his watch. "Time for me to make contact. See you at breakfast."

Trevor returned to his cabin. Though designed for two, he was the sole occupant. He powered up his satellite phone and iPad. After typing a brief message, he used a USB cable to connect the units. He aimed his phone out the window and at the horizon, receiving a satisfying beep when he established connectivity. It took milliseconds to transmit his message.

*To: Topaz*
*From: Black*
*Deployment underway. Now in the Med—nothing to report at this time.*

\*\*\*

Two days later, the *Ventrusco* approached Port Said. The ship maneuvered to an open berth in the container terminal. Once secured, crew hustled to the top level of containers. A crane hovered above, waiting for connection to the first one.

"*Vieni qui!* (Come here!)" Luigi waved his arms. Men swarmed like bees to unhook and remove straps, waiting for the crane to select their container. Once connected, they stepped aside as the hoist pulled the heavy load skyward and swung it onto a waiting flatbed truck.

The crane removed several more containers, only to replace them with new ones bound for Mombasa and South Africa.

This activity mesmerized those watching. "Can't believe how efficient the crane and crew worked today." Trevor turned around as someone tapped him on the shoulder.

"You and Marco go to the refrigerated hold. There's another container to unload." Luigi handed Trevor a piece of paper with a number scrawled in block letters.

Trevor and Marco headed into their designated work area to prepare the specified container. Trevor disconnected the cooling pipes from his side, waiting for Marco to finish.

A piercing scream rose above the hold's normal noises. Trevor dropped the cable he held and rushed to the source.

Marco lay on the deck, writhing in pain, his hands clenched to his face. An errant hose splashed coolant on him, saturating his clothing.

Trevor hit a red emergency button on the bulkhead by the entry hatch, summoning help while he traced the hose to a shutoff valve. Once the deluge ceased, he rushed back. Stripping off his shirt, he used it to wipe Marco's exposed skin.

By this time, Luigi and several crew members had arrived. One opened a first aid cabinet and two men treated Marco. Two others readied a stretcher to take him topside.

Luigi approached Trevor. "What happened?"

"No idea. I disconnected the hose on my side and waited for Marco. The next thing, he screamed."

Luigi nodded. "This happened before. Fast action by crew should mean minor but painful injury—I hope."

"Is there an—" Trevor glanced behind Luigi and caught a glimpse of a long shadow ascending the stairs in the back of the hold. The shadow disappeared, and Trevor focused on Luigi.

"Step back." He pointed upward as the crane lowered its boom to grab the container. Once lifted clear of the hold, Luigi stepped closer to Trevor.

"An ambulance is on the way. Marco will remain in Port Said until we return. I'll work with you until a replacement arrives. Perhaps tomorrow."

\*\*\*

Late in the afternoon, as the workday finished, Trevor headed off the ship to a nearby food stand. After he had grabbed a bite and a Coke, Trevor found the other Bedlam members gathered around a rickety table.

His demeanor casual, he scanned the area for eavesdroppers before addressing his team. "At first I thought an accident led to Marco's injury—there appeared to be a damaged area on one side of the hose. Now, I'm not sure. Before the crew put Marco on a stretcher and moved him, I caught a glimpse of a man heading up the back stairwell. If the person was a member of the crew, wouldn't curiosity bring him to the scene to find out what happened? Did he sabotage the hose?"

"Ag, perhaps so." Gerhard waved a beefy arm in the air. "But not if he caused the accident."

Before turning out his light, Trevor sent a short message.

*To: Topaz*
*From: Black*
*Arrived Port Said today. Italian partner injured in accident. Foul play cannot be ruled out.*

Trevor spent the night tossing and turning, replaying the scene. *Can't figure out what happened. First, the incident with Gerhard and now this. Too close for comfort.*

Morning came too early. Trevor slapped at the offending alarm, bringing calm to his cabin. He dragged himself out of bed and stood in the shower for two minutes. After he dressed, he headed for breakfast. When he entered the canteen, Luigi called him over.

A slender man with curly black hair stood with him. "Trevor, meet your new partner. This is Rooble."

Trevor shook the extended hand. "Hello, call me Trev. Where're you from?"

"Somalia."

## Chapter Twelve

An Abandoned Warehouse
Victoria, Seychelles

A man slumped on the concrete floor stirred. He raised his head and an eye eased open. Light filtered through narrow slats nailed across the window. Dust particles shimmered in the sun's beams.

He pushed himself to a kneeling position. A whimper escaped from swollen lips. He touched his face. Dried blood crusted his upper lip. He collapsed.

\*\*\*

Soo awoke to darkness. Something scurried across the floor. A blanket was draped over him. Underneath—naked. He passed out again.

\*\*\*

After he regained consciousness, a ceiling fixture bathed the room in light. Next to him, a cup of water, a hunk of bread, and some cooked rice.

He drank half of the lukewarm water. He wet his fingers and dabbed around his nose and mouth to rinse off the dried blood. Voices in the distance—strange, yet familiar.

Soo struggled to his feet. He wrapped the green blanket closer and glanced around the room. A closed gunmetal gray door was centered on the wall opposite the blocked window. Near the door, an armless chair, his clothes in a neat stack.

In the distance, a door slammed. Footsteps. Voices. Growing louder.

He hobbled to the chair, picked up his clothes, and dressed. As he finished, someone banged on the door. A key turned in the lock and the door swung open.

Soo stood in the middle of the room, his right shoulder slumped. No longer naked, his normal haughtiness returned and he clenched his fists. "What's the meaning of this? Who are you? Why did you kidnap me?"

Four beefy men formed a semi-circle in front of him, faces hidden behind latex party masks. One retrieved the chair, placing it under the light. "Sit."

Soo remained standing, testing them.

"Sit. Down. Now. Or my colleague will assist you." The speaker pointed to an associate, twice the size of Soo, muscles pushing at the seams of his clothing. "He won't be gentle like me." He spoke to Soo in stilted Korean, as if it wasn't his native language.

Soo dropped into the chair, keeping his eyes focused on the speaker. "I demand you let me go. I'll see you are rewarded."

"You're in no position to demand anything. I'll ask you questions. You'll answer them. If I don't like the answers—" He nodded toward the muscle-bound man. "He'll help you."

Soo stared back. Bile rose in his throat—he swallowed, almost gagging, as he forced the sour taste down.

"First question—why are you here?"

"I'm on vacation."

The leader glanced at the behemoth who had moved behind Soo. The leader nodded again.

Soo's head whipped to the side as a massive fist smacked him. His cheek stung from the blow and his jaw ached.

"I'll ask again. Why are you here?"

Afraid of another blow, Soo cringed in the chair. "I-I'm meeting someone. A friend."

"Who's this friend?"

"S-she. He's helping me with a problem."

"What kind of problem?"

"Personal."

The leader glanced beyond Soo.

The chair yanked from under him, Soo collapsed on the floor. Unprepared for another blow, Soo gasped, and clutched at the sharp pain surging through his side.

"You want another kick?"

The chair yanked upright, Soo was hauled back to a sitting position.

"Well?"

"M-my wife, sons. Taken from me. He will help me get them back."

"Who took them?"

"Supreme Leader ... Wook Sung." *The bastard.*

The man pulled out a cell phone and typed a text. He glanced back at Soo.

"Who'll help you? How? Why?"

Soo rocked back at the rapid-fire questions. *How much should I say? Will it matter?*

Something hard smacked his head, knocking him out of his reverie. Tears formed. He shook his head.

"I asked questions. Have you forgotten the rules of the game? Answer. Now!" He gave a nod for another blow.

Soo wiped his eyes with his sleeve. "Dacar—the man's name is Dacar. H-he's a pirate. He hijacks tankers in exchange for weapons."

"Why?"

"North Korea needs oil. We've asked our friends—no one will help us. I-If Wook wasn't blackmailing me with my family's lives, I wouldn't help him." *I wouldn't be in this situation, either.*

Silence. Black piercing eyes. A nod.

He cringed in anticipation of another blow. Nothing happened.

The leader strode out the door. The others followed, giving Soo threatening glances as they left. The key turned in the lock and their footsteps faded in the distance.

Soo waited, in case this was a trick and they returned. He leaned forward in the chair, elbows on knees, and stared at the floor. *Did I give too much away? What if this is all set up by the Supreme Leader? If he's testing my loyalty then I just failed. I panicked.*

The filament in the light bulb popped—darkness descended.

Soo lay on the floor, dragged the blanket over him, and sobbed.

What seemed like hours later, a key rattled and two men entered. One carried a flashlight, the other a stepladder.

They replaced the bulb and left.

They didn't turn the key. A test?

Soo edged toward the door. He reached for the handle as four masked men barged into the room.

"Where do you think you're going? Sit down."

He complied with the demand, draping the blanket around his shoulders. Drained, Soo had nothing left in him to ward off any further punishment. He groaned in despair and clutched his head. *Is this the end?*

"I've checked your information. You've done well by not lying." The leader waved the others forward.

A short man held a small leather pouch while another approached Soo. He stood and backed away when the muscle-bound man grabbed him in a bear hug. He grabbed one of Soo's arms and forced a sleeve up.

The man with the pouch pulled out a syringe. He pulled the cap off the needle and checked for air bubbles.

Soo struggled but couldn't break free.

Satisfied there wasn't any air in the syringe, the short man jammed the needle into Soo's arm and shoved the plunger until the liquid emptied into his veins.

He felt faint, his thoughts drifting away—a sense of falling. Soo collapsed.

\*\*\*

For four days, Major Kim scurried about the streets of Victoria. Like a lost soul, he haunted the bars, restaurants, hotels, and shops as he searched for his missing charge. He asked taxi drivers and spoke to passing tourists. No sign of Soo—anywhere.

Kim spent twenty hours a day, pausing for a few hours of restless sleep in the middle of the night. Exhausted, dark circles formed under his eyes. He had lost weight.

"If he's not dead when I find him, he will be," Kim muttered and grimaced as he realized the irony of his words. "I must find him before Wook questions our time away. Hope he believes we can't do anything until Dacar's group lets us know if the new arrangement is acceptable to them."

Kim wandered down a street, glancing left and right, hoping to spot Soo. His stomach rumbled when he neared the Lai Lam Food Shop. He approached the take-out window and ordered shredded chicken cooked in sesame oil and noodles. Armed with his first meal in almost two days, he sat on a nearby bench.

He devoured his food with the chopsticks, savoring the delightful aroma as he filled his gnawing stomach. Once satiated, he rested the empty container on the bench and leaned back. Something tugged at the corners of his mind.

*This bench—Soo sat here when he disappeared. Except for his Ray-Bans, no sign of a struggle. Did he wander off and get mugged? Or did someone grab him?*

Kim knelt by the bench and checked the area. Some garbage had been caught along the legs but nothing worthwhile. He stood, tossed his container in a nearby receptacle, and scanned the area.

He strolled toward the Victoria Botanical Gardens. *Perhaps Dacar is in his apartment.* Walking up to the building's entrance, he tried the handle. Open. *The janitor would be in prison back home for such negligence.*

He climbed the stairs and edged toward Dacar's apartment. He checked the door—locked. Kim tapped but no answer. He knocked harder.

No response.

Kim glanced around but there was no one. Pulling out a small burglar's kit, he picked the lock, and entered. A quick check confirmed an empty apartment. Basic furnishings and a few personal items, indicated occasional use.

Kim headed toward the door when he spotted a photograph stuffed partway inside a book on the coffee table. He grasped the picture and tugged, a second one fell out. Both showed Soo wearing his Ray-Bans and Panama hat. One when they left the airport, and the other as they entered their hotel. *Who took these?*

He searched the room, checking for further evidence. He found a large unsealed envelope taped underneath the coffee table. Inside, more photos of Soo at various locations around Victoria.

A smaller envelope was inside the larger one. Kim opened this and found his own face staring back at him. Three photos, including one when he found Soo's sunglasses under the bench.

Kim stuffed the pictures back in their respective envelopes, replaced them under the coffee table, and left the apartment. Reaching the building's front door, he peered outside. Nearby pedestrians appeared occupied with their own business, and he didn't spot anyone sitting in any of the cars parked nearby, so he left, heading toward the park.

He sat on the grass and leaned against a tree. *Who's helping Dacar? Were we set up? Where's Soo?*

He closed his eyes, trying to concentrate on events which took place between their arrival and Soo's disappearance. *Did I miss surveillance? If so, who?* Kim's eyes snapped open. *Soo! Did he meet with someone when he left the hotel and went for a walk?*

Kim stood and resumed his search. *I better find him. No telling what Wook will do to me if I don't.* Pessimistic about the odds of finding him, he retraced their journey through the gardens. He stepped into a small grotto, an area Soo had enjoyed. On a bench shrouded by leafy branches from Coco de Mer palms, someone slept.

He turned to leave and stopped. Glancing over his shoulder, he spotted a bundle squeezed between two of the palms. He circled the bench, moving closer.

A man, dressed in dark clothing and covered in a green blanket with scattered dark brown splotches lay on the mulch, his head resting against a palm tree.

Kim bent down. Part of the blanket covered the man's face. He pulled it aside—and gasped. *Who is it?*

He pulled the blanket away.

"Soo!"

Battered, bruised, but still with a pulse. Kim tapped Soo's face—no response. He grasped him by the shoulders and gave a light shake. Soo's head moved and his face twitched, before his hand reached out and grabbed Kim's arm.

"Help. Me." Soo's hand fell to the ground.

Kim glanced around the area. The man on the bench groaned and appeared to be passed out, two empty wine bottles held in his arms. No one else around, Kim helped Soo to his feet and half-dragged him out of the palms.

He leaned Soo in a more comfortable position against a tall, leafy tree and dashed to a nearby pond. He pulled an unused handkerchief from a pocket, soaked the cloth, and ran back.

Kim dabbed at Soo's face, removing dried blood, grass, and soil. The water stimulated Soo, who opened his eyes and stared at his savior.

"T-hey took me. I-I don't know where." Soo gasped for air before shaking his head. "I told them nothing."

"Questions later. We'll go to my room and more first aid." He helped Soo to his feet. "Food, too. For both of us."

Together, the men lurched toward the park's exit. Kim found an empty bench and helped Soo to sit. He stepped into the street and flagged a taxi. The driver pulled over to the curb.

"Help me with my friend." Kim pointed to the bench. "I think today's excursion in this heat was too much for him. We must return to our hotel."

Thirty minutes later, Kim guided Soo into the room, aided by the taxi driver. After giving the man a generous tip—by North Korean standards—Kim closed the door.

"Thank you, Kim." Soo's pallor returned to its more normal condition. "I'm feeling better. I'm hungry and thirsty."

"There is a store nearby. I'll buy some fruit, bread, cheese, and water. Stay in the room—don't open the door unless you hear my voice."

When Kim returned, he knocked on the door—twice. Soo let Kim into the room, rubbed his eyes, and yawned.

"Didn't I tell you not to open the door until you hear my voice?" Kim glared at Soo and shook his head.

"I ... uh ... forgot. What did you bring?"

"Nothing fancy, but the fruit and cheese will give you energy. Tell me what happened."

Soo rubbed his arm where he received the injection. Bruised tissue surrounded a red welt. "I sat on the bench by the Lai Lam Food Shop waiting for your return. A man stopped in front of me. Before I knew, someone from behind pulled a black bag over my head. My glasses fell to the ground."

"What happened next?"

"They pulled me to my feet and marched me away. A car door opened and they shoved me inside. Some time later, they dragged me out and threw me into a cold room. I have no idea where." Soo hung his head. "T-they beat me. Asked me questions. If they didn't like my answers, they hit or kicked me."

"What did they ask?"

"One man spoke, but there were four—all wearing masks. He wanted to know why I came to Victoria. I told him for a vacation. Would you open the window, please? I need fresh air."

Kim pushed aside the curtains and shoved against the frame until it opened. He returned to Soo. "What else did this man ask?"

"He wanted to know the names of who traveled with me—I told him I was on my own."

"Did he believe you?"

"Not at first. They kicked me, but I gave the same answer."

"What happened next?"

"Someone gave me an injection and I passed out. I awoke when you found me in the gardens."

Kim rubbed his chin, gazing at Soo for telltale signs of a lie. He asked a final question. "Did you tell them about me?"

"No."

"Hmm. I must arrange our return to Pyongyang. Are you sure you didn't mention my name?"

"I'm sure. I told them my wife and sons lived in Korea—nothing else."

\*\*\*

In the building opposite the hotel, a man grinned when Kim opened the window. He adjusted his zoom lens and snapped a photo of Kim's face. He took another picture, this time of both men. He pushed back through the bushes, dropped his camera inside a Lufthansa airline bag, and departed.

*How to proceed—threats? Blackmail?*

## Chapter Thirteen

Kidnapper's Camp
Outside Kidi Faani, Somalia

The fifteen members of the raiding party dragged their captives from the Jujubba Refugee Camp north across the border into Somalia. Ropes linked the ten women in a single line. Far from civilization, the group pushed their way through scrub brush and across sand dunes under a sky packed with stars.

The kidnappers kept warm with blankets wrapped around their upper bodies. All but two under the age of fourteen, the captives shivered in the cold night air, clad in what they wore when taken from the camp.

Exhausted, they tried to maintain the grueling pace barefoot, their skin scraped by thorns. Weak from hunger and disease, they collapsed. When they slowed too much, sharp jabs from rifle butts hurried them along. Each impact against their frail bodies elicited painful cries.

After more than an hour's march, the leader called for a halt. "Short break. Some water. Then we go."

The oldest prisoner, twenty-five-year-old Jamiila Shamso, approached the leader with caution. "We need more rest. Some food, too." She pointed downward. "We need something to protect our feet."

Asad Nuur gazed at Jamiila. He let the silence build until she trembled. "Ten more minutes. No food—didn't bring any. Drink more water." He reached into a pocket and pulled out a plastic bag. "Perhaps some khat?" He shoved a handful of the dried flowers into his mouth. "Controls hunger and will help ease the pain."

Jamiila sneered at him. "No. I don't use drugs."

He shrugged. "Suit yourself." He spat a stream of juice on the ground, some splashing on his worn sandals.

"Disgusting."

"Don't challenge me." Asad raised a hand as if to strike her. "I've allowed you to walk without being tied up as I expect you to keep the other captives under control."

Jamiila turned up her nose before she turned away and rejoined the others.

Asad laughed and spat again. "Time to move." One of his men yanked on the ropes tied to the prisoners as they labored to their feet. The sudden movement caused several of them to fall headlong into the sand.

The raiders laughed. Jamiila rushed forward to help. On their feet at last, the group trudged north.

Hours passed. The band of kidnappers and captives fought for each step while the continuing cold sapped their energy. As they moved onward, the horizon changed—a sliver of light, a sign the new day would soon be upon them. A hint of moisture in the air and the promise of water rejuvenated the stragglers, quickening their steps.

Within minutes, sunshine and welcoming warmth became a reality. Darkness gave way to a cloudless blue sky. At the top of a dune, the group spotted a narrow, dark ribbon not far away. Water.

They hurried forward, kidnappers and captives alike, all seeking refreshment from the small stream. On the banks, shade from several babbaay trees invited the weary travelers.

Asad ordered the captives untied and allowed everyone an opportunity to drink and soak in the water. They were led to an area where overlapping trees created a canopy. Used by the bandits before, abundant stacks of thorny bushes became the walls of their temporary prison as the kidnappers moved them into place.

"Eat." Asad pointed at the trees laden with papayas. Two men took machetes, scaled the trees, and hacked until the fruit fell. They cut the juicy fruit, passing out pieces until hunger and thirst were satiated.

"We'll stay here until dark." Asad grabbed Jamiila's covered arm. "You're responsible for the others. Make sure they don't run away—or you die." He turned to his men. "Two guards. Make sure there's no trouble."

The captives lay on the warm sand in a huddled mass, their hands still secured. An occasional whimper squeaked out as the exhausted women gave in to their weariness.

The golden orb passed through the heavens toward the horizon. The heat of the day calmed as temperatures dropped. Members of the group stirred, waking others. They chewed on discarded papaya skins, seeking the last bits of juicy and flavorful moisture.

Unlike the first night, the prisoners were tied into two groups. The youngest were linked with Jamiila.

"We go." Asad pointed across the water. "Many hours tonight. Tomorrow, sleep in compound."

With water somewhere beneath the surface, the footing became easier. They moved at a steady pace, the designated lead navigating by the stars.

Asad weaved between the captives, slicing a papaya and handing out pieces. He kept them moving for several hours until midnight when he called for a halt.

"Rest."

Everyone sank to the ground, eager for a brief respite. Jamiila curled into a ball, seeking to maintain body heat. Her eyes drifted shut.

"Move." One of the guards, his left arm missing from the elbow, jerked on her arm, dragging her upright. Once on her feet, he shoved her forward, leading the way for the four other captives.

*So tired—must have dozed. I miss my children.* Like an automaton, Jamiila placed one foot in front of the other, stumbling over exposed roots from nearby bushes. *My children—will I ever hold them again?* Tears fell unchecked.

Monotony set in. No one spoke. Heavy breathing from exertion and the occasional fall were the sole noises marking their passage. Their progression slowed as the moist sand gave way to dunes, trees replaced by thorny bushes and shrubs.

Jamiila became numb to the tedious trek, lost in her thoughts about her son and daughter—Abuukar and Bayda. *What will happen when we reach our destination?*

She fell, dragged backward as two of the younger girls collapsed from exhaustion. A kidnapper approached and raised a whip. Before he struck, Jamiila blocked his way. "No. They're tired—we all are. They're weak. They need food and water." She placed her hand on his arm.

The guard stepped back, raised his whip again, and lashed at Jamiila, knocking her to the ground. She crawled to the young girls, sheltering them with her body. He went to strike again, but Asad blocked his blow.

"What are you doing? I gave no orders to hit anyone." Asad snatched the whip and thrust his hand against the man's chest. "Go. Bring up the rear. Help any who fall—but if you strike them, you'll answer to me."

The guard glowered before lowering his eyes in acquiescence.

Asad extended a hand to Jamiila. She hesitated, fearful of what might happen. "Take my hand. I understand we're not married and shouldn't have physical contact. However, he embarrassed himself—and me."

She reached up, allowing Asad to help her rise. "Thank you." She glanced at those attached to her. "Why take these young girls? You said they would be the future wives of your men. Don't they deserve more care and respect?"

"Some of the men want wives. Others don't."

"They're too young."

"Perhaps, but they will age. In the meantime, they will cook, clean, and take care of their man."

Jamiila shook her head. Frightened to say anything more, she remained silent. *Animals. Nothing but animals.*

Asad glanced around—no one appeared to be paying attention. "Do you have children? A husband?"

"Y-yes. One boy, a girl. My husband—"

"Where are the children?"

"At the camp in Kenya—where you kidnapped me."

"Husband?"

"H-he died. He was sick, but we had no money for medicine or better food."

"Perhaps one day, you will have a new husband. More children." Asad tugged on her sleeve. "Come, a bit farther and we'll take another break. We must be in Kidi Faani before sunrise."

\*\*\*

The first inkling a new day would be upon them was a band of shimmering reds and oranges along the skyline. The kidnappers hurried their charges through the shallows of another river, toward a small enclosure outside the village of Kidi Faani.

They approached a walled compound of whitewashed concrete blocks. Two guards, each cradling an AK-47, sat on wooden crates by the closed entrance. Dressed in faded jeans, Western-style long-sleeve shirts, and bush hats, they wore sandals. They jumped to their feet when they spotted the group and pushed the gates open.

Inside, six single-story stone buildings and two wooden huts filled the area. A lone tree took center stage in the courtyard, several wooden benches arrayed in a haphazard manner in its shade. Chickens and goats wandered around the compound, searching for something to eat. Two women carried buckets, reaching in with a bare hand and sprinkling water on the sandy soil to keep the dust under control.

Asad led them to the tree. "This is our camp." He gestured toward two of the buildings, each painted pink, with a single window near an open doorway. "Five will stay in each of these buildings. Jamiila and the other four tied to her will be in the one closest to the wall."

He issued an order. Men rushed forward and removed the bindings. As the women rubbed their chafed wrists, he stared at them.

"You will be free in the compound. No harm will come to you as long as you follow a simple order—obey. Attempt to escape—you will be killed. If someone is successful, you will be caught and killed. Everyone from your building will also die."

Azad pointed at Jamiila and the next oldest-looking woman in the other group. "You are both in charge. Keep everyone in line, and you will be safe and happy."

When he finished speaking, he walked away, followed by the other men.

\*\*\*

Jamiila led the four girls into their new home. Concrete floor, with several blankets piled in a corner. A bucket full of water and a single ladle by its side. Nothing else.

"We must rest. Have a drink if you're thirsty. We don't know what will happen next." After each one had finished drinking, Jamiila handed out blankets. She gave each of them a hug and they stretched out on the floor, using the blankets as pillows. Soon, silence reigned as they fell asleep—all but Jamiila.

While the others whimpered in their sleep and uttered names in their nightmares, Jamiila tossed and turned, her thoughts on Abuukar and Bayda. *I hope the foreigners treat them well in the camp. Perhaps, one day, we will be rejoined. Can I trick Asad into letting me escape?*

Tears trickled down her face as she drifted away.

\*\*\*

Darkness and cooler temperatures replaced the blazing sun and heat. The captives remained in their shelters, asleep. Asad wandered around the compound, ensuring the guards' positions, one for each wall and two at the gate.

A fire crackled and popped and two men prepared meat for roasting. Earlier in the day, when their women had finished watering the compound, they made *kibhis,* an unleavened bread.

Jamiila stirred, the aroma of roasting meat caused her mouth to water. She woke the others, and they peeked outside. They smacked their lips, involuntary moans escaping as their stomachs rumbled.

Asad spotted Jamiila and waved her over. She obeyed, the others following.

"Eat." Asad stabbed at the roasted meat with a sharp knife. "Take the kibhis and I will cut you a piece of goat."

With their first nourishing meal since being abducted, the women ate in silence, gobbling the bread and meat, licking the juice from their fingers.

"When you are finished, you may go to the wooden huts." Asad nodded toward the structures. "The one on the left is for females. Afterward, return to your building. Remain until the sun rises above the horizon. There's a bucket in each building for the women to use when they aren't permitted to leave."

A calm settled over the compound as kidnappers and captives alike bedded down for the evening. With a full stomach, even Jamiila struggled to remain awake. Her head drooped and she eased herself onto the floor, pulling the blanket over her.

A gunshot broke the silence. Another. A third.

Jamiila peered out the doorway. Men carrying torches gathered at the wall. On the ground, a body lay motionless. Her eyes were wide open, a pool of blood seeping out from beneath her body. A pungent odor similar to copper permeated the area.

Asad turned to glare at the prisoners. "I told you the penalty for trying to escape." He kicked the body until it rolled over.

## Chapter Fourteen

Bedlam Headquarters
Whitehall, London, England

Sir Alex placed the final tome of *War and Peace* on the ornate bookshelf and stepped back. He faced the Queen's portrait, raising a corner to level the frame. Satisfied, he nodded. "CC was right. I spend most of my time here, so it shouldn't be austere. The plants Winnie ordered should arrive today and will spruce up the place. Wonder if I should get one of those office putting cups?" He shook his head. "Never have time for it."

A light tap on the door stopped his perusal of his handiwork. Winnie pushed a serving cart into the office, bearing tea for two with crustless cucumber creations, scones, and strawberry tarts. She arranged the snack on the coffee table and sat in a chair closest to Sir Alex's desk.

"What do you think of the office now, Winnie?" He pointed toward the bookcase and the portrait before helping himself to a sandwich as she played mother and poured the tea.

Winnie swept her long, red hair over her shoulder. Freckle-faced, in her mid-40s, a bit on the plump side, she had worked for Sir Alex for almost a decade.

"Glad you listened to reason. I told you long ago the room had the appearance of a dungeon in the Tower of London."

"No matter. It's fixed now. What's on the calendar for this afternoon?"

"Don't forget your call with the Prime Minister. His office will call at 16:50. You have a meeting with Signor Radicci, the Italian Ambassador, at their embassy at 18:15.

In between, you must attend to your paperwork. It's stacking up. At the end of the day, you're supposed to ring Admiral Blakely in Washington. He's expecting your call at 20:00 our time."

"Yes, Mother." They both laughed.

After they finished their tea and Winnie removed the remnants, Sir Alex tackled the mountain of paperwork stacked in his inbox.

The afternoon sped by.

His intercom buzzed. The flashing red light indicated Winnie wanted to speak with him.

Sir Alex pushed a button on the console. "Yes, dear."

"The Italian ambassador has rescheduled. Also, it's time for your call. They're putting you through to the Prime Minister."

Several clicks echoed on the line, before a deep and mellow voice spoke. "Afternoon, Sir Alex. How are you?"

"Fine, Prime Minister. Yourself?"

"Couldn't be better, although I took a beating at yesterday's Prime Minister's Questions." He chuckled. "I should know better than to let the opposition party needle me."

"Sir, as long as we've known each other, the opposition always maintains the upper hand."

"Quite. As you're aware, I'm flying to America next month to meet with the new president. I'd appreciate a candid appraisal from you before I do."

"Yes, Prime Minister. I'll sort something out for you."

"Outstanding. Oh, by the way, we'll be going to Chequers the weekend after next. Will you join us?"

"An honor, sir. Thank you."

"Jolly good. Talk with you later."

Winnie eased the door open as he set the phone down. "Sir Alex, I'm off to my dental appointment—unless you want me to stay longer. I can always reschedule."

"No, go right ahead. I'll be ringing Admiral Blakely in a few minutes. If I can catch him now, I'll be leaving early. Have a meeting to attend at the club—something about raising fees."

"Okay. Good night, Sir Alex."

He nodded as he perused another file. After ticking several boxes on the attached routing slip, he tossed the file aside. He stood, stretched his back to work out the kinks, and reached for the gray and brown secure telephone.

"Hello." Admiral Blakely's gruff voice rifled through the line.

Sir Alex held the receiver away from his ear. "Richard. Alex here. How are you?"

"Still breathing. Yourself?"

"The same." Both men chuckled. "Winnie mentioned you're withholding some hush-hush information from me?"

"Yes. Sorry, I couldn't pass it to her. From sensitive sources and she's not cleared for the details."

Sir Alex glanced at the ceiling and rolled his eyes. *Yanks. Hung up on security, yet their government's a sieve.* "I understand. Loose lips and all that."

"Here's the situation. An intern, almost young enough to be my great-grandson, if I had any children, stumbled across something interesting. The day before the *Napoli* and her crew were released, the owners transferred two million dollars to a bank in Malta. They haven't used this institution before."

Sir Alex whistled. "Is the money still there?"

"Yes. We've established electronic tracking around the account to let us know the moment there's any movement of the funds."

"This might be the break we need. Any other details?"

"Yeah. You'll like this. One person is associated with the account. Arrogant SOB if you ask me. The first two letters of the account are his initials. His name's Dacar Khadaafi."

"Fantastic, Richard. Please pass my thanks to your great-grandson." Sir Alex propped his feet on the edge of his desk and laughed. "Knowing how you don't care for children, I couldn't resist."

"Go ahead, laugh all you want, Alex. Remember—turnabout is fair play."

"Anything else? If not, I have a meeting at the club. Someone wants to double our membership fee. Oh, before I forget, the Prime Minister will be in Washington next month to meet with your president. Any chance of a paper on him?"

"I'll get you something in the next few days regarding him and his ongoing shenanigans. Something else for you. A NOC reported a possible connection between the North Koreans and Somali pirates. He hasn't provided any details yet but will pass them along as they come in."

"How did someone under non-official cover come up with this tidbit? Never mind—I shouldn't ask."

"Nothing further from this end, Alex. Enjoy your meeting and knock back a Glenlivet on the rocks for me."

"Perhaps a double, I think. Thank you for the information."

*Better alert the team.* Sir Alex dropped the receiver in the cradle, settled back into his chair, and pulled a miniaturized keyboard out from its cupboard. He pecked at the keys with his index fingers.

*To: Black*
*From: Topaz*

*New intel. Keep eyes peeled for linkage between North Koreans and pirates. Also, possible break with the discovery of a money trail. More to follow when available. Proceed as planned.*

He turned out the lights, and locked the office door. His driver waited outside the building. Sir Alex hopped into the black Daimler, which whisked him to the club.

Once settled in a soft, black leather easy chair, he ordered a double Glenlivet on ice. He raised the glass in a silent salute to the admiral's fictional great-grandson.

## Chapter Fifteen

Al-Shabaab Camp
Outside Kismaayo, Somalia

A cockerel crowed, breaking the morning's silence. Tahliil shrugged off his blanket and struggled to his feet. He rubbed his hands over his head and face before venturing into the morning's warmth. The cockerel crowed a second time, as if reminding Tahliil he had slept late. In the distance, a lone baboon whooped and yapped, calling to his troop.

He grabbed his jaw, testing for pain after spending the better part of the night chewing khat. *Hmmm. Missed morning prayers. Too much khat. I know better.*

Satisfied everything appeared in working order, he sat on a bench in front of his tent. "Dacar! Come."

Dacar poked his head from underneath a nearby tarp. "Yes, Tahliil?"

"Bring others. Meet me in command tent. Ten minutes."

Tahliil broke off a branch from one of the nearby shrubs and gathered several stones.

When Dacar and the three lieutenants entered the tent, Tahliil sat on a three-legged stool. At his feet, a pile of rocks and a short, thin stick. He smoothed an area of sand with his palm.

"Sit. New plan. Came last night." He drew a rough outline of the Somali and Kenyan coasts in the sand with the branch. Picking up several stones, he placed two in Kenya, one in Somalia, and one in the Indian Ocean.

"Dacar. No more freighters. Need weapons. Take tankers for North Koreans." Tahliil tapped the stone in the area representing water. "Not near canal. Too close foreign navies. Here instead—east of Kismaayo. Big ocean, make harder to find."

Dacar nodded. "When should I begin?"

"Today. Take Sahid and others. Capture ships. Change name and go Si-Sihan—"

"Sihanoukville."

"Yes. Try not kill crew. Perhaps more money." Tahliil pointed to the rock farthest away from the Somali border. "Harbi. Your target is Mombasa. Attack whatever you want. Keep Kenyans too busy to help tankers."

"Understand, Tahliil. I must scout the areas for targets before choosing one."

Tahliil glanced at Busuri. "You like girls, don't you? Go to refugee camp. Take more. No kill."

Busuri's eyes brightened. "What about ra—"

"No rape, Busuri. No torture, no kill. Hostages." Tahliil glared at him until the gleam in his eyes faded. "Or I do same to you."

"What about my team?" Gari glanced at the stones. "One left, but it's in Somalia."

"Yes. Best target for you. Take Kenyan uniforms, weapons. Pretend Kenyan military. Attack Kismaayo. Come from South. Kill some—not many. Cause confusion."

The five men chuckled. Tahliil stood and wiped his feet through his crude map. He gathered the stones and tossed them outside. "Go. May Allah keep you."

Tahliil returned to his private tent. One of the women brought him sweet tea and fruit for breakfast. He mulled over the future while he ate. *Soon many weapons, money. Plan new attack—against all infidels.*

\*\*\*

Dacar and Sahid gathered some personal items and pistols from the tent they shared. They bid Tahliil farewell and hopped in a battered white Subaru for the short drive to Kismaayo. Arriving in the city, they meandered through the streets before stopping at a small shop near the Haji Jama Mosque in the Faanoole district.

The store sold a mixture of home implements and dried foods. A front for al-Shabaab, the owners were fervent supporters of the group. Behind the shop, stood a small one-story house built out of rubble. Primitive, with electricity and running water unavailable, it was a perfect location for Dacar and his men to meet as few people ventured inside.

He waved a hand at the shop's proprietor, who was busy with a customer, and shuffled down a narrow aisle to the back counter. Sahid grabbed a handful of dates as he shimmied through an area crammed with baskets and barrels. They ducked out the open back door.

Inside the house, the fourteen men waiting for them filled all available space. A small propane stove heated water for tea. Cups in hand, the men waited for Dacar to speak.

Dacar twitched his nose at the smell of unwashed bodies in the Somali heat in such close quarters. "We have a new mission." He gazed at the eager faces. *I remember my first time—excitement, full of energy. Didn't realize I might die. Now I know different.* "We want oil tankers now. No freighters."

"Will owners pay as much to get their tankers back?" one of the men asked. Missing two fingers on his right hand and a ragged scar rippled across his right cheek, he chewed khat and spat on the floor.

Dacar grimaced at the man's actions. "Even better than money."

"What's better?" the same man asked.

"Weapons."

Cheers erupted as the men thumped their feet on the floor.

Dacar motioned for quiet. "We'll take the ships when they are passing Kismaayo. They'll be taken to Cambodia. Their transponders will be disabled so they can't be tracked. The names, homeports, and flags will be changed. Once in Cambodia, a different crew will take over, and our men will return, ready to seize another one."

He glanced at the others. "We begin tonight. Two boats. Eight men in each."

The men cast lots to determine who sailed with Dacar and who went with Sahid.

After the crews were decided, Dacar issued his final order. "We meet at the boats after dark."

\*\*\*

A moonless, starry night provided sufficient light for the passage of the two small speedboats along the river and into the Indian Ocean. The latest information from Rooble indicated a tanker had left the Suez Canal during the previous afternoon, bound for South Africa.

Off the coast, the boats turned north, before heading farther east. They planned to attack from the port side, and Dacar wanted them well out in the ocean as the tanker passed. Previous attacks always came from the coast.

The repetitive motion of the speedboats as they bounced across calm water at twenty-three knots caused many of the pirates to doze. Hours passed with no ships in sight.

Dacar mulled over his plan. Rather than use their mother ship, which was still positioned close to the Gulf of Aden, he hoped to launch a new surprise attack to capture their first tanker. *These boats are too small for their ship to pick up on radar. They'll be alert for attacks from starboard.*

As the first rays of dawn shimmered over the glass-like surface, Dacar reckoned they were about 300 miles east of Kismaayo. He whistled, waking the men on his boat.

"Up. Time to prepare." Dacar grabbed his AK-47 and checked his ammunition. The others gathered their weapons. Metal clicks indicated magazines were seated and ready to go. Two of the men loaded their RPGs, additional rockets lay ready nearby.

"Dacar! On the horizon—a ship!" One of the men pointed to the north. "Is it our target?"

Dacar pulled a pair of binoculars from a pouch on his belt. He tried to focus on the shape but failed. "Samatar, stop the boat. We'll wait for them to come toward us."

They slowed after Samatar cut the engines. The other pirate boat approached them and did the same.

Dacar raised the glasses again. With a more stable platform, although the boat rocked with the waves, he determined the approaching ship was their target—an oil tanker.

"We wait until they pass. Perhaps three hours. The sun will be in their eyes if they scan the area where we are." The others nodded their understanding. A couple of men nudged each other and grinned. They glided knives across small whetstones, sharpening the blades.

The ship edged closer but hugged the horizon. The men became impatient. Dacar shook his head when they gave him questioning glances.

"Go."

Samatar fired up the twin inboard engines and the boat sped after its prey, the second craft following as if they were linked. They closed the gap, with no indication their target had altered speed or direction.

The chase on, Dacar waved to the other boat. Sahid waved back, gave a thumbs up and began separating. Dacar's crew lined the starboard side, weapons at the ready. Samatar pushed the controls to their stops, the vessel appearing to leap forward as it gained on the slower ship and approached its bow.

Dacar turned to one of the men holding an RPG. "Fire a warning shot in front of them. Don't hit the ship."

A wavering contrail signaled the flight of the grenade, which sailed over the bow. A plume of water shot into the air as the grenade exploded underwater. With a prearranged signal, the others shot above the deck, not aiming at any target.

Sahid's crew sped along the tanker's starboard side. Two RPGs sailed forward as gunfire raked the upper structure of the vessel. Their pilot steadied the craft while the others prepared to board.

The speedboats approached the steep sides of the tanker, which had slowed. Hooks and ladders launched, the pirates climbed aboard to take charge.

The first pirate to reach the railing fired his AK-47 into the air. He lifted his leg to climb aboard. His body jerked. Blood spraying from his wounds, he fell into the sea. Replaced by another pirate, this one savvier than his deceased companion, he raked the bow.

A cry of pain escaped from an injured man somewhere nearby. The pirates scrambled onto the ship. One found the wounded man and raised his weapon.

"Wait!" Dacar rushed forward. "No killing—yet. I will decide if it's necessary."

The chastised pirate reversed his AK-47. His rifle butt smacked into the injured man's head, knocking him unconscious.

"Sahid. Take your team and round up the crew. Leave one man in the engine room. Put the rest in the galley."

"It will be done." Sahid grinned.

Dacar and the others headed to the bridge. A locked door provided no barrier—a burst from his AK-47 shattered the locking mechanism and the door bounced inward on damaged hinges.

"Where is the captain?" Dacar glanced around the bridge while his men rounded up the crew.

A small, white-haired man limped forward. "I'm the captain. Don't hurt my men. What do you want?"

"Simple, Captain. Your ship now belongs to me. Behave, and no one will be hurt—except for the injured man who killed one of mine."

Dacar pulled a slip of paper from his pocket and handed it to the captain. "Here are the coordinates for your new destination. Take us there. No tricks." He pointed at the young-looking helmsman. "Or he dies."

Finished, Dacar motioned to one of his men to remain behind. The others herded the crew to the galley while he located the radio console. After he found the ship's satellite phone, he punched in digits memorized long ago, and spoke when someone answered.

"The prize is ours. Proceeding to planned destination."

# Chapter Sixteen

Al-Shabaab Camp
Outside Kismaayo, Somalia

After Dacar and Sahid left the camp to launch their new operations, the others gathered under a tarp to shelter themselves from the sun. Gari passed a bag of khat leaves to Busuri and Harbi. The men chewed and relaxed on the sand.

"I hope Dacar and Sahid are successful." Harbi waved an AK-47 in the air. "These are excellent weapons, but we need more firepower to take on the army."

"What do you want? Perhaps we can make a trade." Busuri launched a stream of spit into the shimmering sand, where it sizzled in the intense heat.

"We have a few mortars, RPGs, grenades. I want—Hummers."

Gari stared at Harbi and shook his head. "Dreamer."

"What for?" Busuri laughed and stood. "Your men ride in technicals. Are you too important to go with them? I don't have any."

"No. The technicals are old. Parts are scarce." Harbi rubbed his chin and pursed his lips. "If I can't steal or buy a Hummer, some other type of armored vehicle would be okay."

Busuri waved a hand at the other men and departed.

"When are you planning to attack Mombasa?" Gari scratched his crooked nose and forced himself from the sand.

"We'll leave tomorrow and be in place during the night. We'll attack at dawn in two days."

Gari nodded. "Okay, my men will hit Kismaayo. Two attacks at the same time might cause chaos."

"Perhaps more difficulties if Busuri hits the refugee camp during the other attacks."

"Agreed, but Busuri does what he wants when he's ready." Gari spat out the khat leaves. "Don't know why Tahliil puts up with him."

"Easy to understand—they're both from the same clan—the Darud." Harbi shielded his eyes as he gazed at his men. He spotted Wardi and whistled.

Towering over the other Somalis, Wardi Galad turned and trotted over.

"Wardi, gather the men in the command tent. We'll leave for Mombasa this afternoon." Harbi clasped the younger man's shoulder. "It's time to show the Kenyans who owns the shoreline."

\*\*\*

When Harbi entered the command tent, twenty men jumped to their feet. Like almost all members of the Digil tribe of the Rahanwey clan, they revered Harbi for his success against outsiders. Dressed in traditional *macawiis* or *khameez*, some favored colored sarongs while others wore white. Embroidered caps sat atop each man's head. Several also sported shawls, useful for wrapping around the face during a sand storm.

Settling into Tahliil's chair, Harbi tilted his head to acknowledge their tribute and motioned for them to sit. "Yesterday, I sent five men with technicals to Mombasa. We will leave after dark in two boats from Kismaayo and join them north of the city. As dawn rises, we shall strike."

Feet thudded into the sand and the men clapped their hands, grins plastered across their faces.

"When we join them, we will divide into five groups." Harbi pulled a folded Mombasa map from a pocket and spread it on the ground. The others gathered around as he pointed at targets.

"We will attack the airport, the Kipevu Power Station, the oil storage tanks, and the Oceanic Hotel. We will use mortars and RPGs. Use your AKs to shoot anyone you find."

A short man called 3M, a nickname given to him since his first, middle, and last names were the same, raised a gnarled hand at the back of the group. Perched on his head was a 3M hat, a gift from a previous American employer. "Harbi, you provided four targets. What will the fifth team do?"

"They will protect the New Nyali Bridge until the other teams return, heading out of the city on Malindi Road. Before they depart, they will destroy the bridge."

The hand shot forward. "I want to blow the bridge."

"You shall, 3M. I count on your expertise." Harbi glanced around the eager faces. "Eat, rest, and prepare your weapons. We begin our journey in two hours."

\*\*\*

The sun disappeared over the horizon as four technicals loaded with Harbi's group left the camp, a cloud of dust marking their transit. After an uneventful trip, they entered Kismaayo, and the convoy meandered through the city before taking the road for the port.

They entered the harbor and pulled up to a dock as two speedboats approached an empty pier. The men gathered their equipment and jumped from the SUVs, hustling to the idling boats. The battered Jeep Cherokees departed on their return journey to the terrorist camp.

With the last man aboard, the men pushed the boats away from the dock. They turned around, skimming over the water away from Kismaayo.

Hour after hour, the boats bounced over small waves as they traveled south. In the distance, a glow appeared—the lights of Mombasa now guiding their way.

Four lights blinked from the shore.

On. Off.

Repeated three times.

Harbi used a battery-operated spotlight to repeat the sequence. A final flash from the shore indicated it was safe to approach.

The boats veered toward the signal. In the shallows, the pilots cut the engines, allowing the crafts' momentum to carry them to the beach. Men hopped out and used ropes to pull the boats closer.

Once the human cargo exited, the boats were pushed from the shore. Reaching deep enough water, the pilots restarted the engines and headed out to sea to await the signal to return.

Harbi and his men trudged across the soft sand, climbed a steep dune by grabbing small bushes, which had somehow managed a foothold in the barren landscape, until they reached a row of waiting technicals.

Everyone onboard, the lead technical departed. The others followed at one hundred-yard intervals to keep out of the dust clouds churned up by the vehicles ahead. They reached a narrow asphalt road and turned left toward Mombasa.

"The potholes are worse than hitting the waves with the boat." Harbi ground his teeth against the jarring. "Is it possible to miss the larger ones?"

The driver glanced at Harbi and grinned. "You suggested this road because there isn't much traffic. Now you know why. Have you forgotten?"

"Ugh." Harbi's head connected with the roof as they rammed through a series of deep depressions gouged in the washed-out road. "How much farther?"

"About three kilometers. We found an abandoned barn. Should be able to keep prying eyes away."

The driver turned off the road, back into the sand. He drove toward the shell of a barn, the lone headlight showing two wooden poles shoved into the ground, holding a pair of doors closed. He hopped from the vehicle and removed the poles, allowing the doors to swing open.

Back in the Toyota Land Cruiser, he pulled inside, followed by the other vehicles. A man jumped out of the last SUV and closed the barn doors, propping the poles back in place. He entered through a narrow side door as Harbi inspected the interior.

"Perfect. No one would suspect anyone to hide here." He glanced up and studied the myriad of stars through the rafters. He turned to his men. "One hour rest and we disperse to our targets."

\*\*\*

The convoy neared the New Nyali Bridge. Two Kenyan police officers lounged in chairs on the far side of the bridge near their guard shack. They stood as the vehicles drew closer, hands reaching to their pistol belts.

The lead vehicle ground to a halt, scant feet from the officers. Dressed in the uniform of a senior Kenyan police officer, Harbi jumped out of the vehicle. The officers snapped to attention, quivering.

Harbi glanced at their wrinkled uniforms and smelled beer on their breath. "Why were you drinking on duty? Your appearance is appalling. Give me your names."

"I am—"

While Harbi kept the officers occupied, two of his men crept behind them. After one identified himself, Harbi's men used handmade coshes to render them unconscious. Bound and gagged, they were hauled inside the shack. Once hidden, Harbi's men replaced the officers on the bridge and waved the convoy forward.

The final SUV remained on the bridge. 3M jumped out, carrying a backpack. Two others joined him, each with an identical bag.

"Come, while the others tend to their attacks, we'll prepare our surprise." 3M grinned at the others. "A farewell boom for when we leave Mombasa."

***

The remaining four technicals continued in a convoy until they reached Jomo Kenyatta Avenue. The first three vehicles turned right toward their targets, while the final one swung left to weave through the streets near the Oceanic Hotel. Although still early in the day, pedestrians scurried about as family-owned shops opened.

People ducked their heads into pharmacies, grocery stores, and others, seeking purchases. The street filled with the various aromas of food cooking.

One of Harbi's men complained. "All we ate was old bread made from weevil-infested flour. How I wish we might stop to get something, anything, hot to eat."

"At least you had protein with your bread." The driver laughed. "If we stopped now, more people might recognize us later. We want to hit our targets and leave."

"I know." The first man sighed. "Still, I'm hungry."

The vehicle screeched to a halt by the traffic circle near the Stragglers Cricket Club. Two men jumped out of the back, one hauling a mortar tube and the other laden with a heavy burlap bag containing rounds and headed to a nearby bus shelter. As soon as the men were clear, the SUV continued toward the water, turned left on Mama Ngina Drive and parked adjacent to the golf course, the Oceanic Hotel in view across the fairway.

The remaining men set up a second mortar in a sand pit. The driver called Harbi. "*Eber* (zero) this is *Kow* (one). In position. Over."

"Kow this is Eber. Wait for my signal."

"*Haa* (yes)."

\*\*\*

Two of the technicals approached Mombasa's industrial area near the Kilindini Harbor as Harbi's vehicle crossed over the Makupa Causeway, proceeding to Moi International Airport. Their destinations: the Kipevu Power Station and the oil storage tanks.

Harbi's SUV raced along the road running parallel to one of the airport's runways. They stopped near a copse of stunted trees. His radio crackled.

"Eber this is *Labo* (two). Ready. Over."

"Labo this is Eber. Wait for my signal."

"Haa."

"Eber this is *Saddex* (three). Also in position."

"Okay."

Harbi and his team set up their mortars. One was positioned to bracket the taxiway leading to the runway. The other was aimed at the terminal building. Ready, Harbi took a deep breath and exhaled. He grabbed his radio and keyed the mike. "Fire!"

*Whoomph.*

Mortars shot from the tubes. Harbi noted the impact of the first one—missed the apron but hit the runway, creating a small crater.

The second mortar round landed on top of the terminal. Glass shattered and screams carried on the slight breeze as a plume of smoke shot into the air. They launched two more rounds before running for their vehicle.

Swinging around, the SUV sped toward the Makupa Causeway.

\*\*\*

Receiving the word to fire, the teams targeting the Oceanic Hotel launched their attack. A round shot into the air from the traffic circle, missed the building and burst between two Mercedes in the parking lot. The cars bounced into the air. Alarms blaring, flames crackled as the vehicles became expensive piles of scrap metal.

The team near the golf course fired a single round. The trajectory, too short to hit the building, caused a towering splash when the projectile smashed into the hotel's swimming pool. Two broken bodies, guests having an early morning swim, turned the frothing water red.

The men abandoned their mortar, which had split after they fired their round. They hopped back in their SUV and tore across the grass to pick up the team by the traffic circle. The driver paused long enough for the men to jump in. Everyone inside, the vehicle rocketed along the street, back toward Jomo Kenyatta Avenue.

\*\*\*

Labo and Saddex launched their mortars as soon as they heard Harbi's command. Positioned near each other, Labo fired at the power station while Saddex targeted the Kenya Petroleum Company's storage tanks.

A brilliant flash obscured the power station when two projectiles hit the facility. Alarms sounded, men scurried from the burning building as the city's sole electrical source faltered.

Not to be outdone, Saddex's team bracketed two storage tanks. According to large red and white signs, one contained diesel while the other held gasoline.

The primary source of fuel for hundreds of vehicles in the city and surrounding area vanished in the roar of heat and flame. Explosions rocked the storage facility, the concussion from the blasts knocked the mortar teams to the ground.

Thick, black smoke filled the air as flames shot upward. Metal shards from the destroyed tanks pierced nearby pipelines, their contents spewing into the spreading area of destruction.

Saddex and Labo clambered to their feet, climbed into their SUVs and sped away, beaming faces glancing back at their success.

\*\*\*

Team *Afar* (four) witnessed the success of the attacks, each marked by the black clouds caused by the explosions. Sirens became incessant as police and emergency services responded to the disaster. Sporadic gunfire echoed across the city.

The team piled into their vehicle, parked at the entrance to the New Nyali Bridge. 3M waved his arm in a circular pattern, urging the four technicals heading toward him to move faster.

The vehicles shot over the bridge, 3M's vehicle bringing up the rear. While the others continued out of the city, 3M glanced at the men in his vehicle and smiled. "Boom."

He twisted a knob on a small handheld device. Four explosions rocked the bridge. One side tipped as the supports gave way under the force of 3M's handiwork. Concrete chunks fell away as a third of the bridge toppled into the water.

"Yes! I love to blow up things!" 3M swatted the man next to him as they broke into cheers and laughter.

\*\*\*

An hour later, the five technicals dropped Harbi's men back at the beach and headed toward Somalia. The two boats waited for the men, the pilots having seen the explosions from a distance. They piled onboard and proceeded north.

Harbi gazed back at the black smoke plumes hovering over Mombasa. "This should keep the Kenyans too busy to worry about Dacar and the ships he's taking."

## Chapter Seventeen

Al-Shabaab Camp
Outside Kismaayo, Somalia

Three hours after Harbi's team left the camp for Mombasa, Gari's men changed into Kenyan Defense Force camouflage uniforms. They grabbed AKs and M4s and jumped into three Land Rover Defenders and an Oshkosh troop carrier.

Gari grinned. "What do we need with armored vehicles like Harbi wants? We'll take what we want from the Kenyans." He pressed his hands down the front of his captain's uniform to smooth out the wrinkles.

His driver, a gray-haired man named Hasan Fido, laughed. "You are a handsome captain. But why not a general?"

"Generals don't chase across the desert. They send captains and sometimes majors."

"Next time, I want to be a lieutenant."

"We'll need to find a lieutenant willing to part with his uniform."

The vehicles bounced along the tracks in the sand until they reached the Kismaayo-Kolbio Road. Not much better than the path they had departed from, but where the asphalt hadn't been ground into pebbles, the convoy picked up speed.

An hour later, they turned off the road toward the village of Anole. A few lanterns shone in the fading light. Hasan glanced at Gari. "When we reach the square, should I stop?"

"Yes. Make plenty of noise when you do. Use your Swahili. Stick with me and yell at anyone that gets in our way. It should only take a few minutes to establish we're a Kenyan military unit chasing al-Shabaab terrorists."

"Aah! I understand. No one will suspect us when we pursue the terrorists."

People peeked out of huts and shacks painted in pale shades of pink, blue, and white as the vehicles pulled into the square. The lead vehicle stopped in front of the town's lone mosque.

Hasan grabbed a bullhorn. "Do not be afraid. We are chasing a group of al-Shabaab terrorists. They attacked a village in Kenya and fled in this direction."

People remained indoors, so Hasan repeated his message.

An old man ventured from the largest hut. "They went north, along the road. Toward Kismaayo."

Through Hasan, Gari spoke to the elder. "Thank you, grandfather. We will give chase and apprehend them."

The convoy left the village, retracing their route back to the Kismaayo-Kolbio Road. They turned right, gathering momentum over the bumpy highway.

As they approached the outskirts of Kismaayo, the vehicles left the road and climbed over the sand dunes to the beach.

"We'll camp here until dawn." Gari twirled a finger in front of them. "Park in a circle. We'll sleep inside. No fires. Dried food."

His men scurried, following their orders. Within minutes, the trucks were arranged in a ragged circle. The drivers hunkered down in their vehicles to rest while the others grabbed their blankets and curled up on the soft sand. Before long, light snoring, the crackling of cooling metal, and the soft lapping of waves on the beach lulled the restless to sleep.

\*\*\*

Gari woke before the rest of his men. He dreamed of death during the night. *A premonition of what might happen today? My death or someone else's?*

He shook his head to clear the muddiness and wandered to the water's edge, using a hand to shield his eyes from the intense reflection of the sun's rays. After relieving himself, he turned and gazed at his men.

Gari cupped his hands around his mouth. "Wake up, you lazy camel jockeys! Time to move."

The men jumped. One pulled his AK from under his blanket, searching for whatever disrupted his sleep. The others laughed.

"We're late! In the time it takes for water to boil for tea, we must depart."

By the time Gari hopped in the lead Land Rover the camp had been cleared of any evidence of anyone's presence, aside from footprints in the sand.

Hasan started the engine and revved it up when someone banged on the side. He poked his head out the window.

"The last vehicle is stuck—buried to the axle."

Gari glanced to the heavens. *Late rising and now this. Hope these aren't omens.* "Get the truck in front of you to tow yours out. We'll meet on the highway."

\*\*\*

The red shades of dawn behind them, Gari's convoy entered the outskirts of Kismaayo. Unlike Harbi, who spread his men out to attack multiple targets in Mombasa, Gari selected two: the Hotel Ceenu Shamsi and the Jubba Fish Cooperative.

The first two Land Rovers broke away from the others, turning right before reaching the hotel. They skidded to a halt in front of their target, six blocks away from the cooperative.

Gari fired his AK at the cooperative, emptying his entire magazine as fishermen and customers alike dove for cover. His men continued the barrage as he turned to Hasan. "Tell them the market must be shut down. Kenyan fishermen cannot catch enough because of the Somali fishermen."

Hasan used the bullhorn to convey Gari's message. No one answered. He tried again. "Close your mark—"

Return fire erupted from the building. Customers screamed as the gunfire intensified.

"Gari, what should I say—"

Gari slumped toward the door. Hasan shook Gari, who didn't stir. When Hasan tried to move him, he pulled his hand back.

*Blood.*

"Allah, help us!"

Gari groaned as he placed a bloody hand on Hasan. "Time ... to ... leave ...." Gari passed out.

Hasan blew the horn as he swung the vehicle away from the cooperative.

A man leaning out a window, and aiming a weapon at Hasan's vehicle fell to the ground with the unexpected movement.

The second Land Rover followed in close pursuit, bouncing over the man rolling in the street.

Gunfire continued from the building, strafing the back of the second truck. Windows exploded, shards of glass burrowed into the men seated in the rear. One tried to fire back at the cooperative, his head blown off as an incoming round made contact.

A loud siren pierced the racket as a Somali ambulance raced toward the fish market. It slammed to a stop as the two Kenyan vehicles sped down both sides of the street, one smashing the side of the ambulance.

The two Land Rovers reached the primary thoroughfare and turned left, heading south toward Kenya.

Crazed with fright and the loss of Gari, Hasan didn't wait for the second truck, but zoomed down the narrow street. Two men, talking to each other, didn't spot Hasan until it was too late. Their broken bodies flew into the air before falling in a heap.

The second SUV tried to swerve around the obstacle, but the sudden maneuver unbalanced the vehicle, which tipped on its side, sliding along the street until crashing into an oncoming bus.

The bodies of local Somalis and those dressed in Kenyan uniforms littered the area. Women and men screamed in anguish as they searched through the deceased for their loved ones.

Hasan continued out of the city, not stopping until he approached the area where they rested overnight. Of the eight men entering Kismaayo in these two vehicles, two fled the scene, battered and bruised, but for now, alive.

They wept.

\*\*\*

The remaining Land Rover and the Oshkosh troop carrier halted in front of the Hotel Ceenu Shamsi. As the men piled out of the troop carrier, an antiquated deuce and a half with Somali Army markings blocked the street. Fixed to the cab's top, an unattended fifty-caliber machine gun.

Soldiers jumped from the back of the Somali vehicle, brandishing weapons. A major stepped forward. "Put down your weapons. You have invaded our country. Surrender now, and you won't be harmed."

Dressed in the uniform of a Kenyan Defense Force sergeant, an older man named Shidane stepped from the Land Rover, his left hand out of sight.

He saluted. "We are in pursuit of al-Shabaab terrorists. We've followed them from the border."

"There aren't any terrorists at this hotel, Sergeant. You've been misinformed."

Shidane shook his head. He raised the concealed pistol and shot the major.

Gunfire erupted on both sides. Shidane scooted back behind the steering wheel and turned the vehicle around, the Oshkosk following. Screams filled the air, rounds finding targets on both sides. Rumbling shook the street as a Somali tank maneuvered into position.

The Land Rover rocked on two wheels as Shidane threw the vehicle into a tight right-hand turn and sped away from the hotel.

An elderly Somali man scurried across the street to escape the carnage. Out of breath, he stopped in the path of the Kenyan troop carrier. The vehicle avoided the old man, smashing through an empty newspaper kiosk before chasing after the Land Rover.

The tank's turret tracked the Oshkosh. With a roar, a cloud of smoke, and a whistling sound, an armored-piercing round streaked toward the fleeing vehicle. Injured men bailed out as the projectile ripped through the rear of the truck, detonating when it reached the cab.

The troop carrier disintegrated, flames shooting skyward as the chassis sailed into the air before flipping over and landing on its top, crushing the driver and another man.

The tank sighted in on the Land Rover and fired.

A miss.

The errant round pulverized a parked car, sending fragments into Shidane's vehicle. He struggled to maintain control, a piece of metal lodged in his chest.

Shidane called out to the other men for help. No response. He ventured a glance. One man had vanished. The other one's body had its arms outstretched, as if grasping for its missing head.

\*\*\*

Hasan waited at the designated rendezvous point. In the distance, a vehicle's engine misfired, a burst of black smoke billowing upward. It appeared to struggle as it approached.

Shidane brought the damaged Land Rover to a halt. He labored to open the door, a screeching sound announcing his success as it fell off its hinges. Losing his balance, he collapsed onto the sand.

Hasan rushed to his side. "Where are the others?"

Shidane coughed, blood seeping out of his mouth. "Tell ... tell them we died with bravery in our hearts." The man's head lolled to the side as his body sagged.

Hasan dragged a hand over the man's face, closing his eyes. He returned to Gari. Eyes closed, a slight motion of his chest indicated he was still alive.

Putting the truck into gear, Hasan and Gari drove back to their base, determination etched on their faces, two survivors of the day's fateful attack.

\*\*\*

Hasan stopped the Land Rover on the top of a dune overlooking the camp. "We made it back, Gari."

He glanced at his team leader. "Gari?" Hasan gave him a slight nudge. Gari's body shifted forward, his head hitting the dash. He didn't move.

"Gari!"

Tears streamed down Hasan's face. He realized his friend and mentor no longer breathed.

Hasan leaned on the horn to alert the camp of his return. He spotted Tahliil near the command tent and brought the bullet-riddled vehicle to a stop in a cloud of sand. Clothes saturated with blood, he grabbed Gari's pistol, checked for ammunition, and stepped out of the truck.

"Gari—he's dead. The others, too." He glared at Tahliil. "The fish market was filled with men carrying weapons. A Somali tank demolished the troop carrier."

Hasan's chest heaved as he tried to keep his emotions in check. "They knew we were coming."

Tahliil nodded. "I told them. We needed dead Kenyan soldiers to create confusion between the Somali and Kenyan governments. They'll be too busy to worry about Dacar's mission."

"But ... But, Gari was your friend."

"At one time, perhaps, but he wanted to take over al-Shabaab." Tahliil shrugged, his lower lip covering the edge of the upper one. "He died for our cause."

Hasan stared at Tahliil, searching for some sign of humanity, a glimpse to indicate his decision to inform the government about the fake Kenyan attack was for the greater cause and not for himself.

Nothing.

Hasan raised the pistol as Tahliil lunged forward to stop him.

Too late.

He pulled the trigger.

## Chapter Eighteen

Kaeson Youth Park
Pyongyang

Soo paid the entrance fee to Kaeson Youth Park and merged with the throng enjoying one of the few pleasures in the city. Not many people rode the attractions, the cost being more than half of the average monthly salary. Most of Pyongyang remained in darkness, but the amusement park blazed with colorful lights.

A long line waited for their turn to ride the Ferris wheel. Soo joined the queue and shuffled along with the others toward the ticket booth.

A nudge from behind caused Soo to jump. He glanced back—just a couple of excited kids pushing each other.

Soo shook his head and faced the front. A stranger stood in his space. Brown hat, gray clothes, bottle-cap glasses, and a small goatee, without any physical identifiable markings.

"Move." The man pointed away from the crowds.

Soo hesitated.

The man gave a slight push on Soo's shoulder.

"Be careful, or I'll yell for the police! Do you understand who I am?"

"You are Ambassador Soo, and you'll do as you're instructed." He gave another push and prodded Soo in the back, leading him toward the empty picnic area.

A second man, dressed in similar clothing to Soo's escort, sat at one of the tables. He motioned to the other side of the table.

Soo paused and the first man shoved him into the seat.

"What is the meaning of this?" Soo's chest heaved with fright.

"We met in the Seychelles." Black orbs like bottomless pits gazed at Soo.

"Y-you tortured me."

"We did no such thing. Your mind is playing tricks." The man stood. "Remember, we are watching."

The two men disappeared into the shadows, leaving Soo alone at the table. Shaking, he stood and trudged back to the line for the Ferris wheel.

He listened to the laughter and chatter around him. *Who are those men? Why are they watching me and making threats?* He made his way forward in the line, one slow step after another.

A hand grabbed his shoulder.

Soo gasped and swung at the unknown assailant.

Kim caught Soo's arm in mid-swing. "Ambassador Soo. What are you doing?"

"I-It's you."

"Yes. We were supposed to meet fifteen minutes ago." Kim gave Soo a glance from head to toe. "Did something happen?"

"No. Yes." Soo's shoulders sagged and he gulped. "T-The men who kidnapped me. They're here."

Kim glanced around. "Where?"

"They were here a few minutes ago. One took me to the picnic area. They warned me." Soo gazed over the queue and toward the picnic area. "I don't see them." He heaved a sigh. "They were the ones who kidnapped me in Victoria."

"Let's skip the Ferris wheel. You need a cup of tea to calm your nerves." Kim guided Soo out of the line and led him by an elbow to a small tea kiosk.

"Three teas, please." Kim paid for the drinks and nodded toward an empty table away from the kiosk. He put one drink in front of him and gave the rest to Soo.

"Drink, Soo. This will help you relax. There is much to talk about."

Soo took a careful sip of the hot drink. Even though the evening wasn't cold, he wrapped his hands around the cup for warmth.

"What is the problem?" He finished the first cup and started on the second.

"We must put our story together. Wook will ask why we stayed out of contact for several days. He might ask both of us."

"I can understand him asking me, Kim, but why you? You're my aide, nothing more."

"True, but Wook is devious when he suspects anyone." *If you realized the truth, you'd require more than tea.* "When do you meet with our leader?"

"In two days."

Kim picked up his cup to hide his grimace. *I meet him tomorrow. Our story must be convincing.* "What will you tell him?"

"I might tell him I needed a few days to myself before returning to Pyongyang."

Kim shook his head. "It won't work. We always seek permission to take personal time. Even more important when we are out of the country."

Soo nodded. "You are correct as always. Hmm." Soo rubbed his chin, his eyes closed. He remained in this position for several moments. Slapping his hand on the table, he smiled. "We tell him I went for a walk. I collapsed in the intense heat. Someone called an ambulance, which took me to Seychelles Hospital. No one knew about you, so you needed time to search for me."

"Yes, a reasonable explanation. Let's go over the details, so you are ready." *I must also be prepared.*

\*\*\*

Major Kim was ushered into a small antechamber to wait for Wook. He would try not to show any nervousness in front of his leader, although perspiration dotted his forehead, and sweat made his skin clammy.

A door opened and Supreme Leader Wook strode into the room, two generals accompanying him, their notebooks and pens ready to capture the meeting.

Kim jumped to attention and saluted.

Wook waved a hand in the air. Kim dropped his salute and shifted to a parade rest position.

"Report." Wook skimmed the contents of a thin folder he brought with him as he sat at a small, unadorned table.

"Supreme Leader, Ambassador Soo and I met with the Somali pirates. The ambassador conveyed your change of conditions from two tanker ships to three for every shipment of weapons."

"How did they respond?"

"At first, they weren't happy and threatened us. When we informed them they would receive weapons in advance, they smiled throughout the rest of the negotiations."

"I'm sure they did." Wook gave a thin smile. "I would like to watch their faces when they receive the weapons."

"Supreme Leader?" Kim frowned at Wook's words, his eyebrows arched, not expecting a response.

Wook chuckled. "We are sending them weapons, most of which are inoperable. The ammunition is old and might explode when used."

"Yes, sir."

"Kim, relax, we're dealing with pirates. They can't retaliate. We'd wipe them out like …." Wook snapped his finger. "A bug."

"It would be an honor to do so, Supreme Leader."

"I want you and Soo to fly to Sehouk ... Seehan—"

"Sihanoukville, Supreme Leader."

Wook nodded. "Yes. You will meet the pirates and orchestrate the handover. No mistakes. They must leave with the shipment without testing the weapons."

"What if they insist?"

"Let them test weapons from the crates with my photograph. The weapons inside will work. The others won't." Wook gazed at Kim. "You will be in charge, not Soo. I'll tell him tomorrow when we meet."

"Yes, sir."

Wook stood and headed toward the door. He stopped and returned. "Kim, aren't you forgetting something? Why were you late returning?"

Kim glanced at the floor before staring into Wook's eyes. "Yes, Supreme Leader. We were late because Ambassador Soo became ill."

"Didn't your orders require you to notify me at once when something changed?"

"Yes, sir." Kim sighed. "I lost him."

Wook stomped his foot and slammed a fist into the palm of his other hand. "How can you lose him? At times, he's a pathetic, dim-witted man, although I admit he does show occasional creativity. You're an intelligence officer. Are you saying he's smarter than you?"

"No, Supreme Leader. He left the room while I took a shower. When I finished, I couldn't find him. I searched the hotel, the grounds, and the nearby area. He was gone. Vanished." He glanced downward, trying to hide any indicator he might not be revealing what did happen.

"Did you involve the police or government officials?"

"No, sir. I kept searching for him. After four days, I found him in the local hospital. A nurse said some tourists brought him in, suffering from heat stroke and dehydration."

"Hmmm." Wook pursed his lips and glared at Kim. "I suppose you acted in the best manner. But ... I should have been informed."

"Yes, Supreme Leader."

"Your new orders will be sent to you in a day or so. Remain in Pyongyang. I might require your services."

***

Soo tossed and turned throughout the night. He dreaded his upcoming meeting with Wook. *Kim never called. Why not? Did Wook arrest him?*

He covered his mouth and raced to the bathroom. He threw the toilet lid up as his stomach heaved. Soo's head and face became damp with perspiration as sharp pains racked his body.

His body ached. Emptied, he wiped his face with a wet cloth and scooped water with his hands to drink. *Why not tell Wook the truth? What is Kim afraid of?*

Soo glanced at the clock, 5:35 a.m. *Might as well stay up and rehearse for my meeting.* He paced the room like a caged animal, all the time expecting a disastrous outcome.

A knock at the door startled him. He checked the time—two hours had passed. He opened the door. Two men waited for him. Without a word, Soo locked the door and allowed himself to be herded to a black vehicle.

After they had arrived at Wook's compound, the car continued past the normal drop-off point and followed a narrow road. At the rear of the facility, a small white gate beckoned. Unseen guards opened an access point. The vehicle stopped and one of the men climbed out. He motioned to Soo. "Come."

They entered the building and walked down a marble-floored hallway. A giant photograph of Supreme

Leader Wook hung on the bare walls, the eyes seemed to look down at Soo. His escort stopped at a plain white door. Twisting the knob, he pushed. "Wait inside."

After Soo had entered, the door slammed shut. Soo glanced around. An armless chair stood near a small table. Otherwise the room was empty.

Moments later, an inner door popped open and Wook strode into the chamber. He gazed at Soo before sitting down.

"Tell me, Soo, why did you not stay with Kim as instructed? Who did you meet with? What did they want?" Wook slammed a hand on the table, causing Soo to jerk back.

"I-I wanted fresh air. I didn't meet with anyone." Soo swallowed, his mouth dry. "I forgot my hat. The heat and intense sunlight became too much for me. I collapsed in the street."

Wook crossed his arms but remained silent.

"Supreme Leader, I realize now it was wrong to venture out without Kim. My actions caused you unnecessary concern." Soo's body trembled, as he feared his leader's response.

Wook nodded. "How are you feeling?"

"Much better now. Our climate rejuvenated me."

"Good. You and Kim leave on a new assignment. You are to travel with the shipment of weapons to Cambodia. When the transfer is complete, return here. I will grant you five minutes with your family if everything is satisfactory."

"Thank you, Supreme Leader. This makes me happy." *Why does he keep torturing me? He should release my family. They have no part in this. Innocent. They are innocent.*

"Do as you're told without any further mishap." Wook stood, signaling the end of the meeting. "You know the penalty."

***

Two days later, Soo and Kim scampered up the loose gangway of a rusty freighter, traction pads long since stripped off the rusting metal, safety line too slack to provide security. Peeling paint, discarded containers, and broken equipment littered the deck.

Soo stopped a crewman. "I am Ambassador Soo, and this is my aide, Kim. Take me to the captain."

The crewman glanced at Soo from head to toe and spat, missing Soo's polished shoes. "Follow me."

Rats scurried from garbage piled in corners, squeaking at the interruption as the men passed. They entered the bridge, which appeared no better than the rest of the ship.

The crewman walked up to a wide-shouldered man with a swarthy complexion, wearing a food-stained uniform. "Hey, Cap'n. This is …." He spat on the deck. "Oh, yeah. Ambassador Soo." With a chuckle, the man left.

"Please have someone take me to my quarters." Soo sneered at the captain with disdain. "I want tea once I'm settled in."

"This is my ship, and you'll work like everyone else. No time for self-important people. If you want tea, you'll go to the galley and make it yourself."

The captain pointed out a door on the other side of the bridge. "Your cabin is located out there. The door is open. You share."

"You must know, as a senior official for our Supreme Leade—"

"On this ship, I am the Supreme Leader. You do as I say, or I'll toss you overboard."

Kim grabbed Soo by the shoulder before he angered the captain. "Let's find our cabin and the galley. We'll unpack and get accustomed to the ship's layout."

Soo nodded. *I hope we don't get sick on this floating garbage pit.* "Lead on, Kim."

"We must keep a sharp eye on the captain and his crew. There's something—I don't trust them."

## Chapter Nineteen

Greek Oil Tanker Zeus
Somewhere on the Indian Ocean

Dacar paced the bridge wing, struggling to contain his excitement after hijacking their first oil tanker. Turning away from the others, he allowed a ghost of a smile to appear before masking it.

Pushing past several of his men, Dacar entered the wheelhouse. He strode toward the captain, a small white-haired man, who remained in his chair. "How did you get your limp?"

"I fell during a severe thunderstorm and broke the femur in two places. Never been the same since."

"Captain, what is your name? Since we will be together for some time, we might as well be pleasant to each other."

"What about my men?"

"As promised, they are contained in the mess."

"What about the injured man?"

"He's with the others. He'll have a headache, but he'll survive. Now, what is your name?"

The captain stood, several inches shorter than Dacar. "I am Sandie Stavros of the Greek Merchant Navy and captain of the *Zeus*."

"Hello, Sandie Stavros. I am Dacar, the leader of this group of opportunists. Thank you for your ship. I gave her a new name, *Zebu* and a new flag, too. From the Bahamas."

The captain gazed around the bridge. Except for the on-duty pilot and himself, the three men were alone as their guard had stepped outside when Dacar returned. "I examined those coordinates you gave me. We are going to Cambodia?"

"Perhaps. Why?"

"No reason, except I'm nosy." Stavros shrugged. "Since you changed the name, the flag, and are going to Sihanoukville, there can be but one reason—ransom."

"Hmmm." Dacar scratched under his right arm. "What would you know about ransom?"

"Others have seized ships and done the same. I assume you are no different."

"Well, Captain Stavros, you are mistaken. This hijacking is not about a ransom. We work for a higher purpose." *Bet you want the information. It's much better than a ransom.* "If you and your crew don't—"

"Dacar." Breathless, Sahid entered the bridge. "I-I must speak with you. Now."

The pirates moved away from the captain, who showed no apparent interest in this interruption.

"What is it? I'm interrogating the ship's captain."

Sahid took several deep breaths to calm himself. "I went into the mess and counted the crewmen. We had twenty-three prisoners with three of our men watching over them."

"What's the problem?"

"Three are missing!"

"Are you sure?"

"Yes, Dacar. We checked everywhere. All doors are locked. We opened closets, cupboards, anywhere a man might fit. I don't understand how, but they've disappeared."

Dacar rushed over to Stavros and backhanded him.

Blood seeped from the corner of the captain's mouth, which he wiped away with a finger.

Dacar hit him again. He went to strike him a third time when Sahid grabbed his arm.

"Enough, Dacar." Sahid pulled a knife from a sheath on his belt. "Let me speak with him."

"Don't kill him—we need answers."

Stavros grinned, his teeth covered with blood. "What's the matter? Are my men too smart for you?" Stavros spat on the deck to clear his mouth.

Sahid placed the point of his knife under the captain's left eye. "How did they escape? Where did they go?"

Stavros glared at Sahid but remained silent.

"Answer me!" Sahid pushed the blade forward, and blood dripped from a small cut.

Stavros closed his eyes, a whimper escaping from his swollen lips. "Do what you want with me. You'll never find my men until it's too late for you."

Dacar pushed past Sahid, using the rifle butt of his AK to smash the side of the captain's head. Stavros stumbled forward and toppled to the floor, dazed.

Dacar kicked him in the ribs and turned to Sahid. "Find those men. Take Samatar with you. Tear the ship apart if necessary. Select a member of the crew to kill if they won't talk."

\*\*\*

The tanker was long overdue at the oil refinery in Durban, South Africa and frantic contact calls ensued. They were unsuccessful. Naval ships along the east coast of Africa were notified about the missing vessel.

"Commander, a signal from the South Africans."

"Thank you, Lieutenant." Commander Ben Pierce, commanding officer of *HMS Snapdragon*, a type-45 destroyer, glanced at the short paragraph. He handed the paper back.

"Seems the Somali pirates might be causing more problems again."

"Yes, sir. Shall we give pursuit?"

Commander Pierce laughed at Lieutenant Brown's enthusiasm. "Since we don't know where the *Zeus* is, how do you propose we give pursuit? It appears the transponder failed or was switched off. Pass the word to Navy Command Headquarters. We'll wait for orders."

"Yes, sir."

Two hours later, the lieutenant approached Commander Pierce. "Sir, our orders came through." He handed over the document.

*To: Commanding Officer, HMS Snapdragon*
*From: Navy Command HQ, Whale Island*
*Initial report confirmed. Proceed with best possible speed from current position along the African coast to Kismaayo. Greek Naval frigate will join you for the search mission. Additional information will be provided when available. Acknowledge.*

"Not quite a pursuit, Lieutenant, but the next best thing. Acknowledge and initiate orders."

"Yes, Commander." The lieutenant smiled as he picked up the intercom to commence his first operation.

\*\*\*

One of the pirates guarding the sailors in the mess lit a khat cigarette and passed the joint around. At the rear of the room, Kallias Markos, the chief engineer, leaned against the wall, flanked by his assistants, Phelix and Vasilis.

He tapped each one on the knee and tilted his head toward a closed door four feet away. Keeping a close eye on their captors, the three men inched their way along the floor to a swivel door.

When he saw the three guards facing away from them, Kallias nudged the kick panel on well-oiled hinges with his foot. He slid inside the galley.

Phelix and Vasilis joined him moments later near an extended air vent cover.

Pulling out his Swiss Rescue Tool, Kallias selected the Phillips screwdriver and attacked the four screws holding the screen in place. Once removed, a metal tunnel was revealed, wide enough for an adult to enter.

"Glad we created this escape hatch." Kallias motioned for Phelix to enter. "In you go. Be quiet and head to the engine room. We'll join you as soon as possible."

Phelix nodded and disappeared into the tunnel. After he was out of sight, Vasilis followed. Kallias entered and reached through an access panel to re-secure the cover. Satisfied they hadn't been missed, he crawled through the maze, popping through an open cover near the engine room.

In his domain, Kallias paced the crowded area. "We must send a message about the hijacking. Vasilis—make your way to the old radio room. The equipment still works."

"Yes, Chief." He grabbed a heavy wrench for protection and departed.

Kallias turned to Phelix. "Go to the captain's quarters. There's a shoebox in the bottom of his closet containing a pistol and ammunition. Bring it here."

"What will you do?"

"First, I'll slow the *Zeus* down. Not too much, but enough to delay our journey. Once I have the captain's pistol, I'll try to rescue him."

\*\*\*

Sahid, Samatar and two others searched for the missing crewmen. They began at the bow and continued throughout the ship until they ended up at the stern.

"Where are they?" Samatar shook his head. "Are you sure the numbers were correct?"

"Yes. I counted the ship's crew twice. I'm positive three are missing."

Samatar released a deep sigh as he shrugged. "Should we check again?"

"Yes." Sahid pulled out his knife and grinned. "In the meantime, I'll talk with the captain again. I'll be more persuasive this time."

Sahid returned to the bridge. The captain's face was impassive, unlike the smirk he wore before. Sahid grabbed the captain by his shirt and poked him with the knife's point, just below his Adam's apple, drawing blood. "Where are the missing men? How did they escape? Tell me, or you'll—"

Dacar stopped Sahid. "Wait. The captain might still be of use. Don't kill him—yet. We'll broadcast a message through the ship for the sailors to surrender or else."

"He knows where they're hiding. All he needs is some encourage—"

"Dacar!" A young pirate, his chest heaving, rushed up to the pirate leader. "A plane is approaching. Fast. I think—"

Loud engine noises drowned out whatever the man planned to say. Dacar rushed to a window as two military aircraft circled the ship. "I think the Americans call those planes Hornets."

"What should we do?" The young man's eyes widened with fear.

"Go out—"

The windows rattled as the planes thundered past on either side of the ship before gaining altitude.

"Go out and wave. A normal crew would do so."

After several additional passes, the aircraft waggled their wings as they zoomed upward, the sound of their engines fading in the distance.

"They must be satisfied we're not the missing *Zeus*." Dacar laughed. "Good thing we altered the name on the bow and stern as quick as we did. We paid a hefty bribe to have the name registered."

"Yes. Should I continue searching for the missing crewmen?" Sahid shoved his knife back in its sheath.

"Not yet. I want to speak with Tahliil and ask his opinion."

\*\*\*

*H*MS *Snapdragon* joined forces with the Greek frigate *HS Navarone*. Maintaining a distance between ships of five miles, they steamed east, searching for the missing *Zeus*.

"Commander, another signal from HQ."

*To: Commanding Officer, HMS Snapdragon*
*From: Navy Command HQ, Whale Island*

*Three hours ago, U.S. Naval aircraft located an oil tanker proceeding in established shipping lanes towards India. They identified the ship as the Zebu, flying a Bahamian flag. No sign of the Zeus.*

*Maintain current operation with Greek frigate. Will advise.*

"Lieutenant, how difficult would it be to change *Zeus* to *Zebu*?"

"With calm seas, the same color paint and appropriate stencils, no time at all."

"That's what I thought. I believe the Americans were duped. They had spotted our missing tanker, but since they focused on the name and the flag, they didn't think outside the box." Commander Pierce shook his head. "Send a message to HQ requesting the coordinates where the Americans spotted the tanker. As soon as you receive the information, plot a course. Inform the Greeks, too."

"Aye, Commander."

\*\*\*

Dacar tossed the satellite phone on the desk. "Three hours! Must be another sandstorm in Kismaayo."

He cracked his knuckles as he paced, swearing beneath his breath. Dacar waited another five minutes before dialing Tahliil's number.

"Allo?"

"Tahliil! At last, I've reached you. I've been trying for hours."

"We had bad sandstorm. It stopped. The sky is clear."

"I need your advice, Tahliil." Dacar explained what had transpired since they captured the oil tanker.

"Dacar, make Greeks fear you. Kill one."

# **Chapter Twenty**

Jujubba Refugee Camp
Malindi, Kenya

After David announced terrorists had kidnapped ten female refugees and killed another, George, Alf, and the other volunteers sat in stunned disbelief. Minutes passed as muted sobbing and sniffling invaded the silence.

"How? Why? Who would do this?" Alf clenched his hands into tight fists, his knuckles whitening. An occasional tear escaped, unbidden, down his face as he tried to come to terms with the human brutality he'd witnessed firsthand.

"May I have your attention, please?" David stepped onto a small crate. "We volunteered to help those in this camp who are in distress and require assistance. Sometimes, evil forces take advantage of people who are weak."

David wiped his eyes before continuing. "We must be strong for those who remain and depend upon us. We'll never forget what's happened, but we must continue our work."

Heads nodded as they listened to David's calm voice.

A lone voice hummed a popular song. One by one others joined in, holding hands and swaying to the offbeat tune. When the song finished, the group hugged one another and grew silent.

"We'll hold a memorial service this evening." Ian clapped his hands. "Now we must focus on the living. Should you want to speak with David or me in private, we'll be available for you."

As the camp staff left the communal area, Alf rushed over to George. "How are you able to be so calm with what's happened?"

"I've been trained to keep my emotions inside. In private, my emotions come out, but the public persona remains steadfast."

"How do you manage? I mean …. I understand you're an heir and must receive training. But … this is a disaster."

"Shh. Keep your voice down. David, Ian, and you are aware of my secret, but no one else is. They might suspect, but no point in confirming for them who I am. Everyone leaves me alone, and they know me as George, one of the volunteers."

Ian walked up to the pair. "Are you guys up to working today? David said more refugees are approaching, so if possible, he needs your help."

They joined Ian and meandered through the camp to the processing tables. David and two other volunteers prepared for new arrivals. In the distance, a small dust cloud marked the arrival of displaced people.

"Hey, George, Alf. Thanks for helping out. With so many shook up over what happened, I understand most of our aides want time to themselves."

"Hi, David. We think it's better to work." George pointed at Alf. "We'll do our grieving in private later. More important to keep busy."

Alf nodded, but remained silent. He brushed aside a trickling tear and joined the other volunteers.

"George, I must take care of some things. Will you oversee the others and register our new arrivals?" David's hand shook in the air as he spoke. "Remember to ask for documentation, although most won't have any. Ask their names, where they're from, and age. Write the information on a form and have them sign."

"We'll remember, no problem."

"Thank you. I'll send others with extra water bottles and high-energy food. The doctor is in his tent, ready to examine the refugees after they're registered."

"I understand." George smiled and shooed David away. "Take care of your business. If any difficulties arise, someone will find you."

David glanced at the ground before gazing at George. "Thanks for being understanding. This has been a tremendous blow to everyone here. I don't know how you've held up given your past."

After David departed, George grabbed a chair from under a nearby canopy, sat and dropped his head into his hands.

*Why's the world so violent? Wish I could speak with Granny.*

Alf sauntered up to George, putting an arm on his friend's shoulder. "The refugees are approaching, appears to be about twenty-five. Will you be okay?"

"Yes. I was reflecting on the situation. Horrible."

Alf assisted George to his feet, and they prepared to help those in need.

\*\*\*

One person after another approached the tables and waited for processing. Unlike the first group George and Alf assisted, the latest refugees arrived in better physical shape. However, all showed signs of trauma, though a few managed to talk about marauders attacking their village and razing it to the ground. Several bled from small knife wounds and one sported a long welt where a raider tried to brand her before she escaped.

Deep brown eyes peeked from under long unkempt hair. The girl clutched her mother's hand as she stared at George.

"What's the little one's name?" George knelt beside the child. Her mother smiled as her daughter grasped George's extended hand.

"Rihana. She is seven years old."

"A beautiful name. Hello, Rihana. My name is George."

Rihana giggled and hid behind her mother's skirt. Moments later, she shifted her head to peek at George.

"Boo!"

Peals of laughter erupted from Rihana.

"I must stop now, Rihana." George stood and spoke to her mother. "I know her name, but what is yours? I must list it on the form."

"I am Nagan."

George turned to Alf. "Please enter Nagan's name on the form and add her daughter, Rihana."

"All done. Nagan, are you able to write your name?"

She nodded. "I learned English in Mogadishu at the American Embassy. I worked there as a translator for four years, before the fighting."

After completing the forms, a British nurse named Rachel led Nagan and Rihana toward the doctor's tent.

George shook his head. "Imagine someone branding Rihana like she was a possession. What's the world coming to?"

"It's a hard life here. At home, we complain about the most trivial matters as if the world will end." Alf closed the ledger while they waited for any further arrivals. "Most of us would collapse trying to survive in these conditions."

\*\*\*

Two nights later, after the evening meal, the volunteers huddled around a small campfire. Rather than a boisterous group, conversation remained muted and laughter almost nonexistent.

Since the abductions and murder, George served as the de facto leader. He stood, backed away a few feet, and clapped his hands for attention. "The shock of what happened will remain with us forever." He gazed at each person. "We can't let it ruin our lives. I speak from experience."

Alf chuckled, breaking the silence. Soon, others joined in until a ripple of laughter circled the campfire.

"Rihana, who joined us a few days ago, came to me this afternoon." George gazed at his friends and colleagues sitting around the campfire. "She doesn't know much English, but she used two words: 'Thank you' before giving me a hug. We must pull ourselves up and continue our work before returning home. These people are counting on us."

\*\*\*

Short and rotund, Busuri lay on his stomach, peering at the refugee camp through a night scope. He studied the foreigners around the fire and grunted. *Perhaps a new target this time? Something to raise fear in those who don't belong here?*

Busuri left his vantage point and crawled back to the wadi. Not a sound escaped from the eleven men waiting for his return. A small backpack and weapons of choice lay within easy reach of each man. Some chewed khat while others dozed.

In a quiet voice, Busuri spoke. "Change of plans. I found something better than entertainment to take from the camp."

"What's better?" Looshan asked.

"You're the youngest member of the group, so there is more to learn. Foreigners—we'll be able to ransom them as Dacar does with the ships."

"Aah. I understand."

"Take the goggles and monitor the people around the campfire. Make note of where they go. Take someone with you. When you find out where the foreigners are staying, report back."

"Yes, Busuri."

"Pay particular attention to the tall man with a white bandage or something plastered on his nose. He might be worth something."

Looshan took the proffered goggles, but hesitated.

Busuri waved him off. "Go."

\*\*\*

After George's speech, the abysmal attitude of the volunteers improved. Before long, spontaneous laughter covered the normal nocturnal noises. Conversation erupted, and the group returned to its pre-attack positive interactions.

Alf walked over to George. "You handled things well. You're a natural at helping others."

"Thanks. It's something Granny taught me."

"I wish I had a granny like yours."

"She's not always easy to deal with, but she's always right." George yawned, stretching his arms in the air. "Think I'll call it an evening."

Alf nodded. "Sounds like a plan."

George and Alf left the few remaining people at the campfire and headed back to the tent they shared. Lights were extinguished throughout the camp as others also retired.

\*\*\*

Looshan slid down the embankment into the wadi, searching for his leader. "Busuri, we know which tent the tall man is using. Another man is with him."

"Excellent. We'll wait for the camp to fall asleep before our attack. Tell the others to prepare. We'll break into three groups—you'll be with me."

"At once, Busuri."

Minutes stretched into hours as Busuri bided his time. *Two or three hostages would be perfect. I'll show Tahliil I'm as successful as Dacar.*

Busuri gazed at the heavens, thousands of stars twinkling. He found his omen—the narrowest sliver of moonlight, shaped like a *billaawe*, the Somali double-edged dagger. *Perfect tool for this evening.*

He nudged Looshan, who did the same to the man next to him until they all stood, circling Busuri.

"We attack now. Looshan and two others will follow me." Busuri divided the remaining men into two groups. "Each team will hit one tent, grab whoever is there, and depart. Be fast but quiet—don't wake anyone else. They will panic when they find empty tents."

The men grinned as they climbed to the top of the wadi and crawled through the brush and grass toward their prey. Silent, they slithered into the camp, until they reached their targets.

Two men pulled the tent flaps open, allowing Busuri and Looshan to enter. Knives drawn, they rushed to the sleeping foreigners.

George stirred, eyes opening when the hilt of a dagger clipped the side of his head. "What? Who's there?"

A hand covered George's mouth as a dagger traced a line down his chin to his throat.

"Sshhh. Make a sound—you die."

George froze until hands grabbed and pulled him out of his bed. He lashed out, landing a right hook to Looshan's jaw.

Busuri swung his knife. Before he connected, George dropped to the floor.

One of Busuri's men stood over George's body grinning, a wooden club in his hand.

"Grab him and let's go."

Looshan and the other man subdued Alf before he woke. The four men left the tent, pulling their captives. Except for an occasional rustle of clothing and soft grunts from dragging their captives, the camp remained quiet.

Back at the wadi, Busuri's team assembled. With them, George, Alf, and a foreign woman with long, dark hair.

"Well done. We have our prizes. Let's head home."

\*\*\*

Several hours later, a phone rang twice before someone answered. "This is the British Embassy in Nairobi. How may I direct your call?"

"Hello, I'm Ian Jones, the Jujubba Refugee Camp coordinator near Malindi. We need help. Prince George has been kidnapped!"

## Chapter Twenty-One

Aboard The *Ventrusco*
Port Said


Trevor shook Rooble's hand. *Is he part of the Somali pirate gang? I need to watch out for him.*

"I'll leave you two to become acquainted." Luigi headed to the food line as Trevor and Rooble followed.

Once Trevor and his new partner had filled their plates, they joined Gerhard and the others. Introductions made, the men dug into their meal.

"Ag, man, you're not eating any meat. You need to eat proper food." Gerhard flexed a massive bicep. "See this? Comes from the right food and plenty of weightlifting."

"Where I grew up, meat was a rarity. I get my protein from an egg a day. We lived near the ocean, so we also ate a lot of fish." Rooble spooned eggs into his mouth and chewed before frowning. "Like rubber."

"Today's are worse than normal." Trevor pushed his plate back and stood. "Rooble, if you're finished, I'll show you the duties Luigi gave us."

\*\*\*

After Trevor and Rooble had departed, Fergus shook his head. "I don't like Trevor's new partner. There's something about him—I'm not sure what, but he bears watching."

"I caught Trevor's nod toward the guy when he stood." Nate drained the last of his coffee. "Our duties don't begin for an hour, so let's tour the ship, and keep an eye on him."

Pun jabbed Gerhard in the stomach before jumping back and standing. "You eat too much. Work now."

\*\*\*

Trevor and Rooble made their way to the refrigerated hold. As they checked the connections on the cooling pipes, Trevor pointed to an open space.

"This is where Marco received his injuries yesterday. We must use caution when we remove any connections."

"Okay. What's next?"

"After we finish examining the joints here, we'll move to the next hold and do the same. Luigi said several refrigerated containers will be removed this afternoon." *Let's hope there aren't any more accidents.*

The day sped by as they continued with their tasks, Trevor showing Rooble the procedures he had learned from Marco.

In the mess for a quick lunch, Luigi approached their table. "Here are the four containers to be unloaded this afternoon." He handed a bill of lading to Trevor.

"Should Rooble and I handle these alone or will someone else help?"

"Since this is the last of the containers to be removed today, Fergus and Nate will help you. Your shift will be finished once they're transferred. Enjoy the rest of the day and evening in Port Said—we transit the Suez Canal tomorrow."

"What time should we be back on board?"

"By seven a.m. We depart an hour later."

\*\*\*

After the chilled containers were removed from the hold, the work teams left the ship to spend some time roaming through Port Said before their departure.

Rooble turned to the others. "I'm meeting a friend later, so I'm going to change. What are you doing this evening?"

"I'll have a quiet dinner and an early night." Trevor glanced at the others. "Don't forget to be back on the ship by seven a.m., or we might leave you behind."

"Ha ha. Wouldn't be the first time a ship sailed without me. Enjoy the evening."

"Anyone up for a stroll through the city before dinner?" Nate nudged Fergus.

"I tink a brisk walk to stretch my legs is what I need."

Nate whispered to Trevor. "We'll give Rooble a chance to go ahead before following. By the way, this afternoon he slid a wrench into his belt while you worked with him. It makes me wonder if he's the mystery man who clobbered Marco."

"I thought the same thing." Trevor rubbed his chin with his thumb and index finger. "Might be a good idea to figure out what he's up to."

"Pun and I are staying in a room next to his. If the door is open, we'll check his belongings." Gerhard shrugged. "If it's locked, I'm sure Pun will find a way inside."

"Everyone be careful. Why don't we meet for dinner at the El Borg around eight p.m." Trevor yawned. "I'll take a snooze, check for updates, and meet everyone later."

When Trevor arrived at the Port Said Pensione, where the ship's crew stayed while in the city, he climbed the rickety external stairs to the third floor. His room was to the right as he entered.

Trevor checked the thin piece of filament he had stretched across the bottom of the doorframe when he left in the morning. Still in place.

He booted his laptop and sent a short email.

*To: Topaz*
*From: Black*
*Injured Italian partner unable to return to work. Replaced by a Somali named Rooble, who is under our surveillance. Ship scheduled to depart Port Said tomorrow morning.*

After sending the message, Trevor took a shower, changed, and headed to the restaurant. *Something about Rooble is off-kilter. Wonder what my team will learn?*

An hour later, the team straggled in, joining Trevor at a circular wooden table on the waterfront terrace. Various ship names were carved in the top, an informal record of those passing time in the city.

An attentive waiter took their seafood orders and scurried away. Nate leaned forward to speak over the cacophony of shouts, whistles, singing, and clapping.

"Rooble met three men at a dingy restaurant about four blocks away." Nate scanned the immediate area, ensuring no one paid attention to them. "Couldn't hear what they said, but they appeared to know one another. After a waiter brought them food, we headed here."

"Pun and I gained access to his room." Gerhard smiled as he nudged Pun. "Our little friend here opened the door in under ten seconds. We searched the room, and he made an excellent discovery."

"He bad man." Pun shook a finger in the air. "I find knife, garrote, and satellite phone in plastic bag in toilet."

Gerhard took over. "I checked the phone. One number in the memory, with calls to and from." He slid a slip of paper over. "Here's the number."

"Excellent work, guys. I'll forward this information tonight. Gerhard and Pun, after you eat, pick up Rooble's trail and find out what you can."

Pun jumped to his feet. "We go now. Eat later."

"Ag, man. Let me grab something—I'm starved." Gerhard grabbed a couple of rolls from a covered basket, downed his Coke, and followed Pun out of the restaurant.

After a meal comprised of a seafood combo, pasta, and soft drinks, Trevor, Nate, and Fergus returned to the pensione. Trevor provided an update.

*To: Topaz*
*From: Black*
*Additional information regarding the Somali named Rooble. Team infiltrated his room, locating a knife, garrote, and Sat phone with single number. Met with three men, believed to be Somali. Identify number and advise.*

\*\*\*

Pun and Gerhard followed Nate's directions to the restaurant where he and Fergus left Rooble. A ramshackle building, wooden shutters clung to either side of small windows. Grease stains streaked the glass, but the aroma of cooking meats and vegetables drew a steady if somewhat seedy clientele.

When they arrived, Rooble was leaning against the counter near a cash register. He dropped a few bills on his check and headed out the door. Alone, he wandered toward Pun and Gerhard.

Pulling back into the shadows, they ducked behind an overflowing dumpster. Putrid odors seeped from the refuse, several cats screeched and yowled as they fought over delectable morsels. After giving Rooble time to pass, they eased forward to the street, Pun swiping at something clinging to his right shoulder.

Rooble sauntered along the narrow streets, lined with still-open shops, merchants hawking their wares: food, clothing, and perfume. The scent of a marijuana cigarette floated in the air, bringing him to a halt.

He glanced over his shoulder before crossing the street. Laughter erupted from a group of teens shoving one another as they raced around several public benches and street lamps.

Gerhard tapped Pun on the shoulder. He pointed ahead for Pun to remain on this side of the street while he used a slow-moving car as a shield. He ducked while he crossed over, staying well behind their target.

Rooble maintained his stroll, paying little apparent attention to his surroundings. At the entrance to a narrow alley, he glanced to his right and stepped over some trash piled by an overflowing bin.

Gerhard remained behind two couples walking arm-in-arm. They stopped at an open doorway and headed into an apartment building. Gerhard passed them and approached the alley. As he crossed the broken pavement, his senses kicked in.

Too late—an arm shot out of the darkness, a knife swiped across Gerhard's right shoulder before he responded. Blood streaming from the wound, he grabbed the knife hand as a tall, thin man stepped forward, attempting to impale him.

With a twist of the man's hand, he shoved the assailant against the corner of the building, snapping the radius bone near the wrist.

His attacker screamed. The knife clattered on the ground. He ran away as a second man swung a long pipe at Gerhard's head.

Falling to the ground, Gerhard used a cross block, taking control of the pipe. He smashed the man's right knee, hit him in the kidney, the liver, stepped around, punched him in the other kidney and then hit him in the temple.

By the time Gerhard dispatched both assailants, Pun had raced across the street. A third man, dressed in black from head to toe, aimed a pistol at Gerhard's back.

Pun pulled his kukri and released it with the accuracy he'd acquired from past experience. A dull thud, followed by a banshee wail from the attacker, demonstrated Pun's aim. The assassin fell against the side of the building, unmoving. Retrieving the kukri, Pun searched the area for further danger.

Satisfied the danger had passed, Pun helped an unsteady Gerhard back to his feet. "We go ship. Visit doctor."

Gerhard nodded, the blood loss making him dizzy. "Lead the way, Pun. Call Trevor and tell him."

After Pun had spoken with Trevor, he placed an arm around the back of his friend, and they staggered toward the port. They moved in the shadows as much as possible to avoid any awkward questions.

Back at the ship, Trevor waited by the gangway. He rushed forward as Pun and Gerhard approached. "The doctor's waiting for you." *What next? Attacks are escalating.*

Trevor and Pun assisted Gerhard up the gangway. They entered sick bay, where the doctor, a bald and stooped man, waited. He helped Gerhard remove his shirt before he staunched the bleeding. "Tsk, tsk." The doctor shook his head. "We'll fix you."

"Ag, man. No needles. I hate needles."

"You require stitches, young man. Let this be a lesson—no fighting." He cleaned the wound. "Hmmm. I think you'll need a tetanus shot, too."

Gerhard rolled his eyes and grimaced but remained quiet while the doctor closed the wound with nine stitches.

"Ow! You stabbed me."

The room filled with laughter after Gerhard received his tetanus injection.

Luigi, with apparent concern etched upon his face, appeared next to Trevor. "What happened?"

"Nothing to worry about. Pun and Gerhard went out for an evening stroll, when a gang attacked them. They defended themselves, but Gerhard received a small cut on his shoulder."

Luigi nodded. "Perhaps a good idea to return to the ship early for safety."

"I agree. After the doc takes care of Gerhard, we'll collect our things from the pensione and come back."

\*\*\*

Their meager belongings retrieved, the team returned to the ship. They sat in the mess, a pot of strong, black coffee on the table. Trevor poured the steaming drink for those who wanted it. He sipped the brew before adding sugar.

"Right. Events appear to be escalating around us. Will be interesting to find out if Rooble returns to the ship before we sail. If he does, I want Nate and Fergus to continue monitoring his activities."

The two men nodded.

"What Gerhard and I do?"

"Pun, you'll continue your duties and stay away from Rooble—for now. Unless advised otherwise, we'll continue our mission. Questions?"

Fergus raised a hand. "If Rooble returns and does something suspicious, should we capture him?"

"Yes. We'll worry about fallout from Luigi later. If nothing else, let's call it a night."

Trevor returned to his cabin and booted his laptop. A message waited for him.

*To: Black*

*From: Topaz*

*Sat number associated with al-Shabaab leader Tahliil. Continue to monitor Rooble's activities and apprehend if necessary. Acknowledge.*

Trevor nodded as he read and composed a response.

*To: Topaz*

*From: Black*

*Instructions acknowledged.*

*This evening Green was attacked by three men, believed to be those seen with Rooble. Minor cut, stitched by ship's doctor. One attacker escaped, another rendered unconscious, final man terminated. No identity papers. Believed to be Somalis.*

\*\*\*

The *Ventrusco* departed from Port Said as scheduled. The ship followed others into the blue-green water as intense sunlight beat down upon the travelers. The canal's banks contrasted with the water: sand, swatches of green, and scattered signs of civilization.

Luigi approached Trevor. "The transit takes about fifteen hours. Every five hours check the refrigerator connectors. The rest of the time, enjoy the sights. We are making an unscheduled stop in Port Safaga. The owners want several containers picked up and dropped in Mombasa."

"Okay, Luigi. I haven't seen Rooble since we departed. Did he return to the ship?"

"No. Not sure why. Have your friends assist with the connector checks."

"Right." *Wonder what happened to Rooble.*

The remainder of the day passed without incident. Before docking in Port Safaga, Trevor checked his email.

*To: Black*

*From: Topaz*

*Team to disembark from ship upon arrival in Port Safaga. Situation is evolving but primary mission may become secondary due to the abduction of Prince George.*

*Further information will be provided forthwith. Prepare for team split into two groups and if possible, continue with both missions.*

*Ship's owner informed. Replacement crew is waiting in Port Safaga.*

Trevor acknowledged the latest communiqué and gathered his team to explain the kidnapping of Prince George. "We'll leave the ship in Port Safaga. We're splitting up. Pun and Gerhard will head to Somalia to track Prince George's kidnappers. Nate, Fergus, and I will proceed to Mombasa, where we'll wait for further instructions."

"Any intel about the kidnappers?" Nate worked a six-inch knife along a whetstone as he prepared one of his favorite weapons.

"Nothing definitive yet. They're believed to be a different faction of al-Shabaab than the hijackers."

Nate finished sharpening his knife and ran the blade along his forearm to test its sharpness. "I hope I meet them."

\*\*\*

After the *Ventrusco* docked in Port Safaga, the Bedlam Bravo team stopped at the top of the gangway where Luigi waited for them. "Thank you for your hard work while onboard. I don't know where you are going, but good luck."

"Ag, man, we make our own luck." Gerhard shook Luigi's hand, followed by the others. Nearby, a British Royal Navy Sea King helicopter waited, its rotors moving in the breeze.

A crewman helped them board. "Not sure who you guys are, but the captain said to pick you up. The *HMS Swansea* was diverted from our mission by the Admiralty, so must be something important."

Trevor shrugged. "We go where they send us. Not always important, but interesting all the same."

# Chapter Twenty-Two

Liberian Freighter *Krumen*
Outside Cambodian Waters

A rusted freighter chugged through the evening's calm waters toward Sihanoukville. Thousands of stars twinkled in the heavens above Cambodia, while a sliver of a new moon ventured forth. Concealed in the hold, a shipment of weapons, an advance payment by the North Korean government to Somali pirates in exchange for much-needed oil.

The *Krumen*, flying a Liberian flag of convenience, had departed from the North Korean port of Wonsan seven days ago on its journey to Sihanoukville. Upon arrival, Ambassador Soo would hand over the weapons to a representative from the pirates.

He leaned over the rail, dropped pieces of paper, which twirled toward the frothy water and disappeared. *I hope Jung Gi and the boys are okay. I miss them.* Soo wiped the tears trickling down his face. *I miss them so much.*

He heard soft footsteps approach. He turned as Kim approached, carrying two glasses. "Tea."

Soo sipped the lukewarm beverage and grimaced. "No sugar?"

"They didn't bring any." Kim waved toward the water, emptying his glass over the rail. "Should have drunk the water—room temperature, but better than this." He faced the ambassador. "Is something the matter?"

"No. Yes—I don't know." Soo wrung his hands. "I—perhaps later." He turned and headed to a door leading inside the freighter.

***

The following morning, Soo and Kim met for breakfast. They grabbed a table in the corner, away from the crew. Several men stared at them, one running a finger across his neck, and uttered a chilling laugh.

Soo shook his head as shivers ran down his spine. "I don't like the crew. No respect for us."

"Never mind, Ambassador. We hired them to transport our weapons. Once they're delivered, we won't use this crew again."

"You're right." Soo pursed his lips and squinted. "I deserve better."

Kim pushed his plate away. "The food is worse every day. Do you suppose someone is trying to poison us?"

Soo dropped his fork with a clatter. "What? Do you think so?"

"Relax." A smile creased Kim's face. "I'm trying to lighten things up. We're getting too serious. If you're finished, let's go for our morning walk around the deck."

Dressed in a white jacket and black trousers, Soo slipped on his sunglasses. Kim followed, wearing his usual black attire.

They weaved their way along the deck, stepping through trash-strewn areas. Reaching the stern, they leaned against the rail, watching the white foam in their wake.

Soo reached into his pocket and pulled out a small gift-wrapped package. "I almost forgot. This is for you."

Kim took the offering and bowed. "What is it?"

"Open the package and find out."

With a grin like a child receiving a present for the first time, Kim removed the wrapping. Inside was a gold-colored box. He opened the gift and removed the contents from a cushion of red velvet paper.

Soo clapped his hands with delight as Kim donned a pair of Ray-Ban sunglasses, a perfect match for those perched on his own nose.

They continued their walk when a crewman rushed up to them. "Captain wants you. Now. Come with me." The man turned and stormed away.

Soo and Kim glanced at each other. "Wonder what he wants now?" Kim shook his head. "Another bribe?"

"He's received plenty of our country's hard-earned foreign currency. We'll have to send more of our workers abroad to earn more."

They scurried to catch up with the crewman. Entering the wheelhouse, they found the captain waiting, hands resting on his hips, a scowl etched upon his scarred face.

He pointed a long claw-like hand at Soo. "You. No tell crew what to do. Eat food like everyone else."

"I am Ambassador Soo. You will address me in the proper manner. My country hired you to transport our cargo without interference." A newfound courage pushed Soo forward. "This rust bucket will be fortunate to complete the voyage."

The captain stepped back at Soo's onslaught, a brief smile showing broken teeth. "So, the pudgy man has a little bite. Well, Ambassador, on this ship I make rules. My crew not servants." He glanced at Kim. "You have own servant—make him do jobs."

*Insolent man. Back home he'd go to prison—or worse.* "I shall report your behavior to the Supreme Leader."

"You do that." The captain snapped his fingers. "We have other business. You remain in hold."

Four crewmen appeared, two grabbing each Korean. They manhandled Kim and Soo out the door, force-marching them onto the deck.

Down in the hold, they were shoved into a dark, windowless room and the door slammed shut. The twisting of a key in the rusty lock echoed over the laughter of the four men.

Soo pounded on the door. "Let us out of here. At once!" He worked the handle up and down.

Kim tried the door but it didn't budge. "Ambassador, save your strength. We're locked in and nothing we can do about our situation at the moment. We will wait for our opportunity and take action."

Soo turned and pressed his back on the door and slid to the floor. "How can you be so calm? This can't be happening."

Kim continued his search of the room. "I can't find anything. The room appears empty, except for us." He returned to Soo and sat on the floor next to him.

"My life—my life is in ruins." Soo slapped the wall with the flat of his hand. "Ever since Wook took my family, nothing remains as before."

"What do you mean about the Supreme Leader taking your family? Why?"

*Do I tell him? What's the difference?*

"I grew up with Wook and we were best friends. He even attended my wedding."

"What happened to make Wook take your family?"

"He wasn't pleased with how I represented the country to the Chinese—said I gave in to them without pushing for our birth rights."

"What did he do?"

"He took my boys and is holding them as ransom for me to do his bidding. Even worse—he sent my precious Jung Gi to the Chongori correctional facility." Sobs racked Soo's body. "His own sister!"

Kim's eyes bulged at the revolution, but he remained silent as Soo wept.

After several minutes, he regained some composure. "Please don't tell anyone about my secret. No one outside Wook and my family is aware of my connections."

*Of course, Nari knows—she knows everything.*

"Your secret is safe with me." Kim noticed the ship slowing, the vibrations from the overworked engines coming to a halt. "I think the ship is stopping. We're still far from land—must be another ship approaching."

Unable to check the time, they had no idea how long the ship remained stationary. After some time, the engine vibrated.

*Craack. Craack. Craack.*

"What?" Soo grabbed Kim's arm.

Muffled screams rose in intensity as additional AK-47s opened up. The anguish of the injured diminished as they appeared to succumb to their wounds.

"Perhaps a mutiny or maybe pirates have attacked. We'll know soon."

A large explosion rocked the ship as it gathered speed. The ship righted itself, and continued on its journey.

A few minutes later, voices echoed in the hallway. Soo jumped to his feet, banged on the door, and yelled. "Let us out."

The key screeched in the lock. The door yanked open, four armed crewmen stood in the narrow passageway. "You can come out now. Our private negotiation with a business associate is finished. No more competitor."

The men grabbed Kim and Soo by the arms and hurried them along the corridor and back to the captain.

"Welcome back, my friends." He spat on the floor. "You help cook, make tea for crew. When finished, I want new weapons. From you." The captain waved a hand in dismissal, and the crewmen took them to the galley.

Grease splattered the floor and work surfaces. Soo and Kim helped the cook prepare the tea. As before, they used lukewarm water.

Soo grumbled to Kim. "This is beneath us. We've paid them to deliver us to Sihanoukville. What does this mean for us? What will the Supreme Leader say if I relay the captain's demand? What about my wife and children?"

"Calm down, Ambassador. We should be at our destination in a day or so. Once our cargo is unloaded, we will be finished with the captain and his crew."

"I still don't like this."

\*\*\*

Two days later, the *Krumen* pulled into a berth in Sihanoukville. Their cargo wouldn't be transferred until after dark, so Soo and Kim headed ashore for a prearranged meeting.

A tuk-tuk deposited them in front of the Orange Supermarket on Ekareach Street. They paid the driver and walked along the street, Kim using shop windows to monitor for any possible surveillance.

Oblivious to Kim's tradecraft, Soo hurried from one storefront to another. Music blared from speakers anchored in the walls and the cacophony added to the din caused by tourists. The aroma of spices, grilled meat, and seafood wafted on the warm air currents.

Kim guided Soo into a crowd waiting to cross the street at a traffic light. Tired of waiting for the light to change, people surged forward, taking Kim and Soo with them. Noting their destination on the other side of the street, they stopped at a nearby shop.

Satisfied they had no obvious tail, the men dashed through a myriad of tuk-tuks, motor scooters, and wandering pedestrians before entering the Holy Cow Restaurant.

Out of breath, Soo slipped his sunglasses to the top of his head and sat at a table by the door. Kim shook his head, indicating an area at the back of the restaurant.

As they approached, Soo recognized a man seated at the table. *Dacar.*

The Somali stood and gave a short bow to Soo and Kim. He turned to another man at the table and made the introductions. "Ambassador Soo and Kim, this is my second-in-command, Sahid."

After the four men sat, a waiter brought tea and departed. Dacar acted as host and served the others. He lifted his cup in the air. "To a successful conclusion of our business."

Soo returned the gesture while the others remained stoic.

"Ambassador, since you are here, am I correct in assuming the shipment arrived?"

"Yes. The captain of the *Krumen* can verify this or I can show you."

"You may introduce us to the captain. Sahid and I will sail with the ship when she departs tomorrow."

"When should we expect the first oil tanker?" *I must complete this arrangement to show Wook I'm doing my best.*

"As we agreed, the ship will be handed over in about two weeks." Dacar wriggled his right hand in the air, open palm. "A second tanker is being tracked now and should be in our possession soon."

Soo stared at Dacar. "We expect you to uphold your commitment." *Or my family is finished.*

"Don't worry—you'll receive your oil, as long as the weapons keep flowing." Dacar pushed his chair back and stood. "Let's go to the ship. I want to inspect the weapons."

\*\*\*

Sahid dry-fired several weapons. He didn't know the firing pins had been sabotaged and smiled when he pulled the trigger and received a satisfying click.

Dacar looked over a few opened weapon crates and nodded at the Koreans. They left the ship, feeling as if a weight was lifted from their backs. A warm and starry night, they strolled through the port.

"It's been a long day, Ambassador." Kim put a hand on the ambassador's shoulder. "Let's head to the hotel."

Soo yawned. "I can't wait to return to Pyongyang and inform the Supreme Leader we've completed this stage of the mission."

"It will still be two days before we arrive. There are three flights before we return home." *Perhaps the freighter will be approaching Somali waters before the pirates check all the weapons. Soo doesn't know what I've done.*

\*\*\*

A heavy-set man, his face hidden behind a latex clown mask, lowered the night scope. "Follow them."

The unmarked, battered van edged along the quay. The two Koreans seemed to pay no attention to the vehicle until it sped forward.

Tires squealing, the van skidded to a stop. The side door opened. Four men wearing balaclavas jumped out. They grabbed Kim and Soo and bundled them into the vehicle. The door slammed shut, the driver floored the accelerator. The well-tuned engine revved and raced through the port's gate and into the night.

The man in the passenger seat glanced at Soo and Kim. "We meet again."

Soo stared at the man. "You!"

## Chapter Twenty-Three

Kidnapper's Camp
Outside Kidi Faani, Somalia

A lion's roar shattered the pre-dawn calm. Baboons screeched and sought safety in the trees.

Jamiila Shamso listened to the morning sounds as the sun rose. Unable to sleep, she'd laid awake for the past two hours. *I miss my children. My handsome Abuukar and beautiful Bayda. I long to hold them in my arms.*

She struggled to her feet, picked up the blanket, and walked over to the corner. Four young girls remained asleep on the concrete floor, using their blankets as pillows. Jamiila covered them with her blanket. *Sleep my darlings. Block out the nightmare we are living.*

One of the girls whimpered before settling. Jamiila stepped away and tiptoed to the water bucket. *Almost empty.* After quenching her thirst, she picked up the bucket and approached the open doorway.

Jamiila crossed the compound toward the well. Chickens pecked at the dust for seeds and goats rummaged among a rubbish heap for something to eat, while two guards maintained a watchful eye on her.

"Where are you going?" Asad, the leader of the raiding party, appeared next to Jamiila.

"We-we are out of water. I wanted more for the children."

He took the bucket from her. "I will help you—this time. In the future, let the children draw the water. There's a small wooden bucket attached to a rope, which is lowered, filled, and pulled back up. The contents are poured into the larger ones."

After Asad finished filling her bucket, Jamiila thanked him.

"No problem. Remind the girls in your building not to leave the compound. Or you." Asad pulled an index finger across his throat.

She shuddered. "I will remind them. What do we do for breakfast?"

"This isn't a hotel. You must help the other women prepare the food. Go under the tree—they will show you what to do." Asad walked away.

Jamiila took the bucket to their building and joined two women by the lone tree in the center of the compound. "*Subax wanaagsan* (good morning). Asad sent me to work with you."

The women glanced at each other before introducing themselves. "Subax wanaagsan. I am Maryan. This is my sister, Khalli."

"Hello, Maryan and Khalli. Pleased to meet you."

"Thank you." Khalli, the taller of the two sisters at almost six feet, stepped forward and shook Jamiila's hand.

A moment later, Maryan followed. "We shall teach you how to survive in the camp. Feeding the men is one of our most important tasks."

The three women sat on a nearby bench under the massive damal tree. Its broad, overlapping branches and foliage provided the perfect shelter to escape the intense sunshine and heat.

Khalli laughed. "Along with washing their clothes and cleaning their buildings. Some of the men think we should bed them, too."

"Jamiila, Asad must be obeyed at all costs." Maryan glanced at Khalli and motioned for her to be quiet. "He is my son, and I love him. But, he's become a bit distant since joining al-Shabaab."

"Be careful around the men and try not to be alone with any of them." Khalli's eyes seemed to darken as they almost closed. "One of them tried to rape me. He would have except I pulled my knife and threatened to castrate him and feed his parts to him for breakfast."

Khalli clasped her arms around herself and shuddered. "I never told Asad—he would kill the man."

"All of them are a bit deranged." Maryan put her hand on Jamiila's arm and smiled. "Asad must like you. You're the first captive he sent to work with us."

"Do you think he will let me go?"

"He's not married—yet. Perhaps, he's considering you for himself. You're about the same age."

"I have two children. They are still at the Jujubba Refugee Camp."

"We must wait to find out what he's thinking. Allah will guide him. Come, we've talked enough and the men will be wanting their breakfast when they return with some fruit."

As Maryan spoke, several guards walked past, empty sacks over their shoulders and machetes in their hands.

Khalli and Maryan showed Jamiila where they kept food supplies in the closest building. Although musty inside, the floor remained dry. Onions and strings of hot peppers hung on hooks from the rafters while several bags contained rice, sorghum, chickpeas, and corn. Different baskets held tomatoes, carrots, and eggs. The aroma of various spices, including cumin, cardamom, cinnamon, and sage floated on the warm air currents. In the darkest corner, ten covered pitchers held fresh goat milk.

"This morning we have a treat. We've gathered enough eggs for every person, including those brought from the refugee camp, to receive one." Maryan beamed as she made this announcement. "This happens perhaps once a month."

"If the men wouldn't steal the eggs before we collect them, there would be more." Khalli rolled her eyes.

"Some of the men eat them raw, holding the egg over their mouth and cracking the shell. Disgusting!"

***

The guards returned laden with fruit they picked from the trees along the nearby river's embankment. They dropped their loads by the community benches and wandered away.

Jamiila helped Khalli and Maryan sort through the fruit. "My mouth's watering from seeing the ripe mangoes, papayas, and bananas."

Maryan laughed. "Since we prepare the breakfast, we sneak some for ourselves. I'll start on the papayas and Khalli will cut some mangoes. Jamiila, peel a dozen bananas and slice them into one of the empty buckets. We'll add the other fruit to it."

Once they prepared the fruit, Khalli returned to the storage building. She returned carrying a dented metal pail. Struggling with the weight, she almost dropped the container when she stumbled.

"Oops. Almost dropped the *sabaayad* (chapatis)!" Khalli set the pail next to the fruit. Jamiila added a stack of dented metal plates, scoured clean in the sand.

Maryan stepped forward, a small bell in her hand. A twist of her wrist and twin chimes summoned everyone for breakfast.

Khalli used a ladle and scooped fruit onto the plates, passing each one to Jamiila. She dropped a chapati on them, before handing them to Maryan, who doled them out.

Asad approached and received a plate ahead of the others. Before finding a seat, he stopped by Jamiila. "After you fill your plate, come sit next to me."

Jamiila nodded and blushed. She kept the last plate she filled for herself. Walking over to Asad, who sat on a small bench in the depths of the tree's shade, she waited for acknowledgment.

Asad poked a piece of banana wrapped in chapatti into his mouth. "Sit." He glanced around. "Please."

Jamiila sat and tore off a piece of the day-old bread and scooped up a slice of papaya. She bit off a small piece and chewed. *Seems so peaceful here. I wish Abuukar and Bayda were with me.*

Asad finished the last of his breakfast and stood. "After you eat, you will work with my mother and aunt in the vegetable garden."

"What do you grow?" Finished eating, Jamiila stood.

"Onions, carrots, peppers. Some corn. We can't grow much because we don't want the government to become nosy."

*You'd be arrested or killed. Perhaps soldiers will come and save us.* "I will do as you say."

"Instruct two of your girls to carry water from the well. The other two will obtain fertilizer and feed the plants."

"Where is the fertilizer?"

"Where else? The latrine. Not my first choice, but we must do what we can to survive."

*Ugh.* Jamiila shivered from the thought.

"Remind the girls the guards will be watching them. If they try to escape, well—they know the penalty."

"Yes, Asad."

"Go." He shooed her away. "Khalli and Maryan are waiting for you." Asad turned and strolled to the area where his men lounged.

*I hope we are saved. If not for my children, I'd try to escape, even if they kill me.*

\*\*\*

By the time the sun reached its zenith, everyone except two guards had retired to the buildings to escape the heat.

Jamiila ushered the girls inside. They leaned against the wall, the cool concrete providing some respite.

Jamiila almost gagged on the putrid odor filling the confined space. "You two! Go wash—everything! You stink like you fell in the latrine. Return after you are clean."

"Yes, Jamiila." The twin sisters ran from the hut.

Thirty minutes later, the girls returned. Jamiila gave them a sniff. "Much better. Time for rest."

Jamiila tossed and turned, dreaming of her children. *My babies!*

A hand touched her shoulder. Startled, Jamiila opened her mouth, but a scream was trapped in her throat when a calm voice spoke to her.

"Psst. It's Maryan. Time to prepare the evening meal."

The women headed to the communal area where Khalli swung a machete.

Whack!

She pushed something aside. The machete reached for the heavens when she struck again.

Whack!

As Maryan and Jamiila approached, the scent of fish and blood became strong.

Khalli glanced up and smiled. "One of the men caught some fish today. We'll make a curry."

Jamiila shuddered. "I don't like fish."

"We must do with what is provided. Two days ago, a goat." Maryan picked up a sharp knife and began filleting. "Now fish. Those living along the coast love fish, but not everyone does."

"I-I will try it." Jamiila reached out and touched the scales of the lifeless fish. "I must maintain my strength even if I must eat something new." *For the sake of my children. I pray we are united soon.*

\*\*\*

Once the women had prepared the meal, Maryan rang the bell. As before, the men ate first, followed by the captives, although Asad waited to the end.

"Jamiila, join me." Asad walked to his normal seat, Jamiila bringing a plate of stew for each of them.

She nibbled at a piece of white, flaky flesh and grimaced.

"First time eating fish?" Asad smiled as he scooped a handful of stew into his mouth.

"Yes. It-it's a strange flavor."

"I grew up on the Indian Ocean, so we ate fish most of the time. Healthy for you." Asad stared at Jamiila. "Food from the sea will make you strong, excellent for expectant mothers."

Jamiila blushed. "I'm not with child. Remember, I am a widow."

"Things change. Who knows what the future will hold? I've watched you with the young girls. You must be a good mother." Asad stared at the sky, filled with stars. "Will you remarry?"

"I-I don't know. Perhaps if I find the right man. First, I must find my children."

"Tell me about your village and your husband."

"Our village was small—no name. Five families, each with a cow and a few goats." A smile etched across Jamiila's face. "We slept under a huge tree with thorn bushes used as a fence. The breeze would shift the branches and rustle the leaves as if they were alive.

"We always ate at a communal table. Men first, followed by the children. The mothers ate the leftovers."

"What about your husband?"

"He was a distant cousin. At first, I didn't want to marry him. He was tall—and handsome." Jamiila gazed at Asad. "Like you."

Asad bowed his head.

"He is gone, so my children are my life."

"For the right incentive, perhaps they might be rescued."

Jamiila's heart jumped, a gleam in her eye. "What reason would create a rescue?"

"Marriage."

"I-I must think."

"No rush. Perhaps tomorrow or the next day we will leave here and head north to our main camp."

A commotion stopped their conversation. The four remaining captives from the second hut were brought in front of the men, tied to each other with small pieces of rope.

The men walked around the women, poking and prodding. Soft laughter floated on the breeze, as the men knelt in a circle while the women remained standing.

"Asad, what is happening?"

"One man will pick a woman tonight as his wife. They will play *shax* until one wins."

"They have no board."

"No, they will trace squares in the sand and use sticks and stone as the pieces. The final winner will choose his bride."

*How disgusting.* "What if the woman doesn't want the man?"

Asad shrugged. "It is our way."

\*\*\*

While the men continued their game, Jamiila helped Khalli and Maryan clean up. Afterward, she ushered her young charges into their building for the night. She sat on the floor near the door, watching the game.

Sporadic laughter and shouts continued as the game reached its climax. The victor shouted, jumped to his feet, and raced to the women.

He grabbed the arm of one and dragged her to an empty building while the losers whistled. The remaining women dashed back to their building. Jamiila moved to her makeshift bed.

Silence descended over the camp. The embers from the evening fire winked out one by one.

"*Aarrgh!*"

Jamiila jumped to her feet and glanced outside. Asad ran past, brandishing a small flaming branch, and entered the building where the shax winner had taken his bride.

Curious, everyone crowded around the hut.

Jamiila pushed through to Asad's side. "What happened?"

"The bride carried a hidden knife. She slit her husband's throat."

Jamiila moved forward but Asad stopped her.

"Don't. There is blood everywhere."

"Where is the bride? I will comfort her."

"She's beyond help." Asad glanced at the ground. "She used the knife on herself—a single blow to the heart."

## Chapter Twenty-Four

Jujubba Refugee Camp
Near Malindi, Kenya

A five-vehicle convoy with the Union Jack attached to the front fenders pulled into the refugee camp. Clouds of dust billowed as the brown Range Rovers slewed to a halt in the sand in front of the whitewashed administrative building.

Men in desert camouflage uniforms jumped out of the lead and trail vehicles, brandishing weapons and scanning for potential threats. The driver of the middle Range Rover opened the rear door as two additional soldiers took up defensive positions.

Out stepped a tall, thin man with silver hair, his gray suit a stark contrast to the soldiers' uniforms, pant legs flapping in the breeze. Brushing his shoulders to remove any dust, he glanced around, a grimace etched across his features.

Ian left the shade of the building's veranda, scrambled down the three steps, and approached the man. "Hello and welcome to Jujubba. I'm Ian Jones, the refugee camp coordinator." He held out his hand.

The man gazed at Ian with apparent disdain and ignored the proffered hand. "I am Reginald St. James, the second secretary at the British Embassy in Nairobi."

"Well, Reginal—"

"You may address me as Sir Reginald. Now, take me to the building used by Prince George."

"George, as we addressed him, didn't stay in a private building. He slept in a tent, like the rest of us."

"My God, man! You put the future king in a common tent?" He stared at Ian as if he wanted to squash him like a bug. "Have you no shame?"

Ian clenched his teeth, facial muscles rippling with anger. "When George arr—"

"Prince George."

"Once George arrived, he wanted to be treated like the other volunteers. My assistant and Alf, his tent mate, knew his true identity. No one else did."

"Oh, yes. Alf. Where is the incompetent moron who let the prince be captured?"

Ian crossed his arms and indicated with his head. "He's with your security people. Might be comparing notes."

"Hmmm. Trying to find an excuse for his dereliction of duty, more to the point."

"Aren't you being a bit hard on him?"

St. James turned and stared down at the shorter man. "No excuse is acceptable. Since he's still alive, it is quite apparent he did nothing to defend the prince or to prevent his abduction."

"You don't know the circumstances regarding George's disappearance."

"Have no doubt, after acquainting myself with the facts, my report for the ambassador will contain the smallest detail of this lamentable situation. I wish to speak with you before I converse with him. Should I detect a hint of collusion, that too, will be included for the ambassador to deal with as he sees fit." Hands behind his back, St. James glared about the compound. "In the meantime, can you manage a spot of tea and perhaps a scone or two? I'm parched after the long journey."

"No scones, but some Earl Gray. There is raspberry jam to spread on a chapatti."

"Heavens. You do live rough here. No matter, it will do for now."

\*\*\*

Alf approached the men milling around the middle Range Rover. They spoke in quiet voices, but conversation ceased when he joined them.

The team leader nodded at Alf, before grabbing him in a bear hug and lifting him off the ground. "Alfie! Way to go, losing an heir to the throne!"

"Put me down, Mikey. What will the others think?"

Both men broke into laughter and slapped each other on the back.

"Guys, may I introduce the former Corporal Alfred Livingston of 16 Air Assault Brigade. You wouldn't know by his appearance, but Alfie's done a number of hush-hush operations—Iraq, Afghanistan, and a few places we've never admitted to visiting."

After a round of handshakes, Mike and Alf moved away for a private conversation.

Mike tugged a red beret from his head and used a shirtsleeve to wipe the perspiration from his face. "How do you handle the heat here? I'm soaking."

Alf laughed. "The climate hit me the same way when I first came to Jujubba. I became accustomed to the heat and humidity, so it's no longer an issue."

"You can keep it, mate."

"So, what's with the prima donna? You along to wipe his nose and pick him up when he falls?"

"Ha-ha!" Mike glanced at Ian and Sir Reginald. "He's a hereditary peer. His father used his influence to acquire a posting to Nairobi. When the defense attaché learned Sir Reginald was coming here to investigate Prince George's disappearance, he asked me to provide personal security and run interference."

"What kind of interference?"

"To be honest, the colonel wanted me to undo any problems created by Sir Reginald before a major diplomatic row erupted."

"From the commotion in the few minutes since you arrived, I believe the colonel's assessment is correct."

"So. How did you lose Prince George?" Mike waved a hand in dismissal. "A big strapping lad like you should have been able to handle a few intruders."

"With the right weapons, sure. However, George stated in no uncertain terms I would be only allowed one pistol and a knife. Nothing else. I agreed to abide by his wishes."

"What about your hand-to-hand combat experience? How did they—"

One of the local boys who helped the volunteers ran up to Alf and tugged at his sleeve. "Come, Mr. Alf. You must come. Mr. Ian and the man who speaks funny want to talk with you."

"Off you go, mate. I'll catch up with you after the interrogation." Mike laughed and returned to his team.

\*\*\*

Alf trotted up the stairs and across the veranda to Ian's office. After brushing the dust from his clothing, he knocked on the door and walked in.

"You wanted to speak with me?" Alf noted Sir Reginald occupied Ian's seat behind his desk, while Ian sat on a straight-backed chair. He motioned to an empty chair next to him, and Alf slid onto the hard seat.

Sir Reginald glared at Ian. "I demand—"

Ian waved his hands and shook his head. "You may ask questions, but you won't demand anything. The embassy maintains no jurisdiction over Save the World, which is an international organization headquartered in Switzerland. Your concern should be for the prince's safety—nothing else."

"Harrumph!" Sir Reginald scribbled in a notebook. "I suppose you're right. So, young man, why didn't you protect Prince George?"

"I didn't hear anything in time to respond. When I awoke, a man stood over George with a knife to his throat. I tried to reach under my cot for my SIG S—"

"What's that?"

"My pistol, a SIG Sauer P226. I kept the SIG in a holster under the corner of my bed. I had pulled it out when my arm was yanked back, causing me to drop my weapon."

Alf closed his eyes as he focused on the events. "I struggled with the intruder when something hard hit the back of my head. I-I blacked out."

"What did you do next?"

"When I came to, I was bound and gagged, and in what appeared to be a narrow wadi. The moon cast sufficient light—across from me sat George and a foreign woman with long, dark hair. They were bound and gagged."

Sir Reginald took additional notes before nodding to Alf to continue.

"My hands were also tied, but I worked them free. I pulled out the gag and scanned our area for a means of escape. About a dozen armed men rested nearby. I removed George's gag and as I went to untie him and the woman, someone spotted me.

"The man yelled and fired his AK in my direction. George told me to run for help. I took off as several weapons opened fire. Two rounds hit me—a graze along the left side of my head and the other nicked my arm.

"The kidnappers gave chase, but I hid until they gave up. Afterward, I returned to the camp and notified Ian."

"Well, young man, in my opinion, you panicked. Concerned about saving your own worthless life, you abandoned the others." Sir Reginald's face wrinkled with disdain. "My report will indicate this and I'm recommending charges be made against you."

Alf jumped to his feet. "You arrogant ass! I did as George instructed. In hindsight, I should have stayed with him and been taken to wherever." He jabbed a finger at Sir Reginald. "We have a chance to find him and if you or anyone else dares to stand in my way, I won't be responsible for the consequences!"

Ian stood in front of Alf. "Go outside. I'll finish this." He put an arm on his shoulder. "I understand you did what you thought best under the circumstances. We'll find George."

"Yes, sir." Alf stormed out of the room without a backward glance, slamming the door behind him. He jumped down the steps and stomped towards Mike.

"Hey, Alfie, what happened? We caught the shouting."

"Th-that pompous buffoon riled me. Said I'm to blame for George's capture. He's going to have me charged!"

"Relax, Alfie. Sir Reginald's a blithering idiot. Give me the details and I'll pass them to the defense attaché, who will file his own report through the Defense Ministry."

The men leaned against the middle Range Rover, while Alf relived the events of the fateful evening. Mike pulled a small binder from his pocket and made periodic notes. When Alf finished, Mike replaced the notepad, bringing out a small envelope.

"This is from the colonel."

Alf ripped open the buff-colored envelope.

*To: Corporal Alfred Livingston*
*From: Colonel John Parker*

*A dreadful situation. I've spoken with a representative from the Royal Family and they insist you be included in any attempts to rescue Prince George. They assign no blame to you, knowing George would insist on minimal security.*

*Within the next forty-eight hours, a small team will arrive. You will render them all assistance. They will identify themselves as Topaz.*

*Good luck and may you find our future king.*

Alf gave Mike the note to read.

"Who is Topaz?" Alf pointed at the sheet of paper in Mike's hand. "Don't recollect the name."

"Someone associated with Topaz contacted Colonel Parker. He said they know their stuff, even if they might be a bit unconventional."

"I'll do whatever I can to help rescue George."

The door to the administration building flew open and bounced off the wall as Sir Reginald and Ian stepped out. They walked to the Range Rover.

Sir Reginald gazed at Alf before turning to Ian. "I'll be in touch. Keep me informed of any developments." Once again ignoring Ian's hand, he climbed into the vehicle.

Mike shrugged. "Take care, Alfie. I'll send you any scuttlebutt I learn."

"Thanks, Mikey."

\*\*\*

Thirty-six hours later, Ian and Alf had finished a light dinner and sat in the office. Subdued conversation ensued, centering on the kidnapping of George and Silvia Stefani, the Italian aid worker seized with the prince.

The whispery sound of a well-tuned engine floated on a warm breeze. The motor silenced, the nighttime chorus of insects returned. Ian and Alf jumped to their feet, but before they checked on the new arrival, someone knocked on the door.

The door popped open. Two men entered, one bald and built like a wrestler, the other at least a foot shorter, with a swarthy complexion and piercing dark eyes. Both were dressed in black uniforms, boots, and berets. They scanned the room before their eyes rested on the occupants.

The tall man pointed at Ian. "You are Ian, the camp coordinator." He turned his attention to Alf. "You are Corporal Alfred Livingston. Please confirm."

After they verified their identities, the hulk pointed to himself. "I am Gerhard Badenhorst from the South African Special Forces Brigade. My friend is former Gurkha Sergeant Agam Bahadir Pun of the Second Battalion, the Royal Gurkha Rifles."

The four men shook hands. As Ian extracted crumpled fingers from Gerhard's grasp, he asked, "We know your names, but why are you here? This is a refugee camp, not a military base."

"Ag, man. We are Topaz."

## Chapter Twenty-Five

Bedlam Headquarters
Whitehall, London, England

A black hackney carriage rumbled across Vauxhall Bridge, carrying the sole passenger away from his meeting with the heads of various intelligence agencies. Dressed in a navy-blue Saville Row suit, Sir Alex stroked his trimmed black beard with a manicured hand. His other hand beat a rhythmic tune on the locked attaché case perched on the seat next to him.

After crossing the bridge, the cab meandered through London's streets until arriving at the Old War Office Building in Whitehall. Lost in thought, the distinguished gentleman made no attempt to disembark.

"Ahem, Guv'nor." The taxi driver tipped an imaginary cap as he glanced at his fare in the rearview mirror. "Your destination, squire."

He shook his head to clear the cobwebs. "Thank you, Giles. We'll settle our account with your company. Until the next time."

Giles opened the door and smiled. "Always a pleasure, Sir Alex."

He walked a short distance along the pavement before entering through an unobtrusive side door. The armed Ministry of Defence police officer checked his identification and waved him forward.

"Good day, innit, Sir Alex." The guard clicked a button, allowing an inner door to open.

"Afternoon, Arthur." Sir Alex stepped into the hallway and headed to his office.

The door popped opened. Alice Worthington, his personal assistant, smiled at him. "Tea is on your desk, along with two McVitie's Rich Tea biscuits."

"Thank you, Alice. I could murder a couple of scones with jam and cream."

"You must manage your weight, Sir Alex. M'lady said no more scones until you lose a stone."

After the outer door latched shut, she grabbed a pad from her desk and followed Sir Alex into his inner sanctum. He sat in a pale gray brocaded armchair next to Alice, they clinked teacups, and each took a sip. Sir Alex picked up the plate of biscuits and offered them to Alice before helping himself.

Alice, almost as tall as Sir Alex and around the same age, smiled as her hand played with her youthful-looking ponytail. She nibbled on her biscuit, chasing the crumbs with another sip of tea.

"I don't understand how you always remain slim. You eat biscuits and cakes every day." He shook his head. "All I need to do is glance at them, and I gain weight."

"Must be in the genes, Sir Alex. Did you realize I'm not eating scones today? I didn't want you to be tempted."

"Thank you for your support, but a bit of temptation is always food for the soul." Both laughed, knowing Alice would keep Sir Alex's wife informed about his eating habits at the office.

"How did the meeting go?"

"As expected—frustrating. Plenty of talk but no action. Even though we're tied up with North Korea and Somali pirates, I insisted we be the lead organization to recover Prince George."

"I imagine everyone breathed a sigh of relief."

"Yes, none of them wanted to take charge of finding him in case a damned fiasco ensued, causing the death of the young man or a whopping ransom demand. Wimps!

Concerned about their own careers and perspective knighthoods rather than doing what is right."

Sir Alex drained his cup, glanced at the closed pack of biscuits, and sighed. "Back to work. Would you be a dear and contact Admiral Blakely?" He glanced at the wall clock. "It's 8:30 a.m. in Washington. No doubt he's been at work for hours."

"At once, Sir Alex." Alice picked up the tea tray and left the room.

Two minutes later, Alice stuck her head back inside. "I contacted the admiral's office. He's in a meeting at the White House. He'll return your call as soon as he gets out of the session."

"Thanks, Alice. The new president is stirring things up around the world, so I suspect Blakely is trying to offer guidance, although I don't think his help will be accepted."

\*\*\*

Two hours later, the red phone rang on Alice's desk. She answered and buzzed Sir Alex. "Admiral Blakely's on the line." After making sure the two friends and colleagues had established contact, she continued with her regular tasks.

"Richard, thanks for returning my call. How are things in D.C.?"

"Hi, Alex. Normal situation here—total chaos. My prediction came true, but from time to time, I sense a glimmer of hope. What can I do for you? Perhaps switch jobs?" Admiral Blakely chuckled.

"No, thanks. As bad as things might appear here, I'd rather stay on this side of the pond." Sir Alex sighed. "I met with the intel chiefs earlier today. Appalling! Things seemed bad enough with the North Korean issue over oil and their dealings with Somali pirates. With the abduction of Prince George from the refugee camp, things are turning bleak."

"I don't envy you one bit. How can we help?"

"Against my better judgment, I've split Bedlam Bravo into two groups. I realize we agreed to keep the teams working as a single unit, but I could use a man from Alpha."

"As you're aware, they each bring specific skills to the teams. What are you searching for?"

"Someone who knows his way underwater and with explosives."

"We have the man, but I'll verify with CC. Hold the line for a minute."

While Sir Alex waited, he gazed at the ceiling, whistling an old sea shanty, "Drunken Sailor." After two renditions of the chorus and the first verse, Admiral Blakely came back on the line.

"CC's keeping his team busy while they wait for another assignment. All of them volunteered to help you, but based on your requirement, CC selected Willie Campbell, a former Navy SEAL. He worked for the CIA before joining us."

"Sounds perfect."

"One thing, though. He's from South Carolina and sometimes he's a bit hard to understand."

"No problem—we'll take him."

"Where and when do you want him? He's not far away, and it won't take him long to prepare."

"Two of Bravo arrived last night at the Jujubba Refugee Camp where unknown miscreants kidnapped Prince George. They'll receive some assistance from a Corporal Livingston, who went with the prince to the camp. He's young looking, Richard, but a smart lad, former member of 16 Air Assault Brigade. I believe he pulled a couple of your SEALs out of trouble in Afghanistan near the Pakistan border."

"A few SEALs ran into problems—they were lined up on their target when some innocent Afghans walked into their firing lanes. The mission commander aborted, not wanting to cause unnecessary casualties. All hell broke loose, with the SEALs pinned down and unable to extract themselves.

"Alex, this mission in Somalia might be an excellent opportunity to check the corporal out for a possible spot on Bedlam Charlie. If he performs well, I'll support him. Who met him at the camp?"

"Gerhard and Pun. He'll have his work cut out for him with their practical jokes, but they are serious when the job's at hand."

"Nothing wrong with a bit of levity to break up the monotony during downtime."

"Agreed. I'd like Willie to join the others in Mombasa as soon as possible. With his addition, we can still break into additional two-man teams, should the need arise."

"Consider it done. I'll pass the word for Willie to head out ASAP. Anything else, Alex?"

"Yes. Your young intern's information regarding the money associated with the release of the *Napoli* paid off. After some arm twisting with the Maltese bank, the account for Dacar Khadaafi is frozen."

"How did you get the bank to cooperate?"

"We played on their loyalties as a former member of the British Commonwealth. We reminded them how we protected their island during WWII. They're assisting, at least for now."

"My intern reported a fence appeared around the money. Now we know why."

"Sorry, I didn't make time to inform you earlier."

"No harm done—at least we've cornered part of the pirates' ill-gotten gains. What about the oil tanker they hijacked?"

"It appears our information regarding the name change from *Zeus* to *Zebu* is correct. The ship is flying a Bahamian flag. The transponder's been disabled and satellite coverage hasn't provided any trace so far. *HMS Snapdragon* and a Greek frigate are working in tandem to locate the ship."

"As always, you British are on the ball. I have something for you. An American contact spotted North Korean Ambassador Soo and another Korean disembarking from a battered freighter in Sihanoukville and passed the information."

"Did the contact provide the name of the ship?"

Richard laughed. "Yes, she did. The contact is a cook in one of the restaurants near the port. She was taking a break and spotted Soo. The ship is the *Krumen*."

"Ah, yes. Purveyor of nefarious cargoes for anyone with the funds."

"Our contact didn't provide any additional intel, but if she comes up with something of interest, I'll call. Anything else?"

"That's all I have for you. Thank you again for loaning us one of the Alpha team." Sir Alex paused. "Our leaders might learn a thing or two from our 'special relationship.'"

"No problem—just give a shout. Agree with your assessment of our current leaders, but at least we will outlive their mistakes. Toss a Glenlivet for me."

Sir Alex chuckled. "One for you and a couple for me." He broke the connection and turned to his computer.

*To: Black*
*From: Topaz*
*Alpha agreed on the loan of Rebel to augment your team. He will arrive Mombasa ASAP. Upon his arrival, prepare to split into two teams. One will transfer to HMS Snapdragon and render assistance as soon as she locates the hijacked oil tanker, now called Zebu. The other will head to the Seychelles to meet with local contacts.*

*Funds associated with ransom for the Napoli frozen. Account holder identified as Somali named Dacar Khadaafi. Arrest warrant passed to Interpol.*

Sir Alex closed down his computer. He reached into the bottom right drawer of his desk and extracted a new bottle of Glenlivet and two glasses. He poured a generous measure into each glass before glancing at the ceiling and closing his eyes.

"Here's to our mission's success. May God watch over Prince George until we recover him and then look away as we deal with the perpetrators."

Sir Alex opened his eyes, picked up the first tumbler, and downed the contents in a single gulp and reached for the second one.

"Amen."

# Chapter Twenty-Six

Al-Shabaab Camp
Outside Kismaayo, Somalia

Hasan raised the pistol as Tahliil jumped forward to stop him.

Too late.

Hasan pulled the trigger.

The bullet whizzed by Tahliil's head, missing his ear by the thickness of a feather. He grabbed Hasan's arm, forcing him to drop the weapon. "What you doing? You might kill me."

Hasan glared at him. "Your actions killed Gari and the others. I thought friendship mattered—I was wrong."

"They martyred for cause. Their deaths will protect Dacar's mission—most important."

Hasan lunged for the pistol.

Tahliil kicked Hasan's head, knocking him out. Turning to the others who had gathered, Tahliil scooped the weapon from the sand and pointed at Hasan. "Clean him up. Put him in tent under guard. He still one of us."

Two men grabbed the unconscious man and dragged him away. Tahliil shook his head as he monitored their departure before walking to the command tent.

Inside, he sat in his chair. *Why men don't understand? Sacrifice is for best reason. Survival. I must think.*

Tahliil jumped from his seat and paced in the sand from one corner of the tent to another. He stopped and dropped to his knees. Allah provides!

He sketched a rough map of Somalia in the sand, using small rocks to mark four locations. Next to the stones, he drew letters: K, A, M, and B. Satisfied with his artwork, Tahliil stood, circling the crude drawing several times. *Yes. This work. I am sure.*

Tahliil stuck his head outside the tent and called to the nearest man. "Tell lieutenants come here thirty minutes. Hasan and 3M, too."

"Yes, sir."

At the appointed time, the four men stood before Tahliil. After gazing into the face of each one, he rose from his seat. His eyes remained fixated on Hasan. "First, thoughts for martyrs. Gari and others helped cause."

Tahliil and the others bowed their heads and offered silent prayers. After a suitable amount of time had passed, Tahliil returned to his seat.

"Sit. New plan. Bigger. Create more problems for government."

The four men nodded, grins breaking out across their faces. They stomped their feet and chanted.

Tahliil raised a hand. "Good news, yes? Busuri, when Dacar not here, you senior lieutenant."

"Thank you, Tahliil. I shall not let you down."

Tahliil stood and clasped Busuri's shoulders. "Be not like Gari. Remember place."

Busuri nodded and remained silent.

Tahliil walked to his crude Somali map, motioning for the others to follow him. Picking up a stick, he pointed at the letter K. "We here outside Kismaayo. Must increase attacks."

"Will we attack Kismaayo again?" Hasan kept his gaze pinned on the map.

"Yes, but not you." Tahliil turned from Hasan and pointed at Harbi. "You will lead. Hit and run."

"Yes, Tahliil. How many men?"

"We divide into three groups." He turned to Busuri. "Tell Asad to bring half his men and the older women from Kidi Faani. Young ones remain."

"At once."

"Harbi, where Warsame? He has men and foreign captives."

"They will arrive in two days."

"Excellent." Tahliil pointed at the letter A. "We move camp to Afgooye. More food, water." He moved the pointer to the letter M. "Busuri, after new camp made and rest, you attack Mogadishu—power station and airport. If time, perhaps more targets."

"I am honored. My men and I will wreak havoc and put fear in their hearts."

Tahliil turned to Hasan. "One letter left—B. You lead attack on Boosaaso."

Hasan tipped his head, trying to hide his grin.

Tahliil returned to his chair as the others resumed chanting and stomping their feet. He raised his hands in the air. "We hurt government with ecol—economy targets. Dacar returns soon with more weapons from new friends. Go now. Plan. Tell 3M what bombs you want. Discuss here in three hours."

The four men paused to shake Tahliil's hand as they departed.

Hasan, the last to leave, grabbed Tahliil's arm. "I do this in Gari's name—not for you." He glared at Tahliil before storming out of the tent.

\*\*\*

As dusk fell, lanterns bathed the inside of Tahliil's command tent and entrance with pale yellow light. Shadows cast a myriad of shapes around the area, moving in the light breeze.

Inside, two tables were loaded with roasted goat, rice, chapatis, and vegetables. Pitchers of milk stood like sentries, interspersed among the steaming platters. The mixed aromas of the prepared food filled the tent.

Tahliil's lieutenants entered. "Eat, eat." He waved at the tables. "First food, then talk."

The men rushed forward, grabbing food and tossing it onto metal plates. Using their right hands, they dug into their choices. Grunts of delight echoed throughout the tent as the dishes emptied.

Satiated, everyone gathered in front of Tahliil and knelt.

"Now, talk. Busuri. You first."

"We have picked our targets. In addition to the power plant and the Mogadishu airport, we will attack the refinery and the police barracks near the palace. If there is time, we will also hit the port."

"Excellent. Remember, everyone to Afgooye first. Except Harbi. He attack Kismaayo before come to Afgooye."

"Yes, Tahliil." Busuri glanced at the others. "Asad will arrive tomorrow with half of his men. Not many women—three."

"How come not more?"

"One died the first night at the camp trying to escape. The other killed her new husband and then committed suicide."

"Enough—one each team. Harbi, about Kismaayo?"

"We will hit targets in the north of the city. I also want to attack the fish market where the military ambushed Gari."

Tahliil turned and tipped his head for Hasan to speak.

"The port is the primary source of income for Boosaaso. We will concentrate our effort in destroying the fish processing plant and the tannery. If possible, we will disable some of the cell towers." Hasan gazed at Tahliil, his eyes glancing to the ground before remaining steadfast. "I want Gari's pistol. His bullet-ridden Toyota will be my transportation."

Tahliil nodded and turned to 3M. "How bombs coming?"

The smallest man in the group, 3M cleared his throat. "I will make as many as possible. Busuri, Harbi, and Hasan want more than I have materials to make."

"Okay. Soon, Dacar provide supplies. More bombs, ammunition, guns. No more talk. Meet tomorrow."

\*\*\*

Two dust-laden vehicles approached the camp, midmorning the following day. Recognizing the Toyota Land Cruisers and the lead driver, the guards fired their weapons into the air. The camp alerted, most of the men rushed forward to greet them.

Busuri met the passenger of the first vehicle as the man jumped down. They shook hands and gave each other a brief hug. "Welcome back, Asad! How many men did you bring?"

"I brought ten—and three female captives."

"Excellent. You and your men will be on my team. You'll be second-in-command."

"I'm honored, Busuri. What should I do now?"

"Bring your men and the captives into the camp. Eat and rest. Later, we will be moving to Afgooye."

No sooner had the two vehicles entered the compound than someone shouted an alarm. Busuri ran to a wooden, two-story structure about fifteen feet high and six feet wide, where two men pointed to the southwest. He climbed the watchtower.

A man handed a pair of binoculars to Busuri. "Over there—a cloud of dust. Not sure what is disturbing the sand. Many vehicles, I think."

"Inform Tahliil. It might be Somali soldiers or a Kenyan military patrol."

"At once."

Busuri trained the binoculars on the dust cloud. *Too fast for heavy troop trucks or tanks.*

"What …?" Tahliil spat out the word as his chest heaved from the exertion of climbing the tower.

Busuri pointed to the cloud and handed over the glasses. "There—several vehicles coming this way."

"Yes. We ready to fight." Tahliil handed the binoculars to Busuri. "Stay here. Direct men."

The dust cloud continued its advance toward the camp. Two miles away, the hidden source of the disturbance stopped forward movement.

Busuri continued to monitor the area. Dust settled.

Technicals.

With a whoop, Busuri ran to the edge of the platform. "Technicals! Three of them—it must be Warsame."

Excited voices heralded the news, accompanied by gunshots as weapons were raised and fired into the air. Tahliil and his lieutenants met the technicals when they arrived at the gates.

A smile plastered across his face, Warsame shook hands with the men. "We brought two captives, a British man, and an Italian woman."

Cheers erupted and others slapped Warsame on the shoulders. Four of his team pulled the captives from the middle vehicle and shoved them in front of Tahliil.

The woman screamed and fell to the ground. The man reached down and helped her stand, his eyes locked on Tahliil.

Dressed in tattered clothing too small for him, George sported a black eye. Peeling skin and brown scabs dotted his nose. Scratches and insect bites covered both arms and his ankles. He held himself erect, almost regal, as he faced his captors.

Silvia wore pants too long and baggy for her and a long sleeve shirt buttoned to the neck. Her unkempt hair tied in a greasy ponytail reached to the middle of her back. Despite her darker Mediterranean skin tones, Silvia's sunburned face bled from a myriad of scratches and blisters. Unlike George, she seemed ready to topple over.

Tahliil leered at the woman, who shrank back, and moved closer to George. "Take them my tent. Guard. No escape."

After the excitement of Asad and Warsame's return, Tahliil's men wandered back to their previous tasks, while he strolled to the command tent. "Lieutenants. Follow."

Perched on the edge of his seat, Tahliil glanced at his men. "Everyone leave for Afgooye before dawn." He turned to Harbi. "Attack Kismaayo dusk tomorrow. Head to Afgooye after."

Harbi nodded.

"Warsame and men go with you."

"As you wish, Tahliil."

"May Allah protect us." Tahliil stood. "Finished now. Eat. Interrogate foreigners."

\*\*\*

Dusk fell with its normal abruptness—daylight one moment and dark a few minutes later. Lanterns and torches scattered around the compound provided flickering light. As the hours passed, the sounds of human inhabitants diminished, giving way to nocturnal activity.

Tahliil stepped past the guards into his tent. Huddled together on a blanket on the ground near his bed, one of the foreigners gazed at him with defiance while the other cowered, unable to face him.

He sat on a camp chair a few feet from the bed. "Sit on bed. Better."

The captives moved as directed. Settled, they appeared to wait for something to happen.

"Names. Where from? Why in Kenya?"

"My name is George. My friend is Silvia. I'm from England while she is Italian. We both finished our university degrees and took a year out to donate time to help others."

"Who you help?"

"Somalis, Kenyans, anyone who came to Jujubba Refugee Camp."

"Where go university? What study?"

"I went to St. Andrews and studied art history and geography. When I finish at the refugee camp, I will join the Royal Air Force. I want to fly jets and helicopters."

Tahliil glanced at the woman and motioned for her to speak.

"I-I studied medicine at the University of Bologna. When I leave the camp, I will go back to the university and learn to be a surgeon. One day, I want to return to Africa and help others."

George squeezed Silvia's hand and turned to Tahliil. "We've told you a bit about ourselves. Who are you? What do you want with us?"

"I am Tahliil. I lead one wing of al-Shabaab."

"Isn't al-Shabaab a terrorist group?" George rubbed his peeling nose. "I seem to recall reading about an attack on a shopping mall in Nairobi and something about pirates."

"To some, terrorists. Freedom fighters better description."

George gazed at the dark eyes of the man. "I believe you are smarter than you show. Why the charade?"

Tahliil clenched his fists and closed his eyes. *Should I tell the foreigner the truth?* He sat in the same position for several minutes. When he opened his eyes and glanced at George, his eyes were red and brimmed with tears.

"Many years ago, my father was the leader of a small but important Somali clan. He became the vice president. Two years later, the government was deposed in a coup. The plotters killed the president when they overran the palace."

Tahliil gulped and brushed away a tear threatening to dribble down his cheek. "The traitors grabbed my father, accused him of corruption, and dragged him to the beach. They made my family and I witness his execution.

"Afterward, I was thrown on the streets without any identity papers. The army found me. Without proper identification, I was tossed in the back of a truck and taken to an army training camp."

George shook his head. "What a horrible story!"

Wracked by sobs, his shoulders heaving, Tahliil appeared to shrink in stature. When he finished, he wiped his eyes with his sleeves. "I went from the elite to something less than human. I modified my speaking patterns so everyone would dismiss me as an ignorant fool.

"I joined al-Shabaab for revenge. I want to kill every person involved in my father's death, even if I lose my life. Even my men think I'm dim-witted, which is why some plotted to replace me. I arranged their deaths in Kismaayo."

Tahliil stood. "We've talked enough. We leave this camp early in the morning." He stepped to the tent's entrance. "Guards, take foreigners to tent with other captives. Death if escape."

Alone in his tent, Tahliil cleansed himself with sand. Facing Mecca, he prayed. Once finished, he slid on top of his bed, but sleep remained elusive.

*George, who are you? You're not cowered by captivity. You portray a privileged upbringing but cover it up well. Will someone pay for your return? I must find out.*

# Chapter Twenty-Seven

Hotel English Point
Mombasa, Kenya

Trevor Franklin, Bedlam Bravo's leader, stood on the open-air terrace of the Hotel English Point's penthouse. He took a sip of his tea and gazed at the spectacular view of Mombasa's Old Town, the old port, and Fort Jesus.

After a final glance at the scenery, Trevor sighed and returned inside. He sat at the eight-place dining table and pulled his laptop closer.

He shook his head as he reread the latest communiqué from Sir Alex. *I think we're stretching ourselves too thin. Still, must follow orders.*

A rap on the door—a key turned in the lock. A poor imitation of a chickadee's tweet followed.

Trevor closed the laptop and strode to the door. Standing to the side, he glanced through the peephole. Smiling, he unlatched the deadbolt and yanked open the door.

Laden with plastic shopping bags from several nearby stores, Nathaniel 'Nate' Webster and Fergus Mulligan stepped inside. They wandered to the dining table and dropped their purchases.

Trevor closed the door and joined them. "Did you buy out every store?" He laughed. "Anything worthy of keeping?"

"I tink everything is rubbish." Fergus rubbed a hand over his short, red hair. "Mission accomplished—we visited loads of shops today."

"Locals in every shop for about ten blocks are aware two freelance photographers want to speak with those traumatized by the al-Shabaab attacks." Nate's eyes twinkled as he smiled. "We spread the word we would pay for photos or videos of the terrorists."

"Any takers?" Trevor pursed his lips.

"Yes. We promised twenty pounds if what they supply us is used." Fergus danced a small jig and laughed. "They are to take their material to the nearest police station. We already talked with a police sergeant. After we agreed to give him a cut and hinted about taking his photograph, he'll help us out."

"Greed." Nate rolled his eyes and twirled a finger in the air. "Makes the world go 'round."

"I must hand it to you guys. An outstanding job—not what I might have done, but it should reap the desired results."

Nate pointed at the laptop. "Any news from—?"

Trevor waved a small black box, about the size of a smartphone with a six-inch antenna. "Checked the room out. Didn't find any critters, but to be on the safe side, I suggest we go on the terrace."

After they settled into chairs overlooking the old port, Nate glanced down.

"I checked everything on the terrace, too. If someone has a directional mic on us, we won't know." Trevor smiled at Nate's concern over their security. "Right. Received an email from Topaz. Bedlam Alpha is providing someone to help us—Willie."

"I guess we'll be doing some underwater work. Since I was a Special Branch diver, I assume I'll partner with him."

"Correct. He'll arrive at Moi International tomorrow night at 00:45. You'll pick him up."

Fergus nodded.

"We'll give him a day or so to recover from jetlag before transferring to *HMS Snapdragon*. Nate and I will be travelling to the Seychelles to meet with local contacts."

"Did Topaz provide any further details?" Nate stood and walked toward the terrace's glass wall.

"Not about our mission. They'll provide an update later. However, I did receive a short email from Gerhard."

"What's the big oaf up to?" Nate chuckled.

"He says they arrived at the Jujubba Refugee Camp and met with the administrator and Prince George's sole security man. The guy, a former corporal with 16 Air Assault Brigade named Alfred Livingston, will take Gerhard and Pun to the wadi where he left the prince."

"If anyone is capable of picking up the trail, Pun will. I witnessed him in action, and he has a natural gift."

Nate laughed and switched to one of his favorite topics. "Not sure about you guys, but I'm so hungry I could eat a gazelle."

"Not much else we can do at this time, so I agree with Nate." Trevor patted his stomach. "Always room for a bit more grub."

\*\*\*

The following morning, Nate and Fergus arrived at the police station to meet with Sergeant Jomo. Painted in the colors of the Kenyan national flag, the building stood out from those nearby covered in pastel colors. Oversized Masai shields and spears attached to the wall guarded the entrance.

Despite the pristine appearance of the exterior, the building's interior displayed chipped green paint, greasy floors, and battered desks. Two ceiling fans failed to improve the airflow, their movement almost nonexistent.

"May I help you?" A young woman at the information desk interrupted the appraisal of their surroundings.

"Yes, good morning. We have an appointment with Sergeant Jomo—Webster and Mulligan."

"One moment, please." The woman hopped from her stool and sauntered between the other desks. She stopped in front of a closed door at the rear and rapped her knuckles on the glass.

The door opened. A heavyset man with curly black hair and dark eyes filled the doorway. He stepped forward, his face beaming. "Mr. Webster and Mr. Mulligan. Welcome! Come into my office."

After they seated themselves in designated chairs, Sergeant Jomo pointed to a small pile of photographs on the edge of his desk. "Many responses to your requests. Most are pictures, but two people brought cell phone videos."

"Fantastic. We hope to find faces cropping up during the recent al-Shabaab attacks so we can create a photo display and sell our work to various newspapers around the world." Nate's eyes twinkled as he laid out their plan. "We'll begin with photos of those with weapons."

"Three or four men are holding guns. Some are from different angles, so most facial features are provided."

"Excellent. I will work with Mr. Webster to select the best. I spoke with a friend at *The Irish Times* in Dublin, and they are keen to view our material." Fergus pointed at the sergeant. "Since you are helping us, they want your photo, too."

Jomo's face threatened to split as a new smile appeared. "I will help my new friends. We must remove the terrorists and criminals, so tourists will return to Mombasa."

"We've another meeting to attend." Nate pointed at the photos. "May we take these now and we'll check back again later?"

"By all means, my friends."

\*\*\*

Armed with an oversized envelope stuffed with twenty-two photographs of varying quality, Nate and Fergus returned to the penthouse. They joined Trevor, who waited for them before digging into a late breakfast.

Once the men finished eating, they placed the empty dishes on a cart and wheeled it into the hallway. Nate dumped the photos on the table and spread them out.

Each took a photo and scanned the others for duplicate images. They identified multiple photographs of three men holding AK-47s.

Trevor booted his laptop. "I'll upload these and send them to Topaz. In the meantime, go through them again in case we missed anything."

*To: Topaz*

*From: Black*

*Blue and White's plan to obtain photographs of possible al-Shabaab terrorists involved in recent Mombasa attacks resulted in over twenty snaps so far. The images of three men holding weapons were captured multiple times (attached). Please advise any confirmed identities.*

*Acquisition program is continuing at this time. After we depart the area, local contact will continue to collect images.*

"Right. Put everything in the safe in the walk-in closet and bring your cameras. Time to play tourist."

\*\*\*

Fergus left the hotel at 23:45 and grabbed a random cab outside the hotel. At Moi International Airport, he paid his driver and stepped inside the expansive entrance area, packed with people waiting for new arrivals. He leaned against a pillar as he gave the crowd a once-over. Armed soldiers patrolled throughout the terminal. Two dog handlers threaded their way through the throng, German Shepherds sniffing at random people and luggage.

The PA system announced passengers arriving from Nairobi would exit the building in a few minutes. People inched forward, creating a thin opening for arrivals to squeeze through.

Among the local arrivals pushing their way out of the building, a muscle-laden foreigner with close-cropped brown hair bulldozed his way toward Fergus. A massive green backpack was strapped to his back.

A bit shorter than Fergus at five-feet-eleven-inches tall, William Campbell's hazel eyes sparkled as he approached. "You must be Fergus. I'm Willie."

The men shook hands. "Sorry for the delay. After I cleared customs in Nairobi, the airlines insisted my bag be transferred to the hold. No problem on my first two flights, but the last plane was tiny and my duffle came off last."

They stood in line waiting for a taxi. Once their turn came, they deferred to the couple standing behind them and took the next cab. After providing the name of their hotel, Willie and Fergus remained quiet, shrugging off questions from the driver.

Fergus paid for the trip when they reached the hotel, giving a small tip. The man glanced at the money. "Cheapskate." His tires screeched as he departed.

"I gave him the going rate for a tip according to a police sergeant we met." Fergus shrugged as they went through the doors.

"The guy must have figured we would overtip like most foreigners." Willie glanced around the lobby as they strode to the elevators. "So, this is how the other half lives."

"Wait until you see the penthouse—outstanding view, plenty of space. I might become accustomed to this."

When they entered the penthouse, Fergus introduced Willie to the others. They filed onto the terrace.

"Well, shut my mouth. Fergus didn't exaggerate about y'all's view. Your boss must have deep pockets to spring for this. I can't imagine Admiral Blakely reimbursing us for a suite like this."

"We haven't explained to Sir Alex about our accommodations. We took the last room available with visual access to the city." Trevor smiled. "It'll be a battle with the accountants, I'm sure."

Fergus handed everyone a Tusker Lager as they sat.

Trevor took a swig of the cold beer before setting the bottle on a coaster. "Right. Business. Willie, you and Fergus will be heading to *HMS Snapdragon*. Her crew is working with a Greek frigate to locate the oil tanker we're interested in, now called the *Zebu*."

He turned to Fergus. "While you were picking up Willie, a new signal came in from Topaz. Rather than a couple of days for Willie to overcome jetlag, two Typhoon FGR-4 aircraft will pick you up in fifteen hours at the airport and take you to Diego Garcia."

"How will we transfer to the *Snapdragon*?" Willie smothered a yawn with a ham-sized hand.

"They didn't specify, so perhaps it's still being worked out. Nate and I will take a commercial flight to Mahe Island, Seychelles. We'll leave for the airport in about four hours, so Nate and I need to call it an evening. We'll all meet again at 05:30."

\*\*\*

At the appointed time, the four men met again. Trevor checked for any last-minute updates from Topaz. Nothing.

Nate and Trevor said their farewells and headed for the airport. They checked in and followed other travelers to the boarding lounge. At 08:10, their flight departed for Nairobi where they would change planes for their connection to the Seychelles.

Fergus lounged around the penthouse throughout the morning and paid a visit to Sergeant Jomo while Willie caught up on his sleep. When Fergus returned, Willie's bag sat on the floor in a heap, the contents strewn across the dining table.

"Willie, what's all this?"

"Never know when these 'toys' might come in handy on our mission. Our technical whiz made them before I left to join you. When we get to Diego, I'll demonstrate."

A knock on the door interrupted their preparations. Fergus crept to the peephole while Willie ducked around a corner.

Knuckles rapped on the door, more urgent and louder. Weapon drawn, Fergus glanced outside. A foreigner, dressed in a flight suit, prepared to knock a third time when Fergus yanked the door open.

"Sorry, I'm early. There's a bit of a ruckus at the airport and the pilots want to get airborne."

"Two minutes and we'll be ready." Fergus nodded to the bar area. "Grab a drink while we finish."

While the man poured himself a soft drink, Fergus and Willie finished packing and dragged their bags to the door.

Their escort tried to pick up Willie's bag, but let it tumble to the floor. "What's in this thing? Bricks?"

"Naw, jest a few things which might make the mission a bit easier."

They hauled everything into the elevator. While Fergus checked them out, the others carried the luggage to a small battered Jeep with Kenyan military plates.

"How'd ya nab this vehicle?"

"I work with the Kenyan military. They're the ones who provided the vehicle and arranged landing permission for the planes."

Fergus joined them and the driver merged into traffic, blowing the horn as a bus tried to overtake. "Crazy drivers—can't wait to finish my posting and return to London."

As they approached the airport, traffic slowed.

The Jeep's driver squeezed through the congestion, and sped toward a private gate into the airport.

After showing his identification to the guards, they opened the gate and the Jeep shot through, careening around airport vehicles until he reached a cordoned area. Two Typhoon jets sat side by side, the pilots going over their planes before departure.

Fergus and Willie jumped out of the Jeep, grabbed their bags, and waved farewell. They walked over to the aircraft where the pilots joined them.

"White and Rebel. Glad you made it. Seems to be a bit of a hubbub brewing." Both pilots were tall and thin, with one sporting a sparse brown mustache. "Two minutes and we'll get you loaded up and we'll be off. I want to depart before the crowd does something stupid."

"What do y'all think is going on?" Willie glanced at the people hanging on the perimeter fence shouting and throwing objects onto the tarmac.

"The locals have been stressed over higher taxes and loss of jobs. They use the airport to protest their frustration with the government. Rebel, I'm the flight leader and you're with me. Let's climb aboard."

Given permission to taxi by the control tower, the jets moved forward.

*Whoomph. Whoomph.*

"Flight leader this is two. Incoming!"

"Full throttle. Now!"

The sudden acceleration forced the men deeper into their seats. They sped along the runway and rotated upward as additional rocket-propelled grenades peppered the area.

"British military aircraft. What are you doing?" An unknown voice from the control tower squeaked at them in anger. "No permission to go. Return at once."

"Sorry, Control. Your transmission is garbled." The flight leader grinned. "Thank you and have a good day."

Grenades burst around a jet fuel bunker, rupturing the metal container. A thunderous explosion followed, the ensuing fireball billowing skyward, flames and thick, black smoke encompassed the airport.

"Holy crap! Rebel, did you and White have something to do with this?"

"Not us, Flight Lieutenant." Willie laughed. "Scout's honor." *Not this time, anyway.*

The pilot shook his head. "Never mind, I don't want to know. Next stop—Diego Garcia, compliments of Her Majesty's Royal Air Force."

## Chapter Twenty-Eight

Sihanoukville, Cambodia
Merchant Ship *Krumen*

Dacar and Sahid stood with the captain of the merchant ship *Krumen* as he gave instructions to cast off from the dock. Normal procedures required a local pilot to remain with every foreign craft until they cleared the port. A small craft followed the *Krumen*, waiting to collect the pilot.

"Captain, when he returns to the port, I'm going with him." Dacar waved a hand at the Cambodian pilot. "I must take care of some personal business. Sahid will remain onboard with you."

"No problem. Don't forget the fee. If not pa—"

"What fee?" Dacar glared at the greedy captain. "The North Koreans paid you to deliver their cargo to the Seychelles."

"The price has increased. I want twenty-five thousand dollars to offload. There'll be expenses and bribes to pay."

Dacar bristled at the attempted price increase. He pursed his lips and let out a huge sigh. "Very well. I'll meet the ship when you arrive at the destination and provide the money, okay?"

"Cash." The captain grinned as he rubbed his thumb and index finger together.

"Yes, cash."

"Captain." The local pilot approached, holding out a hand. "I ordered the ship to slow. We've reached the point where your pilot may continue without me."

The captain glared at the interruption but remained silent. He reached into a back pocket and removed a smudged envelope. "Here is your fee. Until the next time."

The Cambodian tipped an imaginary hat. "I enjoy doing business with you—always punctual with your payments."

"Remember, the extra is for keeping your mouth quiet. Go now." The captain pointed at Dacar. "Take him with you. Seems he wants to remain longer in Cambodia."

After the two men transferred to the local craft, the *Krumen*'s single screw churned the water before the ship moved forward. The pilot and Dacar jumped onto the small boat, colliding with each other when they fell and rolled across the deck.

Climbing to his feet as the boat headed back to port, Dacar scratched his chin and smirked. "Who says ships can't be fun?"

"We must discuss what fun means." The pilot rubbed a banged knee as he stood upright. "I think of being with my wife, having a splendid meal, and laughing with friends as fun. Jumping from a ship to a small boat? Not so much."

"Ha! You're spoiled by your easy life. Never mind—I require your assistance."

The pilot's eyes gleamed. "Will it involve ships? Will I make money?"

"Yes, to both. In the not too distant future, a ship will pull into port. Before departing, I want some new artwork—change the name, homeport, and ship's logo. A new flag, too."

"Those things might be arranged—if someone has connections with the right people. For you, I will make contact, but it will cost."

Dacar watched the man's face flush with excitement. "How much?"

"Twenty thous—"

Dacar's nostrils flared. He crossed his arms and glared at the smaller man.

"No. I mean fifteen thousand. Dollars."

"Twelve thousand dollars—in cash and we are agreed."

They shook hands before they staggered to the seats while the boat bounced on rippling waves. A horn blew when another freighter headed out of the port. The pilot waved before turning back to Dacar. "Would you like a cold beer?"

"No thanks—I don't drink alcohol. If you have a cold Coke or Dr. Pepper, I'll join you in celebrating our arrangement."

\*\*\*

The following morning, a man in a light gray suit with a white shirt and red-striped tie stepped out of the inexpensive G'Day Mate Guest House. In his right hand, Dacar held a black attaché case. He glanced both directions before strolling along Ekareach Street to the ANZ Royal Bank.

Inside the building, Dacar stood behind several people waiting for a teller. When his turn came, he stepped forward. "I wish to make a hefty money transfer."

"Yes, sir." An elderly Cambodian woman motioned to a waist-high railing with a swinging gate. "Step over there and someone will assist you."

A tall, slender man with thinning black hair met Dacar at the rail. "Come this way, sir." He held the gate open for Dacar, pointing to a nearby desk. "Would you like tea or coffee? Perhaps some water?"

"No, thank you. I'm fine."

"How may I help you?"

Dacar opened his case and removed a single sheet of paper and a forged American passport. "I would like to transfer one hundred thousand dollars from my account at the Freedom Bank in Malta. The number is DK90123."

The clerk scanned the document and compared Dacar with the photograph in the passport. "Everything appears to be in order. Is the money to be transferred here?"

"Yes. I want sixty-two thousand in mixed denominations. Non-sequential bills in pristine condition. The balance will remain on deposit in your bank."

The clerk's eyes gleamed and he grinned. "I'll be able to take care of this transaction for you within fifteen minutes."

Dacar fidgeted while the minutes ticked by on a wall clock.

Fifteen minutes later, the clerk reappeared, a frown etched across his face. He sat, reread a note he brought with him, and cleared his throat. "Mr. Khadaafi, the Freedom Bank is unable to initiate the transfer."

"Why?"

"They're willing to make the transfer. However, someone froze the account. You are unable to make deposits or withdrawals until you visit the bank in person."

*Hmmm. Can't go to Malta. The Maltese Police Force want me.* "Suggestions?"

"There isn't anything I can recommend." He glared at Dacar. "Should you be able to sort out your, ah, difficulty, I shall be happy to assist with your transfer request."

Two security guards approached, taking up station on either side of Dacar's chair.

"These men will escort you out of the bank. Good day."

The guards each grabbed an arm and pulled Dacar toward the exit. They let him leave the building without a scene.

"*Wallahi!* (I swear to God!)" Dacar fumed at the indignant behavior of the bank clerk. *How dare he*! He straightened his ruffled clothing, rolled his shoulders and marched away from the bank.

He pushed his way through the crowds on Ekareach Street until he reached the guesthouse. In response to a polite greeting from the desk clerk, Dacar slammed the empty attaché case on the counter. "I'm checking out. Arrange a taxi to take me to the airport."

"Is there something I might do to help?"

"There's nothing anyone can do. I must leave." Dacar rushed to his room, threw his meager belongings into a worn and battered leather suitcase, and returned to the desk. He tossed money on the counter and raced to a waiting cab.

"Airport—hurry!"

\*\*\*

The taxi skidded to a halt in front of the terminal. Dacar dropped a handful of bills over the front seat and dashed inside. He raced to an Air Asia ticketing desk. Chest heaving, he tried to calm himself. *Relax. Things will work out.*

"May I help you, sir?"

Dacar took a deep breath and exhaled. "Yes. I want to travel the quickest way possible to Djibouti."

The ticket agent pointed at a small row of red plastic chairs. "Please take a seat. This will take several minutes."

Dacar tried to make himself comfortable in one of the chairs. He propped his feet on his suitcase and shut his eyes.

Twenty minutes later, the clerk tapped him on the shoulder. "Sir, you fell asleep. I have your tickets arranged. There will be three flights and it will take over forty-eight hours. You depart in ninety minutes."

\*\*\*

Three days later, dressed in the same clothes he wore when departing Sihanoukville, a bedraggled Dacar stepped out of Djibouti-Ambouli International Airport. He raised a hand to his forehead, blocking out the intense rays.

Jostled by others leaving the terminal, Dacar scanned the waiting throng for his contact. *Hope he received the message.* Dacar's eyes roamed over the crowd. *He's not here.*

Dacar grinned as he recognized a familiar figure approach from the edge of the crowd. *Rooble!*

They clasped hands and gave each other a hug. "Sorry, I'm late." Rooble raised his right hand and pointed over the crowd. "The next stage is prepared. One of our boats is waiting in the harbor."

"Let's go, my friend. I'm seething over the shame from Sihanoukville." *If only I could kill someone—anyone—who stands in my way.*

Rooble pushed his way to the exit, Dacar following. They weaved their way through narrow, dusty streets. Everyday life existed here—children played, goats wandered about, chewing on pieces of discarded paper as older children herded them. Adults laughed and shouted, adding to the din. A slight breeze brought salt air, cooking aromas, and the smell of dung.

A few minutes later, Rooble blew a whistle and waved both hands in the air. A small, blue and white boat coasted up to the dock and banged against tires hung over the edge to prevent damage.

Dacar and Rooble climbed aboard. After a round of handshakes and hugs, the boat pushed away and headed out of the harbor.

"How was the trip?" Rooble's eyes gleamed as he handed Dacar a long dagger. "Did you check the weapons?"

"Good and bad. I inspected them before the *Krumen* departed. Sahid is still on the ship." Dacar heaved a sigh. "I tried to transfer money from Malta, but someone froze the account." He clenched his fists until the knuckles turned white. "I'll find out what happened and deal with whoever caused me inconvenience and embarrassment."

"What happened?"

"I don't know." He ran a finger along the dagger's blade, a thin line of blood forming where he nicked himself. "A wise suggestion to hold some of the *Napoli*'s crew until I transfer the funds, even though Tahliil wanted them released."

Dacar wiped the smear on his trousers. "Since I'm unable to access the money, Engineer Smith will pay."

\*\*\*

The boat skirted the coastline, heading toward the pirate compound near Ras Hafun. The pilot entered a narrow bay and continued to a small, rickety pier. After dropping off Dacar and Rooble, the boat turned and left the bay.

A one-armed man met them as they plodded through a dusty street to a two-story house surrounded by a whitewashed stone wall. The wooden gate opened and they squeezed past a sentry wielding an AK-47.

The entrance secured behind them, Dacar turned to their escort. "Bring Smith next door. Blindfold and gag him first."

"At once."

Dacar stormed into the adjacent building as he attempted to control his anger. He sat in a threadbare upholstered chair, the original colors faded beyond recognition.

The door opened and the engineer stumbled into the room after receiving a kick to his lower back. He regained his balance and stood with military bearing. Clothing in tatters, a thick black beard streaked with white, but power still radiated from his features.

Dacar waved a hand and two guards grabbed the captain, forcing him to sit on a wooden chair. His feet were tied to the legs, while ropes looped through the back of the chair held his upper body.

"So, Smith. We meet again." Dacar spoke in a quiet, raspy voice. He stepped forward and yanked the gag from the engineer's mouth.

"What do you want? The owners paid the ransom yet you still detain another crew member and me."

"Shut up! Don't lecture me—the money is frozen and can't be transferred."

A grin appeared on Smith's face.

Before he could reply, Dacar strode forward, grabbed the captain's hair and yanked his head to the side. "Don't make fun of me. Your life is in my hands." *And right now, I want to cause you pain.*

Dacar pulled down the blindfold and forced the point of his dagger near the bridge of the engineer's nose. "Perhaps I should send one of your eyes as a gift." He traced a circle around the right eye and switched to the left. "Which one?"

"Kill me and the owners will see you in hell before they pay another penny."

"I don't require more money—access to what I have will be sufficient."

Smith screamed when Dacar applied pressure to the blade. It slipped under the engineer's skin, rivulets of blood cascaded down his face.

The knife moved again, ever closer to an eye.

A blood-curdling scream, louder than the first, echoed throughout the room. A third one split the air, then silence.

## Chapter Twenty-Nine

Victoria, Seychelles
Sunrise Small Hotel

The screeching of the hard rubber from the landing gear was lost in the screams, and shouts rippled throughout the cabin as the Kenyan Airways flight sped along the taxiways and past airport support staff before coming to an abrupt halt. The ground crew waved red and green paddles in the air at the aircraft, their eyes growing round with fright before the pilot shut down the engines.

"Must be a former carrier pilot." Trevor shook his head as he collected his luggage from the overhead bin.

Nate glanced at the passengers scurrying to disembark. "Perhaps we blew a tire." He shrugged. "Not the first hard landing I've had at this airport. Happened two years ago. Might be the same guy."

They followed the signs to customs. A surly agent snapped his fingers and glared at each passenger who approached his desk. Trevor and Nate received the same unwelcoming attitude, but after a thorough review of their documents, paying particular attention to their photographs, the agent stamped their passports and waved them through.

"Not a very pleasant fellow." Trevor shielded his eyes and pointed to the right. "Doesn't appear anyone is waiting for us."

"Agreed. Let's grab a taxi—the lady behind the third one seems competent."

Trevor laughed. "She might be a looker, but how does her appearance equate to her competence as a driver?"

"I suppose there's no comparison." Nate grinned as he shifted his bag from one shoulder to the other. "But it works for me."

***

Prior to exiting the taxi at the Sunrise Small Hotel, Nate obtained the driver's phone number. When they entered the hotel's primary block, he eyeballed the piece of paper. "Never know, might come in handy."

Trevor rolled his eyes. "Uh huh."

They identified themselves at the counter as Smith and Jones.

The clerk located their reservation, hemming and hawing as he read. "Two adjacent rooms for a week." He glanced at the pair. "Anyone else in your party?"

Trevor shook his head. "No, but we want our privacy."

Nate turned from viewing the hotel's interior. "He snores, too."

The clerk laughed. "You are in luck. With your arrival, the hotel is full. Each room comes with its own bathroom, but you share a small kitchenette."

"Perfect." Nate rubbed his stomach. "I'll be able to make something whenever I'm hungry."

"Always thinking of your stomach. I don't understand how you remain so fit." Trevor finished signing the registration document and passed the pen to Nate.

"Must be in the genes." Nate scrawled on the form and slid it to the clerk.

He gazed around the dated lounge, with its black leather chairs, red and gold floral carpet, an unlit fireplace, and an old television. "Is there somewhere I can pick up a local newspaper? I don't see any here."

"Sorry, sir, we are out." The clerk gave Nate a sheepish grin. "Down the hill a short distance is a small store by the main entrance to the National Botanical Gardens, which should have what you desire."

"I'll be upstairs when you return." Trevor waved as Nate headed out the door.

After dropping his bag and laptop case on the small coffee table, Trevor opened the door to the private veranda and stepped outside. Across the street, a tiny kiosk stood by a secondary entrance to the botanical gardens. He breathed in the fresh air, a hint of various floral scents carried on the warm breeze.

Trevor returned inside, removed the laptop from the bag, and powered it up.

*To: Black*
*From: Topaz*
*Fireworks at Mombasa Airport—unable to determine if related to the mission. Multiple casualties. Rebel and White en route destination, compliments of RAF. Arrival time TBD.*

*Your rendezvous scheduled for 09:00 at the Hindu Temple. If no show, contact will call you with a new time/location. Will identify as Kumquat and has access to relevant information. No details available from across the pond regarding your contact so proceed with caution. Acknowledge.*

While Trevor typed his response, someone tapped on the door. A poorly whistled rendition of "Yankee Doodle" ensued.

Trevor smiled and stepped to the entrance. He glanced out the peephole, confirmed the whistler's identity, and unlocked the door.

Nate stepped inside, waving a local newspaper. "Check this out. Someone blew up a jet fuel storage tank in Mombasa about the time Willie and Fergus were scheduled to depart. Several deaths and almost 100 people injured. The incident's described as a local protest gone bad."

Trevor gestured toward the laptop. "Sir Alex reported the men are on their way to Diego." He shook his head and laughed. "Your whistling needs a bit of improvement. I almost didn't recognize the tune."

"Oh, well." Nate shrugged. "Music never came easy to me."

"Our meeting is scheduled for 09:00 so the evening is ours. I suggest we do a quick reconnoiter of the location while we're out for a meal. Sir Alex mentioned we're meeting with a contact the Americans use, but didn't provide any specifics."

"Knowing American government agencies and their territorial mentality, it's not a surprise. Anyway, sounds like a plan. As long as I pick tonight's restaurant."

Trevor returned to his laptop.

*To: Topaz*
*From: Black*
*Acknowledge latest communiqué. Will approach meeting with due diligence.*

\*\*\*

On their way to dinner, Trevor and Nate headed toward the Arul Mihu Navasakhti Vinayagar Temple. The sun inched across the horizon as they threaded their way through the narrow streets, checking for surveillance by using storefronts as mirrors. They shifted from one side of the street to the other and doubled back on themselves as if they were lost.

A temple priest, dressed in long, multi-colored robes, opened a door when Nate and Trevor approached. Tourists wandered inside, removing their shoes as a sign of respect. An unrecognizable melody filled the air, created by a drum and a flute.

"Whoa! Didn't expect this." Nate whistled. "What intricate architecture and amazing colors. Must have taken ages to build."

"The mountain backdrop is a perfect setting to dramatize the temple's exterior." Trevor shifted from one spot to another while he gazed at the building. "Appears to be a door on either side, perfect for potential egress if required."

"Excellent." Nate snapped a few photographs and lowered his voice. "I wonder if our contact chose this location? Seems he knows his stuff."

Trevor nodded. "So, where's this restaurant you found? What type of food—creole?"

"The Marie Antoinette Restaurant—it's about a ten-minute walk from here and is a former colonial mansion. The restaurant is located in a residential neighborhood so it'll be easier to spot a tail."

"But what's creole?"

"Nothing to worry about. Creole's a blend of French, Spanish, and African cuisines, with a bit of spice added for extra zing."

"Ohhh." Trevor rubbed his stomach and bent over.

"What's the matter?"

"Nothing—practicing for when the spices hit me. I enjoy the eating experience but my stomach doesn't."

"Maybe they'll ease up on the spices for you—but I doubt it." Nate stopped and crouched, pretending to retie a shoelace. "We might have a shadow. Appears to be a local."

Trevor paused outside a shop window and pretended he was interested in the store's display. "Black jacket, jeans, mirror glasses, carrying a backpack?"

"He's the one."

"We'll find out later if he has any friends. Lead on to Marie Antoinette's."

"Just a couple of minutes and we'll be there."

Moments later, Trevor and Nate stood in front of the restaurant. Rough-hewn logs, painted a dark brown dominated the exterior, while a reddish-pink roof and lime green shutters made the building stand out among its more subdued neighbors.

Escorted to a table for two, they scanned the menu and made their selections—chicken curry for Trevor while Nate chose battered parrotfish.

Nate asked for directions to the restroom. Once he returned, he took a sip of his Coke. "Our tail has company. Another guy dressed the same."

After an enjoyable meal, they approached the counter to settle their bill. Nate paid while Trevor stepped to a corkboard covered with business cards left by previous customers. He fumbled in his wallet for a card and gazed out the window before pinning his to the collection.

Nate joined him and they headed toward the door. "Are they still waiting?"

Trevor laughed and shook the hand of the waiter who had scurried in front of them to escort them out. "Yes. Let's head back to the hotel and find out what the lads want."

They continued their aimless walk through the streets, pausing from time to time as if trying to find their way. Before long, they approached Victoria Market, one of the city's landmarks.

Although the market was closed for the evening and shutters drawn, tourists still wandered nearby. As Trevor and Nate approached, two men stepped out of the shadows.

"Appear to be clones of the two behind us." Nate glanced over his shoulder. "Yep, still there but not closing on us."

The two thugs in front of them stepped forward, pulling small knives from their pockets. The shorter man removed his glasses and gave Trevor and Nate a wicked grin while waving his dagger in a figure eight. "Hand over your money. Not be hurt. You are rich tourists, so you give to us."

Nate pulled a beat-up wallet from his back pocket and tossed it on the ground. "Here—take my money and let us go."

The robber put his knife back in his pocket. He inched forward and bent down to pick up the wallet.

Nate lashed out. His right foot connected under the man's chin. The man's head snapped back and he collapsed motionless to the ground.

The other man rushed toward Trevor, leading with his knife. Trevor threw a cross block and stepped back from the thug's outstretched arm. He grabbed the knife hand and squeezed a pressure point until the weapon clattered to the sidewalk.

Trevor followed with a left-handed punch, catching the fellow near the temple. Wordless, he dropped and hit the pavement with a thud.

Meanwhile, Nate faced the potential threat from the rear. The two men, who appeared younger, never attempted to join the fray.

Two police whistles resounded through the narrow street. Galvanized by the approaching officers, the young men dropped their knives and raced away.

A police sergeant and another officer approached. One glance at the scene and the sergeant appeared to understand what had happened. He turned to the second officer. "Cuff those two. Call for a vehicle to transport them to the station."

He gazed at Trevor and Nate. "Don't recognize either of you. I assume you're tourists who met some of our more unpleasant citizens?"

Trevor pointed at the one he punched. "Sergeant, we didn't mean to cause problems. We defended ourselves when they demanded our money and attacked with knives."

"Are either of you hurt? Might be a wise decision to visit our hospital. The doctors and nurses are first-rate."

Trevor and Nate shook their heads.

"We're fine." Trevor pointed up the hill toward their hotel. "We'll be at the Sunrise Small Hotel for another day or so if you require further information from us."

"I don't think it will be necessary. Please enjoy the remainder of your visit."

\*\*\*

The following morning, Trevor and Nate approached the Hindu temple about thirty minutes prior to their scheduled rendezvous. No sign of surveillance, they remained in the shadows waiting for the designated signal.

Nate glanced at his watch—fifteen minutes past time. "A no-show."

Trevor nodded. "A few minutes more and we'll return to the hotel."

When they entered the hotel's grounds, Nate headed to the garden, while Trevor went to his room.

A few minutes later, Trevor plopped on a bench next to Nate. "This setting is a perfect spot to relax. However, Topaz informed me I'd receive a call to arrange a new meeting location and time. We've visited several locations. I think we should use cover terms in front of the contact in case we must relocate."

Nate nodded. "Agree. Suggestions?"

Trevor handed Nate a hand-written note. "How's this?"

*Point Able – Hindu Temple*
*Point Bravo – News Café*
*Point Charlie – Natural History Museum*
*Point Delta - Marie Antoinette's*

Nate scanned the list. "Good suggestions. I spotted the sign for News Café near the Victoria Market. Seems a logical choice as we're familiar with the area."

"Wonder how long befo—"

Trevor's phone rang. He glanced at the number—local. "Hello?"

A synthesized voice responded. "Kumquat. Meet me at Victoria's clock tower in one hour." The call terminated.

"We're on. Remember the clock tower down the street? In an hour."

"A bit exposed, but maybe we can move to one of the chosen locations."

"Agree."

Minutes from their hotel, the tower dominated the roundabout at the intersection of Independence Avenue and State House Avenue. Trevor and Nate separated, taking turns walking past the clock, stopping and glancing at maps, before continuing their strolls.

Nate waited for traffic to clear and stepped into the roundabout to snap a photograph. Finished, he returned to the sidewalk and once again consulted his map.

Trevor joined Nate as a short, slender Asian man wearing a blue and orange baseball hat and black-rimmed glasses exited a nearby three-story building. He stumbled and slipped toward a two-foot-high stone wall topped with plants, a hand extended to arrest his fall.

Nate rushed over and grabbed the man, helping him to lean against the wall. "Let me help you."

The guy wrenched himself free from Nate's grasp and stood. He pulled off his cap and glasses. Long, black hair cascaded onto narrow shoulders as she tilted her head from side to side, framing her dark eyes, narrow lips, and pert nose. "I am Kumquat."

Trevor and Nate glanced at each other before focusing on the woman. "We are Topaz."

Trevor spoke with the woman as Nate stepped back, checking for surveillance. "Since we've established contact, it would be a prudent idea to relocate—to an area not so exposed."

Kumquat nodded.

"Nate, take point about one hundred yards ahead. We'll go to Point Bravo."

Trevor, Nate, and Kumquat climbed the green-railed steps of Trinity House a few minutes later and entered the News Café. They obtained a table along a wall near the rear of the busy shop.

"I'll order tea and cake. Okay for everyone?" Trevor flagged down a waitress and placed their order.

"What shall we call you?" Nate raised opened hands in the air. "You're a beautiful woman and I can't keep calling you a piece of fruit."

She giggled, covering her mouth with a hand. "My name is Mi-Cha." She glanced around and lowered her voice. "I work for the South Korean government."

Both Trevor and Nate nodded but remained silent.

"I request your help. My cousin lives in North Korea—he's in extreme danger. If his true identity is discovered, he'll be executed."

## Chapter Thirty

Munsu-dong Diplomatic Area
Pyongyang, North Korea

Three days after disembarking from the freighter *Krumen* in Sihanoukville, Soo unlocked the door to his government-provided apartment. He dropped his luggage on the floor and walked around, hoping his actions with the *Krumen* had prompted Supreme Leader Wook to release his family.

Located in Munsu-dong adjacent to the diplomatic area, Soo's family had been overjoyed with the expanse of their new home on the thirteenth floor of the dun-colored building. They enjoyed meeting other government functionaries who shared the building.

Silence.

Soo's heart sank—without his family, an empty apartment, more like a prison than a home. He collapsed on a sofa, head between his hands. *No more. I can't take any more.*

Time passed before he walked to an ornate desk—one of the wedding gifts from Wook. Two photographs in silver frames stood in the middle. One held a photo of Soo and Jung Gi on their wedding day. The other, taken last year, showed their two grinning boys.

He smiled. *I must be strong for them. Otherwise, everything is a sham—the government, position, power.* Soo snapped his fingers. *It can disappear in a moment as if nothing existed.*

He turned over a glass on the desk, uncorked a decanter of Jinro, and poured a healthy amount. Gazing at his wife's photo, he lifted the glass in a silent toast and downed the spirits in a single gulp. *I'd do anything to get my family out of Wook's control.*

Soo prepared a second drink and stepped back to the sofa. He lifted the glass of potent vodka-like soju and stopped. He hurled the glass across the room, where it shattered after striking the wall. *No!*

He stretched out on the sofa, an arm across his eyes. Sobbing, he remained in the same position, calling the names of his wife and children.

\*\*\*

After Soo departed Pyongyang Sunan International Airport in a government limousine, Kim hailed a taxi.

"Where to, please?"

"The Taedonggang Beer Shop. I'm tired—no more questions."

The taxi driver nodded and pulled away from the curb.

Kim closed his eyes.

"Sir? Sir? We are at your destination."

Kim jerked out of a light sleep and fumbled in a pocket for money. Without a word, he paid, left the taxi, and entered the shop.

A place for working-class men to meet at the end of the day, the Taedonggang Beer Shop was packed to capacity. No stools or chairs, the customers stood around tall tables, talking, laughing and drinking.

Kim scanned the crowd. There—at the rear, with two others. He pushed his way toward his objective. When he approached, the two men left, leaving his contact alone.

The short, stocky man eyed Kim before sliding a beer toward him.

Kim nodded in appreciation and downed half of his drink. "Tell our friend the task is finished."

"Welcome back. I will tell him. He wants to meet."

"In two days—usual place. I'm waiting for a summons, which I must attend."

"I'll pass the word."

Kim finished his beer and worked his way out of the bar. He meandered through the streets until he arrived at his apartment block in the workers' section of the city.

***

The shrill ring of the telephone startled Soo. Still dressed in the clothes he wore when he returned home the night before, he jumped from the sofa and ran to the phone.

He answered on the fourth ring. "Hello?"

"Good morning, Ambassador Soo. Did you enjoy your vacation?"

"Y-yes, but my jet lag is terrible. How are you, Nari?"

"I am fine, Ambassador. Your appointment is at one p.m. at the Ryongsong Residence. The driver will pick you up from your apartment thirty minutes before the meeting."

Soo stifled a gasp at the mention of Ryongsong.

"O-okay, Nari. Anything else?"

"No. Will you be in the office after your appointment?"

"I hope so." Soo dropped the receiver into its cradle. *What now? My last visit to Ryongsong ended in disaster.*

He paced the room, contemplating the summons. *Perhaps Wook is pleased with my efforts and will return my family.* He shook his head. *No. Wook doesn't forgive even a perceived slight. Until the oil flows, they will remain hostages.*

His stomach gurgled. *Time to eat.* Soo sniffed an armpit. *A shower first.*

Revitalized, Soo reviewed the transfer of weapons to the Somali pirates. *No issues, except for the Krumen's captain wanting more money.*

The intercom buzzed.

Soo jumped, unaware of the passing time. He left the apartment, locked the door, and hurried down the stairs. Floor after floor he went, cursing the lack of a working elevator. *Hasn't worked for weeks.*

When Soo exited the building, the driver waited by the car's door. Unlike the last time when Soo opened and closed his own door, the driver smiled, and assisted him into the vehicle.

As before, he paid no attention as the vehicle hurried through the streets. Once at the Ryongsong Residence, the driver escorted him to a more appropriate room, befitting his position.

No guards waited with him. Soo sat at an ornate cherry table laid with two informal place settings. *Tea and dim sum?*

Before long, the inner doors opened. Wook entered with a single guard, followed by a servant pushing a cart laden with a tea service and several covered dishes.

"Welcome back." A smile crept across Wook's face. "My congratulations on a job well done in delivering the weapons."

Soo shook the proffered hand and bowed. "Thank you, Supreme Leader. Not easy dealing with a lower-class crew and a scoundrel of a captain, but I insisted they follow my instructions."

Wook sat at the table, motioning for Soo to sit across from him. The servant poured tea, uncovered the dishes, and served portions of the appetizers to both men.

After eating in silence, Wook pushed his plate away and drained the cup. He gazed at Soo. "I have a surprise for you."

"I am honored, Supreme Leader." *Now what?*

Wook clapped his hands, and the inner doors opened again. Two young boys, Jae and Ki, entered the room. They bowed toward Wook before rushing to their father.

"*Appa! Appa!*" The boys ran to Soo who threw his arms around them in a smothering hug.

Wook acknowledged the boys and turned to Soo. He clapped his hands and the doors opened a third time.

Jung Gi!

Soo bowed to Wook. "Thank you, Supreme Leader. My most private wishes have come true."

"I'll give you fifteen minutes with your family—no more. Remember, they are still my guests until you complete your mission." Wook stood and left the room, the guard following.

Jung Gi hurried to Soo. "My husband—I missed you so."

"Did anyone hurt you? Wook told me he sent you to Camp Fourteen." Soo shook with rage at the vision of his wife at the mercy of the prison guards.

"No. One of my brother's guards took me with three other women to the camp. He left the others but brought me back. They've locked me in a room ever since." She placed a hand on Soo's arm. "I am unharmed."

Soo pulled her close so she wouldn't notice the tears welling in his eyes. *She's lost weight. No spark in her eyes.* He clenched her tighter. *I must free my family—somehow.*

Six guards entered the room.

Jung Gi kissed Soo as the guards pulled her from his embrace. "I must go now, my husband. Take care of yourself and one day we will be reunited." She knelt and kissed Jae and Ki. "I love you, my sons. Be strong." She held back her tears and kissed them again, giving each one a final hug.

Soo stood with the boys on either side of him as two of the guards escorted Jung Gi from the room.

"Appa, we want you to stay with us. Please?" Jae, the older of the two by a year, stared at his father with pleading eyes.

"No, my sons. The Supreme Leader wants you to remain here where you'll be safe while I conduct government business. We'll be together again, soon." *I hope.*

Guards grabbed the arms of the children and escorted them away, leaving Soo alone. He sat and pounded his fists on the table. He glanced at the door, hoping for another glimpse of his children. Nothing. He cradled his head on his arms and wept.

***

Soo entered his office and smiled when Nari rushed to him. He gave her a brief hug and stepped away.

"I'm glad to be back." He wiped his red eyes. "Wook allowed me a brief visit with my family, but I have more work to do before we are reunited."

"The Supreme Leader cares about his people, Ambassador. You are one of his instruments to keep our country safe."

Soo smiled. *She doesn't realize how evil Wook is. I didn't either until he took my family.*

"I brought you a present from Cambodia." He handed a gift-wrapped box to Nari.

She squealed with delight as she removed the paper, using caution so it might be reused at a later date. A black and silver box hid the gift.

Opening the cover, her eyes widened and a smile spread across her face. "Oh, Ambassador! What a beautiful checkered scarf. What brilliant colors. I will always treasure it."

Soo smiled and waved a hand. "It's called a *krama* and will help keep you warm during our winters."

Nari bowed. "Thank you, Ambassador."

\*\*\*

Major Kim sat in an antechamber waiting for his meeting with the Supreme Leader. Impatient, he crossed and uncrossed his legs before standing and examining a series of photographs depicting the Supreme Leader from childhood to the most powerful man in North Korea.

Doors swung inward and two guards entered. After confirming Kim's identity papers, one tilted his head toward the exit. "Come."

Kim left the room and marched along a nondescript hallway, flanked by the two men. They stopped at an unmarked door. "You may enter."

Kim stepped inside and found Wook waiting for him.

"Welcome back, Major Kim. Sorry for the delay. I dangled bait in front of Soo first."

"What did you bait him with, Supreme Leader?"

Wook laughed, a sinister snarl filling the room. "His family. He seems to think if he completes this mission to my satisfaction, I'll return his family."

"Very generous, Supreme Leader."

"I haven't forgotten Soo's incompetence which put our country and my leadership in an awkward position. I might allow him another visit, but I'll keep his family under my control."

Kim nodded. "A wise decision, if I may say so, Supreme Leader. Do you have a new mission for me?"

"Yes, for both of you. Return to the Seychelles in two days. Learn more about this pirate named Dacar." Wook thrust a hand toward Kim. "Kill him as a lesson to the others not to play games with me. I'm still waiting for delivery of the first oil tanker."

"I'm under the impression it's on the way, Supreme Leader."

"Never mind. You have your orders." He handed a sealed envelope to Kim. "Additional details are inside. You are dismissed." Wook turned and left the room.

The guards escorted Kim out of the palace. He went to a nearby taxi rank. Devoid of cabs, Kim waited with other passengers. He glanced around, sensing an unknown presence.

Shaking it off, Kim scanned the area. *Perhaps I'm overtired. Nothing out of the ordinary.*

Once an empty taxi stopped in front of him, he gave instructions for the driver to take him to the Taedonggang Beer Shop. Still early in the day, few customers occupied the tables. Kim ordered a beer, went to his accustomed spot at the rear and opened the envelope.

*Complete your mission as ordered. Should Soo meet with an unfortunate accident, no blame will fall on your shoulders. Do not fail.*

A hand grabbed Kim's shoulder. His heart raced as he prepared to attack.

"Relax. Here's another beer." His contact pushed over a fresh drink. "How did your meeting go?"

"I'm returning to the Seychelles. He wants the Somali pirate leader killed as a lesson to the others."

The man shrugged. "You've handled this type of mission before. What's another?"

"I'm to take the ambassador with me." Kim bowed his head. "He will die, too."

## Chapter Thirty-One

Jujubba Refugee Camp
Malindi, Kenya

Ian and Alf stared at the muscular bulk of Gerhard and the diminutive Pun. Alf grinned and stretched out a hand. It disappeared within Gerhard's grasp.

"I'm Corporal Alfred Livingston. My friends call me Alf." He wrenched his hand free, flexing his fingers to restart the blood flow. "Where is the rest of your team?"

"Ag, man. With your assistance, we won't require additional support. Pun is one of the best trackers in the world. I'm not too bad, either."

"Welcome to Jujubba." Ian smiled and motioned for Gerhard and Pun to sit. "I wish we'd met under better circumstances. Would you care for something to eat or drink?"

Pun remained silent, letting Gerhard carry the conversation. "Might be wise to refresh ourselves. We've been on the go for several hours. Afterward, we want to visit Prince George's quarters."

"George and I shared a tent." Alf laughed when Gerhard and Pun appeared puzzled by his familiar reference to the prince. "He didn't want any special treatment, so we always called him George. Ian and I are privy to his true identity, but no one else."

"Did you post guards in the evening?" Gerhard scratched the stubble on his chin as if something occurred to him.

"Before the initial kidnappings of several women, we didn't post guards." Ian glanced at the floor. "Jujubba is a quiet refuge, designed to help those in need. After the first incident, we hired two men."

"Did they remain at a static post or did they patrol?"

"They monitored a post near the main gate, but I asked them to patrol the perimeter every two hours."

"So, anyone paying attention would be able to time their attack when the guards were out of sight." Gerhard nodded. "How did they find out George worked here—perhaps inside help?"

"I don't think George was a specific target." Alf peered at Ian. "All of the male volunteers shared tents near the north side perimeter with the females located in the second row."

"I can't believe anyone inside this camp would aid kidnappers." Ian shook his head and frowned. "The refugees are almost dead when they arrive. The locals we employ earn an excellent wage by local standards. Why would they jeopardize a steady income when well-paying jobs are hard to find?"

Stifling a yawn, Gerhard stretched and struggled to his feet. "Ag. I suggest we quit for tonight and begin anew after daybreak." He shifted toward Ian. "Do you have a spare tent Pun and I might use? If not, we brought one."

"There's an empty one near Alf. He'll show you the way."

"Excellent. In the morning. I want to view the tent where you stayed. Perhaps we'll pick up some clues."

\*\*\*

Gerhard opened his eyes as a rooster crowed. Pun sat on his camp bed, dressed and sharpening his kukri against a well-used whetstone.

Pun smiled at him. "Get changed. Time to work."

"Ag, man. I thought I gave the orders."

Gerhard dressed and they stepped outside. Two rows of brown, two-person tents, lined an area close to the fence.

Alf approached. "Sorry about the accommodations. These are excess British officer supplies, complete with a canvas floor. The best we can do."

Gerhard laughed. "Plenty of space."

"I suppose for one night. As you'll notice in the tent I shared with George, we also kept a small chest for personal items and a lantern." Alf led them to a tent on the outer row.

"This is where we stayed. I moved my personal belongings to my new tent but tried to preserve things the way they were prior to the kidnapping."

Inside, both beds were overturned. Reddish-brown splotches stained both the pillows. The lantern lay on the floor, smashed. The chest had been tipped over.

"Not much to see. The stains are blood—both of us received some minor injuries during the scuffle."

"Enough." Gerhard nudged Pun. "Any clues to help us?"

Pun gazed around the tent before shaking his head.

"Okay, show us the fence where the kidnappers entered the compound."

Alf led them to a spot about twenty yards away. Four strands of barbed wire stretched from post to post, but the two lower pieces had been cut.

"This is where they entered and forced us out and dragged us out there." Alf gestured to several sand dunes about 100 yards away.

"Thank you, Alf. Let's eat breakfast and talk with Ian before we depart."

As they walked past the small tents, they neared rows of larger ones.

"The green tents are for the refugees. Each one will hold twenty people, but sometimes we squeeze in a few more. There are one hundred of these tents, so we can handle at least two thousand refugees." Alf's chest swelled with pride. "The five camps near Dadaab can hold almost two hundred fifty thousand people. They receive most of the aid donations, but we do a decent job."

They jumped up the three steps to the veranda and entered the camp office. Ian wasn't inside, so Gerhard powered up his iPad. One new message.

*To: Green, Black*
*From: Topaz*
*Sensitive source confirms a couple from Europe had been held captive at a small compound in the vicinity of Kidi Faani, Somalia. Current whereabouts unknown but believed heading north.*

*Locate and determine whether the couple is the missing George and the Italian woman. Acknowledge.*

Gerhard acknowledged the message and closed his iPad. "Prince George and Silvia might be located near a village called Kidi Faani in Somalia." He leaned toward Pun. "Plot the fastest possible course to this village."

Pun nodded and pulled out his tablet. Head down, he poked a few characters.

Alf snapped his fingers. "One of the kidnappers mentioned 'kidifani' or something similar. Didn't realize it might be a location. Sounded like a local word."

"Ag, man. No worries. Let's chat with Ian, grab our kit, and begin the hunt."

"What about breakfast?" Alf rubbed his rumbling stomach.

"Ag, man. I almost forgot. Must eat first."

Ian entered the office in time to overhear Gerhard's words. "Breakfast will be here soon. Two of the volunteers are bringing our food."

"While we wait, I must inform you we've identified a lead on Prince George's whereabouts." Gerhard gazed at

Alf. "I can't provide specifics, but we might find him soon."

"Excellent news!" Ian's eyes brightened. "Do you require anything else before you depart?"

"Two things: breakfast and a translator."

Everyone laughed. They ate a quick meal of fresh fruit and chapatis, washed down with mango juice.

"An excellent repast." Gerhard burped to emphasize his enjoyment. "Much better than field rations eh, Pun?"

Pun chewed and nodded.

"When you're ready to depart, Dalmar will join you. He's one of the older Somali youths working at the camp. He translates for me, so there shouldn't be any difficulties. Dalmar speaks Swahili, too."

"Thank you, Ian." Gerhard offered his hand. "We better be on our way."

The four men climbed into the battered Toyota Land Cruiser and departed. Gerhard handled the initial driving duties while Pun and Dalmar discussed the best way to reach Kidi Faani. Alf sat in the front passenger seat, a carbine across his lap.

Sand dunes and rocks baked under the relentless sun. Stunted shrubs scratching an existence out of the harsh terrain dotted the various shades of brown. The monotony of the bleak landscape and the rocking of the vehicle soon lulled Alf to sleep.

They crossed into Somalia, following a dusty trail. Several hours later, with Alf driving, they approached a small river.

"Kidi Faani not far now." Dalmar's face beamed. "On the other side of the river, perhaps eight kilometers or five of your miles, a bit to the east."

Pun took over the driving duties after they found a shallow area to ford the river.

"Ag, man. Keep your eyes open." Gerhard charged his SA-80 assault rifle. "There's a village ahead."

They entered the village and stopped by a well in the square. Goats, a couple of sheep, and several chickens appeared to be the primary occupants. The buildings leaned upon one another for support. Once painted in shades of blue, white, and pink, the colors now blended together.

A man stepped out of the largest building and trudged toward the vehicle. Dalmar climbed out and spoke to the man for several minutes, punctuated by various animated gestures.

They shook hands. Dalmar turned, grinned, and gave a thumbs up.

Gerhard jumped out of the Toyota, hauling a duffle bag with him.

"Mr. Gerhard, this is the village elder, Mohammed. The villagers know of the camp we seek, but they avoid contact except when two women come to the village to buy supplies. He says the camp is about two kilometers north and west of Kidi Faani."

"Please thank him for us and give him this." Gerhard handed over the duffle. "It's a token of our appreciation for his assistance."

Dalmar struggled with the bulging bag and set it on the ground at Mohammed's feet. Like a child opening a present, Mohammed opened the zipper and pulled out the contents. His eyes grew wider as he delved through the array of staples: corn, rice, flour, and millet. At the bottom of the bag, a package of hard candy, each contained in a colorful plastic wrapper.

Mohammed shook Gerhard's hand before putting the items back in the bag and dragging it toward the building.

\*\*\*

Pun advanced the vehicle toward the camp. No one responded to their approach. A gap between the gates, broad enough for a person to slip through, narrowed as a shadow stretched toward them.

*Bleat. Baa.*

Curious, two kids approached the now-silenced vehicle, the heated engine creating a series of clicks as the metal cooled.

"Young goats." Alf tightened the grip on his weapon. "Are they loose, wandering around, or did someone send them toward us as a distraction?"

Pun pulled out his kukri, eased the driver's door open, and snuck up to the gates. After a glance inside, he shook his head and entered.

"Stop!"

Pun turned to his left and followed the command.

A woman appeared, her eyes wide with fright. She held a machete in her right hand.

Pun relaxed and whistled.

Gerhard and Alf rushed through the gates, weapons at the ready. Their translator followed.

"Ag, man. What's this?" Gerhard faced Dalmar. "Ask who she is. Explain we are searching for a foreign man and woman."

Dalmar spoke with the woman. As they talked, two other women came closer, both carrying machetes.

"She says her name is Jamiila. The other women are Maryan and Khalli."

"I speak English." Jamiila stepped forward. "Come with me. You must be thirsty."

The men relaxed and followed. The women took them to benches underneath a massive damal tree. Khalli brought water and fruit. Jamiila went to one of the buildings and returned with four girls.

"This is the camp of Asad, a member of al-Shabaab." Jamiila's hand swept across the air. "Maryan is his mother and Khalli is his aunt. They attend to the men when they are here."

"Where are you from?" Gerhard took a bite of mango. "Your English is excellent."

"I am Somali. I used to work as a translator for the American Embassy before the Americans left my country. I worked there for five years, not long enough to receive a relocation visa, so I ended up homeless and fled south with my children to escape the fighting and starvation."

"It must have been difficult for you. What brought you here?"

Jamiila's eyes brimmed with tears. "Things were no better in the south, so I took my children to a refugee camp in Kenya. Asad kidnapped these girls and me."

"The man and woman we're searching for were taken from Jujubba Refugee Camp."

Jamiila gasped, her hands flying up to hide her face. "Asad kidnapped me from Jujubba." She sobbed. "My children are still there."

"Miss, I work for Mr. Ian." Dalmar pointed to the south. "If you help these men, I will return to the camp and let Mr. Ian and your children know you are safe."

"Yes, I'll help. My children are Abuukar and Bayda. Please tell them I love and miss them. We'll be together soon."

"Yes, Miss." Dalmar turned to Gerhard. "May I return to Jujubba?"

"Ag. Yes, of course, as long as Jamiila assists us."

Alf glanced around the compound. "Where's everyone? Are there other captives?"

"Asad and the others went north—to a camp near Kismaayo. They took three female captives with them."

Gerhard stood and stretched. "What about the foreigners?"

"Men brought them here a few days ago. They stopped long enough to eat and rest. The man was tall, with red hair and a sunburned nose. He had many scratches and a black eye. The woman had long, greasy hair. Her skin was darker, but not like mine. Her face had cuts and blisters."

Jamiila finished a slice of papaya and wiped her hands on her brown skirt. "They left several hours later with the hostages. I overheard them saying they were joining the others."

Maryan turned to Jamiila and spoke for several minutes. Jamiila nodded and asked a few questions before speaking again in English.

"Maryan says she overhead the leader say they were taking the hostages to Tahliil. He's one of the al-Shabaab leaders. She also pleads with you not to hurt Asad. He didn't kidnap the foreigners." Jamiila dropped her head, gazing at the ground. "H-he also protected me from the others."

"Ag." He shook his head. "If the foreigners are there and he hasn't hurt them, as long as he puts down his weapons and surrenders, I'll do what I can."

"Please." Maryan grasped Gerhard's arm. "If it's Allah's will, everything will have a positive outcome."

"Anyone pointing a weapon at me will find I have little patience." Gerhard clenched his jaw, his eyes darkened like flint. "I will protect my team and the foreigners—even if someone tries to stop me. To my last breath."

The ever-quiet Pun twisted his face into what passed for a smile and unsheathed his kukri. "Me, too."

## Chapter Thirty-Two

Al-Shabaab Camp
Outside Kismaayo, Somalia

Livestock and fowl alike remained in their normal resting spots within the compound. A line of twenty vehicles, comprised of Toyota Land Cruisers, Land Rovers, Jeep Cherokees, and old army trucks, formed. Tahliil's men climbed aboard.

A hint of dawn twinkled on the distant horizon as Tahliil completed a satellite phone call. Away from the others, no one overheard his conversation.

"Yes, today in Kismaayo …. Tonight in Afgooye …. Captives, too …. Yes, thank you."

Tahliil terminated the call and placed the phone in his pocket. He grabbed a backpack and his AK-47 and walked to the lead vehicle.

After he stowed his pack at his feet and cradled the weapon on his lap, he turned to the driver. He waved a hand in a forward motion. "We go now Afgooye. Take break in two hours."

The driver nodded, engaged the gearshift, and led the battered convoy out of the camp toward Kismaayo.

Tahliil rocked to the movement of the Jeep, going over his plan. *Attack in Kismaayo today. Everyone else will rendezvous at the Afgooye camp. Tomorrow brings offensive in Mogadishu and two or three days later, it's Bosaasso's turn. What to do with the foreign captives?*

The driver turned left on the road outside Kismaayo and headed north toward Jamaame en route to Afgooye.

By the time the two-hour mark approached for their first rest stop, the convoy had driven through Jamaame.

They pulled to the side of the road. Drivers topped off their fuel tanks from five-gallon containers, while the remainder of the men stretched.

In the middle of sand dunes, sparse vegetation, and almost non-existent traffic, the foreign hostages were allowed a few minutes to work kinks from cramped limbs. The Somali captives remained tied in the back of a stolen troop carrier.

Tahliil whistled and waved his right arm in a windmill fashion. Busuri and Hasan hustled to his side. "Where Asad and Warsame? Want them, too."

Once the others arrived, Tahliil gave a quick update. "Busuri, I want Mogadishu attack tomorrow. Warsame, help Hasan with Boosaaso. I go Nairobi—Asad you run Afgooye camp."

The lieutenants nodded. Busuri pursed his lips, a frown etched across his features. "What is so important in Nairobi for you to be away when our attacks are ready to begin?"

Tahliil glared at him, his jaw clenched and eyes like small lumps of coal. "Al-Shabaab business. Tell later. Back to vehicles—time to go."

The convoy inched onto the road, gathering speed as the group continued north.

*Why don't they obey without asking questions?* Tahliil dug a finger into an ear, scratching an itch. *Always problems to deal with. The meeting in Nairobi will help.*

\*\*\*

Harbi waited until the sun was overhead before leading the remaining men out of the camp. The technicals—two Jeep Cherokees, and two Toyota Land Cruisers—bristled with weapons. His men remained relaxed, laughing and joking.

*I wonder how they will respond. For many, this will be their first attack—and their last. Will they be brave or flee when bullets chase them?* Harbi pulled the magazine from his AK-47 and checked the spring action. Satisfied, he replaced the magazine and chambered a round.

The four vehicles entered Kismaayo and continued on the main thoroughfare in the direction of the city center. Two blocks later, traffic became congested. Buses lined both sides of the street. On the left, hundreds of people shouted support for their favorite soccer team.

*How I miss playing.* Harbi shook his head. *All in the past—my country requires my services as we rebuild.*

Without warning, the driver slammed on the brakes, Harbi's head smashed into the windshield. About to shriek abuse, he swallowed his words and stared as a Somali tank blocked the middle of the street.

"Back! Hurry!"

Harbi turned and glanced out the back of the Toyota. Another tank blocked the street behind them.

"Ambush!"

Soldiers popped up from hidden positions along the rooftops on either side of them. The tank blocking the convoy lowered its barrel, aiming at the center of Harbi's vehicle.

He reached out with his AK-47 and fired. In moments, the four vehicles were in flames as multiple tank rounds and rocket-propelled grenades smashed through the unarmored technicals.

Men tried to escape, firing their weapons at the rooftops. Showing no mercy, the soldiers continued to shoot until the bodies stopped moving.

Harbi gasped. "We've failed. Tahliil set us up." His body relaxed as he expired, reunited with his nineteen men in death.

\*\*\*

Several hours later, Tahliil's convoy entered a massive compound outside Afgooye. A ten-foot concrete block wall concealed within the sprawling fields of a banana plantation surrounded the compound's perimeter, with a watchtower on each corner.

The convoy stopped in front of a two-story whitewashed building. Tahliil dismounted and called for Asad, who rushed forward.

"Take command. Bring foreigners. Put them in room." Tahliil pointed to the second floor. "I talk again."

"Yes, Tahliil."

"You take room on bottom floor."

Asad nodded as Tahliil entered the building. He went to his bedroom and packed a small carry-on.

A knock interrupted his packing. "Come."

Asad entered and reported. "Tahliil, the foreigners are locked in a room down the hall on the right—the one with the deadbolt outside the room. They are still tied up."

"Take bindings off. Nowhere to escape. Give water and fruit. I come soon."

When Tahliil entered George and Silvia's makeshift prison, he noted Asad had done as instructed. *Good lad—follows orders well. Does he have an evil heart like so many? Or is he trapped like me? Must find out.*

George and Silvia sat on the edge of a bed, eating bananas. They stopped and stood.

Tahliil motioned for them to sit and pulled a straight-backed chair forward. "I'm leaving soon for the airport, but I wanted to check on your condition."

George glanced at Silvia. "We're fine. Your man, Asad, made us as comfortable as possible during the journey and since arriving. May I ask where we are?"

Tahliil pursed his lips as he pondered the question. *Why not tell them?* "We are in the middle of a plantation, which was not taken from my family. When we acquired this property, my father put it in my great-great grandfather's name. Everyone had forgotten about him.

Those who attacked the government in the coup took everything else—including my family."

"When will you return? I've enjoyed our chats. You're a very intelligent person who has endured much." *Similar to my family.*

George nodded and rubbed his peeling forehead.

"The flights are twice a week, so I'll return in four or seven days." Tahliil stood and pushed the chair back in its original position. "I instructed Asad to ensure you remain in good health. We'll speak again soon."

\*\*\*

At eight p.m., Asad returned to the room where George and Silvia were held. Another man accompanied him, both bearing trays. After setting his on the foot of George's bed, the man departed.

"We bring you food and water." Asad pointed to the trays. "The same as we ate—mutton stew, chapatis, and bananas."

"Thank you, Asad." George picked up a spoon and sampled the stew. "Hot. I'll wait for it to cool."

"When I first saw you at the camp outside Kismaayo, you both wore clothes which didn't fit. Why?"

"They took us from Jujubba in the middle of the night. We weren't dressed for traveling."

Asad nodded. "Makes sense. How are the new clothes I sent you?"

"Snug, but a much better fit."

A frown etched across Silvia's face. "I'm still wearing men's clothing, but at least these are clean and closer to my size."

"I'm sorry, but the only other option was to provide you with what Somali women wear."

Silvia shook her head.

"How soon will we be released?" George gazed at Asad until he glanced away. "Is Tahliil making arrangements?"

"I know not what Tahliil is doing. But, he instructed me to protect both of you until his return. I will do so." Asad reached out and twisted the door handle. "I'll leave so you can eat your meal. We'll speak tomorrow."

***

Busuri and Asad shared breakfast as night faded. Both lost in thought, it was a quiet and solemn affair.

"Asad, pray to Allah we are successful with our efforts today." Busuri rubbed a hand over his face. *We will be victorious. I hope.*

"I will do so, Busuri. We'll be waiting for your return. May Allah guide you and your men."

Asad walked with Busuri to the waiting line of vehicles. Busuri climbed into the front passenger's seat and the ten trucks departed.

About forty-five minutes later, the convoy entered Mogadishu and continued toward the city center. At the K-7 roundabout, they turned right in the direction of three of their targets.

The group remained together, passing the Mogadishu International Airport. The vehicles slowed when the asphalt road gave way to sand. They continued south, away from the city. A tall, brown building appeared on the left—the electrical plant. The first five trucks pulled over while the remainder headed to the refinery, now within view.

Busuri spoke into his radio. "Laba (two) this is Kow (one)."

"Go ahead, Kow."

"Plant your parcels and set the timers for ten minutes and return here."

"Understood."

Busuri jumped out of the Jeep Cherokee. His men climbed out of the other vehicles and followed. They dropped into a shallow depression where he scratched a rough sketch in the sand. "Place the charges at the four corners of the building. Once the bombs detonate, shoot at any workers fleeing the building."

"Question, Busuri. What will we do next?"

"After the attacks on the refin—"

"Kow this is Laba. Five minutes to detonation."

Busuri turned to his men. "Hurry! The others are ahead of schedule."

The men scooted up the embankment and rushed toward the plant.

*Boom! Boom!*

Thick black smoke and flames shot upward from the refinery, visible to Busuri two miles away. A shockwave rolled past, rocking him back on his feet. "Laba this is Kow. Come in. What happened?"

"Kow this is …. This is Laba. The bombs exploded early. We don't know why. Many of the men are dead or injured!"

"Hurry—join us."

*Boom!*

The closest corner of the power plant disintegrated in a cloud of dust. Broken pieces of concrete blocks hurled through the air, one almost decapitating Busuri.

His men rushed at him, some carrying their weapons, other empty-handed. Of the ten vehicles, four remained.

Busuri's driver died when a chunk of masonry smashed through the windshield and embedded itself in his chest. Dragging the corpse out the door, Busuri climbed into the blood-soaked seat, started the engine, and headed back toward K-7. The other three vehicles followed.

\*\*\*

Hasan, Warsame, and their men arrived outside Boosaaso late in the afternoon, having traveled the longest distance. While the men rested, Hasan, accompanied by Warsame, headed into the city, using the bullet-ridden Toyota in which Gari led the first Kismaayo attack.

"We'll check out the port so we can plan our approach to the fish processing plant and the tannery." Hasan pulled Gari's pistol from his holster and rubbed the barrel along his jaw. "We will make the government pay for killing my friend."

"When do you want to attack?"

"Tomorrow evening, after the plants close for the night. Unlike Tahliil, I don't believe in unnecessary bloodshed." *I wonder how the other attacks have gone?*

\*\*\*

The Kenyan Airways flight touched down on schedule at Jomo Kenyatta International Airport. With a short taxi, the plane soon reached its gateway. Seated near the exit and with a single carry-on bag, Tahliil was one of the first passengers to disembark.

After flashing his false diplomatic passport to the customs official, he was ushered through. Beyond the baggage area, people waited for loved ones while others waved signs to catch the eye of people they were charged with collecting.

Tahliil nodded to the man holding a sign with his false name and followed him out of the airport to a waiting limousine.

"Sir, your room is ready at the Hilton Hotel, and a table is reserved for you in their restaurant whenever you wish to eat."

"Thank you." Tahliil yawned. "Were there any messages for me?"

"Yes, sir. Dinner reservations are set for tomorrow evening at the Carnivore Restaurant. Your dining companion will meet you there."

Tahliil nodded and yawned again.

The driver remained silent as he drove into the city. When they arrived at the hotel, the driver escorted him to check-in.

"Sir, I'll collect you at six tomorrow evening."

"Thank you." Tahliil reached into his wallet and pulled out some money.

The driver shook his head. "It isn't necessary, sir. Your friend took care of things."

A bellhop took Tahliil's luggage and escorted him to a suite on one of the upper floors. Tahliil washed and changed. After eating alone in the hotel's restaurant, he returned to his suite and retired early. *Should be my first decent sleep in weeks.*

\*\*\*

A do not disturb sign on the door, Tahliil slept late the following morning. When he arose, he soaked himself in a hot bath, before heading to the breakfast buffet.

He enjoyed a satisfying meal of scrambled eggs, beef sausage, fried potatoes, toast, and tea. Finished, he stopped by reception to purchase a local newspaper and returned to his room where he changed into swimming trunks.

Tahliil went to the hotel's pool for a swim.

Skin wrinkled from being immersed for so long, Tahliil dried himself and settled on the lounger to read the *Daily Nation*. Two articles on the front page caught his attention.

He read the first story, a smile spreading across his face. At the end of the four paragraphs, he laughed. *The Somali Army verifies they killed forty terrorists when they thwarted an attack in Kismaayo. Harbi took nineteen men with him—so they're all dead.*

The second article detailed attacks on the Mogadishu electricity-generating plant and the oil refinery. *More excellent news—both are still operational but the police killed and captured twenty al-Shabaab terrorists. Hmmm.*

Tahliil scanned the paper for other reports of interest. Finding nothing, he dropped the paper and settled in for an afternoon snooze.

\*\*\*

The clock struck six p.m. in the hotel lobby as a well-groomed man in a dark pinstripe suit, white shirt, and blue tie, stepped out of the elevator. He shrugged away offers of a taxi and watched his driver approach.

Twenty minutes later, the limousine stopped in front of the Carnivore Restaurant in Langata, on the outskirts of Nairobi. As Tahliil entered the restaurant, a smiling host welcomed him. He mentioned his reservation and the host led him past a massive barbeque pit. The aroma of various types of meat cooking on Masai swords over a charcoal fire made his mouth water.

They approached a table for two at the rear of the restaurant, reserved for diners who request privacy. A woman glanced up, a smile on her face. She stood, adjusted her black sleeveless dress, and walked toward Tahliil with a slight limp. They shook hands and kissed each other on both cheeks.

"Tallie, I'm glad you made the trip. There is so much to discuss. How is your daughter?"

"Hello, Evelyn. You're radiant as always. I find it difficult to determine who is more beautiful—you or Jamiila."

# Chapter Thirty-Three

Permanent Joint Operating Base
Diego Garcia

The two British Typhoon FGR-4 aircraft streaked toward Diego Garcia. They left Kenya far behind, although the Mombasa control tower continued to call until they faded away. The flight leader ignored the pleas for them to return and switched the radio to a new channel.

"No way I'm responding to his demands. Okay, Rebel, what's so important we've been hijacked to provide door-to-door delivery service for you and White?"

"Yeehaw! Never been in a taxi which can travel faster than the speed of sound."

"Bet no cab can do this either." Without warning, the pilot rolled the aircraft, so the bottom of the plane faced the sky.

"Fer sure." Rebel's voice tapered off. "Don't suppose you might flip us back? My stomach isn't where it should be."

"What's the matter? Is the poor newbie suffering from a little disorientation? Need your sea daddy?"

"How'd you know I was in the Navy?"

"Wasn't sure but didn't think you belonged in the Air Force or you wouldn't be hugging the panic strap."

"How do you know I grabbed the panic strap?"

"Experience. I did the same when a senior pilot rolled the aircraft on me."

Rebel chuckled. "Excellent observation skills. What will I be doing next?"

"Beats me—I'm not clairvoyant. Just escorting a fellow serviceman to his destination."

"Former serviceman. I'm a civilian now."

"Uh huh. I understand—hush-hush."

Rebel yawned. "I'm bushed."

"Another hour or so before we land in Diego. I'll keep the flight smooth and let you take a kip."

\*\*\*

Rebel woke when he overheard the flight leader speaking with the Diego control tower. When the conversation stopped, Rebel coughed.

"Oh, you're awake. We'll land in a couple of minutes."

The jet angled toward the ground. Rebel searched for the runway.

"Five miles out."

"Uh, where's the runway?"

"Hang on." The pilot banked to the left, throttled back to idle, and pulled up in a crosswind turn to reduce speed. The aircraft continued descending.

"Holy crap!" Rebel closed his eyes, bracing for the impending crash.

The gear and flaps extended as the jet banked again and continued to slow.

Rebel's stomach forced its way upward. He gulped as the aircraft kissed the runway. After sighing with relief, he shouted, "Yeehaw!"

The flight leader laughed. "First combat landing? We practice whenever possible. Gets you on the ground much quicker than commercial aircraft. Less chance of being left vulnerable to enemy aircraft and ground fire."

"I feel safer underwater. You flyboys can keep the skies."

The two aircraft taxied behind a pickup truck with a sign in the rear stating: 'follow me.' They continued to a revetment area where a Navy vehicle waited, with a British Petty Officer standing nearby.

The four men descended. After removing their helmets, the flight leader twirled the end of his mustache. "Our bit's finished. Good luck with your mission."

"Well, thank y'all for a mighty fine ride, Squadron Leader."

Still pale from the flight, Fergus shook his head. "I tink I'll fly commercial next time. Glad someone provided a barf bag. I didn't use it, but the bag gave me great comfort."

They shook hands as the petty officer stepped forward and saluted. "Sirs, I'll take you to your quarters to clean up before your first meeting." He handed each of them a massive envelope. "Your room keys and a welcome package."

\*\*\*

An hour later, refreshed after hot showers and a change of clothes, Rebel and White rejoined their escort. They hopped in the Land Rover and the driver took them to a small building set apart from the others. A six-foot-tall fence topped with concertina wire surrounded the one-story facility. Unlike nearby buildings, no signs identified its purpose.

"You must show identification to enter. Someone will let me know when to return for you." The airman saluted and withdrew.

After showing their identification at an entry booth manned by armed Marines, an unsmiling able seaman took them inside. Rebel and White followed as the man marched to the end of the corridor and knocked once on a door. He opened it and stood aside, allowing them to enter.

A short man with a balding head and wearing civilian clothes and thick glasses stood behind a gray metal desk. Two chairs faced the workspace, which held a small lamp, the base in a shape of an anchor. A folder lay in front of him. He joined the men.

"Greetings. Sir Alex instructed me to invoke his name when meeting you. I'm Commodore Smithers. I'll be your coordinator until we hand you over to *HMS Snapdragon*. He provided a physical description and photos of you, so I know with whom I'm speaking. Please use Rebel and White with everyone. We're used to hush-hush comings and goings."

"Thank you, sir. I hope we're not any nuisance." White shook the offered hand.

Rebel followed suit.

"Please be seated. Would you like tea or coffee?"

Both men shook their heads.

"Right—to business. *HMS Snapdragon* will arrive tomorrow morning, stopping long enough for you to hop aboard. The remainder of your time on the 'Footprint of Freedom,' as the Americans like to refer to our island, is up to you."

Commodore Smithers gazed at Rebel. "I understand you've brought some, ah, parcels with you. Do you realize Diego Garcia is subject to British Customs? Explosives are on the controlled list."

"Yes, sir, we're aware. They're disguised as toys and they weren't scanned when we arrived. If Customs had done so, we carried a sealed letter signed by the British Prime Minister requesting a waiver to the controls."

"More of Sir Alex's work, no doubt." The commodore waved a hand in the air. "We've arranged for a discarded barge to be anchored about four miles away for your practice."

Rebel's eyes lit up. "Thank you, sir. I must show White how these things work before we deploy. Don't want to blow ourselves up."

The commodore chuckled. "I would like to see how they function—from a distance, of course."

"Aye-aye, sir."

\*\*\*

Rebel steered the rented powerboat toward the barge while White conducted another check of their equipment. The craft skimmed over gentle waves as they neared their destination.

White tossed a drift anchor over the side when Rebel cut the engine. Remaining about half a mile from the barge, the men donned their diving gear.

Rebel opened two small Styrofoam containers. Nestled inside, two action figure toys, painted red, white, and blue.

He handed one to White. "Check this out. Dr. Charles Edwards, who handles our computer requirements, loves engineering and designed these for us. He's the guy who came up with fake gas canisters to swap with those holding sarin gas during our mission in Turkey."

White turned the toy over, examining the details. "I remember playing with toys like these in the early eighties when I was a kid."

Rebel laughed. "Ah think these pack more of a wallop. Each one contains over a pound of military-grade C-4. It's molded into the shape of some of the original parts, with magnetic strips added to the snap-on accessories. Shove in a detonator, clamp onto the desired target and clear the area."

"I can't wait to give them a try."

Rebel nodded and handed the second one to White. "Here ya go. We'll work together under the barge—you'll secure both toys and I'll be there to assist."

Thirty minutes later, they climbed back on the boat. Rebel started the engine while White grabbed the anchor. They headed toward shore and stopped.

"Now."

*Whoosh!*

Two plumes of water erupted skyward from either side of the rocking barge.

"Well, hush my mouth." Rebel slapped White on the back. "Excellent work—you can be my swim buddy anytime. Now to prepare for the *Zebu*."

\*\*\*

Their escort from the day before arrived at 08:00. White and Rebel loaded their gear and they set off. After a short drive, they pulled up to a gangway providing access to *HMS Snapdragon*.

"This is as far as I take you, sirs. The buzz says you're on a secret mission. Good luck." He shook hands. "Someone will escort you to the wardroom for a spot of tea, before you meet the old man."

Rebel glanced at White. "So much for our mission being under the radar."

"Must not be much news here, so we've stirred things up." White laughed. "Let's be on our way."

They climbed the gangway of the type-45 destroyer and showed their identification. A seaman verified their names with information held on a clipboard.

"Follow me, sirs. Commander Pierce is waiting for you on the bridge."

They entered the bridge where a tall, slender man, with blond hair and blue eyes, sat in a captain's chair reading a report. "Ah, our guests are here." He stood and shook hands.

"I'm Commander Ben Pierce, Commanding Officer." He gazed at the men. "You have friends in high places to pull this ship from its mission. I've been given orders to resume our duties. We'll proceed at flank speed as soon as we're five miles from DG."

"Ah beg your pardon, Commander." Rebel laughed. "We're part of the same team, and like you, we understand orders—at least most of the time."

Commander Pierce chuckled. "That's what I like—someone who will stand their ground. We'll get along fine. Let's go to the wardroom and I'll buy you a tea."

As they sipped on the hot brew, the commander pulled the report from his pocket. "A few minutes before you boarded, we received a signal from the Greek frigate *HS Navarone*."

He drained his cup. "She's been tailing the *Zebu* but got too close. Several RPG rounds fired from the stern of the *Zebu* hit her, causing minimal damage but several injuries. The *Navarone* is continuing to follow but at a safer distance."

"How close will you be able to take us, Commander?" Rebel pursed his lips as he rubbed his chin.

"The *Zebu* doesn't appear to be in any hurry to reach their destination and made little headway during the night. If we approach during darkness, we'll get as close as you want."

"I don't mind a short swim, but shorter is better." White nudged Rebel. "I'm a diver, but don't care for long swims, while my friend is a natural in the water."

Rebel shrugged. "I served with the SEALs in a former life."

The commander tapped his nose and glanced at Rebel. "We'll get you on top of the *Zebu* if need be."

\*\*\*

Fifteen hours later, *HMS Snapdragon* approached the Greek frigate's position. Three miles beyond, the *Zebu* lay in darkness, moving at steerage speed.

Commander Pierce met with Rebel and White on the bridge. "The Greeks will continue to creep closer, masking our approach. At one-mile separation, they will match the *Zebu*'s speed."

Both Rebel and White nodded but remained silent.

"When we secure our position to starboard and ahead of the *Navarone*, the gangway will be lowered. Seamen will assist getting your Seabobs and equipment into the water. Lieutenant Brown will show you the way. From there, it's up to you. Godspeed."

"Thank you, Commander." Rebel appeared calm as ice. "We'll proceed underwater until we can pop up under their stern. Once we attach our packages, we'll zip back. We'll be back onboard before detonation."

With Lieutenant Brown leading the way, the Bedlam duo collected their gear and joined the others on the gangway. Donning their wetsuits, flippers, oxygen tanks, and goggles, Rebel and White slid into the sea and grabbed a Seabob. In a pouch hooked to their belts, each man carried two of the action figure explosive devices.

Capable of twelve miles per hour underwater with the Seabobs, they covered the short distance between *HMS Snapdragon* and the *Zebu* in minutes. They placed a magnetic package on either side of the rudder. With sufficient time remaining before the one-hour duration of the Seabobs' batteries expired, Rebel pointed downward toward the propeller. With a nod, White followed him.

The tanker was almost at a standstill as they neared the propeller hub. Rebel shook his head and swam away, waiting for White.

With a sudden spurt of energy, Rebel swam forward, grabbed White's right ankle and yanked. Pulled away from the hub, White twisted his body and glanced behind.

Rebel pointed up. The slow-moving propeller would have caught White if it weren't for Rebel's quick action.

Thumb and index finger forming a circle, White signaled he was okay. Rebel patted him on the back and they swam back to the rides.

Forty minutes after leaving the *Snapdragon*, the men climbed back onboard. Stripping off their gear, they shook each other's hands.

"Many thanks, Rebel. Dat propeller would have made fish food out of me."

"No pro—"

"Your packages must have worked!" Lieutenant Brown pointed in the direction of the tanker. "Lights have snapped on and men are running around the deck."

Smith led Rebel and White back to the bridge.

Commander Pierce laughed as he shook their hands. "Excellent work, gentlemen. The *Navarone* reports the *Zebu* is dead in the water. They've offered to assist any personnel who want to leave the ship. No takers, so far, but the Greeks are arranging a tow."

"I tink dat I enjoyed meself." A grin stretched across White's face.

Rebel glanced up from a flimsy paper handed to him by Commander Pierce. "Fire up your tablet." He showed White the note.

*To: Commanding Officer, HMS Snapdragon*
*From: Navy Command HQ, Whale Island*
*Instruct guests to check email. New orders.*

Their bags remained on the bridge while they conducted their mission. White reached inside his, grabbed the iPad, and logged into his account. A flashing light indicated a new message.

*To: White, Black*
*From: Topaz*

*Proceed to the Seychelles. New packages for Rebel en route from Alpha. Probable target scheduled to arrive within forty-eight hours. Details to follow.*

After sending a confirmation, White turned his tablet so Rebel could read the message. "I tink dat we will be having more fun!"

Rebel's eyes sparkled. "Agreed. I hope they allow us to blow something up this time."

# Chapter Thirty-Four

Somali Pirate Compound
Near Ras Hafun

The moment before the knife pierced Engineer Smith's left eye, Dacar flicked his hand, forcing the blade away. He wiped the blood from his earlier gouge on the engineer's stained shirt.

"You're in luck, Smith. You might still be worth money to the ship's owner, so I won't cut any parts off—yet."

"You—you're an evil bastard! I hope you rot in hell!"

"I might be evil, but I know my father. Besides, name calling won't gain your freedom."

Dacar grabbed Smith's hair and yanked his head backward. "I want my money released and you'll make it happen."

Smith struggled against his bindings. "Big talk while I'm tied up. If I were free, I'd teach you a lesson."

Dacar released him. "You might not be scared, but I think something else will be persuasive." He nodded at one of his men standing by the door.

The pirate disappeared, returning moments later with a young man, his swollen right arm wrapped in a filthy rag, and tied him to a second chair.

"Perhaps you'll be more cooperative if I cut pieces from your friend?" Dacar grabbed the man's ear, raised his knife, and drew it across the lobe. Blood oozed from the thin red line.

"*Argh!*"

The man struggled, trying to move away from the blade.

Dacar shifted the knife behind the top of the ear. He glanced at Smith and smiled.

"*Aaaahh!*"

Blood seeped from the new cut as the man's efforts to free himself intensified.

"Stop!"

"Don't hurt the boy." Tears trickled down Smith's face. "I-I'll do as you want."

"Now, that wasn't so hard, was it?" Dacar laughed as he dropped his blade into its sheath. "All you needed was some gentle persuasion."

Dacar turned to the guard. "Get someone in here to clean up this mess. Release him—he has writing to do." He pointed at the engineer.

Smith rubbed his chaffed wrists when he was freed. Seated at a small table in the corner of the room, he composed his plea.

*Please work to release the funds provided to the Napoli hijackers. They've injured young James Patterson and threatened to kill him. Please hurry to meet their demand!*

Dacar grabbed the paper as soon as Smith stopped writing. After reading, he nodded. "Good. Once the company succeeds in freeing my money, I promise to let you go." *Dead or alive, who knows?*

He left the building, slamming the door. *I should have cut his ear off to show I mean what I say.* Dacar stopped one of his men. "Where's Rooble?"

"I'm not sure. He received a phone call."

"Dacar! Dacar!" Rooble rushed up, out of breath.

"Why are you so excited? What's happened?"

"I received a call from Qaalib, who's in Safaga. Another oil tanker is in the Red Sea and will be heading south."

Dacar sat on a three-legged stool, and frowned. *Should we go after it? We told the Koreans we'd take another ship soon.* "Prepare the men. We'll take the mother ship and the two small boats—ten men in each. You'll be with me."

Rooble's eyes widened with excitement. "Thank you, Dacar! This will be my first hijacking."

*Pray to Allah it won't be your last.* "After all your work in the Suez, I thought it time for you to join us. Find Samatar and tell him to join me. We'll plan our attack."

\*\*\*

The mother ship waited in the Gulf of Aden for Dacar's attack boat to arrive. Once a fishing trawler, the mother ship, painted blue and white, and now called the *Barre-3*, sailed under a Mozambique flag.

Twenty Somali pirates patrolled the main deck, their eyes peeled for their leader. Several men prepared the second attack boat, tethered nearby, loading RPGs and AK-47s. Others loaded thirty-round banana clips for the rifles and stored grenades for the launchers.

"Ahoy!" A pirate waved to those on the attack boat and pointed west toward the Somali coast. "Dacar!"

Thirty minutes later, the boat carrying Dacar, Samatar, Rooble and three others, joined the mother ship and the other attack boat.

Dacar called everyone together. "We're going after another oil tanker, the *Sea Bird*. It should pass us about five miles to the east before dusk."

The men whistled and stomped their feet. Several fired their AK-47s before Dacar waved for quiet.

"Both attack boats will depart in a few minutes and close on the tanker's estimated course. The mother ship will follow later. The *Sea Bird* will pick it up on their radar but won't spot our small boats."

Men nodded at Dacar's words and grinned.

"I'll take charge of one boat. Samatar will captain the other. Ten men for each one. Who wants to go?"

Every pirate raised a hand, some raised both. Dacar laughed. "Everyone will get a chance as we'll be going after more tankers." Dacar gestured toward several men. "You'll join Rooble and me. Samatar, pick your crew and prepare to cast off."

\*\*\*

The sun dropped toward the horizon as the two pirate speedboats wallowed in the ocean, waiting. With lights popping on across the oil tanker, the unsuspecting *Sea Bird* passed.

The pirates used their time-tested attack approach—one boat charging on either side of the intended target. Expecting an unarmed crew on the tanker, the pirates began their attack.

Samatar's boat raced along the starboard side of the ship. When they neared the bow, a man fired an RPG to warn the ship to slow. Several others strafed the vessel without aiming, to cause confusion and fear among the crew.

*Craack! Craack!*

Without warning, return fire from the deck of the tanker bracketed Samatar's boat. Men toppled into the water as the unseen enemy used force to keep the pirates from closing and boarding the ship.

"Shoot! Kill them!" Samatar emptied the AK-47 clip at the ship. His head lurched backward when return fire punched him again and again as rounds found their target. He collapsed, his feet caught under the seat he'd been standing on, while his body, arms flailing, hung over the side.

The air was filled with continued weapons firing and the screams of the dying.

On the port side, Dacar's crew fared no better. His men died, one by one, under a controlled onslaught. Dacar blew a whistle to break off the attack.

Firing stopped as the tanker continued on its journey. Dacar's pilot, blood soaking the left side of his shirt, steered his boat toward the second craft.

"Samatar, speak to me." Dacar called for his friend. "Samatar!"

"He's dead—they're all dead but me." A young pirate stood, teetering as the boat rocked. "Help me."

Dacar pointed to three of his men. "Take the other boat and follow. We're going back to Ras Hafun." *Is there a traitor in our midst?*

\*\*\*

The two speedboats halted, the keels scoured and the vessels jerked as they slammed into the rocky shore to stop their transit. The *Barre-3* remained offshore, men hopping off to attend the injured.

Dacar stormed through the streets to their compound, a battered and dazed Rooble in close pursuit. Villagers chased their children indoors, out of harm's way.

The pirates arrived at the gated property and banged on the door.

No response.

Dacar slammed his hand against the door. Moments later, someone unlocked the gate and pulled it open.

"Take me to the prisoners—now!"

The man hastened to do his bidding, tugging at his arm. "We've moved the prisoners, Dacar. Their building stank. It's been hosed down but needs to dry."

"I don't care about that. Bring me the young one—the one with the injured arm."

The man returned with the prisoner in tow. His faced bruised, eyes swollen, he stood erect in front of Dacar.

"Kneel in front of me."

The man spat at Dacar.

"Down on your knees."

He grinned and gave a two-finger salute, the back of his hand facing Dacar.

Dacar's face turned red, spittle flew from his mouth. He shoved the man to the ground and stomped on his injured arm.

Screaming, the hostage kicked at Dacar, catching him in the right kneecap.

Dacar bellowed with rage. He pulled a pistol from his pocket, aimed at the prisoner, and fired.

"Bring Smith in."

Two men dragged in the engineer, who fought to escape. His resistance ceased when he noticed the body of his young friend. "You bastard! Your time will come and I'll spit on your grave."

Dacar stared at the engineer. "If your company hasn't released my money by the time I next check, you'll meet the same fate. Or worse." He turned and walked away.

\*\*\*

Two days later, Dacar arrived in Victoria, Seychelles. After clearing customs, he grabbed a taxi and went to his apartment.

A musty smell greeted him when he unlocked the door. *Must hire someone to clean this place.* He dropped his luggage and opened the blinds. Most of the time, the view of the botanical gardens provided a calming effect. Not today—things appeared to be getting worse.

Dacar shook his head as if the effort might release pent-up anger. He slammed the door of the apartment when he left. On the ground floor of the building, a small shop provided an assortment of prepared sandwiches.

He bought a bottle of water and a cheese sandwich and returned to his apartment. After eating, he went to his bedroom. Not a religious man, he still prayed to Allah before shutting off the light.

At ten a.m. he entered a local bank, HBL Pakistan. A regular customer, the manager greeted Dacar before he reached the tellers.

"Hello, Mr. Khadaafi. What brings you to our bank this fine morning?"

"Good morning. I want to arrange a transfer of funds into your bank." Dacar set his briefcase on the floor next to the chair and adjusted his tie and coat.

The manager nodded. "Please, come this way. Would you like some tea?" They sat at a desk outside the manager's office.

"No, thank you. My schedule is tight on this trip. Perhaps next time I visit Victoria."

"As you wish. Where will the money be coming from?"

"The Freedom Bank, Malta, account number DK90123. I want to transfer one hundred thousand dollars into my HBL account."

"This will take a few minutes. Please be patient and I'll return as soon as the arrangements are completed."

The manager returned twenty minutes later, a frown creased his face. He shook his head as he returned to his seat. "Mr. Khadaafi, I've terrible news for you. It appears Interpol froze the funds in this account. Something to do with piracy?"

Dacar slumped in the chair. "I have no idea. Are my funds here still available?"

"Oh, yes. I checked before rejoining you. The problem is with the account at the Maltese bank."

"Okay, I want to withdraw ten thousand dollars."

"No problem at all. As per our standing agreement, the money will be ready for your collection in twenty-four hours. I hope this is acceptable?"

*I forgot about the waiting period. Can't be helped—might raise additional alarms.* "Yes. I'll return tomorrow morning. Thank you for your help."

Dacar returned to his apartment, threw his empty briefcase across the room and picked up his satellite phone from the coffee table. He placed a call to Rooble. After four rings, he terminated the call.

As prearranged, five minutes later Dacar dialed again.

Rooble answered on the first ring. "Halloo? Who's calling?"

"Dacar. The owners of the *Napoli* haven't had my money released. They must be reminded who they're dealing with. Send them the photographs of the man I killed and tell them they have forty-eight hours to fix the problem."

"Okay, right away."

He sucked in a lungful of air and exhaled. "If I can't move the money, I want you to kill the engineer."

## Chapter Thirty-Five

Hilton Hotel
Nairobi, Kenya

Tahliil and Evelyn finished their meal at the Carnivore and returned to the Hilton Hotel in Nairobi. They collected their room keys from the desk and checked for messages.

"Should we stop by the hotel restaurant for coffee and dessert?" Evelyn draped her arm across his, as they headed upstairs. "I could go for a crème brûlée."

Tahliil patted Evelyn's arm. "Why not? What time is your flight?"

"I leave for the airport at ten p.m. I'll be in London before you wake up tomorrow."

A handful of diners remained in the restaurant when they entered. Escorted to a table away from the others, a waiter took their order and left.

"Tallie, are things becoming dangerous for you?" Evelyn gazed into his face. "I read the newspaper accounts of the botched attacks in Kismaayo and Mogadishu."

"Of all people, you should know not to believe everything released by the Somali government." He laughed and shook his head. "They ramped up the number of insurgents and fed it to the press, who were obliged to publish the story. Where did the others come from? Simple—embellishment of the truth."

Evelyn grimaced after taking a sip of the strong coffee. "I realize this, but I'm also referring to your continued efforts to cause dissension. Will this backfire on you?"

Tahliil shrugged. "As long as I set the record straight and my Jamiila's protected, I'll die a happy man." *Bold words, but I still require British assistance.*

"Tell Jamiila I said hello the next time you meet with her. Where is she now?"

*I'll give her aces for effort.* "I'm not sure. We're supposed to meet next week to make plans for a holiday—we're thinking somewhere in Europe."

"The next time you're in London, please give me a ring. I'd be happy to show you around." Evelyn glanced at her silver wristwatch. "Dear me, the time has flown. I'd better collect my things. My taxi will be ready in fifteen minutes."

"Shall I lend a hand?"

They stood and she gave him a peck on the cheek. "I'm fine. Go relax—you'll be in the thick of things soon enough."

"You're right, of course. My flight's tomorrow afternoon. Our time together has been a pleasure, as always. Give my best to your cousin."

\*\*\*

Back in war-weary Somali, Tahliil exited the airport terminal. Nearby, one of his faithful followers waited. The man took Tahliil's case and led him to a Toyota Land Cruiser.

They left the airport and headed toward K-7. Tahliil glanced out both sides of the SUV. *Traffic lights not working—electricity out again. Wonder how much damage we caused and how much is incompetence?*

After they turned left at the K-7 traffic circle and took the road toward Afgooye, Tahliil relaxed. "How camp morale?"

"Bad, Tahliil. The failed attacks resulted in many casualties."

The driver sucked in a lungful of air and exhaled as if trying to clear something away. "The men are unhappy and grumbling about lack of leadership. They walk around the compound with their heads down. No laughter or joking. Yesterday, two men dropped their weapons at the gate and left."

"Hmmm." Tahliil rubbed his right index finger near his ear. *Is this a positive sign for me? Perhaps.* "How many men in camp?"

The driver's face twisted into a grimace. "No one returned from the attack in Kismaayo. Busuri took forty men to attack the electricity plant and the refinery. He returned with sixteen, but most were wounded."

"Boosaaso?"

"No information yet. They attacked last night."

Tahliil frowned. "How Asad do running camp?"

The driver smiled. "Asad is a competent administrator. Perfect choice for the job and the men respect him."

"Excellent." *Jamiila appears to like him, so I'll protect him—for now.* "Enough talk. Wake before camp if I asleep."

\*\*\*

The driver stopped a mile from the compound. He turned around—his leader appeared to be asleep.

"Psst, Tahliil. Wake up."

Tahliil jumped at the driver's voice. "Sorry. Tired. Fell asleep."

"The camp is about a mile away. Would you like some water before we enter?"

Tahliil waved his hand. "No. Go now. Meet with Asad and Busuri."

The driver parked in front of the two-story whitewashed building—Tahliil's headquarters.

Asad rushed down the steps as Tahliil stepped out of the vehicle. "Welcome back, Tahliil. How was your trip?"

"Thank you. Trip long but profitable."

"Come inside. Food is ready."

"Join me. Tell about camp."

As they stepped into the building, Tahliil's stomach rumbled at the aroma of roasted goat, vegetables, and rice. "Eat first, talk later."

Asad led Tahliil to a table holding two place settings and a pitcher. He clapped his hands, and two young women entered, one carrying a laden platter. The other woman ladled the food onto the plates and they withdrew.

Both men scooped goat and rice into their right hands and ate in silence. Once finished, Asad filled two glasses with goat milk.

Tahliil patted his stomach and belched. "I ate too much, but happy. How are prisoners?"

"The Europeans remain in their locked room. I allow them to use the toilet under escort. They also walk around inside the compound for one hour each day."

"So healthy, yes?" *Not sure what to do with them, but they might be worth some money.*

"Yes, Tahliil. The man doesn't appear to be afraid of anyone, but the woman yelps and shakes all the time."

"I talk them later. How men?"

"Angry. Worried. Upset. Busuri thinks we might have a spy in our midst."

*Little does he know.* "Hmm. Did he mention any names?"

"One, but the man died in the attack on the oil refinery."

"Who?"

"Shire."

Tahliil sat back in apparent surprise. "Shire staunch fighter. Good comrade." He shook his head. "Where Busuri?"

"Resting. Both of his shoulders received minor shrapnel wounds. The doctor treated him and gave him some strong pain pills. They make him sleep."

Tahliil stretched his arms above his head and yawned. "I talk Busuri tomorrow. You did well. Now, I speak with foreigners."

\*\*\*

Asad unlocked the door to the Europeans' room and departed, a guard remained in the hallway. Tahliil stepped inside. The guard relocked the door.

George jumped to his feet, followed by the slow-moving Silvia. She lowered her head, refusing to meet Tahliil's gaze.

Tahliil waved them back to the seats on the beds. "Your injuries appear better today. New clothes, too?"

"Yes. During your absence, Asad took care of us." George pointed at his Western jeans and t-shirt. "He arranged for the clothes from a foreign charity in Mogadishu. I'm not sure where the medicine came from, but it worked on our scrapes, sunburns, and cuts."

"I will make him my camp administrator. When I returned from Nairobi, I noticed several improvements. Everyone told me Asad made the changes."

"When will we be released? Silvia's condition worsens as each day passes. She requires better medical care."

Tahliil gazed at the woman. *Do I arrange for her release—perhaps a show of good faith?* "I will think on this and make a decision soon." *I must find out more about George. There's something about him—I'm not sure what. Who is he? Nothing on the Internet about missing foreigners named George and Silvia.*

"We're both grateful for the time we're allowed into the compound. Thank you for arranging this."

Tahliil nodded and covered his mouth as he yawned. *Asad arranged their time outside but isn't taking credit. What's his game? I must keep an eye on him.*

"I'm feeling tired. We'll talk more tomorrow."

\*\*\*

Alone in their makeshift prison, George sat beside Silvia, holding her hand. She leaned against him, sobbing.

"No need to panic." George put his arm around her. "Tahliil appears to be a decent chap, although he's leading a band of cutthroats. Asad also seems to be a kind person—he didn't need to find us decent clothes and extra medicine."

Silvia wiped away her tears. "Yes, you're right. My stomach hurts but the drugs help." She patted her abdomen. "I'm afraid of the others—they stare at me as if I'm not wearing any clothes. I feel … I feel molested."

"We'll take things as they come—together. My granny says, 'Tomorrow will take care of tomorrow.'" *I hope she's right. Are they searching for us? They must be by now.*

\*\*\*

After retiring for the evening, Tahliil lay awake, restless. Faces of the dead, some one-time friends, flashed through his mind. *Is my plan too ambitious? Have I moved too fast?*

Despite his exhaustion, sleep remained elusive. Toward dawn, Tahliil nodded off.

The nightmare returned—he relived his father being dragged to the beach by a mob. Forced to kneel, his head on a bloodstained block of wood, the executioner swung the machete. Again, and again, until his father's head rolled onto the sand. The executioner kicked the body away from the block and grabbed the head, holding it aloft, as the people laughed and cheered.

They grabbed his mother—Tahliil jumped, his body drenched with perspiration.

***

After morning prayers, Tahliil shared breakfast with the injured Busuri. When they finished, they moved to the room Tahliil used as an office.

"Why did you go to Nairobi? As our leader, you should have remained with our attacks underway."

"I told before—business. You not need know."

Busuri's eyes hardened into pinpricks of light as he glared at Tahliil. "I disagree. Somehow, the government learned of our plans. First, Gari and several of his men die in an attack in Kismaayo, and now Harbi and his entire team are wiped out."

"Maybe too many attacks." Tahliil shrugged. "Perhaps Allah's will?"

"Don't invoke Allah unless you believe." Busuri shoved a finger into Tahliil's chest. "My attacks in Mogadishu didn't work. The bombs provided by 3M didn't detonate as promised. Either the detonators or the material was faulty."

"We talk with 3M. Find out if prob—"

Tahliil's satellite phone rang. He checked the caller ID.

"Hello, Hasan. How Boosaaso?"

"Horrible. We arrived as planned. While my men rested, Warsame and I checked out the port. Couldn't find anything suspicious, so we planned to attack after the fish processing plant and the tannery closed for the day, to avoid unnecessary casualties."

Static burst through Tahliil's phone. "Hasan. Hasan. Cannot hear you."

"Sorry, Tahliil. I dropped the phone when we went over a boulder. We're being pursued by government forces—at least those of us who are still alive."

"What problem?"

"They knew we were coming. When we approached the tannery, soldiers poured onto the docks from both ends, trapping us. They fired, over and over. Several men tried to surrender but were killed."

Hasan's voice trembled. "They shot others in the back when they threw down their weapons and ran away! The rest of us fought hard, but Warsame and two men are all who remain with me."

"Where now?"

Hasan laughed. "I won't say. Who informed the authorities about our attack? Was it you? I—"

"No, not me. Why accuse me? We will find." *I hope nothing points to me—they'd kill me without hesitation.*

"I'm sure you were behind our betrayal. You didn't shed a tear over Gari's death after he attacked Kismaayo for you. How dare you betray your friends. Did you plan the same for us? For me?"

Tahliil yanked the phone away from his ear as Hasan's voice continued to rise in intensity.

"I pray to Allah to allow me to live. I will take pleasure in using Gari's pistol—"

The call went silent as if they were disconnected. The connection resumed in time for Tahliil to hear Hasan utter a curse.

"I'm going to kill you."

## Chapter Thirty-Six

Office of the Chairman, Joint Chiefs of Staff
The Pentagon, Arlington County, Virginia

Admiral Blakely, Chairmen of the Joint Chiefs of Staff, rubbed his eyes and ran his hand over his short hair as he strode down the corridor to his office. The click of his heels echoed in the deserted hallway.

He unlocked the door, turned on the light, and set his Starbucks coffee on the credenza. He flicked to one of the twenty-four-hour news channels and sat at his mahogany desk.

Admiral Blakely glanced at the wall clock as it clicked to 04:30. While he waited for his computer to boot, he sipped his lukewarm brew. Emails checked, he picked up the gray phone from the corner of his desk and punched several buttons.

"Hello." A British female voice, bereft of emotion.

"Winnie." A smile spread across his face. "Richard Blakely here. Is he in?"

"Oh! Good morning, Admiral. You're in a bit early, aren't you?"

"Couldn't sleep, so I decided to make a start to the day."

"I'll get Sir Alex for you."

Admiral Blakely tapped his foot as he listened to the classical music.

"Richard! Sorry for the delay—I was on another line. Do you ever sleep?"

"Morning, Alex. I wanted to pass along some new information, which will be of interest to your deployed team. It might be nothing, but we've received rumors of a growing rift between DPRK Leader Wook and one of his ambassadors—Soo."

"We've also picked up something about this, but nothing actionable thus far."

"Our source learned Soo and an aide named Kim will be arriving in the Seychelles soon. Aren't a couple members of your team there?"

"Yes. Wonder if we should make a play for one of them?"

"My thoughts as well, Alex. Perhaps we can turn Soo into an asset."

"An interesting perspective. Will pass the information along to the team. I believe they're still in contact with Kumquat. Do you have time for an update or are you dashing away?"

"Hope Kumquat is of some benefit. Speaking of being useful, I spoke with CC yesterday afternoon. Bedlam Alpha is primed for deployment should Bravo require any additional resources."

"Fantastic news, Richard. Bravo is stretched a bit thin, although your loan of Rebel is helping. Please send them to Brize Norton for now. I've also arranged for the use of two four-man teams from 40 Commando's Recce Troop, should the need arise. With your offer of Alpha, we'll be in excellent shape."

"Glad to hear. What's the status of the *Zebu*?"

"Rebel and White stopped the *Zebu* in international waters. The Greeks arranged a tow, and the ship's on her way to their planned destination."

"Huh? Wouldn't it be better to head to the nearest port?"

"We discussed this with the Greeks. They suggested adding several of their commandos to the ship's complement. When the ship docks, finding out who meets the *Zebu* would be of interest."

"Hmm. Excellent idea—tie up some loose ends."

"Agreed. In the meantime, Rebel and White are on their way to the Seychelles. The *Krumen* is scheduled to arrive there in a day or so."

Admiral Blakely laughed. "It's going to be a crowded island. What about Prince George?"

"I spoke with my cousin, Evelyn, yesterday. She's working with an al-Shabaab source, who is privy to information regarding Prince George and an Italian woman named Silvia. We're hoping this contact will lead us to him."

"Hope you find him soon."

"No doubt we will. By the way, Evelyn informed MI6 she's resigning after the prince is rescued. She's ready to join Bedlam Charlie as soon as she's free."

"She'll be a welcome addition to the family."

"Anything else, Richard? If not, I won't keep you."

"We've covered everything, I think. Catch up later—I need to find more coffee—strong and black."

"Don't know how you can drink the stuff—give me a cup of English Breakfast anytime."

Admiral Blakely laughed. "Enjoy your tea."

\*\*\*

After terminating his call, he stepped into the outer office where the aroma of brewing coffee greeted him. Admiral Blakely glanced around, wondering who had prepared it since it was too early for his secretary to be in the office.

A tall, slender man jumped to his feet. "Morning, Admiral. I thought you might enjoy some fresh coffee." Matthew McMasters, nicknamed 'the grandson' because of his youthful appearance, filled two cups with the steaming liquid.

"What are you doing in so early?" Admiral Blakely took a careful sip and headed into his office, Matthew close behind.

"I couldn't sleep, sir." He stifled a yawn as he stretched. "Something about the Maltese account used by the Somali pirate bothered me. I began searching for any additional accounts he might have—I found one, at least I think so."

"Where is it?"

"Assuming I'm correct, Dacar opened an account in the Seychelles three years ago." He used erratic hand movements punching the air to emphasize his points. "Five noteworthy deposits—each for fifty thousand dollars. There's been a few withdrawals, all under ten thousand."

"Hmm. Keep at it, Matthew. Excellent work."

"Thank you, sir."

Alone in his office, the admiral dialed a number from memory. "Hello, Georgia. Is CC in?"

"One moment, Admiral. He's here somewhere." Georgia, Bedlam Alpha's logistics whiz, paged the team leader.

"Hello, Admiral. Hope you have something for us."

"Morning, CC. Gather your team. You're deploying to Brize Norton. You're aware of the situation regarding the North Koreans and Somali pirates?"

"Aye, Admiral."

"There's a separate issue, which has spread Bravo thin—the kidnapping of the third heir to the British throne from a Kenyan refugee camp. He was helping Somali refugees. We're unsure if he was an intentional target or a random capture. If Bravo requires your assistance, you'll be closer and ready for immediate deployment. They're expecting you."

"Aye, sir. We're packed and ready to go. I'll ask Georgia to make the arrangements for us to depart this evening."

"Excellent. I'll inform Sir Alex."

# Chapter Thirty-Seven

Hotel Bel Air
Victoria, Seychelles

Trevor walked to the window of his first-floor room at the Hotel Bel Air while he waited for his laptop to boot. Surrounded by a myriad of green foliage, ranging from bushes to palm trees, the hotel offered quick access to Victoria's city center.

*Good choice, but if I compliment Nate, he'll go on about his expertise forever.*

Trevor returned to the table and opened his email account. Updates from team members and London awaited his attention. He selected the one from Sir Alex first.

*To: Black*
*From: Topaz*
*Friends across the pond tipped two North Koreans involved with the Somali pirates are heading to the Seychelles. They are Ambassador Soo and Major Kim. Conduct surveillance and apprehend if possible. Kumquat green-lighted to provide assistance.*

*Bedlam Alpha en route to the UK for further deployment if required. Two commando teams are also on standby.*

*Freighter Krumen steaming toward your location carrying weapons for Somali pirates. When Rebel and White arrive, they are to disable the vessel in international waters.*

*Legoland reported they have a source with knowledge regarding the location of the heir. Will provide further details when available.*

After sending an acknowledgment, he opened one from Fergus:

*To: Black*
*From: White*
*ETA Seychelles tomorrow morning around 09:00. Please arrange hotel rooms. Will take taxi into city center and contact you upon arrival.*

*Freighter Krumen, carrying illicit weapons, should arrive in forty-eight hours or so. Standing by for instructions.*

"Must not have received the go-ahead from Topaz." Trevor drummed his fingers on the desk, while waiting for the final email to open—from Gerhard.

*To: Black*
*From: Green*
*First terrorist camp a bust. Added a guide/translator and proceeding to possible location for those missing from Jujubba. Will advise.*

Trevor rubbed the scar by his temple as he reread the emails. He paused when he caught the sound of a key unlocking the door and grabbed his Double Trouble stun gun from his backpack.

Nate entered the room, carrying a black and white shopping bag. He pulled out his purchases and spread them on the coffee table.

"Hats, sunglasses, cameras, and shopping bags I understand." Trevor picked up a set of fake teeth. "Padding, wigs, hats, colorful clothing, fake teeth—isn't Halloween a bit early?"

"These should help us blend in with the tourists." Nate chuckled. "Of course, we might want to visit the city sights again."

Trevor placed his gun on the table and turned the laptop for Nate to read the email from Topaz. "Your disguises might come in handy—appears we'll be busy."

"Where do we start?"

"I'll call Kumquat. Would you contact the front desk and reserve two rooms? If none are available, ask for a recommendation."

"Will do." Nate scurried out of the room and closed the door with a soft click.

Trevor contacted the number Kumquat provided. No answer after several rings, he hung up.

Four minutes later, Trevor's phone vibrated. He glanced at the number—local. "Hello?"

"We must meet tonight. Urgent business arriving soon."

He recognized Kumquat's voice and responded. "Eight p.m., at the first place we met."

"Confirmed."

Nate returned, beaming. "I had an excellent conversation with a beautiful woman at the reservations desk."

Trevor rolled his eyes and shook his head. "Did you book two rooms?"

"Oh, yeah. Did I mention …." He waved a piece of paper. "She gave me her phone number, too."

"Down, boy. Work to be done. We're meeting with Kumquat this evening."

\*\*\*

Thirty minutes before their scheduled contact with Kumquat, Trevor and Nate converged on Victoria's clock tower from different directions. Not spotting any surveillance, they approached the diminutive figure dressed in brown trousers and a baggy blue shirt, with a broad brimmed hat and oversized sunglasses.

"We meet again." Kumquat smiled and linked her arms with the two men. "We'll go to our safe-house. I want to introduce the rest of my team."

They meandered through the streets of Victoria, stopping at window displays designed to entice tourists.

They entered a couple of stores as if they hadn't a care in the world.

Kumquat led them along a tree-lined street to a small housing development. After glancing around, she marched up the steps of a quaint house surrounded by a six-foot high hedge.

Inside, four men waited. Trevor and Nate stared at them for a few minutes before bursting into laughter. The men joined in, while Kumquat stood in the center of the room, a puzzled expression on her face.

Trevor turned to her. "We've met your team before. We thought they might be muggers, trying to find some unsuspecting tourists."

Kumquat smirked, trying to keep a straight face. "They told me they fought with eight men wearing balaclavas." She glared at her men. "I hope they learned a lesson."

"The altercation is behind us, so we can move forward." Trevor walked over, a hand stretched out. After a brief hesitation, each of the four men shook Trevor's hand, following by Nate's.

"What is so urgent to contact me?" Kumquat sat on a ragged sofa, gesturing to the others to sit.

"We received word about the pending arrival of Ambassador Soo and Major Kim. Our orders are to capture and interrogate them."

Kumquat shook her head. "I believe seizing both men will raise questions in Pyongyang. I mentioned before Major Kim is my cousin and he faces execution should Wook ever find out about his real affiliation."

"Yes, I remember." Trevor nodded. "Perhaps it's better to grab him and let the ambassador return to North Korea on his own."

"We can bring my cousin here for a debriefing. When are they scheduled to arrive?"

"In a few hours."

Kumquat pounded a fist into an open palm. "We must prepare for their arrival."

\*\*\*

Trevor and Nate were eating a breakfast of fresh fruit and tern eggs at the Espadron Family Café when Trevor received a call. He stepped outside to answer.

"Hey, Trevor. We're by the city market. Willie grabbed some bananas for us as we're both hungry. Where should we meet you?"

"Welcome, Fergus. We're at Sam's Pizzeria on Francis Rachel Street—easy to spot. Nate booked rooms for you at our hotel."

"I'll ask people for directions if we can't find our way. Join you soon. We're famished."

Trevor and Nate moved to a table for four when one became available. Moments later, Willie and Fergus joined them.

"More food's on the way. Coffee and fruit juice." Trevor motioned to the empty chairs. "Take a seat. After breakfast, we'll take a walk, and I'll bring you up to speed."

When they finished eating, Nate paid the bill, the men left the restaurant, and walked along the street until they came to one of the botanical gardens' entrances.

They found a quiet spot, away from others visiting the park. Trevor glanced around, didn't spot anyone, so he gave Willie and Fergus their orders. "First, excellent job taking care of the *Zebu*. She's being hauled to her intended destination. The Greeks want to catch whoever is working behind-the-scenes."

Willie nodded. "Makes perfect sense. Must be a support network assisting them. You mentioned the *Krumen* is heading this way."

"Yes, you're correct." Fergus tapped Willie on the shoulder. "Should be arriving soon."

"Topaz wants you to disable her—in international waters. Can you do the needful?" Trevor glanced from Willie to Fergus.

"Of course, we can do what's needed." Willie's eyes registered disappointment. "Ah wanted to sink the *Zebu*, but this is better. We kept enough of the toys Dr. Edwards made to sink it twice, but as instructed, we'll disable the ship."

Trevor nodded. "Topaz doesn't want to create an international incident, hence their cautious approach."

"Where's the ship now?"

"The *Krumen*'s about one hundred and fifty miles outside the Seychelles international boundary." Nate provided the details after he completed a telephone call. "*HMS Snapdragon* is monitoring the *Krumen*'s progress and relaying information."

Willie whistled. "Time enough for a couple of hours of shuteye before we get wet."

"Trevor, we must acquire some of these toys." Fergus rocked on the bench, keeping his hands about seven inches apart. "They might be small, but they pack a wallop."

"Let's head back to the hotel." Trevor stood. "What size boat do you want?"

"Something with a bit of speed, I tink." Fergus grinned. "My turn to drive."

"Ah agree with Fergus." Willie yawned. "We want to reach the ship after dark and away from the islands. The explosion might light up the sky, but we'll maintain our 'plausible deniability' factor."

"Nate, will you head to the marina and find something decent to rent. Book the boat for the rest of today and tomorrow."

"Diving gear, too." Willie chortled. "The works."

"On the way." Nate turned from the others and headed in the general direction of the marina.

The others continued to the hotel. After Willie and Fergus grabbed their keys, Trevor pulled them aside. "I'll send a note informing Topaz of your arrival. Knock on my door before you're ready to head out."

Back in his room, Trevor logged in and prepared an email for Topaz. He noted one incoming message.

*To: Black*

*From: Topaz*

*Info from Interpol suggests someone tried to access the account at the Maltese bank of interest. The request came from the HBL Pakistan bank in Victoria. The manager had received the Interpol alert and notified them about Dacar Khadaafi. Talk with the manager. Also, recommend hiring a place to use as a safe-house and interrogation center.*

Trevor acknowledged the latest communiqué, informed them of the demolition team's arrival. *Nate's an excellent scrounger. He'll find a suitable place.* After cracking his knuckles, Trevor rubbed his scar and smiled. *Excellent—haven't conducted an interrogation in some time.*

\*\*\*

Trevor watched a soccer game on the television while Nate took a power nap. A discrete knock sounded. Trevor turned the volume down and stepped toward the door when a louder knock echoed throughout the room.

Snug against the wall, Trevor leaned forward enough to glance out the peephole. Recognizing Willie and Fergus, he opened the door and ushered them inside.

"Hey, guys." Nate jumped to his feet and shook their hands. "Your boat's waiting for you and she's a beauty. I took her out for a spin before claiming an empty berth."

"What did you find? I hope the boat will do the trick."

Everyone laughed as Fergus nudged Nate in the ribs.

"The best one still available, a twin-engine Sport Fisherman called *Lanshore*."

Willie nodded. "Excellent. Where's the berth?"

"This way. We're on our way to eat and find a place to wait for the fireworks." Nate held the door as Willie and Fergus snatched their duffle bags from the floor. "The marina's locked at night, but the manager gave me a piece of paper to show the security guard. Should be a breeze."

Twenty minutes later, they approached the marina. Nate offered the paper provided by the manager and a guard opened the gate. They headed along a floating walkway and turned right for the berth Nate had rented.

Willie nodded in appreciation when he spotted their ride. "This will do the job for us, ah reckon. Well done, Nate."

"I'll leave you to your adventure and join Trevor for dinner. We picked a spot along the promenade to catch the show." Nate pointed at a tarp toward the stern. "A present for you—don't open it until you're in position."

Willie glanced at his wristwatch. "The ship should be outside the Seychelles twelve-mile territorial limit. Expect curtain call in about four hours."

After Nate departed, Willie and Fergus boarded the boat. Once they checked over the scuba gear and wet suits, they cast off and headed out of the harbor.

Nate joined Trevor at a restaurant specializing in seafood. Full of diners, they took a table shoved in a corner. After a filling meal of local delicacies, they claimed a bench on the promenade to wait for the upcoming show. Nate and Trevor sipped on Seybrew Festive Lager wrapped in paper bags as they people watched.

\*\*\*

Two hours after setting off from Victoria's marina, Willie guided the boat to within nine hundred yards from the *Krumen*. Most lights extinguished, the ship appeared stationary.

"Must be waiting for daylight before entering the harbor. Makes our job easier."

"I tink this will be lots of fun." Fergus unpacked his duffle while Willie set a sea anchor.

"Ah wish we had the Seabobs, but no way to haul them from the *Snapdragon*."

Fergus yanked the tarp off the present Nate mentioned. His face lit up. "I don't understand about coincidences, but Nate worked a miracle."

Under the tarp, two gleaming red Seabobs.

"Well, hush my mouth. Appears Santa Claus came early."

They manhandled the two seventy-seven-pound craft into the water, tethering them until they were ready. After donning their diving gear, each man attached a nylon mesh bag to their weight belts. Inside, six parcels.

"As discussed, we'll place the packages along the keel, from stern to bow." Willie grinned. "Once we're back on our boat, we'll head back to Victoria before we detonate. Should be an awesome sight."

Willie and Fergus dropped into the water, disconnected the Seabobs, and set a course for the *Krumen*. They angled their crafts underwater and commenced their mission.

After they arrived near the stern, Willie nudged Fergus and pointed at the screw—stationary.

The men separated from the Seabobs and swam to the keel. With the wide beam of the ship, lookouts wouldn't spot the two swimmers.

Willie and Fergus worked their way along the bottom of the ship, removing the strips from the parcels so the magnets would clamp onto the keel and hold the bombs in place.

They were in position to place the final packages toward the bow when something shoved Willie from behind. He turned and caught a glimpse of a shadow.

*Shark!*

The stealthy carnivore swam past Willie and disappeared in the distance. He removed the strip uncovering the magnets and attached the bomb to the keel, keeping an eye on where the shark went.

Moments later, the shark returned, heading straight for Willie. He pulled his Ontario MK-3 knife, keeping his arm by his side, ready to strike the creature.

The predator swam to within six feet. Willie tensed, bubbles in the water increasing as he breathed faster and faster.

At the last second, before coming into range, the shark veered away, moving beyond the bow of the ship.

*Whew! Close one. Appeared to be a hammerhead or blacktip shark—nosy, but not hungry.*

Getting his breathing under control, Willie swam over to the starboard side of the ship. He spotted Fergus planting his final package and swam toward him. A thumbs-up from Fergus, they headed back to the Seabobs.

Their rides underway, they returned to the boat. Once they stowed their gear, Willie told Fergus about his encounter.

"I tink you were lucky. Might have been fish food." Fergus donned a Guinness shirt to ward off the evening chill. "Are we ready to party?"

"We'll head toward shore for about fifteen minutes. Ah want to give us some distance from the pending shockwave. We'll still be within the detonators' range when the packages explode."

After Willie stopped the boat, both men gazed at the *Krumen*, now almost hidden in the dark. Willie glanced at his watch. "The timers should set off the explosives—now."

"Nothing happened." Fergus pouted. "I expected the ship to go up in flames."

"Wait, my friend. The first two bombs went off but five pairs remain. Look! Three lifeboats leaving the ship. The scoundrels are departing as fast as possible." Willie glanced at his watch again. "Here we go."

The unexploded bombs received instructions from their timers. Still no sound from the ship, but lights popped on across the deck and the bridge.

*Boosh! Bwoom!*

The *Krumen* bucked as if her back was broken. Streaks of flame shot skyward before a massive explosion occurred followed by additional blasts.

The sky reflected reds, yellows, blues, and whites as the ship disintegrated.

Willie and Fergus ducked, the shockwave rolling over them and almost capsizing their boat.

"They had more than munitions on that ship, or something more dangerous." Willie snickered. "Should have been disabled, perhaps listing to one side, but not be a spectacle. Although it will be an excellent display from shore."

"I agree." Fergus slapped Willie on the back. "You're a crazy bastard, but you know your business."

"Let's head back to the marina. I'm sure everyone will be awake and watching the spectacle."

\*\*\*

Ashore, the *Krumen*'s demise came with a roll of thunder, followed by a spectacular fireworks display. People rushed to the promenade, filling every available space.

The unannounced spectacle lasted for almost fifteen minutes. Tourists and locals alike laughed and clapped their hands. One of the cafés cranked up their music and people swayed in time to the beat.

Trevor and Nate stood, gazing out to sea. They joined the throng as they tried to work their way toward their hotel.

"Guess they succeeded." Nate shook his head. "Not sure what those bombs are made of, but they packed a punch."

"Agreed. Glad Willie's on our side."

An elderly couple stopped Trevor. The woman asked, "Young man, is this a local holiday? We wondered about the fireworks celebration. A superb display."

"I'm sure I read about a holiday—celebrating the islands' heritage." Trevor laughed as the couple continued their stroll. "I agree with you—a display worth waiting for."

## Chapter Thirty-Eight

Al-Shabaab Camp
Outside Kismaayo, Somalia

Hues of red, orange, and blue kissed the horizon. An occasional bird circled overhead, searching for an early morning breakfast. A light breeze wafted over the area, stirring soft sand into various shapes.

A man lay beneath a brown tarp, his binoculars focused on a manmade structure. Inch by inch, he scanned the al-Shabaab camp. Other than the small tendrils of smoke and the quiet bleating of goats, no additional signs of life existed.

Pun scooted backward from under his concealment. Crouching, he moved farther away, pulling the tarp with him. When the terrain rose, providing him with cover, he ran out of the area.

A soft scrape alerted Gerhard and Alf. They tightened their grips on their SA-80 assault rifles, relaxing when Pun's face appeared.

"Someone inside the camp. No guards on walls or by the gate." He downed the bottle of water Jamiila handed him.

Gerhard withdrew his knife from a sheath on his belt and traced a rough drawing in the sand. "Pun and Alf return to your observation post. Jamiila and I will head east and close on the camp. If anyone glances in our direction, the rising sun will be in their eyes, limiting their vision." *I hope.*

Pun and Alf set off in a stooped walk toward the camp. Once they reached the location where Pun had first monitored their target, they dropped to the ground.

Separated by six feet, they crawled in a zigzag pattern. The goats' bleating increased, but no one appeared at the vehicle gate.

Gerhard and Jamiila circled around to the east of the camp. Green, leafy vegetation masked their movements. Taller yeheb nut bushes, over chest high, aided their transition. They stopped in a dry wadi, hiding behind an overgrown damal tree. A check of the compound revealed a single opening—a narrow wooden gate. He keyed his radio twice.

\*\*\*

Pun acknowledged Gerhard's notification. He clicked his transmit button once, and continued his slow crawl toward the entrance, Alf following. They arrived at the wall, about twenty feet west of the gate. Pun pulled his kukri, shoved the blade between his teeth, and snaked closer as Alf covered him with his assault rifle.

As Pun reached up to twist the handle on one side of the gate, it turned.

*Creak!*

Pun backpedaled, gaining distance from the opening.

A voice spoke in an unknown language. An old goat, a bell dangling on a blue ribbon around its neck, bleated again and left the compound, followed by five more goats.

As soon as the last one passed, the gate closed.

Pun rushed back to the opening and listened.

Nothing.

He tried the other side of the gate—it opened with a soft click. On his stomach, Pun pushed against a rusted metal band at the bottom of the door and slithered through the narrow opening.

Two massive command tents stood in the center of the compound. Several smaller tents were scattered around the area. A brown, tattered tarp shielded a nearby area, several benches clustered underneath.

From Pun's position, he also spotted a kitchen space, where the smoke he observed earlier seemed to originate. He crawled toward the command tents, which blocked his line-of-sight to the kitchen. *If anyone cooking, they not see me.*

Pun teased the edge of a flap up at the first tent.

Empty.

He tried the second one with the same result.

Pun gave a short whistle. Moments later, Alf scooted beside him, weapon at the ready.

In a slight crouch, they separated, Pun going to the left and Alf to the right. They converged on the kitchen.

"Iieeeee!"

A woman spotted Alf and dropped a basket. Several eggs fell out and cracked. She dropped to her knees and grabbed a few unbroken eggs.

Pun rushed forward, putting a hand over the woman's mouth to silence her, as she appeared to gather strength for another outburst.

A shot rang out—a man hobbled forward, his arms shaking as he leveled his antiquated bolt-action rifle at Alf.

*\*\*\**

Gerhard and Jamiila heard a woman's scream and rushed to the narrow gate. A well-placed kick from Gerhard's size twelve combat boot sprung the door's latch, and they hurried inside, entering not far from Pun and Alf.

"*Istaajin!* (Stop!)"

Jamiila ran toward the gray-haired man, repeating her plea for him to stop. The man lowered his weapon, keeping his eyes on Alf, the closest of the compound's invaders.

The other woman edged her way closer. They conversed with Jamiila in Somali, before the man lowered his weapon.

Jamiila turned to Gerhard and the others. "This is Fartaag and his wife, Zaynab. They are the camp's caretakers. Their eldest daughter, Gargaaro, is hiding in one of the smaller tents."

"Ag. Where are the guards?" Gerhard scanned the nearby grounds while Pun and Alf held their weapons ready should any threat materialize.

Jamiila translated. "Fartaag says all of the men went with Tahliil, the local al-Shabaab leader."

Gerhard turned to Pun and Alf. "Search the remainder of the tents. Find their daughter and bring her here."

Both men nodded and scurried away.

Gerhard faced the couple and Jamiila. "Ask him where they went. Did they have any foreigners with them?"

A lengthy discourse ensued, hands waving in the air, appearing to emphasize Fartaag's words.

"He says Tahliil took his men north, to a family compound hidden in a banana plantation outside the village of Afgo—"

Fartaag jabbered and pointed north.

Jamiila smiled and nodded at him. "He says he will guide you to the camp if you do not rape and murder his wife and daughter."

"Tell him no harm will come to them. What about foreign prisoners?"

The old man appeared to relax after Jamiila spoke with him. He turned to his wife and issued what appeared to be several commands.

Jamiila laughed. "He says since he is in charge here and because you will care for his family, he told Zaynab to prepare breakfast for all of us."

"Nothing wrong with a bit of breakfast." Gerhard rubbed his stomach. "Cooked food is much better than our rations."

"He also mentioned one of Tahliil's men, named Asad, was responsible for taking two foreigners with them." *Is this my Asad? Perhaps.*

"One was a tall man, with red hair and a bad sunburn. The other was a woman with dark hair and a bronze-colored complexion, perhaps from too much sun. Both appeared well cared for."

Before Gerhard asked another question, Pun and Alf appeared, dragging a struggling woman between them.

"We found her hiding in the back of a tent." He held up his arm, blood trickling down. "Pun approached first and called her by name. She threw rocks at him. I grabbed her and she bit me."

Fartaag spoke again, gesturing at the middle-aged woman. She bowed her head and followed Zaynab.

"Ag, man! Hope your tetanus injection is current. Pun, clean and bandage his wound."

Pun nodded and led Alf away.

"Please tell Fartaag we would be honored for him to lead us north. Breakfast first. How long will the trip take?"

Jamiila and Fartaag conversed again. "He says if walking, about a week." She smiled. "But if you have a motorized machine, less than two days."

"Tell him we'll use the Land Cruiser. Be a cozy fit for the five of us, but we'll make do. Did he say anything else?"

"Yes, he wanted to know where we came from. I mentioned the al-Shabaab camp outside Kidi Faani. He asked if Maryan and Khalli were still alive."

Gerhard scratched his shaved head. "Why wouldn't they be?"

Jamiila frowned. "Fartaag mentioned rumors about foreigners hunting women for sport. They rape them before cutting off their heads."

"What? I don't believe it. Please reassure him they were healthy when we left." He gazed at Fartaag. "We protect our women, not use them as prey to be abused and killed for fun."

"I did. He was concerned because they are his sisters. Asad, in charge of the foreigners, is his nephew."

Gerhard shook his head. "Is everyone here related?"

"Most are, either by marriage or tribal affiliation."

Zaynab reappeared and beckoned for them to follow.

Jamiila translated. "Breakfast is ready. Fruit, eggs, bread, and milk. She says this is humble fare to serve their visitors, but it's all they have."

Gerhard's stomach rumbled at the mention of food. "I'm sure it will be sufficient. Lead on."

Under the tattered tarp near one of the command tents, several benches were arranged in two rows. Platters of various fruits, a basket of eggs, another with chapatis, awaited them, along with a perspiring pitcher of goat's milk.

The men and Jamiila sat, with Zaynab and Gargaaro serving everyone before helping themselves.

After they finished, Gerhard walked away from the others. He pulled out his iPad, connected it to his satellite phone, and composed a message.

*To: Topaz, Black*

*From: Green*

*Terrorists moved to camp outside Afgooye. Foreign captives transferred with them. According to caretakers, the group isn't expected to return in the near future. The new location is less than a two-day drive. An old man will serve as our guide. Please advise.*

Gerhard rejoined the others to discuss their next steps. "We must go after the foreigners. From the description Fartaag provided, it might be Prince George and Silvia."

"What about the old couple and their daughter? They might warn this Tahliil about us." Alf's demeanor seemed to improve at the mention of the prince.

"He's going to guide us to the compound. Jamiila, stress to the women not to contact anyone about us being here or where we're going. If they do, Fartaag will be punished."

Jamiila spoke with them. "They won't do anything to jeopardize his or Asad's safety."

Gerhard nodded. "Good enough for me. Let's prepare to head out. I'll report in and check for any updated orders.

*To: Black, Green*

*From: Topaz*

*Two four-man commando teams dispatched to Mombasa. ETA twelve hours. Upon arrival commandos will proceed north, using Kenyan-flagged fishing trawler, Masai Mara.*

*White and Rebel will procure vehicles from the American Embassy in Nairobi and travel ASAP to rendezvous point at Shark's Bay, four miles south of Gezira Beach.*

*Black and Blue, continue current mission. Join others when prudent to do so.*

*Green, join the others and converge on Shark's Bay.*

Gerhard acknowledged his orders and disconnected his equipment. *Who's Rebel? Are the Yanks invading?*

## Chapter Thirty-Nine

The City Streets
Victoria, Seychelles

Dacar roamed the streets of Victoria, his thoughts focused on revenge. *If the money isn't released, I'll send Smith's body parts to the Napoli's owners, one piece at a time.* He kicked a nearby trash receptacle, spreading the contents along the street.

His fists clenched, his jaw locked in a grimace, people stepped aside as he marched through the crowded market area. Distracted, he bumped into a solid mass.

"Excuse me, sir. May I help you?" A tall and thick-set police officer smiled at Dacar, his hand on the head of a baton dangling from his belt.

"Uh—no. I was deep in thought and didn't notice you."

The officer's eyebrows raised about half an inch, but he remained silent.

"Sorry, officer. I'll be more alert." *At least enough to spot the police.*

Dacar gave a polite nod and continued on his way. At a nearby kiosk, he purchased a newspaper and a soft drink. He sat on a bench, drank his Coke, and read the paper.

His face paled as he read about the failed al-Shabaab attacks in Kismaayo, Mogadishu, and Boosaaso. *What's happening? Someone must be tipping off the government.*

He stood, tossed the paper and empty can in the trash receptacle, and entered the botanical gardens. Dacar weaved through the tourist attraction and strolled toward his apartment building.

*\*\**

Dacar never spotted the two men following him. Trevor rubbed the scar near his temple and trained his binoculars on the rear exit of the botanical gardens, while removing his outer clothing. "The target's come back into sight and is heading across the street to his building."

"Told you he hadn't a clue anyone was tailing him."

Trevor noted lights illuminating the apartment, before Dacar pulled heavy curtains across the windows. He replaced his binoculars in his backpack. "Aren't you finished yet?"

"Who planned for me to be dressed like an overstuffed police officer? This padding weighs a ton." Nate removed the last piece of clothing before pulling off the curly, black wig.

"I told you I'd help drag the stuff back to the hotel in case we need it again." Trevor chuckled and ducked as Nate threw the wig at him.

"If someone needs to dress up again, it'll be you."

"Hah! Says you. I enjoyed the experience, you standing in Dacar's way and letting him almost plod into you."

"Perhaps so, but we've confirmed where he's living."

Both men burst into laughter as they gathered up the costume and headed back into the park.

*\*\**

The following morning, they dressed in lightweight suits for their respective meetings. The manager of the HBL Pakistan bank agreed to meet with Trevor, while Nate arranged to view several properties available for rent.

A few minutes before his ten a.m. appointment, Trevor entered the bank and spoke to a teller who directed him to the manager's office. He knocked on the door and stepped inside when a voice beckoned him.

A slim man with wavy brown hair stood, walked from behind his desk, and offered a hand to Trevor. "I must say, this is a first for me to meet someone from Interpol. I'm Jean-Marc Belmont, the bank manager."

They shook hands. "Thank you for taking time out of your busy schedule to meet with me. I'm Trevor Martin, Interpol investigator." He pulled out his credentials and held them for Jean-Marc to view.

After a glance, Jean-Marc nodded.

"We're following up on your response to our fraud alert concerning a Maltese bank account." Trevor replaced his wallet.

"Yes. Not every day someone can assist in stopping international corruption. May I offer you something to drink? Tea perhaps?"

"Thank you, but no. You mentioned in your note you have reservations about a person named Dacar Khadaafi. Does he bank with you or another branch of the bank?"

"Yes, with us. He opened an account here about three years ago." Jean-Marc slid a piece of paper toward Trevor. "This is a copy of his account activity. His most recent visit to the bank was a few days ago. He wanted to transfer one hundred thousand dollars from the Freedom Bank in Malta."

"May I keep this for our records?"

"Yes, of course. I made a copy for you. I tried to transfer the funds and was unable to do so. He made his displeasure known and said some kind of mistake had been made and he would investigate the reason for the failure. Dacar withdrew ten thousand dollars from his account with us."

"Is this his current contact information at the top of the page?" Trevor rubbed his chin as he reviewed the account details.

"Yes. The same telephone number and address he provided when he opened the account."

"Excellent. The funds in this account might originate from nefarious sources." Trevor reached into a pocket and withdrew an Interpol business card. "Would you notify me if he makes another transaction?"

"At once. Should I freeze the account?"

"Hmm. Perhaps leave the account open but monitor the activity. We don't want to scare him away. Once we make an arrest, I'll ensure you receive proper credit. There might be a reward, too."

\*\*\*

Nate met a woman from the rental agency at her office near Victoria market. She came recommended by the hotel clerk and might be her twin—blonde hair, blue eyes, almost as tall as him. Her laugh reached to her eyes.

"Welcome, Mr. Nate." She offered a hand, giving his a firm shake. "I'm Gabby."

"Hello, Gabby. Thank you for helping me find a suitable rental."

"Oh, no problem at all. I'll find you the perfect home for your time on the island." She appraised him from head to toe. "Trust me."

Nate laughed. "Remember, the property must be located in a quiet area, at least two bedrooms, and a basement for storage."

"I can think of a few possibilities, but a basement might be difficult with the houses available. However, one or two come with small cellars. Would one of these work for you?"

"Yes, perfect."

"Shall we be on our way? Perhaps we might stop for a lemonade or something else before we finish."

***

Nate returned to the hotel three hours later. Trevor sat at a table in the lounge area reading a local newspaper, a cold beer in front of him.

"Well, well. Thought we lost you." Trevor used a foot to push out a chair.

"You won't believe this! The woman at the rental office is the older sister of the desk clerk."

"So, what kept you?" Trevor gazed at Nate, a hint of a smile on his face.

"It took time because she showed me everything."

Trevor's eyebrows shifted upward. "Uh-huh. Everything?"

Nate began to nod. "Well, not everything, but close. She helped me find the perfect spot."

Trevor burst into laughter. "I bet."

"You're jealous because you spent your time with some dude in a bank. Anyway, I rented a house for two months, beginning today." Nate jangled keys in his pocket. "The property's in a quiet neighborhood, furnished, with three bedrooms, and is surrounded by a high hedge. No basement, but a cellar, which will meet our needs."

Trevor drained his beer and stood. "Shall we locate our target? Assuming he follows his normal routine, he should be returning home in about an hour."

They left the hotel and hopped in the rental car arranged by Trevor. They parked across the street and about half a block away. The four-door white sedan blended in well with the other vehicles.

Trevor and Nate claimed a nearby bench. Before long, their quarry sauntered along the street, passing them in the dimming daylight. He had pushed his key into the lock at the entrance to his building and turned the knob when they rushed him, shoving him inside.

"What is this? Who are you?" Dacar reached for the knife in his pocket, but Trevor grabbed his arm, twisted it behind his back and forced him to drop the weapon.

Nate secured Dacar's arms with plastic ties while Trevor shoved a piece of duct tape across his mouth.

Nate ran to the car while Trevor held their captive. After Nate parked in front of the building, he scanned for activity.

Still quiet, he signaled, and Trevor forced the struggling Dacar into a duck-walk. Once he was shoved in the back of the car, Trevor sat next to him. Nate shifted the gears and drove away.

\*\*\*

The area in darkness, Dacar struggled against his bindings, his head aching. He tried to scratch his face where the duct tape had irritated the skin when it was removed. His hands wouldn't move nor could he stand.

"Someone drugged me." Dacar wet his lips, attempting to remove the taste of wallpaper from his mouth. He struggled but couldn't free himself.

A light snapped on. He blinked and turned away from the light. Eyes adjusting, he glanced at his surroundings—no windows, brick and mortar walls, and a chair holding him in place. Rats scurried past, attempting to escape the bright light.

"Ah. Our guest is awake." A man wearing black clothes and a gray balaclava stepped in front of him. He held a bottle of water.

"Thirsty?"

Dacar nodded, licking his lips.

The man uncapped the bottle, took a long swig and held the bottle forward.

Dacar tried to catch the dribbling water as the man allowed the remaining contents to fall to the floor.

"Perhaps later, if you answer my questions."

"Why ... why should I? You're holding me against my will."

Trevor slapped him across the face. "You're familiar with holding people against their will, aren't you?" He pulled a black case from a pocket and extracted a syringe.

"No time for games. You will tell me what I want to know." Trevor pushed the plunger, clearing the air from the syringe. He stepped forward. "Everything."

Dacar struggled against his bindings. "No! No!"

An unseen force grabbed his arm, holding it still. The syringe came closer, the needle pricking Dacar's skin.

"*Aaaahh!*"

***

When Dacar came to, his clothes were drenched in perspiration, his right arm unbound. A folding table, not visible before, stood next to his chair and to the right. A cup of steaming liquid sat in the middle of the table, a water bottle nearby.

"Go ahead." The balaclava-clad man came into view. "The drug we used, still experimental and not available to most people, worked well. No apparent physical harm—just a pinprick. Of course, we don't know if there will be any lasting effects."

Trevor laughed. "As I mentioned, it's experimental, so you'll be able to help with the study. In the meantime, you answered every question I asked. Your answers didn't vary no matter how I mixed up the questions."

"Will ... will you let me go? My ... my family relies on me."

Trevor shook his head. "Dacar, don't lie to me. The first questions we asked concerned your family. We spent all night confirming what we could."

"But ... but ...."

"Drink your tea before it's cold. In the morning, we'll talk again, before your trip."

"What trip?"

"To the UK, where you'll be a guest of Her Majesty's judicial system. You forgot. In addition to other crimes, you confessed to killing a young crewman from the *Napoli*—he would have been twenty-four tomorrow."

Trevor left the room, the sound of a deadbolt echoing in the cellar when he secured the door. He went upstairs and made an Earl Grey tea for himself before sending an update. He chuckled, thinking how they convinced Dacar he was injected with an experimental drug—yet it was a simple saline solution.

*To: Topaz*

*From: Black*

*Dacar captured. Bound and gagged in safe-house.*

*Initial interrogation confirmed location of pirate compound near Ras Hafun. One of the two missing Napoli crew still alive. Dacar killed the other one. Fifteen members from another hijacked vessel held at same location.*

*Bravo maxed out with current requirements. Recommend Royal Marines attack pirate compound.*

Trevor sat on the sofa, contemplating what he'd learned. *I'd like to string him up myself. But, must let the legal system runs its course.*

A ping indicated an incoming message.

*To: Black*

*From: Topaz*

*Excellent information. Amphibious assault ship, HMS Neptune, with Royal Marine contingent, will be dispatched to pirate camp. Bedlam Alpha deployed to Brize*

*Norton in the event you require reinforcements. Continue interrogation.*

*Instruct Blue to proceed to Nairobi and join Rebel and White at British Embassy.*

Trevor closed down his computer. He grabbed two bottles of water and headed back to Dacar. When he unlocked the door and pushed it open, a vile coppery odor permeated the air.

*Blood!*

Dacar's head rested on his chest. Blood dripped from a gashed throat, a piece of a broken china cup on his lap. Flies found his saturated clothes, feasting on the unexpected meal.

*No! No!*

Trevor pushed his hand against Dacar's throat—no pulse. He checked the pirate's wrists.

*Dead.*

Trevor staggered away and sat in the other chair, his head in his hands. *What have I done?*

## Chapter Forty

Hilton Northholme Resort
Victoria, Seychelles

Soo and Kim stepped from the Seychelles International Airport terminal into brilliant sunshine and a warm breeze. A cab shot forth from the nearby taxi stand and stopped in front of them. They glanced at each other before climbing inside.

"Take us to the Hilton Northholme Resort." Soo grinned, slapping the seat next to him. "I'm looking forward to a relaxing time." *I wish Jung Gi and the boys were here.*

"Don't forget, we're here on important business. How did you manage to arrange rooms at the Hilton?" Kim raised his eyebrows. "Who will pay for them?"

"Never mind. Nari made the arrangements—I'm positive she drove a hard bargain." Soo's eyes sparkled as he laughed. "We don't have rooms. Nari booked us into a villa—complete with a private pool."

After check-in, a bellhop escorted them to their villa. He deposited their luggage on the floor of the single-story white building and departed. Outside the windows, the rustling fronds of nearby palm trees provided a relaxing backdrop.

"Kim, the guest room is yours. I'll use the main bedroom."

"Yes, Ambassador. Where shall we eat this evening?"

"Make reservations for the hotel's restaurant. Tomorrow evening, we'll dine elsewhere."

\*\*\*

A man dressed in black stepped away from the camera after taking a final photo. Another person took his place and zoomed in on a table where Kim and Soo sat.

"Appears they're settling in for the evening." Trevor tapped notes on his iPad.

"We must separate them before we take Kim." Mi-Cha continued watching the two men.

"I suggest we monitor their activities for two or three days to ascertain any possible pattern where they might partake of different activities."

"Agreed." Mi-Cha backed away from the camera and used her binoculars to scan the hotel complex. "My men will continue to surveil them until we're ready."

"Sounds like a plan."

She handed the glasses to Trevor. "Your friend, Nate, is sitting at a table by the window in the restaurant. Who is the woman?"

Trevor focused on the restaurant, finding Nate. "One of the hotel clerks. I don't remember her name."

"Perfect idea to use her while he covers Soo and Kim."

*I'm sure he has ulterior motives, too.* "Nate's an experienced field operator, and she makes an excellent companion. Who would expect a local woman and a foreign man to be anything other than a couple enjoying a meal?"

"I would be most suspicious. But, I'm wary of everything." Mi-Cha nudged Trevor and laughed. "Where are you taking me for dinner?"

\*\*\*

Two days later in Kumquat's safe-house, she presented her kidnapping plan, and refused to entertain any adjustments.

"It's clear to me Kim goes for a daily massage while Soo is swimming each morning." She pouted, her lips pushed upward. "We should grab him today."

"I'd prefer one more day. But ...." Trevor glared at his not-so-agreeable contact. "But, we'll do as you suggest."

Mi-Cha clapped her hands, a smile sneaking across her face. "I knew you would listen to sound advice. This might be your operation, but I know my cousin." *Why won't Trevor listen?*

Trevor glanced at his wristwatch. "If they keep to their routine, we have about five hours to set things up and be in position."

"Not a problem. My men are at the hotel now, disguised as caterers assisting with a private party a local dignitary is holding at the hotel this evening."

"When did you plan to share this little tidbit?"

*He might excel at his job, but he does not understand my people.* She chuckled. "I just did."

Trevor blew out a breath, threw his hands up, but remained silent.

\*\*\*

Kim changed into loose-fitting clothes while Soo donned his swimwear. After Soo stepped outside to the suite's private pool, Kim headed to the spa for his regular massage.

He entered an empty room and glanced around. No masseuse waited for him. "Hello. I'm ready for my appointment. Hello?"

No response.

Kim called again and a hotel staff member stepped into the room. "The masseuse is behind schedule, working on an important customer. She will join you when she's finished."

Sitting on the table, Kim waited, his impatience growing. He swung his feet back and forth, his hands resting in his lap.

Noise at the door caught his attention—the masseuse. "Fifteen more minutes and I'll be with you. Lie on the bed and I'll cover you with a warm towel."

Kim did as instructed. After the masseuse covered him with a towel, she turned off the overhead lights. A pink glow emanating from a small lamp cast shadows throughout the room. "Rest. I return soon."

The warm towel, combined with the soothing orchestra music of popular tunes coming from a ceiling-mounted speaker, eased Kim's tension. After a few minutes, he began to snore.

Unseen hands grabbed his arms and legs.

"Whaat? Who?"

Kim felt large calloused hands around his wrists, forcing them down, as someone else took control of his arms. He struggled but couldn't break free. What little light existed in the room was extinguished as a rough sack covered his head. The fibers scratched his cheek and the scent of ammonia and cinnamon invaded his sinuses. He soon succumbed to the knock-out drug.

\*\*\*

Four balaclava-clad men wearing gas masks, dumped the unconscious Kim into a commercial laundry hamper with wheels. One checked the hallway, while another headed to the outer door.

The coast clear, the remaining two removed their masks and shoved the hamper along the hallway and outside. One of the men jumped into the driver's seat of a white van. Displayed on the side, 'Victoria Caterers—We Feed You Right.'

The others manhandled the hamper into the back. The last man slammed the cargo doors shut and hopped into the front passenger seat. The driver stepped on the gas and headed out of the complex.

\*\*\*

Once Kim came to, he found himself lying on a bed, his arms and legs secured with plastic ties. Unable to free himself, he studied his surroundings. In the opposite wall, a door. *Might be the way out.* Two chairs, a small table, and a dresser completed the furnishings. No pictures or photographs present. A second door to his right perhaps led to a bathroom.

Kim caught the slight scrape of a key in the lock. He feigned sleep as someone entered.

"Come, Major Kim. We know you're awake—the room has eyes."

He opened his eyes and stared at two people. One tall, the other short, both dressed in black. The tall man's features were visible, while the second person wore a balaclava.

"You're British. Who are you? Why did you kidnap me? Release me at once." *I sound like Soo.*

"Answer our questions and we will make things as painless as possible. You might even be freed."

Kim shook his head. "I won't tell you anything. I'm not a Western lackey, cowed by your feeble threats."

"Perhaps not."

*A female voice, coming from the shorter person. Is this a trick?*

"My name is Trevor." He plugged a soldering iron into an electrical outlet and placed the device on the small table. "You might not be afraid now, but you will be."

*Torture? I'm prepared to hold out.*

The female leaned toward him and whispered, "I know all of your secrets."

*How? The voice is familiar. Who is she?* "I am unafraid."

The woman pushed her thumbs under the balaclava and jerked it upward. She shook her head, letting her long black hair swish and fall into place.

Kim gasped. "Mi-Cha! What are you doing here?"

"Hello, my cousin. You have much to explain and not a lot of time."

Trevor unplugged the iron and stepped closer. Mi-Cha grabbed Kim's arms and held him as Trevor reached forward, the tip of the device glowing red.

"No!"

The plastic smoked and separated as the iron burned through the plastic tie securing Kim's arms. Trevor repeated the process, freeing Kim's legs.

Kim rubbed his wrists, his gaze switching from his cousin to Trevor and back again.

Mi-Cha handed Kim a bottle of water. He twisted the cap and guzzled, not stopping until he drank the last drop.

"What do you want?"

"Kim, your time working in Pyongyang has warped your mind." Mi-Cha brushed a hand across her cousin's face. "Did you forget your mission? Bring the Supreme Leader down."

"A difficult task with surmountable obstacles. I request more time."

"No, Kim. Your time has expired. We know about North Korea's plot to obtain oil by exchanging weapons with Somali pirates."

"Yes, your information is true."

"We also know about your relationship with Ambassador Soo." Mi-Cha stared at Kim. "As Trevor mentioned, you will tell us everything—before you're escorted back to Seoul, either as a traitor or a hero—your choice."

Kim puffed his chest out. "I'm not a traitor and I love South Korea. I will answer your questions."

Trevor glanced at a list of questions he had written down. "What tactics did you use to gain Wook's trust?"

"It wasn't easy." Kim closed and rubbed his eyes. "To prove my loyalty, I executed a South Korean spy."

Mi-Cha gulped. "What? How could you?"

"I'm not making any excuses, but I believed my fate rested in Wook's hands. I'm sure if I had hesitated, I would have died."

Trevor nodded and scratched a few notes. "How did you end up working with Ambassador Soo?"

"Wook didn't trust him, although they were childhood friends. He tasked me to kill Soo if he ever showed any disloyalty. I would have executed him, if it meant my life or his."

Kim gazed at his cousin. "Did you know Soo's wife is Wook's sister? Jung Gi and Soo's two boys are prisoners."

Mi-Cha excused herself. "I must pass this information along right away. There is an operational cell in Pyongyang who might be able to help free them."

Kim nodded. "Wook allows Soo restricted access to his family, most times in the palace. They also went to a guesthouse once outside the palace grounds."

Trevor jotted more notes. "A final question, for now. Who came up with the plan to trade weapons for oil with the Somali pirates?"

"Hard to believe, but Soo came up with the idea. I thought Wook would ignore the suggestion." Kim chuckled. "He instructed Soo to make the arrangements and I became his escort."

Trevor stood and pulled a cable tie from his pocket. He secured Kim's arm to the bedpost. "I'll ask more questions later, but for now we're finished. Would you like some food?"

"Yes, please."

***

Trevor joined Mi-Cha in the safehouse's kitchen. One of the men stirred a pot on the stove. One whiff and Trevor almost gagged.

"I hope he's not cooking something for us to eat."

Mi-Cha laughed. "No. If we must extract Kim from the Seychelles, this will be used to knock him out. Natural ingredients and leaves no residue behind."

"Well, it smells terrible." Trevor pointed toward the bedroom where Kim remained. "What did you make of his answers? Do you believe him?"

Mi-Cha gazed at Trevor before answering. "He's changed—no longer the cousin I remember. I do believe he told us a version of the truth. I contacted the cell in Pyongyang, and at this moment they are investigating Kim's claims."

"I'll send my report, then let's eat somewhere nice to celebrate."

*To: Topaz*
*From: Black*

*Major Kim in custody. Initial debrief indicated he'd been embedded in the Wook government for almost five years. He killed a South Korean intelligence officer to gain closer access to Wook.*

*He stated Ambassador Soo is the brains behind the weapons for oil deal with the Somali pirates. Wook is holding Soo's wife and children hostage to ensure successful completion of his mission.*

*Please advise.*

Trevor sent his report and joined Mi-Cha. They left the safe-house and walked to a nearby restaurant for dinner.

Two hours later, Trevor checked his laptop. Another message.

*To: Black*
*From: Topaz*

*Your report acknowledged and shared with Alpha. Leave Major Kim in Kumquat's care. Proceed to Mombasa.*

\*\*\*

Soo finished his swim, dried himself with a towel, and stretched out along the granite edge of the pool. Before long, he fell asleep under the sun's rays.

When he awoke, the sun had edged toward the horizon. Exterior lights popped on around the resort. He sat, stretched, and went into the suite.

"Hello, Kim? Where are you? I'm hungry—let's eat."

Silence.

"Kim, are you here?" Soo knocked on the guest room door, expecting Kim to jump out at him.

No response, so he pounded on the door. Twisting the handle, he stepped inside.

No Kim, no belongings—nothing to indicate he ever used the room.

Soo changed into casual clothing and dashed outside, calling Kim's name. Other guests stared at him and shook their heads when asked if they had seen another Korean at the hotel.

On the verge of a breakdown, Soo entered the hotel lobby and went to the check-in desk. "Excuse me. I'm Ambassador Soo. My aide, Major Kim is missing. Please find him at once."

"One moment and a security officer will meet with you." The clerk shook his head and picked up a telephone.

Soo sat on a nearby chair, crossing and uncrossing his legs. *Where did he go? Did someone kidnap him? I hate this island.*

A shadow paused in front of him. He glanced up.

"Ambassador Soo? I'm the hotel's chief security officer. When did you last speak with your friend?"

"He's not my friend—my aide. I spoke with him this afternoon before I went for a swim. He said he wanted another massage."

"Any contact with him since?"

Soo shook his head. "Nothing. But something is strange. I checked in his room and all of his belongings are gone as if he never came with me."

"I'll search the premises for you, Ambassador. I'll require assistance, so I'll contact the police and ask them to send a few officers. Please wait here. Someone will bring you a drink."

Soo watched the man disappear. *If he brings the police, they might arrest me and charge me with a crime. I must go, but where?*

A bellhop brought him tea and biscuits. After taking a sip, Soo snapped his fingers. *The airport!*

He stood and wandered around the lobby. No one appeared to be monitoring him.

Soo dashed out of the building and hurried to a nearby taxi stand. "The airport, please. And hurry!"

When he arrived at the airport, Soo handed several bills to the driver and scurried from the cab. Inside the terminal, he found a ticket counter. When his turn came, he sucked in air, exhaling to calm himself.

"I am Ambassador Soo from the People's Democratic Republic of North Korea. Urgent business requires me to return home at once. Please book me on the next available flight out of here. The destination doesn't matter."

# Chapter Forty-One

American Embassy
Nairobi, Kenya

Three foreigners stood within the security booth outside the three-story American Embassy. A Kenyan police officer stared at them while another examined their passports. Once he compared the photographs with their faces for the fourth time, he picked up a telephone.

"I don't understand why the British High Commission wouldn't provide the vehicles." Fergus raked a hand through his red hair.

"Trevor mentioned the British Second Secretary, Reginald St. James, tried to commandeer the rescue efforts." Willie loosened his tie. "I assume Sir Alex became involved, but needless to say, St. James is petty, and so he stopped us from obtaining our transport. A friend posted here will assist us."

Nate pointed through a window toward the embassy. "Is your friend tall, built like you, and a Marine?"

Willie turned and grinned. "Yep, Gunnery Sergeant Jason O'Malley. We've tipped a few drinks together and …. Perhaps I should keep quiet."

O'Malley squeezed into the security booth. After a bear hug between the longtime friends, he escorted them into the compound, away from prying ears.

"Can't show you around the place. After the recent attacks, security is tighter than ever. However, I spoke with the Defense Attaché. As soon as I mentioned your name, he said to provide you whatever you require, within reason."

O'Malley clasped Willie's shoulder. "Three beat-up Land Cruisers with Kenyan and Somali license plates fall into the acceptable category. Head around the side of the compound to the second gate—the motor pool entrance. I'll join you from inside."

Fifteen minutes later, off-white SUVs pulled out of the gate. A blast from the horns and a wave ended their visit to the embassy.

The three vehicles threaded their way through the streets of Nairobi, heading north, with Willie leading the way. Their transports were loaded with provisions and several five-gallon containers of fuel. Multi-storied buildings soon gave way to single story homes and small shops.

They continued their journey until they reached Garissa, their overnight stop. Willie pulled into the parking lot of the Nomad Palace Hotel and alighted from the vehicle.

Fergus joined Willie and pointed at the five-story hotel. "You'd tink there are better colors than salmon pink."

"O'Malley recommended the place, so color aside, it should provide what we need." Willie pantomimed sticking a finger down his throat.

Nate nodded. "Let's grab our rooms, find a petrol station, and a decent restaurant. I'm hungry."

"Agreed. We'll leave early in the morning since we still have four hundred miles to travel." Willie clapped the others on their shoulders and marched towards the hotel.

\*\*\*

The Royal Air Force C-130J Super Hercules dropped toward the runway. Its tires kissed the tarmac as the pilot guided the aircraft to an unused apron. A troop carrier appeared and stopped near the four-engine workhorse.

The loadmaster dropped the loading ramp. Eight men disembarked, each carrying oversized duffle bags.

Dressed in civilian clothing, their physique and bearing hinted at their military stature.

After they tossed their bags in the back of their next transport, the men returned to the craft. They transferred several wooden crates from the plane and climbed into the truck.

One of the men slapped the back of the cab. The driver started the engine and left the area. Before they departed the airport, the C-130J clawed its way into the air, en route to its next destination.

Forty minutes later, the truck stopped in the employee's parking area of Mombasa's port. Trevor waited for them. As the men clambered out of the vehicle and snagged their bags, two of them approached Trevor.

They came to attention but didn't salute. "Colonel Franklin, I'm Sergeant Taylor, and this is Sergeant Davies. We're from 40 Commando and are here to assist with your current mission."

"Sergeants, welcome to Mombasa. We don't stand on military etiquette, so please relax."

"Where's our transport, Col-I mean Trevor?"

"Moored a few berths along the wharf." Trevor pointed over his shoulder. "We've borrowed a fishing trawler for our mission."

The men glanced at each other.

Trevor caught their unspoken exchange. "It might be a fishing trawler, but the *Nakuru* belongs to the Secret Intelligence Service. It's equipped with twin Caterpillar one-thousand horsepower diesel engines and will cruise at twenty knots."

The sergeants smiled.

"Let's grab your kit and get moving. We have a day and a half to cover over five hundred nautical miles to our rendezvous point."

\*\*\*

The *Nakuru*'s pilot, a member of the Secret Intelligence Service, guided the trawler out of the port and into the Indian Ocean. After reaching the Kenyan maritime territorial limit of twelve nautical miles, the craft changed course, heading north.

The pilot increased their speed to twenty knots and the craft seemed to soar over the water. A bumpy ride as the wave action rolled toward the coast, but the men enjoyed the combination of hot sun and cool ocean spray.

A couple of hours into their journey, Trevor opened two coolers filled with sandwiches. The ten men made short work of the cheese and cucumber sandwiches, washed down by Tusker beer.

"Gentlemen, I don't want to give a pep talk, but you must be apprised about the force we're going to face. How many of you served in combat zones?"

Every hand raised. Trevor smiled. "I couldn't ask for a better bunch. The al-Shabaab group will be a mixed bag, from those who never fired a weapon at someone who will shoot back, to those who are long-time fighters."

Trevor gazed at each man in turn. "Be as it may, there are a few things going for us. While they might possess the numbers, our field experience and superior weapons should ensure our success."

"How many will we come up against?" Sergeant Taylor glanced at his team before focusing on Trevor's response.

"Once we rendezvous with my team, we'll have fifteen combatants. The enemy—estimates range from thirty to sixty."

The men nodded as they digested Trevor's information. No one asked any additional questions—yet.

"One thing to remember, though, this isn't a gun and run mission. There are noncombatants in the compound, and our goal is to rescue two of them—an

Italian woman named Silvia." Trevor paused. *They need the truth—how will they react?*

"The woman is secondary to our rescue mission. Our goal—to recover Prince George, Her Majesty's grandson."

"Blimey! Oops—sorry sir." One of the commandos blushed after his outburst.

Laughter engulfed the entire group.

"A couple of my men used much stronger language when they found out. One didn't say a word—he removed his kukri from its sheath and sharpened the blade."

A hand shot up. "Sir, how will we get from the beach to the terrorist camp?"

"We'll be using Toyota Land Cruisers, compliments of the Yanks. Three of my men are driving them north as we speak."

"How will we find the camp? You mentioned a place called Afgan or something similar."

"The camp is located within a banana plantation outside of Afgooye. We have a guide and a translator—both will need protection."

The boat slowed and the pilot shouted. "Time for fishing, guys."

Trevor pointed at several rods and reels tossed on the deck. "Grab your gear and pretend you're having a fantastic time."

\*\*\*

After a filling breakfast of fresh fruit, toasted day-old bread, and hot tea, the Bedlam operatives checked out of the Nomad Palace Hotel. With stuffed stomachs, full fuel containers, and plenty of water bottles, Willie, Fergus, and Nate hopped into their vehicles, turned onto Kismaayo Road, and continued their journey.

Two hours later, a sign indicated ten kilometers to the Kenyan-Somali border. No traffic in either direction, the lead vehicle pulled onto the shoulder, the others followed.

"Best to top up the fuel tanks here and change the Kenyan license plates for the Somali ones." Willie nodded toward the sign. "Might run into bandits hoping to bump someone off, so keep your weapons close."

"Talk about a boring landscape." Nate shook his head before finishing the last of a water bottle. "Sand, a bit of green stuff, and more sand. How does anyone live here?"

"They're a hardy people. Despite the fighting, famine, and harsh living conditions, they somehow survive." Willie wiped the perspiration from his forehead with the back of his sleeve.

"I don't think many Westerners could handle this type of life. Too dependent on modern conveniences."

"We better saddle up—still about ten hours to the rendezvous point." Willie drained his water and climbed back in his vehicle

The border crossing consisted of a ramshackle building and a wooden barricade across the road. Two Somalis manned the outpost, chewing khat to occupy their time.

When the convoy slowed at the barrier, one of the men spat his khat juice into the sand and leaned against the end of the pole, allowing the vehicles to pass.

Willie stopped to show his passport, but the Somalis waved them through without a glance at his document. Nate and Fergus followed suit.

Three miles later, the road dipped behind a rocky cliff. Stunted shrubs grew out of crevices, maintaining a stranglehold on the rock.

Willie slowed and checked his mirror to ensure the others had followed. He kept moving forward into what looked like a sharp bend. The road straightened after the curve and he relaxed. *Must be my nerves—but they serve me well.*

The convoy had cleared the cliff area and increased their speed along a straight section of road when a bullet shattered the side mirror on Willie's vehicle.

He glanced over his shoulder and spotted two technicals chasing from behind, men hanging out the windows and firing at them.

Willie spun the wheel and floored the accelerator, so he faced the oncoming danger. Nate and Fergus followed Willie's lead. As the bandits closed in on them, erratic gunfire continued.

The Bedlam operators leveled their SA-80 assault weapons and sent a dangerous hailstorm toward their attackers.

Perhaps frightened by an armed target, the technicals spun about and fled.

Willie stepped from his Land Cruiser. "Glad we were prepared. Let's hope the remainder of the journey will be quiet."

"I agree. We might have enough excitement later." Fergus pulled an empty magazine from his weapon and slapped in a full one.

"Let's roll." The men climbed back into their vehicles and continued north.

\*\*\*

The *Nakuru* crossed the Kenyan-Somali boundary and shifted closer to the shore. The pilot continued his occasional dashes at twenty knots before slowing down to allow the men to dangle their hooks and maintain their subterfuge as fishermen.

As dusk approached, Trevor broke out the final cooler of sandwiches. With the ice long melted, they were limp but still retained some of the cheese flavor. Several of the men broke out their rations while a few brave ones persevered with the sandwiches.

They continued north throughout the evening. Trevor set up a rotation to allow the pilot to grab some rest. Their speed reduced to ten knots, the temporary pilots hugged the coast, moving further out when they approached pockets of civilization.

The hours ticked by without any difficulties. As the sun rose and commenced its journey across the sky, the trawler passed Kismaayo.

Without warning, water shot into the air on either side of the boat, the distant echo of guns following.

"What?" Trevor turned in the direction of the shot.

"Don't worry, Colonel. I'll show you what's under the hood." The pilot laughed and pushed the controls to their maximum, the twin engines protesting as the *Nakuru* leaped forward.

"Break out the weapons. Prepare to repel boarders." Trevor tried to focus his binoculars on the vessel behind them.

"Somali Navy boat—appears to be a Poluchat-class patrol boat."

Thick, black smoke billowed out of the patrol boat's stern. The trawler increased the gap as the aggressor wallowed in their wake before turning back.

"Hope they don't radio ahead—we might have a warm reception." Trevor replaced the binoculars in their pouch on his belt. "I hope they'll assume we're heading to Mogadishu and set a trap for us."

The pilot laughed. "Since we are stopping miles before reaching the port, they'll have a long wait."

\*\*\*

Two hours before dusk, a battered Toyota Land Cruiser topped a rise and came to a halt. To the left, the land undulated toward the coast. In the water, two rocks pierced gentle-rolling waves.

"Fartaag says this is Shark's Bay. Beautiful, isn't it?" Jamiila gazed at the water glistening in the sunshine. "He says we must park along the road. The sand from here to the beach is too soft to drive on."

"Ag, man." Gerhard rolled his eyes. "We'll have to carry all of our supplies."

"There are three of us to help you." Alf laughed. "Although I thought you'd be able to carry everything in one load."

"There's four—I'll help, too." The tone of Jamiila's voice indicated she wouldn't take no for an answer.

They made short work of lugging the supplies to the beach. Before long, a welcoming fire blazed. Jamiila placed a pot of water on a tripod to boil for tea.

Pun pointed to the south. "Vehicles come."

Gerhard turned and spotted three sets of headlights. His phone rang. "Right on time."

He spoke for a moment and closed the phone. "They'll be here in about ten minutes."

\*\*\*

An hour after darkness enveloped the area, Pun was the first to pick up the sound of a boat's engines. The low-level purr increased as the *Nakuru* veered toward the campfire.

Nate and Fergus rushed to the water, grabbing ropes tossed to them from the trawler and strained to pull it closer to shore. Trevor and the others disembarked, while the pilot killed the engine and dropped an anchor.

"Ag, man. Everyone's arrived." Gerhard grabbed Trevor in a bear hug.

"It's party time." Nate shook hands with Trevor.

"Perhaps later. I'll introduce the 40 Commando members if you do the same with everyone else."

After introductions, the combined team enjoyed stew for dinner. A long journey for everyone, yawns ran through the group.

"I suggest we grab some sleep." Trevor pointed at Fartaag. "Our guide says it's about two hours to our destination, and I want to be in position as soon as possible after daylight. I'll send an arrival message back home."

*To: Topaz*
*From: Black*
*Successful rendezvous at Shark's Bay. Entire Bedlam team plus commandos, translator, and guide will camp tonight on the beach. Four-vehicle convoy will depart early morning to establish perimeter positions around terrorist camp. Anticipate recovery of captives within forty-eight hours.*

\*\*\*

After lights were extinguished and the fire banked for the night, everyone settled down—all but one. Crawling away in the sand, the person traversed the group's path up to the road. On the other side of the vehicles, the individual pulled a satellite phone from a pocket and punched in a number long memorized.

"I'm with a rescue party. Your guest is Prince George."

# Chapter Forty-Two

Tahliil's Plantation
Outside Afgooye, Somalia


A guard slid down the ladder from his watchtower, running to find help. He jumped up the steps into Tahliil's home and glanced around.

"Help! Help me!"

Footsteps thudded on the stairs. Tahliil and Asad rushed to meet him.

"What's the problem?" Asad grasped the man by his shoulders. Realizing he'd overstepped his position, he turned to his superior. "Sorry."

Tahliil shook his head. "You in charge of compound when I gone. Perhaps all the time?"

"Tahliil, I spotted something—from the wall." The man pointed in the general direction he came from.

"What you see?"

"I—I'm not sure. A shadow."

"Take Asad and show."

Without waiting for Asad, the guard raced out the door and scurried up the ladder.

Winded, Asad followed. "Show me."

"Over there." The guard gestured toward several massive banana trees swaying in the wind.

"You mean those trees? I see shadows, nothing else. I think you fell asleep and panicked when something woke you."

"No ... no, I mean, perhaps." Unable to maintain eye contact, the guard stared at the ground.

"Remain on duty and stay awake." Asad gazed at the trees.

Back at the house, Asad joined Tahliil. "Whatever the guard saw is no longer there. Perhaps a wild boar after a breakfast of bananas."

Tahliil rubbed his chin. "Double guards. Might not be boar."

"At once."

Activity increased outside as Tahliil overheard Asad issuing new instructions. *He's a good man, I think. If things work out, I'll make him my aide.*

Several minutes later, Asad returned. "Guards are doubled. I added a roving patrol outside the compound during daylight hours, too."

"Why not nighttime?"

"If the guards fall asleep and are startled by an evening patrol, they might begin shooting."

Tahliil nodded. *Ambitious and smart.* "Breakfast. Join me."

\*\*\*

Busuri leaned against the perimeter wall, five men arrayed around him. On the ground, a rough diagram of the compound.

"I tell you, something is wrong." Busuri pointed to the map of Somalia drawn in the sand. "Two failed attacks in Kismaayo. In the first one, Gari and most of his men were ambushed. Harbi's entire force died in the second one."

"Perhaps the army was lucky." An older man, his hair dyed with henna gestured at Busuri's map.

"What about my failed attacks in Mogadishu? Never happened before. What transpired in Boosaaso to Hasan and Warsame? I overheard Hasan accused Tahliil of informing someone. Now, they are on the run, their men dead."

Several of the men shrugged, rocked back and forth on their feet, but remained silent.

"Why did Tahliil go to Nairobi after planning the attacks, instead of remaining here?" Busuri shook his head. "He should have provided support and leadership to us. He said it was al-Shabaab business. Well, we're part of al-Shabaab."

"He is one of the leaders, so perhaps business required him to go at this time." The red-haired man scratched his head, his dyed palms revealed as he did so.

Busuri slapped a hand against the wall, causing the men to jump. "Are you all like sheep? Follow what Tahliil says no matter if it makes sense?"

"He is our clan leader, Busuri, don't forget." A man with gray, curly hair stepped forward. "Of course, you're an outsider, not part of us."

"My last point—why has Asad become so popular? He's in charge of the compound during Tahliil's absence and responsible for the foreigners. But, he's never fought against our enemies and hasn't earned his position."

Busuri sighed in expiration. "I tell you—Tahliil bears watching or something will happen to the rest of us."

The men exchanged uneasy glances.

\*\*\*

After breakfast, Tahliil decided to visit the foreigners while Asad continued organizing efforts within the compound. He unlocked the door for Tahliil and handed him the key.

"I want to check on the guards. I have a strange premonition—something is going to happen." Asad rolled his shoulders and headed downstairs.

Tahliil stepped inside the room. *Should I surprise George with my knowledge of his identity? Perhaps later, when the time is right.*

"How are you this morning?" Tahliil noted the empty trays. "Appears Asad is taking excellent care of you."

"Yes, thank you." George extended his right hand toward Silvia. "Have you decided when we might be released?"

"These matters take time to arrange." Tahliil slid a finger along the bridge his nose. "We live in perilous times. Listen to anything Asad instructs you to do—it might be a matter of life or death."

Silvia gasped. "But we are innocent! How can we face such matters?"

"Somalia is run by ruthless men, my dear. They will do anything to remain in power, even kill if they believe murder is necessary."

"You're scaring her, Tahliil." George stood between them. "I won't have this."

"Settle down. I'm informing you of the realities regarding your safety while you're here." Tahliil took a deep breath and exhaled. "Perhaps arrangements will be completed soon. Now, is there anything you might need? If not, I have business requiring my attention."

Disturbed by his conversation with George, Tahliil went outside. He left the compound and walked through the banana trees, one of his favorite pastimes.

*Am I overreacting? What will happen when the rescue team arrives? Will they kill every Somali to recover their prince?*

Tahliil strolled toward a corner of the plantation, shaded by the towering banana trees reaching upward for space.

*Leaves rustled.*

He paused in mid-step, searching for the source. *Must be the wind.*

A deep, guttural sound broke the silence. Tahliil whirled around.

"Who's there? Show yourself—now."

More rustling.

A shadow loomed, charging toward him.

Tahliil stifled a scream, pulled his knife, and prepared to meet his enemy.

The undergrowth parted, a wild boar snorted and ran past.

Tahliil relaxed and replaced his knife in the sheath. *Now I'm jumping at every damn noise. Business must be sorted soon before it causes my death.*

\*\*\*

Dinner was a solemn affair attended by Busuri, Asad, and Tahliil.

"Busuri, tomorrow you train men. Help pick new lieutenants—two." Tahliil drained his cup of milk, hoping to ease the knot in his stomach. "We make new plans, new targets."

"I will do your bidding." Busuri crossed his arms. "Two targets come to mind—the police barracks by the port and the presidential palace. Perhaps also the hotel used by foreigners."

Tahliil nodded. "Prepare plans and show in two days. You may go."

Busuri stood and left the room without another word.

"Asad, be wary of Busuri. Him angry, might strike. Guards ready for tonight?"

"Yes, Tahliil. Extra guards within the compound and an additional one in each of the four towers."

"I tired now so rest. Talk tomorrow." *I must think about the future.*

\*\*\*

Once Tahliil headed to his room, Asad stepped outside to survey the compound. No electricity except when a generator was used, torches burned near each of the towers and by the gates, but their light couldn't pierce the oncoming darkness.

Silence descended over the plantation, day giving way to nocturnal creatures venturing from their lairs. Asad returned to Tahliil's home and went inside.

*Aaieeee!*

A scream filled the night, followed by the rapid fire of an AK-47 on full automatic. The sky lit up with tracers, casting an eerie glow.

Asad raced outside, grabbed a torch, and rushed up a ladder to a tower. "What happened?" He shook the dazed guard out of his trance-like stupor.

"I-I heard a scream. Something hanging in the trees. I don't know what. I think it's dead."

"Come with me." Asad scurried to the ground, followed by the guard. At a run, they scrambled to the gate.

"You." Asad directed two men slouching against the wall, AK-47s resting on the ground, khat cigarettes dangling from their mouths. "Grab your weapons and come with us."

When they rounded the corner of the compound, a white sheet appeared to be blowing in the wind. Asad crept closer.

A woman, her throat cut. Asad checked for a pulse—none. He recognized the woman, one of the captives he brought with him, given to Busuri's team.

Asad stood. "Where is the creature you killed?"

The guard led him to an area farther from the wall. "Here. A black creature."

"Bring another torch." Asad bent down to examine the creature. Covered in black, the beast appeared to be a man—no, two of them.

"Please inform Tahliil I killed the intruder." The guard thumped his chest. "I am not afraid of the dark."

"Yes, you killed both intruders." Asad bent down and yanked off the blood-soaked balaclavas. "Examine your trophy—go on. You should be proud of yourself."

Asad glanced at the bodies. "You killed Hasan and Warsame."

## Chapter Forty-Three

Munsu-dong Diplomatic Area
Pyongyang, North Korea

Intermittent city lights twinkled as a car sped through the empty streets. The sole passenger glanced at the scenery rushing by the closed window but remained focused on his current situation.

Once he arrived at his apartment building, Soo staggered inside, exhausted. He unlocked the door, entered his government-provided apartment, and flicked the light switch.

Nothing happened.

*There's electricity in the building—now what's wrong?*

He flicked the switch again with the same result.

"Hmph."

Strong hands grabbed Soo from behind, covering his mouth with a gloved hand. The intruder twisted Soo's left arm behind his back, the grip so tight he couldn't move.

Soo blinked as the lights came on. In addition to the man holding him, two others stood nearby, with a fourth sitting on the sofa, his legs crossed. All wore white anti-pollution masks, a familiar sight in the city.

The men forced him to a chair across from the sofa. The man raised a finger to his lips, suggesting silence.

Soo nodded and the hand across his mouth disappeared. He glared at the intruders. *Now what? They're Koreans. Did Wook decide to be rid of me?*

"Ambassador Soo. We mean you no harm. In fact, the opposite—we offer you assistance." The man pointed to one of the others, who showed Soo three recording devices.

"We removed these from your apartment. We may speak without Wook's people finding out. They'll think it's faulty equipment. We'll put them back before they send someone to repair them."

"Who are you? What kind of help?"

"We are friends who want to assist you and your family escape from this brutal regime."

"Ha! No one escapes from the Supreme Leader's clutches. Are you offering me a bullet to the head?"

The stranger smiled. "To the contrary, Ambassador. We're offering you an opportunity for a new life—a better future."

"What must I do—kill Wook?"

"His demise would be best for everyone." The man chuckled. "We know about the weapons for oil. Your inside information regarding this program will further erode Wook's regime. You'll be aware of inner workings which should be exposed."

"I-I can't help you." Soo rubbed his eyes. "Wook is holding my family hostage. I must free them first."

"We know where your family is being held. We have a plan, but we'll keep the details secret—for now. Are we agreed—your freedom in exchange for your information?"

"Where will we go? When?"

"Somewhere safe, with a new identity and a new job. The timing is fluid, but this will happen in the near future."

Soo nodded. "You promise much. I might be signing my own death warrant, but if you can return my family to me, unharmed and in good health, I'll give you all the information I possess—about everything."

The man stood and offered his hand. "We'll be in contact soon."

\*\*\*

Once the men departed, Soo thought about the conversation. *A new life in a better place.* He shook his head. *Is this too much to hope for?*

Soo prepared for bed and slept well, the first time since his nightmare began. He dreamed of being together with Jung Gi and the boys, a smile etched on his face.

Somewhat refreshed the next morning, Soo ate a light breakfast. He called his office and spoke with Nari for a few minutes, requesting a vehicle to collect him.

When he arrived at work, Nari yanked the door open. "Oh, Ambassador Soo! You had terrible misfortune. Please, tea is ready."

They stepped into his inner office, a cup of steaming tea waited on Soo's desk. Nari turned to leave after he settled in his seat.

"Please wait, Nari. Th-thank you for looking after me. You've been a perfect secretary and an excellent friend."

"Thank you, Ambassador. You must drink your tea. Our Supreme Leader is sending a car. You are meeting with him at the palace."

The mention of Wook caused a sharp pain in Soo's stomach. *Wook will berate me for losing Kim. But, it's not my fault.*

\*\*\*

Escorted to Wook's chambers, Soo steeled himself for an unpleasant meeting. Armed guards lined the walls, staring at him. Two generals stood behind Wook, notebooks and pens in hand, ready to capture the moment.

Dressed in his everyday black attire, Wook sat in his chair, glowering. A cup of tea steeped on a small table to his right. "Did your incompetence cause my current problems?"

"N-no, Supreme Leader. At least, I don't think so. I am a worthy servant."

Wook slammed a fist on the table, spilling the tea. "Where's my oil?"

"T-The oil should have arrived last week. I'll check into this at once."

"You needn't bother. I know where the oil is. The Greeks stole my ship when it sailed into Sehouk—"

"Sihanoukville, Supreme Leader."

Wook snapped his fingers and glared. "Yes. Thank you for correcting me."

"At least the pirates received your gracious offer of the weapons. I will arrange a meeting with—"

"What happened to Major Kim? My sources said you returned from the Seychelles without him."

*What does he know?* "We were waiting for the *Krumen* to pull into port with the weapons for the pirates. I went for a swim while Major Kim decided to have a massage."

"Did you search for him or run away?"

"I conducted a thorough search for him, Supreme Leader. The local police tried to help, but … well, I was better off on my own. I couldn't locate him, so I returned to Pyongyang to provide you with my report."

Wook gazed at Soo. "Hmm. I suppose under the circumstances you acted in a proper manner."

"Thank you, Supreme Leader."

"The entire program is a mess and must be transformed." Wook fixed Soo with an evil grin. "Perhaps some time with your family will reinforce what you will lose if you aren't successful."

Soo's heart thumped with joy. *Dare I ask how much time?* "Thank you for your confidence in me to carry out your orders, Supreme Leader."

"Beginning this evening and through tomorrow night, I will permit you, Jung Gi, and the boys to stay at my private retreat outside the palace. The same one you used for your honeymoon."

"Thank you, Sup—"

"After taking advantage of my generosity, I will grant you two final weeks to fix the mess you created. Otherwise, you'll never see your family again and ...." Wook stood and waved a hand, dismissing Soo. "You'll be executed for being a traitor."

***

Two hours later, guards escorted Soo into Wook's private guesthouse. A stone's throw from the palace, the three-bedroom, two-story house surrounded by lush gardens inside a ten-foot-high brick wall, offered a welcome retreat.

Two boys rushed toward Soo, their mother following a few steps behind. Soo crouched and cradled his arms around his children as tears streamed down his face.

He stood and grasped Jung Gi in his arms. "My wife—I've missed you so much."

"And I you, my husband."

For the benefit of any listening devices, Soo praised Wook. "We've been offered a splendid gift. The four of us are together for the rest of today, all day tomorrow, and tomorrow night. We shall dine well, fish in the little pond, and stroll through the gardens."

Jung Gi fluttered her eyelashes at Soo. "Anything else, my husband?"

"I'm sure we will think of something." He glanced at his wife, a grin spreading across his face. "For now, join me for a walk in the gardens."

***

Hopeful they were away from prying eyes and listening devices, Soo held her hand as they strolled through the grounds. He sat on the brick wall surrounding the koi pond and pulled Jung Gi next to him.

"Do you love me, my wife? Will you accept my decisions without question?"

Jung Gi searched Soo's face for a possible hint of his meaning. "Yes, my husband. I love you with all my heart and will support you, no matter the outcome."

"Our situation in North Korea is dire. Wook controls our lives and can take them away without a thought. I have a plan—it might be dangerous—but we deserve an honest chance at happiness."

Jung Gi's eyes glistened with tears. "Oh, my love. I've longed to hear you will take us to a new life but did not dare to believe it might happen. When?"

"I'm not sure yet, but soon. Be prepared to leave everything behind. I have money hidden in a secret account outside of North Korea. We shall survive."

They held each other for a few minutes, before they were disturbed by the laughter of their children filling the air.

\*\*\*

After dinner, Soo, bolstered by several shots of soju, a Korean drink similar to vodka, regaled his family with stories of his travels abroad. The boys were dressed for bed, while Soo and Jung Gi wore their clothes from earlier in the day.

The children fell asleep long before Soo finished his story. He carried them to bed one at a time while Jung Gi tidied up the living room.

Alone at last, Soo held Jung Gi close. "I enjoyed myself today—how I miss you and the boys when we're apart. No matter what happens, know I love you."

Jung Gi kissed Soo on the cheek and rose to her feet. "Time for us to retire, too." She pulled him up. He gathered her in his arms and carried her to their bedroom.

\*\*\*

A soft noise, not unlike a foot knocking a leg of a table or chair, jostled Soo from his sleep. He glanced at the clock on the bedside table: 1:25 a.m.

"Sshhh. Someone's in the house." Soo climbed out of bed and tiptoed to the door. As he grabbed the handle, the door whisked open and two shadows crept into the room.

*These are the guys who spoke to me in our apartment. It's happening now!*

The man closest to Soo put a finger to his lips.

Soo complied. The man stepped closer to Soo and whispered, "Wake your wife but be gentle. We don't want her to scream."

He edged around the bed, put a hand on Jung Gi's mouth, an arm on her shoulder. He gave a gentle nudge—Jung Gi's eyes flashed open. She tried to sit up, but Soo held her in position.

He leaned down and whispered, "My plan is underway. Don't be frightened—these men are here to help. We must change clothes and never regret the loss of anything we're about to leave behind."

Jung Gi nodded and climbed out of bed. The two masked men stepped out of the room, giving Jung Gi and Soo privacy to change. Afterward, they joined the men in the living room. Two others were there, holding the still-sleeping boys.

The leader went to the door. He peeked out and waved for the others to follow.

Jung Gi gasped when she crossed the threshold. To the left of the entrance, a guard lay on the ground.

"Unconscious. Hurry to the truck." The group ran to the back of the vehicle and climbed inside.

The leader spoke in a normal voice. "Until we leave the city, you must each hide in one of the fifty-five-gallon barrels in the rear. Once things are quiet, you'll be able to sit on the bench."

Soo counted the barrels—eight. "What's in the other containers?"

"Unpleasant gifts for anyone who opens them."

"What?"

The leader laughed. "They contain diesel for the truck. Come, we must hurry."

The driver cranked on the starter several times until the North Korean-built Wookri-58 troop carrier's exhaust belched smoke and the engine kicked over.

Before long, the momentum of the vehicle lulled Soo and his family asleep.

Sounds like several cars backfiring disturbed the night.

*Gunfire!*

The driver increased the truck's speed, the vehicle swaying over several potholes. A few minutes later, the commandeered troop carrier slowed and stopped.

The leader jumped into the back and opened the four barrels. "Nothing to be alarmed about—bandits. A former military vehicle traveling alone at night must be a lucrative target. We're fine now, but I'll give you ten minutes to stretch your legs. When you return, you may sit on the bench."

Wide-eyed, Jung Gi and the boys jumped out of the vehicle and stretched. Soo touched the leader on the arm before joining his family. "How do we address you?"

The man appeared to think about this before chuckling. "Refer to the four of us as the Park Brothers. I am Mr. Park."

"Thank you, Mr. Park, for what you are doing. You're risking your lives for us—why?"

Mr. Park gazed at Soo. "Justice. With your connections to Wook, you know many secrets which should be shared with the outside world."

After the break, Soo and his family returned to the back of the vehicle. They set off again for an unknown destination.

\*\*\*

Hour after hour passed. With the exception of several short breaks for fruit, water, and a stretch, everything appeared the same. Few vehicles traveled on the road.

At their next stop, Soo checked their surroundings. A hint of dawn appeared on the eastern horizon. *South! We're going south. But where?*

Before they boarded, Mr. Park approached. "We must leave this highway and will travel on the back roads. The journey will be rough but hang on and please be patient. Remain in the vehicle until I inform you." He stared at Soo. "No matter what you hear or what happens, stay hidden. After the road becomes smoother, you must hide in the barrels."

As predicted, the vehicle found every pothole in the road. *We'll be bruised at this rate.* Soo held Jung Gi on one side of him, with one of the boys on the other. The youngest clung to Jung Gi.

After an indeterminable amount of time and several stops, the bumpiness of the back roads ceased and the truck's speed increased. They clambered back into the barrels, heeding Mr. Park's instructions.

Hidden in the darkness, no idea where they were, Soo worried. *Where are we? Were we right to trust these strangers?*

Traffic increased around them. Horns blared and brakes squealed as the cacophony of city sounds increased.

The vehicle stopped. Mr. Park helped Soo and his family out of the barrels. They jumped down and found themselves in a warehouse.

"Ambassador Soo. It's been a long journey so far. Your travels aren't over, but you will rest here for a couple of days."

"Thank you, Mr. Park. Where are we?"

A grin spread across Mr. Park's face. "May I be the first to welcome you and your family to Seoul."

# Chapter Forty-Four

Shark's Bay
South of Mogadishu, Somalia

The occasional seagull dove toward the camp by the beach, searching for breakfast. No scraps available, they squawked as they flew higher. The morning light shimmered across the still water, reaching a glistening finish as the waves tugged at the shore.

Jamiila stoked the remnants of last night's fire, adding the remainder of the charcoal Gerhard had lugged from his vehicle when they arrived. She filled a pot with water from the ocean, dropped in a purification tablet as Alf had instructed her, and set the container on a tripod.

The group woke and packed their gear in readiness to embark on their mission. While Jamiila finished preparing breakfast, the others policed the site. All they needed before setting off was fruit, bread, tea or coffee.

Fifteen minutes later, scattered footprints disappeared as a blustering wind drove sand into them. The vehicles loaded, Gerhard led the four-vehicle convoy along the final leg to Mogadishu.

They passed the damaged refinery and power plant, both on their right. Trevor had switched vehicles with Alf, and now rode with Gerhard and the others. "A lot of superficial damage on both facilities. I suspect they'll be operational before long." Trevor glanced out the window.

Fartaag spoke to Jamiila.

"Fartaag says Mogadishu had electrical problems before the attack on the power plant." Jamiila smiled when Fartaag spoke again. "He said one time an engineer tasked to record temperature readings did an excellent job."

She laughed at Fartaag's next words. "But he never informed his supervisor when it went critical. Before he remembered, it blew, sending parts through the roof and the wall, some pieces falling a mile away."

Everyone laughed.

"Ag, man. I bet he lost his job."

Trevor clenched his jaw. "I'm surprised security isn't tighter. With the attacks on the city, I'd expect more military and police presence."

"You spoke too soon, Trevor." Gerhard pointed ahead as they approached the airport. "Tanks and armored personnel carriers—they're waiting for another attack."

"Fartaag says turn left at the K-7 roundabout. This will take us to Afgooye."

\*\*\*

On the outskirts of Mogadishu, Trevor asked Gerhard to pull over. The other vehicles followed and everyone piled out for a stretch.

"Through Jamiila, Fartaag says we're about twenty-five kilometers from Afgooye. For you Yanks—about fifteen miles." Trevor gazed at each person in turn. "Time to put our game face on and tackle the enemy. Any questions?"

The group remained quiet, as they prepared to commence their mission.

"Mount up and move out." Trevor chuckled. *I sound more like Nate every day.*

Thirty minutes later, the convoy veered left off the primary road and continued along a winding trail. Banana trees hugged both sides of the path, dimming the way ahead.

Squeezed in the back next to Jamiila, Pun continued to swipe his kukri along a sharpening stone. He tested the blade on his arm—a thin bloodline appeared. Satisfied, he put the stone away and returned the kukri to its sheath.

Fartaag spoke to Jamiila. "Trevor, we must stop in about five minutes. Fartaag says we're about three kilometers away from Tahliil's compound."

Trevor slapped a full magazine into his SA-80 assault rifle and checked his belt for his Double Trouble stun gun. *Hope we can rescue Prince George and Silvia without bloodshed. But, that's not our decision.*

Gerhard gestured to a faint track leading to the right. "Trevor, suggest we pull off this path and hide the vehicles."

"Agreed."

The men and Jamiila dismounted. Trevor held a piece of paper in his hand, a rough sketch of Tahliil's compound. "Sergeant Taylor, your team has the east perimeter. Sergeant Davies, yours will take the north."

"Sir." Both men acknowledged their assignment.

"Gerhard, take Alf, Fergus, and Pun. You'll cover the south section. This leaves Willie, Nate, and me to hit the west, where the primary entrance is located. Jamiila and Fartaag will stay with my group."

Stern expressions on their faces, no one uttered a sound. A bird flew off when the commandos charged their weapons.

"Let's head out. Radio contact if a necessity. Call sign for each team is their respective perimeter."

Trevor's team took the lead, followed by Gerhard, Taylor, and Davies. The last team crossed the road and disappeared into the trees.

*Snap!*

Everyone dropped to the ground. Trevor scanned the terrain ahead. *Movement. Armed. Did we surprise a guard?*

He signaled for their sniper. Alf squatted next to Trevor.

"Runner ahead. Armed. Track and terminate."

Alf nodded once and scurried forward. No sound indicated his movement, a single branch swayed in the passing breeze.

Five minutes later, Alf returned. He gave a thumbs-up.

Trevor stood, the others following. When he estimated they were about a kilometer from the compound, he paused, his hand in the air moving in a circle. The team leaders approached.

"We separate now to our respective positions. Key a radio once for north, twice for east, and three times for south when you're in position. I'll do four. Thirty seconds after all teams are ready, we go."

The leaders signaled their men and snaked forward, disappearing among the banana trees.

Trevor led his group to the west side and waited for the others to signal. He surveyed the wall, noting four armed guards standing near the vehicular entrance.

He shifted forward for a better view when he overheard two men talking. *A roving patrol?*

Trevor pulled his team back. When they were a safe distance away, he talked with Fartaag through Jamiila. "There are more guards than you mentioned. Also, a roving patrol? Any more surprises?"

Fartaag shrugged. "My information was accurate at the time. Someone made changes."

Trevor shook his head in disgust. *Murphy's law again. Let's hope there aren't any more surprises.*

They moved back to their original positions, weapons ready.

A single click from the radio.

Two more.

Silence.

Three clicks soon followed.

Trevor keyed his radio four times. *Thirty seconds and we begin.* He tightened his finger on his launcher, ready for action.

*Whoosh!*

Trevor fired a single smoke grenade over the wall. The smoke increased as the other teams did the same.

The guards in the towers, in apparent panic, opened fire, long bursts shredding leaves from banana trees. The roving patrol scurried to a gate and forced their way inside, leaving the door ajar.

The more-seasoned guards at the vehicle gate knelt and spread their fire in what appeared to be established shooting lanes. One by one, they toppled over, victims of well-aimed return fire from Willie and Nate.

While gunfire subsided in their section, Trevor realized additional guards must be on the walls in the other areas as the firing increased four-fold.

Smoke and the smell of something burning filled the air. The screams of the dying overwhelmed the sounds of firing.

*Whoomph! Whoomph! Whoomph!*

*The teams are breaching the walls.* Time to move. Trevor gave the signal and his team crept toward the open gate.

Once inside the compound and not meeting any resistance, Trevor edged along the wall toward a two-story building, followed by Jamiila and Fartaag. Willie and Nate went the opposite way, checking bodies to ensure no one was faking their death.

Trevor glanced toward a single-story building, its roof a mass of flames. He continued moving past when a bloodcurdling scream came from an opening. Ablaze, a man staggered toward Trevor brandishing a machete.

*Blam!*

Shot after shot tore into the man. Trevor turned, half expecting Willie or Nate was his savior.

Jamiila stood, her arms by her side, a pistol in her right hand.

Trevor dashed to her side. "I told you to stay back. Are you okay? Have you been hit?"

Jamiila shook her head. "No, he was going to strike you. I had to do something .... I've never killed anyone before." She trembled as she wrapped her arms around herself.

"You did what you had to. Where did the pistol come from?"

"Willie gave it to me."

Trevor frowned. "Okay, we must move forward. The two-story building is our objective."

While the commandos and Gerhard's team cleared the compound, Trevor led his group toward their target.

Willie and Nate rushed up the steps, ready to breach the building. Nate reached from his crouching position and tried the doorknob.

Unlocked.

He nodded at Willie before using his SA-80 to shove the door open. Gunfire erupted from inside. During a pause, Nate hugged the floor and Willie walked high, gaining access to the interior, as Trevor provided rearguard support.

Both fired, catching two Somalis reloading. The guards slumped to the floor, their fighting days over.

Trevor moved toward the stairs, a closed door to his left. He pushed the door open.

A man stood inside, swaying on his feet, a bloody rag around an arm, a weapon in the other but pointed at the floor.

"Asad! Don't shoot!"

Jamiila rushed to Trevor. "He—he's my friend."

Trevor grabbed the man's arm holding the AK-47 and wrestled it from him. He pulled his stun gun and incapacitated the man.

"You've killed him!" Jamiila knelt beside Asad, tears brimming.

"No, Jamiila. I didn't kill him. You saved his life." Trevor helped her to stand. "If you hadn't spoken, I would have shot him. He'll recover."

Once again, Willie and Nate took the lead, creeping up the stairs, SA-80s pointed toward the second-floor opening. At the top of the stairs, they split and began clearing rooms.

Trevor, followed by Jamiila and Fartaag, remained on the landing, waiting.

Willie signaled to Trevor, who stepped toward him, keeping close to the wall.

"We've cleared the other rooms." Willie rapped on the door. "This one's locked."

"Open it." Trevor grinned.

Willie handed his weapon to Nate and lined himself up with the door. A single blow from his size eleven boot proved too much as the door buckled.

A second kick and access was achieved. Trevor led the way inside.

Standing in the middle of the room, a tall man with red hair. Behind him, a shorter woman with long, black hair.

"Did Granny send you?"

\*\*\*

While Pun and Jamiila attended to Prince George and Silvia, the others continued their search for combatants. Satisfied they controlled the compound, Trevor called for the team leaders to report.

"Ag man, we captured six men and four others are dead." Gerhard rubbed his arm. "I obtained a new scratch, but Pun treated the wound. A few stitches, a couple of pills, and I'm good to go."

"Sir, we killed five terrorists, including two outside the perimeter wall. We captured seven—they're trussed up and waiting for collection." Sergeant Taylor shook his head. "Not much fight in these guys when someone can shoot back. One of my men received a through and through in his calf. Painful, but he'll survive."

"Sergeant Davies, what about your team?" Trevor stared at the soft-spoken commando.

"Sir, my team engaged the enemy. Twelve dead—no survivors. One minor injury among my men. A bullet nicked the ear of one. A new bragging point with the ladies."

Fartaag approached and raised his hand.

Trevor gestured to him.

"No ... no Tahliil. He escaped."

"Sergeants and Gerhard. Well done to your teams." Trevor glanced around the quiet compound, the occasional moan from an injured person breaking the silence.

"Gather the captives in a shaded area and treat the wounded. Collect all of the weapons and destroy them. Also, check the terrorists' vehicles. We'll require extra transport to move everyone."

"Sir, what about the dead?" Sergeant Davies asked.

Trevor thought for a moment. "If there's time before we depart, bury them."

"Yes, sir."

Back inside the house, Trevor composed a situation report.

*To: Topaz*
*From: Black*

*Mission completed. Prince George and Silvia Stefani recovered unharmed. Al-Shabaab leader Tahliil missing. Twenty-one terrorists killed, thirteen wounded. Two local captives freed. Three team members received minor injuries.*

*Request extraction from Shark's Bay.*

***

An hour later, ready to depart for the return trip to their rendezvous point, Trevor surveyed the compound a last time. *We were lucky.*

He boarded Gerhard's vehicle, along with Pun, Jamiila, and Fartaag. Before giving the signal to depart, Trevor checked for messages.

*To: Black*
*From: Topaz*
*Well done to all. Proceed to rendezvous point. Two CH-53E Super Stallion helicopters en route. Send Nakuru back to Mombasa.*

*Expect unwanted entourage upon landing in Nairobi. Be polite but firm.*

*Rebel and Blue are to proceed to Seoul to escort multiple packages. Remainder of Bravo return to Headquarters.*

"Back to Shark's Bay, Gerhard." Trevor yawned. "Our next ride is on the way."

***

Mindful of the injured, Trevor had the convoy return to Shark's Bay at a slower pace. Ninety minutes later, they parked along the roadside where their journey to Afgooye began.

The *Nakuru* remained in position where they left her. The pilot and the guard waved at Trevor and his men as they trudged down the hill, escorting their guests, while the commandos secured the vehicles and prisoners.

After introductions, Prince George and Silvia were assisted onto the boat, so they would remain out of the sun's rays. The prince drained the last of a water bottle and turned to Trevor. "What's the plan now, Colonel?"

"Transport will be arriving within an hour. We'll fly to Nairobi, where members of the Foreign Office will see to you and Silvia. The rest of us will disappear—we have a separate mission to conclude."

"I see." Prince George tapped the side of his nose. "No one will hear a word out of me—except, Granny. I hope you haven't been inconvenienced too much by my wayward excursion."

"We're glad your adventure had a happy ending." Trevor stood. "Excuse me, sir, but I must look after my men and prepare for our ride."

Prince George stood and shook Trevor's hand. Silvia stepped forward and gave him a hug and a peck on his cheek.

***

The calm atmosphere along the beach was soon shattered with the arrival of the helicopters. A sling underneath one held a fuel bladder while the other carried a stack of sheet metal.

The lead helicopter descended, releasing the bladder as soon as slack appeared in the cables. The chopper rose as the second one swooped in and dropped its load.

"Colonel Franklin, this is Rescue One." The pilot's voice squawked through the radio Trevor held. "Your men must spread the pierced steel planking in two squares before we can land. We're too heavy and we'd sink to the fuselage in the sand."

"Roger, Rescue One. Give us a few minutes."

The Bedlam team scurried to erect the landing pads. Several of the commandos rushed down the hill to assist.

Fifteen minutes later, the hovering helicopters landed. Even with the metal pads, the craft settled into the sand.

The pilots jumped out and approached Trevor. After saluting, they surveyed the landing site. "No problem—we'll be able to lift off, assuming no heavy loads." Rescue

One unzipped his flight suit. "Who would think it would be so hot with the ocean at our feet?"

Everyone laughed.

"If a couple of your men will assist, we'll refuel and prepare to depart. We thought it best to bring extra fuel—didn't want to run out on the way back."

Stretchers taken from the helicopters were used to remove the non-ambulatory prisoners from the trucks while everyone else made their way to the helicopters.

Willie joined the group last. He grinned but didn't speak.

Trevor glanced at him.

"Ah left a little present on each of those vehicles." Willie laughed. "Ah think someone will receive a nasty surprise."

Once Prince George and Silvia left the *Nakuru* and boarded the first helicopter, the pilot approached Trevor.

"Time we head back to Mombasa." He held out a hand. "It's been a pleasure."

"Many thanks and have a safe journey."

The two helicopters loaded, they whisked their way into the sky and headed south.

\*\*\*

Three hours later, the CH-53Es approached Nairobi International Airport. Instructed where to land by the tower, they followed the taxiways and descended when they reached the tie-down areas.

A group of vehicles and people awaited their arrival. When the rotors stopped spinning, a man in the uniform of a British Army colonel rushed forward, followed by a tall, thin man with silver hair, dressed in a lightweight gray suit.

Trevor alighted first, followed by Prince George.

The suit rushed forward, brushing past Trevor without a word. "Your Highness. I'm so glad we were able to obtain your release. I'm Reginald St. James, the second secretary at the embassy. Follow me, Prince George. I'll be your escort until you are safe back in the UK."

Prince George glanced at St. James before turning to Trevor. "Thank you again, Colonel. I'm sure we'll speak again. Now, I must go with my new 'friend.'"

Once they departed, the British officer stepped forward. "I'm Colonel Parker, the Defense Attaché."

"Hello, Colonel. Thank you for meeting us."

"Sorry about the fuss with St. James. He's quite a handful, but he'll be in his element now. We have an aircraft waiting to take your team and your prisoners back to Britain. All except two." He flipped through the tickets in his hand. "I understand two of the Yanks must catch a different plane. Here are their tickets and a sealed envelope with their orders."

"Thank you, Colonel. Let's reload and depart. The sooner we leave, the sooner things will return to normal for you."

Trevor turned to his assembled men. "We're heading back to the UK—except for Willie and Nate. You have a new mission." He handed the tickets and envelope to Willie and shook everyone's hands. We'll meet again soon in London. Good luck."

Trevor turned away to organize the transfer to the waiting military transport. Willie opened the orders.

"Where we headed?" Nate tried to peer over Willie's arm but couldn't read the fine printed note.

"Do you like chimchi? We're heading to the UK via a quick stop in Seoul. Seems someone there wants our company."

## Chapter Forty-Five

Nairobi International Airport
Nairobi, Kenya

The waiter served the two men their drinks, set a dish of heated cashews on the table, and departed. They raised their glasses in a silent toast and downed their Islay single malt in one swallow as an announcement called their flight.

"So, tell me again why we're traveling all the way to Korea to escort someone to the UK?" Nate matched Willie stride for stride as they joined the boarding queue for their Emirates Airlines flight.

"This is a British mission, we're working for Bravo, and the British government wants to debrief the ambassador first." Willie chuckled. "Why worry? We're flying business class, all the food we want, and an easy few days before we're back in the UK."

"Still seems a long way to go." Nate handed his ticket to a member of the cabin crew who escorted him to his seat, Willie following.

"Let's enjoy our trip—our next one might be more dangerous." Willie laughed and nudged Nate. "You might find a Korean girl to fall in love with, and I'm sure you'll enjoy fermented vegetables."

Nate slipped off his shoes, donned the socks from the comfort kit, and slipped the eye mask over his head. "I think you've spent too much time underwater and aren't getting enough oxygen." Nate reclined his seat, pulling a blanket up to his chin. "Wake me for dinner."

"What would you like to eat?"

"Anything, as long as you eat something else."

\*\*\*

Nineteen hours later, the Emirates flight landed at Seoul Incheon International Airport. Willie and Nate grabbed their belongings and disembarked with other business class passengers.

With nothing to pick up from baggage claim, and a cursory glance at their diplomatic passports by a bored immigration official, they soon joined the throng streaming toward the exit.

Willie and Nate stepped away from the others after entering the chaos of the packed terminal and scanned for their contact.

A short, balding man with an unlit cigar between his teeth approached them. "As I live and breathe, my old buddy, Nathaniel." The man grabbed Nate in a bear hug and lifted him off the floor.

"Put me down, you little oaf. Meet my friend, Willie."

The man dropped Nate and stuck out a hand. "Pleased to meetcha. I'm Wizard."

Willie shook hands. "Ah wonder why they call you Wizard?"

"'Cuz everyone's amazed when I achieve the impossible."

Willie glanced at the two men. "Are you related by any chance?"

"Naw—but we're from the same town."

Nate grabbed Wizard's arm. "Lead on. I'm tired and hungry."

Wizard laughed. "Same old Nate—wants to eat his life away. Come on."

The men threaded their way to the exit and headed to a secured parking lot. Wizard handed the attendant a small envelope and pulled into traffic after the barrier was raised.

One hand on the horn, Wizard nudged through the vehicles until entering the Incheon International Airport Expressway for the trip to downtown Seoul. "Too bad there's no time for sightseeing. I'm an excellent tour guide. Sit back and relax—the journey will take about an hour."

Nate frowned. "We thought we'd spend a couple of days or so, getting over jetlag before picking up our packages."

Wizard shook his head. "No way, bro. Word from on high is for you and your charges to leave ASAP. If the flight had enough seats available, you'd be leaving tonight."

He tapped the horn and swerved around a slow-moving vehicle before cutting back into the lane.

"You'll be staying at a family-run hotel not far from the embassy. We leased the entire building, whether anyone's staying or not, so the owners handle our requests with the utmost discretion."

Wizard took his eyes off the road to check the time. A horn blared nearby as he veered into the next lane.

"About twenty hours before you head back to Incheon. Plenty of time to catch up on some sleep. Two armed security officers are staying at the hotel and will remain with you until your flight."

A short time later, Wizard pulled the vehicle in front of a modern, three-story building, squeezed between two older apartment blocks. Once inside, he led them to their rooms, the keys dangling from the locks.

"Here you go, gentlemen." He presented each of them with a business card. "Next time you're going to be in town, give me a heads-up and we'll party!" He slapped Willie and Nate on the back and strolled down the hallway, whistling.

Willie pointed to the card. "Check this out. No name but a picture of a wizard and a phone number." He glanced at Nate. "Are all of your friends this crazy?"

Nate rolled his eyes. "Would you call yourself sane? Playing with toys made out of explosives?"

Willie looked away, coughed, and changed the subject. "Wizard suggested not disturbing our charges until closer to departure time. Ah think it's an excellent idea. Let's find our hosts and something to eat."

"Did you mention food?"

\*\*\*

An hour before departure time, Willie and Nate knocked on a door down the hallway from theirs. The scrape of a deadbolt echoed in the confined space, followed by the click of a key being turned.

The door creaked open.

A gray-haired man, glasses perched on his nose, stood in the doorway. "Yes? May I help you?"

"Ambassador Soo?" Willie's voice boomed and seemed to startle the ambassador.

"Y-yes."

"Mr. Park sent us. Don't be frightened of my overgrown friend." Nate gave a slight bow. "My name is Nate and this is Willie. We will be your escorts until you are safe in London."

Soo relaxed, a glimpse of a smile appeared. "I thought perhaps my nemesis obtained mercenaries to capture my family and me." He opened the door wider. "Forgive my manners. Please come in."

"Thank you, Ambassador."

Standing in a row by a floral-printed sofa, Soo's family appeared to shake with tension. His wife focused on the floor while the boys stared wide-eyed with mouths open at Willie.

"May I present my wife, Jung Gi." Soo gestured to her and she made a slight bow, keeping her head down.

Willie and Nate returned her greeting.

"These are our two boys. The taller one is Jae and the other is Ki."

Both boys bowed but kept their eyes on Willie.

Once again, Nate and Willie bowed.

"You have a beautiful family." Willie walked over to the boys and ruffled their hair, bringing squeals of delight.

"Thank you. When will we leave for the airport?"

Nate checked the time on his wristwatch. "Soon, so you should pack your belongings."

"I-I'm afraid there isn't much to pack. We had to leave everything behind when we fled." Soo wiped his eyes and inhaled. "The kind people at your embassy bought us carry-on luggage and a couple of changes of clothes, a few toys, and personal hygiene products for Jung Gi. We will be ready in ten minutes."

\*\*\*

Willie and Nate waited while Ambassador Soo and his family cleared customs on their new South Korean passports. After they gained access to the inner terminal, Willie and Nate followed without a glitch.

"Ambassador, time to stretch our legs before our flight is called." Willie picked up the family's four carry-on cases as if they were empty. "Our first trip will be ten hours."

Nate led the way, followed by the family and Willie. Three turns around the gate area, and they entered the boarding lounge to relax.

They were the first to board the Emirates aircraft, Nate having mentioned to a flight attendant about the family.

"Guess what, Willie? Did you spot the attendant with the long brown hair in a ponytail?" Nate held a piece of paper in the air. "She's from California and I have her phone number. The next time I'm home, I'm supposed to call her."

Willie shook his head and chuckled. "Ah guess jetlag hasn't gotten in the way of your favorite pursuits."

After the meal, the lights were dimmed and most passengers took the opportunity for some rest. A few, however, viewed in-flight movies.

Giggles erupted from time to time as Jai and Ki stared at a children's program. Soon they too closed their eyes.

When Willie awoke several hours later, he found a small hand intertwined with his. Jai, sound asleep, rested against Willie's shoulder, a smile on his face.

\*\*\*

When they disembarked in Dubai, Willie and Nate led Soo and his family into the terminal. The family froze in place. People pushed past, but the newest world travelers couldn't believe their eyes.

Ki and Jai ran from display to display, theirs eyes wide. They pointed at various items, their voices squeaking and shrill with enthusiasm.

"Mr. Nate, is everyone here rich?" Jung Gi stared at the bright lights, stacks of every imaginable item for sale. She swayed with the music coming from a nearby store.

"Anyone who can afford the price of an airline ticket may shop here." Nate nodded toward two women passing in their native African attire. "From all over the world."

"I have never witnessed such a display. How do you say … awesome?"

Everyone laughed. They continued walking through the displays until they reached the business lounge.

Willie presented the tickets and the doors whisked open, allowing them access. "We have about six hours before our next flight. Free showers available if anyone wants to freshen up." He pointed to the right. "If you're hungry, there is an assortment of food and drink."

Ambassador Soo lowered his head. "I-I'm afraid I have no money, but we are hungry. Would you loan me some? I shall reimburse you at the first opportunity."

Willie burst into laughter. "Ambassador, the food and drinks are free. Once I handed our tickets to the reception counter, they confirmed us on the next flight."

\*\*\*

Thirteen hours later, their final flight touched down at London Heathrow Airport. The aisles erupted with people trying to grab luggage from overhead bins and pushing their way to the exit.

Nate motioned for Soo and his family to remain seated. "We'll let the others leave. No rush for us—we have friends meeting us."

The mad dash into the terminal over, Willie and Nate stood. Willie grabbed the family's luggage from overhead while Nate helped them move toward the exit.

They left the plane and observed a lighted sign: 'Welcome to London Heathrow.'

Four unsmiling men approached. Jung Gi and the boys hid behind Willie and Nate.

"Welcome to England!" Trevor shook Ambassador Soo's hand, followed by Gerhard, Fergus, and Pun. "Your journey is still at the beginning. You'll stay in a local hotel for the evening."

"Will Mr. Willie and Mr. Nate be with us?" Jai ventured from behind his protection and peered at Trevor.

"Of course, young man. You and your brother have six new uncles to become acquainted with. Shall we go?"

# Chapter Forty-Six

United Nations Security Council Chambers
Manhattan

Two Gulfstream executive jets provided by the CIA touched down at RAF Brize Norton. After brief customs formalities, a four-person security team descended from each aircraft, boarded a small bus, and were taken to on-base visitors' quarters.

The team leaders, AJ Lynn and Rikon Meadows shared one room while the six men accompanying them doubled in three others.

Tall, at almost six feet, AJ's hazel eyes peeked through a long brown fringe and the end of her ponytail lay over one shoulder. Rikon, five inches shorter, maintained her blonde hair in a cropped style, her blue eyes sparkling.

"I'd like some breakfast, but I think sleep's more important right now." AJ yawned as they entered the sparse accommodation.

"Never mind food—give me some coffee." Rikon tossed her black case on the bed. "Eight hours from now, we'll be escorting our charges to the United States. Better sleep now and on the return flight. We won't get much after we land."

AJ nodded. "I feel naked without my SIG."

"Me too. But, British laws are stringent. Once we're back on the planes, our weapons will be handed back to us by the pilots."

"A bit extravagant to hire two planes for this mission." AJ stretched out on her bed. "Plenty of room."

"Yes, but the office stated no collusion between our principals until they testify. What happens afterward won't be our problem."

\*\*\*

An alarm buzzing in the background woke AJ from a sound asleep. She turned over, glanced at Rikon, and rolled back into a comfortable position.

"Oh, no you don't. We tossed—I won, so you get ready first." Rikon laughed. "While you're busy in the bathroom, I'll grab more sleep."

"I'll sing you a lullaby." AJ swung her feet out of bed and snatched her bag.

"I've heard you sing before—do me a favor and don't. It's like a cry for help."

A knock echoed through the room an hour later. AJ and Rikon picked up their cases and headed out the door. They joined their teammates and boarded the same bus for the short trip back to their aircraft.

Once onboard, the teams retrieved their weapons from the gun safe. As arranged, the groups remained on the planes, while British armed police officers escorted a witness onto each jet.

"Where are we going?" AJ's charge glanced around the cabin before asking one of the men. The guy pointed at AJ. "She's the boss."

Tahliil Wardi turned to her. "I'm sorry. I meant no offense. I assumed—"

"No problem, Mr. Wardi. Please take a seat. We'll be departing in a few minutes."

"What is our destination?"

"McGuire Air Force Base—in New Jersey."

\*\*\*

Unlike the lone individual who boarded AJ's aircraft, it was a different situation for Rikon. She glanced at the names on her clipboard and assisted each person over the threshold.

"Welcome, Ambassador Soo. This must be your wife and sons."

Soo began to bow but stopped himself. He held out his hand. "Yes, this is Jung Gi. The taller boy is Jai, and the other is Ki."

Rikon gave a brief bow. "Please take your seats. We'll be departing for America in a few minutes. If you require anything during the flight, please inform me or the cabin crew, and we'll take care of you."

"Thank you, Miss—"

"You may call me Rikon."

Jung Gi and the boys shook her hand before strapping into empty seats. When Rikon walked by, the edge of a seat caught her jacket, lifting the edge above her waist.

Soo noticed the holster clipped to Rikon's belt. *Why is she armed? Is this something else to worry about?*

\*\*\*

Four days later, three black Chevy Suburbans rolled along I-495 toward the Queens Midtown Tunnel. Red and blue grill lights flashing, the convoy was a familiar sight, moving dignitaries to and from events at the United Nations Headquarters.

Exiting the tunnel, the vehicles continued into Manhattan, looping through several streets before turning left onto First Avenue. The convoy slowed as it entered United Nations Plaza, turning right, and stopping in front of the Secretariat Building.

AJ Lynn keyed her Covert-In-Plain-Sight communications device. "Security Team One—check forward perimeter." Responsible for the continued safety of her principal, she performed her duties with utmost dedication.

Two men jumped from the first Suburban and scanned the area. Moments later, one of them responded. "Clear."

"Security Team Two—check rear perimeter."

After the second team reported, AJ turned to the principal. "Are you ready, sir? We'll take you inside to a waiting area near the Security Council chambers."

Dressed in a suit underneath his body armor, Tahliil nodded. "I'm ready. What happens now?"

"I'll remain in the waiting room with you until you're called in front of representatives of the five permanent members on the Security Council. When you're finished, we'll return you to the safe-house."

"I see. Will they allow me to speak?" Tahliil rubbed the deep worry lines on his forehead.

"Yes. They'll also have questions, I'm sure."

The security teams repeated their 'all clear' message to AJ. "Affirmative. Moving now."

She stepped out of the vehicle and assisted Tahliil. They hurried toward the entrance, the security teams closing in on them.

Tahliil stumbled.

*Blam!*

The sound of a shot followed Tahliil's collapse. AJ grabbed an arm and yanked him forward, two of her men assisting. The others scoured the nearby buildings, searching for a position where a shooter might be hiding.

Once inside the building and away from any windows, AJ paused to examine Tahliil.

"No sign of entry or exit wounds. Are you able to speak?"

Tahliil inhaled and let the air out in measured breaths. "I'm fine—a bit winded from the dash into the building. My foot caught on a broken piece of pavement, causing me to stumble."

He grinned at AJ's concerned expression. "Don't worry, my dear. I know the difference between the sound of a vehicle's backfire and someone shooting at me. I'm fine."

AJ nodded. "Okay, if you're positive you're alright. We'll proceed to the waiting room."

\*\*\*

Scheduled to arrive at the UN fifteen minutes later, a different three-vehicle convoy rolled into the Holland Tunnel. Once the black Suburbans left the tunnel, they weaved their way to the Secretariat Building.

Rikon assisted Ambassador Soo out of the middle vehicle. Her men converged on them in a diamond formation and they dashed toward the entrance.

A smooth transition, Rikon breathed a sigh of relief when she had the ambassador secured in a separate waiting area outside the Security Council chambers. *I'm getting too old for this escort duty. Time to find something else.*

"Ambassador, we'll wait here for your appearance in front of the council members. Do you require anything?"

"No, thank you. How long must I wait?"

"Until someone comes for you. I'll remain here until you're called, and I'll be here for your return."

Soo nodded but remained silent, his hands clasped together as if he were praying.

\*\*\*

Someone entered the waiting room from the chambers and beckoned for Tahliil to follow. He stood and glanced at AJ, half-expecting her to join him.

AJ shook her head. "I'm sorry, Mr. Wardi. I'm not allowed inside the chamber." She reached out and touched his arm. "Good luck."

Inside the room, four men and a woman stared at him. A task force representing the Security Council's permanent members—Russia, China, France, United

Kingdom, and the United States—remained silent until he took a chair facing them.

The female representative from the United States was the first to speak. "Mr. uh, Wardi. Tahliil Wardi. Is this correct?"

"Yes, ma'am."

"You are here before us to explain your role in North Korea's weapons for oil campaign. I understand, acting under the aegis of al-Shabaab—a known terrorist group, you controlled a number of pirates."

Tahliil shrugged. "Some call it a terrorist group while others refer to them as freedom fighters."

"Hmmm. Men under your control seized cargo ships for ransom and switched to oil tankers for the sole purpose of obtaining weapons from North Korea."

"Yes, it appears so. But the pirates didn't take orders from me—I made suggestions as part of a three-person ruling council. As you will have read in my written deposition, my true intent was to disrupt al-Shabaab and remove its evil influence from my beloved country. I further wanted to claim my rightful place in Somalia's government."

"I see. No further questions from me at the moment. I'll allow my fellow representatives to speak." She glared at Tahliil. "I will ask more questions later."

\*\*\*

Two hours later, the door to the waiting room opened. A tired-looking Tahliil entered.

AJ stood. "How did things go? You've been with them for hours."

Tahliil shook his head. "I'm not sure. One or two appeared to understand my intentions. Another didn't hear me at all—called me a terrorist."

"You had your opportunity to speak, so try to put things behind you." AJ picked up Tahliil's body armor. "Time for the protective gear so I can take you home."

\*\*\*

Soo paced the waiting room, glancing at the wall clock from time to time. *What's taking so long? I've been here for hours.*

"Ambassador Soo?" A young man held the door open to the room. "Sorry for the delay. The council is ready for you. Would you please come this way?"

Soo entered the council chambers and walked with measured steps to a chair facing the members. Once he sat, he smiled—no one returned the gesture.

"Ambassador Soo." The Chinese representative spoke first. "You are in front of this esteemed group to explain North Korea's attempt to trade weapons for oil."

"Yes, sir."

"Is it not true you were the architect of this program?"

Soo rubbed his chin, weighing his words. "Yes, I created the weapons for oil program to circumvent existing sanctions against my country. But there are mitigating circumstances."

Five unsmiling faces glared at Soo. The Chinese representative continued. "What mitigating circumstances?"

"None of our allies would assist us." Soo stared at the Russian envoy before turning his gaze on the speaker. "Not even Russia and China. Despite my most desperate pleas, not a single country would help."

"I'm sure the Russian representative would agree when I say the UN sanctions prohibited us from helping you. Anything else to say in your defense?"

"Yes. Wook, our Supreme Leader—how I detest his grandiose name—held my wife and children hostage. He threatened to put my wife—his sister—in a prison camp to serve as a prostitute if I did not find an oil source. Who knows what he planned for my sons?"

The Chinese delegate's expression appeared to soften after hearing Soo's words. "Please explain to us everything regarding this program."

Three hours later, the burden of his actions lifted, Soo returned to the waiting room. He smiled at his escort.

Rikon stood and returned the smile. "Well, Ambassador, you spent some time with them. I hope it works out for you."

"Thank you, Rikon. I feel a heavy weight has been removed from my conscience. May I be with my family now?"

"Yes. Once you have your body armor on, we'll return to the vehicles and back to your family."

\*\*\*

After a heated debate behind closed doors, the Security Council released a statement.

*The five permanent members of the United Nations Security Council, having heard testimony from a high-level North Korean defector, have approved by unanimous decision, further tightening of sanctions. North Korea's attempts to bypass existing sanctions to obtain oil through the hijacking by Somali pirates in exchange for weapons cannot be ignored. The new sanctions will be released in a few days.*

*Given the wanton disregard for human life by the Somali pirates and al-Shabaab, new measures, including the potential use of UN peacekeeping forces, will also be announced.*

*In a separate matter, the Council encourages the Somali government in the strongest terms to return all property of the Wardi family seized by unlawful means and return them to Mr. Tahliil Wardi. The Council also requests new presidential elections be called within ninety days, with Mr. Wardi being considered a viable candidate, should he wish to pursue what was taken from his father in the cruelest manner.*

## Chapter Forty-Seven

Bedlam Headquarters
Whitehall, London, England

An overcast sky threatened to unleash a downpour on London's visitors. A light drizzle turned into a torrent as people on the sidewalks huddled beneath umbrellas. They dodged water spraying from tires of passing traffic. Two black cabs weaved their way through Whitehall until they reached the Old War Office Building.

Three men exited each taxi, dashing through the cold deluge toward a side door. An armed Ministry of Defence police officer motioned for their identification. After confirming the group's identity and their authorization to access the building, he nodded to another official who flicked a switch. "Room eleven, gentlemen—they're waiting for you."

Motion detectors controlled the downlighters as the group strolled along the hallway, stopping at room eleven. The shortest one twisted the knob and pushed the door open, allowing the others to enter first.

"Welcome home." Sir Alex stood and shook each man's hand in a two-handed grasp. Evelyn followed with a hug and gave each man a peck on the cheek.

After everyone took a seat, Sir Alex began. "A rough assignment—bad enough with a single complex mission but compounded with Prince George's abduction. Well done to all."

The expanded team and Evelyn nodded.

"Of course, we required a bit of extra assistance—Willie for one. While Bedlam Alpha deployed to Brize Norton, their services weren't needed in an operational role. We put their time to good use, however, when they participated in some joint training.

"Alf, while you misplaced your charge—"

The room erupted with laughter. Alf's face turned red, and he scooted down in his chair, a hand over his eyes.

"I started to say, despite misplacing your charge, your performance in assisting with Prince George's rescue was outstanding."

"Thank you, Sir Alex." Alf's flush faded as everyone applauded.

"Now, Evelyn, my dear. What will become of you since you've 'retired' from MI6? Any ideas?"

"I'm sure something will pop up, Sir Alex."

"You are to be commended for your efforts in working with Tahliil and Jamiila over the years. Now that you've escorted them from Nairobi to MI-6 Headquarters for a debriefing, we need to find something challenging for you."

Sir Alex glanced at his hand-written notes. "There are a few more details to cover. First, thanks to everyone present, Bedlam Bravo smashed the North Korean plot to use Somali pirates to hijack oil tankers in exchange for weapons. The al-Shabaab terrorist group's grip on Somalia has loosened, but they still control much of the country.

"By the way, Royal Marines raided the pirate camp near Ras Hafun. Engineer Smith is safe, and they recovered the body of Patterson, the young seaman, which will be returned for a proper burial. They also freed fifteen crew members who were captured when the pirates seized a freighter over a year ago."

Trevor tapped on the table. "Hear, hear."

"With testimony from Ambassador Soo and Mr. Wardi in front of the UN Security Council's task force, we must hope for a peaceful resolution in Somalia and an end to the terrible North Korean regime. However, I suspect these issues will remain for some time."

"What happened to Major Kim and Mi-Cha?" Trevor asked.

"The last information we received indicated they were back in Seoul." Sir Alex rose and walked to the end of the conference table. "This brings me to Prince George. While I recognize Alf's work in his recovery, there's no doubt in my mind—"

A polite tap and the door opposite Sir Alex swung into the room. Alice, his personal assistant, appeared.

"I'm sorry to interrupt, but you have an important visitor. I didn't think I should turn him away."

Alice stepped away, replaced by a tall man with red hair. Everyone jumped to their feet.

"Please sit down." Prince George, dressed in tan chinos and a blue polo shirt, entered the room. "I wanted to stop by and pass along my personal thanks. If I didn't, Granny would remind me to do so."

Everyone chuckled as the prince worked his way around the table, shaking each person's hand. Once he finished, he sat in the chair vacated earlier by Sir Alex.

"This is a splendid team and shows how international cooperation can overcome impossible odds." Prince George's face lit up. "This will be in the papers I'm sure, but Granny took quite a shine to Miss Stefani. We ate lunch together yesterday."

"Well done, Your Highness." Sir Alex doffed an imaginary hat in the prince's direction.

"Yes, well, things will follow their own course." Prince George stood. "I must be getting back—plenty of things to finish."

"Thank you for taking time out of your busy schedule." Sir Alex waved to encompass the room. "We will always remember this moment."

After Prince George departed, Sir Alex addressed the others. "One more item for the group." He gazed at each member in turn. "You are aware we're organizing a third Bedlam group, which will be under the guidance of Harris Robertson, the Australian National Security Advisor. Bedlam Charlie will be based in Canberra.

"I coordinated with Admiral Blakely and Mr. Robertson—both are in agreement with my announcement." He turned to Alf. "We want to offer you a position on the new team."

The others applauded and left their seats to slap Alf on the back.

"Are you willing to leave Prince George and help forge the newest Bedlam operational team? By the way, the prince supports this offer."

"Yes, Sir Alex." Alf's eyes shone, whether from excitement or tears, no one knew. "I accept."

Gerhard grabbed Alf in a bear hug and lifted him off the floor. "Ag, man. From the first moment we met, I knew you belonged with us."

"Many thanks, Gerhard—I think. Now, put me down."

After the hubbub died away, Sir Alex stepped to Evelyn's side. "My dear cousin, since you're without a job, we want you to be Charlie's team leader."

"Oh, Alex—I mean, Sir Alex. Of course, I accept."

The applause began again, louder than before. Alice reappeared, this time carrying a tray with various liquors and shot glasses.

Several toasts later, Sir Alex pulled Trevor aside. "Before you go, the accountants have been hounding me over a voucher from your stay in Mombasa. Would you please pop into their office and explain why you required a suite?" Sir Alex laughed. "I'm sure they'll accept your explanation."

## Chapter Forty-Eight

London, England
New Homes, New Beginnings

A man dressed in a blue Savile Row suit, blue shirt, and white tie strolled into the Gaucho Grill in London's Canary Wharf area, accompanied by two children. Escorted to his favorite table, he sat and opened his newspaper while the children colored the paper mats placed in front of them.

"Excuse me, Mr. Wardi. Would you prefer your normal breakfast today or would you like to peruse the menu? What about the children?"

Tahliil smiled at the young Somali waiter. "Our usual, if you please."

"Thank you, sir. Here is your tea and two glasses of milk for your grandchildren."

Tahliil nodded and returned to an article of particular interest.

*The Somali government announced plans to dissolve today. New elections are expected to be held in four months' time. The Somali Ambassador to the United Nations called for Mr. Tahliil Wardi to register his interest in campaigning during the election. The ambassador also stated he would endorse Mr. Wardi, should he run.*

Tahliil smiled and closed the paper when their breakfast arrived. He buttered toast and cut sausage for his grandchildren. After eating, he paid his bill and left a generous tip for the waiter.

Once outside, they sauntered back to his two-bedroom apartment on Milligan Close in Canary Wharf. He tucked his grandchildren into the study and tuned the television to one of their favorite programs.

Tahliil headed toward the kitchen when the doorbell rang. Before he reached the foyer, the door opened.

"Hello, Father." Jamiila glanced around the room. "Where are Abuukar and Bayda?"

"In the study learning from a children's program."

"Something educational, I hope?"

"Time for educational stuff later. They're watching 'Wile E. Coyote and the Road Runner.'"

Jamiila rolled her eyes. "Father, when did cartoons become educational?"

"After what they've been through, my dear, I don't believe cartoons will hurt them."

Jamiila grabbed Tahliil's arm and dragged him into the study. "Children, please turn off the television. Your grandfather promised to join Asad and me for a cruise on the river, so we're all going. We've so much to discuss before the wedding!"

\*\*\*

Austin, Texas

Sam Lee stepped out of his three-bedroom ranch in a quiet neighborhood in Austin, Texas. A new manager for Samsung at their nearby chip plant, he rated a company car. Nothing exotic—he drove a blue Kia Sorento.

"Hurry, children or your father will be late for work." Janet helped Jay and Kevin with their books and lunchboxes. Once she shooed them out the door, she grabbed her shopping bag and locked the house door behind her.

Sam glanced at his family and smiled. *Time has changed things for the better. We're away from the madman in Pyongyang, and my family is blossoming.*

After his family joined him in the car and secured their seatbelts, he backed out of the driveway, another suburban family commuting to their daily activities.

# About Randall Krzak

Randall Krzak is a U.S. Army veteran and retired senior civil servant, spending almost thirty years in Europe, Africa, Central America, and the Middle East. His residency abroad qualifies him to build rich worlds in his action-adventure novels and short stories. Familiar with customs, laws, and social norms, he promotes these to create authentic characters and scenery.

He penned A Dangerous Occupation, a winning entry in the August 2016 Wild Sound Writing and Film Festival Review short story category. His first novel, The Kurdish Connection, was published in 2017.

He is currently working on the third novel in the series, Carnage in Singapore. His creative enterprise delved even further into the treacherous sphere of the drug cartel in South America, expanding the manuscript, A Cartel's Revenge, into a future series.

Randall holds a general Master in Business Administration (MBA) and a MBA with an emphasis in Strategic Focus, both from Heriot-Watt University, Edinburgh, Scotland. He and his wife, Sylvia, and five cats are transitioning from the United States to Scotland. In addition to writing, he enjoys hiking, reading, candle making, pyrography, and sightseeing.

**Social Media**

Website: www.randallkrzak.com

Twitter: https://twitter.com/rjkrzak

LinkedIn: https://www.linkedin.com/in/randallkrzak/

Facebook: https://www.facebook.com/profile.php?id=100011369255833

**Acknowledgements**

Many thanks to the folks at Solstice Publishing for giving me an opportunity to share my work and for the guidance throughout the publishing process, especially K.C. Sprayberry, Palvi Sharma, KateMarie Collins, and Melissa Miller.

*Dangerous Alliance* would not be a reality without those who helped me along my journey including: Charles Brass, Oliver F. Chase, John L. DeBoer, Rikon Gaites, D. Gesalt, Preston Holtry, Sylvia Krzak, the Alpha to Omega Review Group, Russell F. Moran, M.D. Neu, Craig Palmer, the Roundtable Pals, Johnathan Pongratz, Mike and Beth Rickerman, Barbara Russell, B. Douglas Slack, Les Stahl, Jeff and Sharon Walby, AJ Wallace, as well as other reviewers from The Next Big Writer and Scribophile. Many thanks!

Made in the USA
Monee, IL
10 February 2020